LOVE'S FIRST LESSON

She saw herself reflected in the green of his eyes and felt the heat from her face course like quicksilver through her veins. For one brief moment, she melted before this man who was so boldly tracing the contours of her face with his fingertips, but then, with a rebellious cry, she pushed him away from her. Instead of thwarting him, her action enflamed him further.

"So my ministering angel's a fighting one, is she?" he chuckled, grasping her by the shoulders and forcing her up against the wall. "I must say you're original, my dear. None of the others ever used a ploy like yours to gain entry to my room."

"I don't know what you're talking about," Sarina gasped, squirming to free herself from his grip.

"Don't you?" he smiled. "Then perhaps you'll understand this." And he cupped her face in his hands and slowly lowered his mouth to hers. . . .

DRAGON FLOWER

DRAGON FLOWER

ALYSSA WELLES

A SIGNET BOOK

NEW AMERICAN LIBRARY

NAL BOOKS ARE AVAILABLE AT QUANTITY DISCOUNTS WHEN USED TO
PROMOTE PRODUCTS OR SERVICES. FOR INFORMATION PLEASE WRITE
TO PREMIUM MARKETING DIVISION. NEW AMERICAN LIBRARY. 1633
BROADWAY. NEW YORK. NEW YORK 10019.

SIGNET TRADEMARK REG. U.S. PAT. OFF. AND FOREIGN COUNTRIES
REGISTERED TRADEMARK—MARCA REGISTRADA
HECHO EN CHICAGO, U.S.A.

SIGNET, SIGNET CLASSIC, MENTOR, PLUME, MERIDIAN AND NAL BOOKS
are published by New American Library,
1633 Broadway, New York, New York 10019

First Printing, March, 1984

1 2 3 4 5 6 7 8 9

PRINTED IN THE UNITED STATES OF AMERICA

PRELUDE

In the pewter half-light of morning, a silken tail of fog entwined the hillside. Great bristling firs, their dark branches severed from their boughs by gossamer filaments of mist, seemed suspended above the earth. Among the peaked stone slabs and wooden crosses, at the site of a freshly dug grave, a minister was reading the final verse of the Twenty-third Psalm.

Sarina Paige closed her father's leatherbound Bible and whispered "Amen." As the first clods of newly turned earth rained down upon his casket, she shuddered, thinking bitterly of her father's abrupt summons to the bosom of Abraham so far from their Oregon home. He should have been laid to rest beside her mother on the banks of the Willamette River and mourned by loving friends, instead of being buried on this bleak San Francisco hilltop and condemned to spend eternity among strangers.

As a parting gesture of condolence, the minister briefly clasped Sarina's hands in his and then motioned to the two men standing silently by the grave they had just filled. They immediately shouldered their dirt-encrusted spades and with eyes respectfully downcast hastened after him. Sarina waited until the three men were lost beyond the rim of the hill before hitching up the narrow skirt of her long kilted morning dress and kneeling beside the grave. In all her nineteen years, this would be her first and final separation from her father.

She stared dismally at the crudely hewn wooden marker which proclaimed that Reverend Thomas-John Paige had been born July 3, 1833, and had died May 17, 1882. How bleak that marker was. It revealed nothing of the man's compassionate and loving nature. It said nothing of the

5

voice which had soothed her while she wept for the mother she had never known. Or the arms which had held her after some nightmare had disturbed her sleep. Or the hands which had turned the pages of his Bible as she learned to read the Scriptures.

Tears welled in Sarina's large golden eyes.

"Father?" Her voice was a tentative whisper. "Oh, Father, what should I do now?"

But there was no answer from the Stygian darkness where her father's soul lay in repose.

"Should I carry on without you?"

Even as she spoke, she knew that to wait for some response was futile. And so, with a sigh of resignation, she slowly rose and made a vague attempt to brush away the bits of earth clinging to the skirt of her gray muslin gown. Once again she felt a pang of remorse at not being draped in the somberness of mourning. But she owned no black gowns and there had been no time to locate and engage a seamstress.

Time. She was grimly reminded of how little remained, for the American clipper *Halcyon*, on which her father had booked their passage, was due to sail the following morning for China. It was in Shanghai that her father was to have continued his ministry, while she was to have taught at the Townsend Mission School there. She had yet to decide whether to continue on alone or return to Oregon City and see her father's lifelong dream defeated.

As if to throw off the mantle of her grief, Sarina straightened her shoulders and stiffened her spine. This was how her father would have wanted her to stand—poised and tall, her head held proudly, her body taut with purpose. Decisions would come later. There was time now only for good-byes. She pressed her fingers to her lips and then bent to touch the rough wooden cross. Running her fingertips over each letter in her father's name, she whispered one last farewell. Then she turned and walked slowly down the hill.

The carriage she had hired made its descent into the city at a clip which set Sarina's teeth to chattering and bounced her body up and down on the cracked leather seat. As they navigated the precipitous streets, Sarina cast about in her mind for some argument to weight her decision in favor of either returning home or setting sail for

China. Now that her father was gone, the prospect of returning to Oregon was painful indeed. The rectory of St. Clement's Episcopal Church was now home to the family of the young minister who had taken her father's place. His own wife was already teaching the eighteen boys and girls Sarina herself had taught in the tiny schoolhouse on Birchtree Road just two blocks from St. Clement's. There would be nothing for her now but knowing smiles and ill-concealed pity in the eyes of those who had castigated Reverend Thomas-John Paige for choosing to desert his loyal parishioners.

Hugging her Bible close, Sarina thought of the children at the mission school awaiting the arrival of their new teacher, even as Dr. Townsend was awaiting his new minister. Her bottom lip quavered. How could she let them all down? Like her spirited father, she too had lived her life fired by a strange restlessness, a sweet compulsion which had seen them both united in the common purpose which had set them forth together on this blighted journey. Dare she leave their common dream to others now?

And then there was China, a world both enchanted and forbidden, mystical and corrupt, a place of almond-eyed beauty and fragrant blossoms, of temples and strange rituals and the pagan worship of those long departed. It was a splendid world which fascinated her, beckoned to her, summoned her. With a sigh, she set the Bible down on the seat beside her and closed her eyes, but its remembered warmth burned like a brand upon her flesh.

A few moments later, the carriage lurched to a halt in front of the dilapidated brown frame building with the name Grand Hotel splashed in large, uneven white letters across the face of it. Sarina picked up her Bible and stepped down from the coach, making her way slowly up the sagging front steps of the hotel and waking a mongrel dog from its nap on the shaded porch. Passing the door to what had been her father's bedroom, she felt the full burden of her grief return, causing her to hurry down the hall to her own room and quickly close and bolt the door.

Untying the yellow satin ribbons on her small gray straw bonnet, she removed the hat and set it down on top of the scarred pine dresser. She unpinned her long hair and then used her fingers to massage away the dull ache the pins had caused. Bending closer to the gold-painted mir-

ror hanging above the dresser, she grimaced at her
reflection. Her cheeks were tracked with the dirt from her
father's grave and her own dried tears.

She poured some water from the white china pitcher on
the washstand into a matching washbowl and used the
lavender-scented soap she had brought with her from
home on her hands and face. After rinsing away the last
traces of the soap, she gently patted her face dry and then
examined herself all over again.

In the gilt-framed mirror, the flaxen tumble of her hair
was dappled with gold, and her hazel eyes, slanted provoc-
atively beneath finely arched blond brows, glowed like
twin orbs of molten bronze. With one corner of the towel
she dabbed at a final speck of dirt near one saucily flared
nostril and then playfully wrinkled her nose. This deepened the dimples in her cheeks and drew her gently pointed
chin taut. Her eyes narrowed as she scrutinized her mouth.
Full and upturned to lend her beauty an air of impishness,
it was now swollen from crying and tugged unhappily
downward. As her bottom lip began to quiver threateningly,
she flung the towel aside and hastily averted her gaze.

Her cheeks reddened in shame as she recalled how
often her poor father had been forced to chastise her for
posturing before her mirror. To him such behavior was
both unseemly and immodest, and especially inappropri-
ate in one intent on spreading the word of God to the
unfortunate heathens of the world. With a dispirited sigh
Sarina flung herself across her bed, ignoring the protesting squeal of the springs, and wrapped her arms around
her lumpy pillow.

Her weary gaze traveled the length and breadth of the
bleak little room and then finally came to rest on her
father's Bible sitting on the dresser where she had left it.
How could she turn back now, when their dream had only
just begun? The sudden surge of excitement welling up
inside her took her by complete surprise. Once again she
could feel the warmth from the Holy Book on her skin, its
strength seeping into her and reinforcing what she was
slowly coming to acknowledge as the only course for her
life to take.

She turned her head toward the open window. Not two
blocks from where she was lying was the harbor, and
somewhere among the sloops and schooners, the fishing

boats and shallow-draft feluccas, a clipper rode at anchor, awaiting the morning tide. She could almost taste the salt of the sea on her tongue and feel the lash of the wind in her face. She saw the canescent sweep of the waves spread before her, a foam-tipped blanket of unending blue, and in her heart she knew.

When the *Halcyon* sailed for China on the morning tide, she would be sailing on it too.

1

Salt spray dampened her face and plastered escaping tendrils of blond hair to her cheeks as she stood on deck in the tangy sea air. A sudden squall sent a stinging shower of sea foam over the side, splotching the fine muslin skirt of her leaf-brown morning dress. Sarina took hold of the rail in both hands and gazed up at the full spread of canvas rippling in the wind high above her.

With her three skysails and full set of mainsails, the clipper was knifing her way through the waves of the Pacific with majestic ease. When the captain had proudly referred to the *Halcyon* as a "greyhound of the sea," Sarina had realized it was no idle boast. The clipper was a formidable adversary indeed for the restless, surging sea, and it was up on deck that Sarina could witness for herself the superb battle being waged between them.

None of the other passengers dared brave the chill Pacific as she did, much preferring the small but comfortable dining parlor instead. There the men would light up their pipes and sip their brandy and talk of hunting or the railroad or of their various business ventures, while their wives took up their embroidery hoops and chatted among themselves. This contented gathering was composed of only seven couples, yet their open disapproval of her and their implied insistence that she not consider herself part of their select company had stung her with a force far greater than their scanty numbers. By traveling alone, without benefit of parent or chaperon, she had obviously flaunted herself as a woman of questionable virtue, and as such had brought about their immediate disdain and her own ostracism.

But in spite of her imposed solitude, she had thus far

borne the sea journey far better than the rest of them. On those occasions when the oil lamps in the dining parlor swung to and fro, and the dishes slid from one end of the table to the other, and the sailors themselves were hard put to maintain their footing, Sarina found herself, more often than not, dining alone. Her hardiness afforded her wounded pride some small measure of satisfaction, but when she was alone in her tiny cabin again, the satisfaction would give way to the loneliness she felt.

"There you are, Miss Paige," called out a melodic voice which scattered her thoughts. "I see you have come once again to view for yourself the wiliness of our mother, the sea."

Sarina turned to acknowledge the man who was making his way toward her. His slippers moved soundlessly across the slippery deck and his black silk jacket and baggy trousers were being flattened against his small frame by the full force of the wind.

"And you, Mr. Loo?" she called back to him as she wrapped her brown wool shawl more securely about her shoulders. "You're either as brave or as foolhardy as I am."

"Whenever man challenges the supremacy of the sea, he is both foolhardy and brave," he told her when he reached her side. His smooth round face was at a level with hers and his black eyes were both warm and wise. "Did you know, Miss Paige, that in China the sailors worship a goddess by the name of Ma Chu?"

Sarina shook her head, awaiting his newest tale, for the kindly silk merchant had taken it upon his narrow shoulders to share not only her solitude with her but also his vast knowledge of China. Like Sarina, he too was traveling alone to Shanghai, but the purpose of his trip was to buy silk for the large fabric house he owned in the Chinese quarter of San Francisco. Being Oriental, he, like Sarina, was considered an outcast by their very haughty and proper fellow passengers, and this had served to draw the two of them into companionship.

"Many sailors carry with them a small red pouch containing the ashes from the incense they have burned before an image of the goddess whenever they are about to embark on a new voyage," Loo Wang was telling her now. "By carrying a part of her with them, they hope to gain her protection for the duration of their voyage. But if a storm should arise while they are at sea, the sailors will kneel down in the bow of the ship, and clutching their sacks of ashes, call out to Ma Chu to spare their lives. It is said that in a storm the goddess will often manifest herself to her faithful by appearing to them in a ball of fire on the mainmast of the ship."

Fascinated, Sarina glanced up at the tall wooden mast, its square white sails puffed out in the wind, crackling ropes snapping, its spars loudly creaking.

"If the ball of fire descends," Loo Wang continued, "the sailors consider it an auspicious sign and they feel certain their lives will be spared. If, however, the ball rises, the sailors believe it to be a sign of impending disaster."

Sarina shuddered at this and her face grew pale.

"Have I frightened you, Miss Paige?" Loo Wang's own face now showed concern.

"I've never been on a ship before, Mr. Loo," Sarina admitted with a shaky smile, "and I tremble to think what I might do to save myself if that ball of fire were going up instead of down."

"I believe that if such an eventuality *did* occur," he assured her in a gentle voice, "you would pray to your own God for deliverance, would you not?"

This made her smile. "Yes," she agreed. "Yes, I suppose I would."

There was much about Loo Wang that reminded Sarina of her father, and at that moment she found herself missing him more than at any other time since his death.

"Your face betrays some grief too fresh to entrust only to the sanctity of memory, Miss Paige." Loo Wang's words took her by surprise. "Might an old man share that grief with you, so that by sharing it you may be granted some healing moments of peace?"

Once again his gentleness touched that ache deep inside her, and so, in halting tones, she told him of her father's death and how she had chosen to realize their long-shared dream alone. As she spoke, a perturbed look crept into his dark eyes, but she paid it little mind, so grateful was she to this sympathetic stranger who was listening so carefully to what she was saying.

"And it is to a mission school that you are going?" Loo Wang repeated when she had finished her story.

"Yes, the Townsend Mission School on the Avenue of Filial Piety."

Furrows deepened in his high, broad forehead. "Forgive me if I alarm you, Miss Paige, but are you not aware of the difficulties being experienced of late by many of the missions in Shanghai?"

As she shook her head, he went on. "Although I myself was born in San Francisco, much of my family still lives in Shanghai. As recently as one month ago, I learned from a cousin of mine that two Christian missions had been burned to the ground. While many of the men and women within the mission fled, some were not as fortunate. Lives were lost."

Sarina thought of the last letter her father had received from Dr. Townsend, a letter which spoke only of the continuing success of the mission school and made no mention of any trouble at all. She suddenly gasped. That letter was now more than three months old.

The wind suddenly seemed too sharp, the air too cold. Was Dr. Townsend truly in danger, then? Would she herself be in terrible jeopardy if she went as planned to the mission? Seized by an icy wave of fear, she began to shiver. Agitation plucked at her even as her own fingers tugged nervously at the damp fringes of her shawl.

"I most sincerely apologize for being the bearer of such distressing news, Miss Paige," the elderly man murmured, "but perhaps the gods have looked with favor upon your Dr. Townsend and spared him as surely as they have spared so many others." He hastily tucked her arm through his. "Come, my dear, set aside your fears, for too many miles still lie between you and the truth, and needless worry cannot alter what the gods have already decreed to be."

Whether it was the pitching of the ship or the wrenching spasm of a nightmare, Sarina was jolted awake close to midnight, her heart pounding, her sheer lawn nightgown clinging to her damp skin. Shuddering, she stumbled from her narrow berth and reached for the long plush cape hanging from a peg on the wall. She slipped her bare feet into shoes still damp from her walk on deck, and after fumbling for a moment with the catch on the door, fled her stuffy little cabin.

With arms out to balance herself, she slowly made her way down the ship's narrow passage. It was clammy with moisture and rank with fumes from the smoke which curled above the glass oil lamps fixed with brass nails to the walls. As she passed the cabin at the foot of the stairs leading onto the deck, she was brought up short by the sound of shattering glass. The cabin belonged to Janson Carlyle, owner of the Carlyle Trading Company and the very ship she was now on. Since she had never seen the man, Sarina assumed he was either an elderly man who suffered sea voyages poorly, or someone who preferred his simple solitude to the questionable companionship available to him. Now as she paused outside his door, she wondered if something was wrong. But when no other sounds were forthcoming, she quickly climbed the narrow flight of steps to the open deck, eagerly anticipating the sweet release of the star-spattered night.

Janson Carlyle considered the smashed bottle with baleful eyes. So much for brandy, he decided as he opened the top drawer of his bureau and took out a bottle of gin. He filled his glass and downed half of it. It hit hard, causing his eyes to water and making him gasp. With his free hand he flicked open the gold pocket watch which had belonged to his father and squinted at the time. Midnight. He snapped the lid shut and raised his glass again.

"To you, Janson Tyrone Carlyle," he toasted himself before he drained the glass.

It helped, but not as much as he had hoped. The pain had already been numbed to a dull ache, and the ache itself was now little more than blurred sensation. A moderate drinker at best, he had decided that this was a night meant for getting drunk. After all, it wasn't often a man got to celebrate all alone both his thirtieth birthday and what should have been his wedding night.

He set down the empty glass and he reached again for the bottle. "Damn you, Hilary!" he cursed as he missed the glass and poured the gin directly onto his bare feet. "Damn you all!" he blurted out, tears bright in his eyes.

He damned his father for being struck down by a heart seizure at the age of twenty-nine, and he damned his older brother, Markham, for dying at the same age of the

very same affliction. Whether it was a coincidence or some
fatal flaw in all the Carlyle men, Janson had no way of
knowing. But it had put the fear of just such an early
death into him and into his younger brother, Garrett.

Now twenty-eight, Garrett had been crippled by his
terror and he lived a cautious and protected life, stunted
by his fear; the boundaries of his life were circumscribed,
his experiences few. Refusing to take any unnecessary
risks, suspicious of change, wary of travel, he visited his
doctor each week in the hope that his self-prescribed regi-
men of passivity would prolong his life. Janson, on the
other hand, fired by the same fear, chose instead to ride
the steed of life with merciless abandon.

He left Garrett in charge of the Carlyle Trading
Company's head offices in San Francisco, thus freeing
himself to travel the world and expand their shipping and
trading empire. He learned to live like a pauper at a rich
man's banquet, filling himself quickly and greedily, savoring each new experience as one savors a precious delicacy.
To him, life was a challenge, a gauntlet to be slapped
across the pallid cheek of inevitable death.

With a fresh glass of gin, he moved on unsteady legs
over to the cabin's one round porthole. Working at the
metal bolt, he finally released the catch and flung back the
heavy glass. He took a deep gulp of the brisk night air and
tried to concentrate on the various business matters requiring his attention once they docked in Shanghai and the
new offices he would finally be opening in Hong Kong.
Business, at least, he consoled himself, was worth a man's
full attention.

But clear thinking was virtually impossible now. He
raised his glass again, only to pause in midair. He blinked
to clear his muddied sight, but instead of melting away in
the translucent spill of moonlight, the vision he had just
seen remained intact. He caught his breath. It was her.
Once again he was witness to her restless prowling of the
sea-spattered deck.

He recalled his first glimpse of her as she had strolled
the deck their second day at sea with an aging Oriental by
her side. He should have known that she would be the
same as all those other golden-haired beauties of reduced
circumstances or lost virtue who came aboard ships like
his in the company of Oriental men. Their destinations

were often different, but their fate was always the same. Lured to China by the promise of marriage to a wealthy American or the prospect of a position in a prominent British household, these exquisite young women, highly prized for their fairness, were ultimately sold into brothels.

He was bitter as he tossed back some more of his drink. The acrid bite of the gin made him cough. His sight began to blur and the golden beauty before him slowly dissolved, yielding to a darker specter. Hers was an image wreathed in a cloud of raven hair, with smoky eyes and parted lips, whose silken skin had summoned up the beast inside him and unleashed a passion too great to be contained. Hilary Woodthrop. At first the virgin temptress. Innocent sorceress. She had bewitched him and coaxed from his cautious heart the pledge of a yearning man's love. Until he could contain himself no longer.

Let's wait, he had pleaded with her that night two years ago as they had lain spent between the twisted sheets of their passion. Wait until he had reached the age of thirty before they married, and he would take it as a sign that he was not meant to die as his father and older brother had. For if he was to have only one more year to live, how could he dare commit himself to a wife and cheat them both so cruelly? Yes, she would wait, she had promised him, her lips warm on his face, her body a torch igniting his. Yet even then he had felt the stab of a chilling fear deep inside him. How could he ever marry and risk passing on a flawed heart to any sons born of their union?

It was four months after they had celebrated his twenty-ninth birthday that Hilary had taken his love and turned it against him. She was twenty-five, she had told him, her voice strangely cool, her touch suddenly cold. If anything were to happen to him now, what would become of her? He had taken her virginity from her and no man of merit would marry her. Some already called her a spinster, others considered her a fallen woman for having kept company so long with a man who had never formally declared himself. It was over between them. She was going to marry someone else.

He had felt his manliness dissolve and all the strength drain out of him. He was stripped naked by her betrayal, and his pride lay a tattered thing at her feet. And so he had taken what little remained of the man in him and had limped out of her life. While he nursed his agony in bleak isolation, she exchanged vows with a wealthy fifty-eight-year-old widower by the name of Prescott Gray in an elaborate society wedding.

The bridegroom was the owner of the prestigious House of Gray, an emporium with branches in New York, Paris, and London, which sold the works of art and ancient relics Gray himself selected on his annual pilgrimages to the many exotic capitals of the world. He was a man who obviously cared nothing about sullied virtue, for he took Hilary, sullied virtue and all, draped her in satins and jewels, and exhibited her as his most priceless of treasures.

Janson's glass was empty. He thought of the pleasures he now took wherever they were freely given, with scant bruising, few tears, and a lack of regret at inevitable farewells. Never again would a woman entrap him, snare his feeble heart, and wring from him the promise of forever. "To you, my elusive moon goddess." He scowled as he raised the empty glass to the woman on the deck. "You'll find no yearning suitor here, sweet Artemis." He smiled, a drunken, leering smile. "A willing partner for the night, perhaps, but one who'll make no promises which either you or I can easily break."

He watched her turn around and lean up against the railing. Haloed by the moon, she now seemed to be shining the full force of her beauty on him. Sparks leaped from each silvered strand of her hair, piercing his flesh and setting his skin atingle. He felt himself being drawn toward her by filaments so fine that he could not see to resist their persuasive pull. Deep in his groin a tongue of desire was beginning to lap at him.

"No," he groaned, closing his eyes as his desire lashed at him with increasing fury.

This bewitching creature, like a siren luring the foolish sailor to his death upon the rocks, had awakened a hunger in him which he had never wanted to feel again. A hunger which could only be his undoing.

"*No!*" He released a savage cry as he wheeled from the porthole and stumbled over to the bureau. He grabbed the bottle and lifted it directly to his lips. This was how he would douse the flame of his treacherous passion. This way, and this way only.

He choked as he took too deep a swallow. Seized by a

paroxysm of coughing, he doubled over in an attempt to catch his breath.

Sarina heard Janson's violent coughing. He *was* ill, after all. Did he need help? she wondered, leaving the deck and hurrying down the stairs. As she neared his cabin, the sound of his coughing grew louder. Without hesitation she knocked on the door. The coughing continued. She knocked again. Finally she simply threw open the door.

His back was to her, his head bowed. Leaning over his dresser, he appeared to be gasping for air. She allowed the door to slam shut.

Janson whirled around, stunned by the sight of her sweeping toward him. His coughing abruptly abated, ending in a sharp hiccup.

Sarina froze, her eyes wide and disbelieving. The man wavering before her was not at all the sickly old man she had imagined him to be.

2

In the glow of the cabin's single oil lamp Sarina saw a young face, sun-bronzed and lean, and thick black hair worn long and heavily salted with silver. Like some dark, avenging demon, he loomed in front of her, clad only in a loosely sashed black brocade dressing gown. Mortified, she lowered her eyes and stared uncomfortably at the bare feet which appeared to be anchoring him to the rough plank floor.

She seemed to have been carved from ivory, he thought, cursing the alcoholic haze through which he was forced to view her. The perfection of her features reminded him of a marble statue of Diana he had found inside a Greek temple he had visited, never once expecting to glimpse such rare beauty again this side of the gods.

Sarina chanced a cautious look at his eyes and found herself thinking of dew-dappled leaves. His nose was an arrogant slash of strength in his granite face, his chin square and firm, and when he smiled at her, a crooked, drunken smile, his white teeth seemed all too capable of devouring her. She wanted to break away from him and yet something held her fast. Although he had made no move in her direction, it was as if he had put out his hand to keep her near him.

"I . . . I thought you were ill," she finally managed in a voice she no longer recognized as hers.

"And like some angel of mercy, you came to save me," he finished for her.

His cutting tone served to restore her voice to her. "I thought you were ill and in need of assistance," Sarina said, and turned toward the door.

"Leaving so soon?"

The mocking edge to his voice caused her to bristle. "You're obviously quite capable of tending to your own needs from now on."

"Oh, but that's where you're wrong. I'm still in need of some assistance."

She was here, wasn't she? Janson thought. She really *was* no different from any of the others. They had all come to him eventually, whether by choice or because they had been sent to him by their obliging Oriental companions, it had never really mattered. And it didn't matter now. What *did* matter was that she was there and that he wanted her. But to his chagrin, when he reached out to touch her, she shrank away from him.

"I won't hurt you," he promised her as his fingers grazed the side of her face.

Her flesh turned to flame, and deep within her something began to soften. She saw herself reflected in the green of his eyes and felt the heat from her face course like quicksilver through her veins. For one brief moment she melted before this man who was so boldly tracing the contours of her face with his fingertips, but then, with a rebellious cry, she pushed him away from her. Instead of thwarting him, her action only seemed to inflame him further.

"So my ministering angel's a fighting one as well, is she?" he chuckled, grasping her by the shoulders and forcing her up against the cabin wall. "I must say you're an original one, my dear. None of the others ever used a ploy like yours to gain entry to my cabin."

"I don't know what you're talking about," she spit, squirming to free herself from his grip.

"Don't you?" he smiled. "Then perhaps you'll understand this." He used the weight of his body to keep her pinned to the wall while he cupped her face in his hands and slowly lowered his mouth to hers. The juniper sting of the spirits Janson had consumed burned her lips, making them tingle and swell with a feeling she had never known before. This new sensation began with her mouth, and when his tongue twined itself around hers, it spread quickly to her own tongue. With her body cushioned by his and her soft breasts flattened against his hard chest, the feeling spread, consuming her, draining her of resistance and dissolving her will.

It was as if he had plumbed her very soul and uncovered the loneliness there. He was neither father nor friend, but a stranger, and yet in her aloneness she was inextricably bound to him. A fluttering deep within her yearning heart warned her that when this forbidden closeness ended she would be more alone than before, and she knew she could not bear to have it end.

She shivered, a cooling wave of abandonment sweeping over her. He had released her just enough to hold her away from him and to study her upturned face with a puzzled frown creasing his brow.

"You seem disappointed," he told her.

"I . . ." Confused and trembling, her lips numb, Sarina was incapable of forming even the simplest words.

"Can it be that my angel's no angel after all, and that she actually craves more?"

Before Sarina could respond, his lips had claimed hers again. All her strength seemed to flow from her and into him.

"Isn't this better than fencing with one another?" he murmured, his mouth gently nuzzling her neck.

"Please . . ." she whispered.

"Please?" he repeated, his tongue lazily following the smooth curve of her throat.

"Don't—"

Once again his lips silenced her protests. Once again she felt her strength give way to sensation. He lifted her into his arms and she became afraid. Even as she cried out to be released, she hoped that he would not abandon her.

"Put me down," she demanded, lashing out at him with weakened fists. "Put me down, I said."

"I fully intend to," he assured her, stumbling only once as he carried her to his narrow bunk.

"You have no right—"

"I have every right," he countered. "You gave me that right yourself the moment you walked in here."

"But I only came—"

"To help me, I know," he cut her off. "Well, now I'll show you just how you can help me."

She had brazenly challenged temptation and now she was about to be punished for her folly. His body was a bruising weight searing her weightlessness; his questing hands, their elegant fingers trailing an aching heat over her skin, were weapons against which she was defenseless. And yet a part of her knew she would have to resist him or be lost. Although no match for his strength and determination, perhaps if she were able to gentle him and calm him, she could effect her escape after all.

"Please . . ." she whispered, straining to put some distance between them. "Please, you're hurting me." She raised limpid eyes to his. "Couldn't you simply hold me for now?"

"Well, if you aren't the most confounding creature," he muttered, giving up in his attempts to unfasten her cumbersome cloak. Settling himself on his back, he obligingly drew her head down onto his chest and wrapped his arms around her.

She allowed him to hold her that way for a while, scarcely daring to breathe, while the rhythmic thumping of his heart echoed in her ear. By tilting her head slightly, she was able to gaze up at his face, so handsome in repose. His eyes were closed, their heavy black lashes lying in fringed crescents upon his cheeks. He appeared to have fallen asleep. She took a deep breath and braced herself for her attempt to slip quietly from his loosened grip. Holding her breath, she raised her head and started to sit up.

He immediately tensed. His eyes opened and in their verdant depths she saw a warning glimmer.

"My arm was all pins and needles," she hastily explained, while she worked to pull her cape from underneath him.

He seemed satisfied with her explanation, for he merely grunted and closed his eyes again. But his hold on her was tighter now. She felt as if she were caught in a vise. Her cloak was stifling, and twisted around her as it was, she now realized that even if she *did* try to escape, her own garments would foil her attempt.

"What the devil are you doing now?" Janson demanded, raising himself on one elbow.

"My cloak," she mumbled, struggling with the ribbons securely tied around her neck.

"Here, let me." He brushed her hands away. "If you hadn't made such a fuss, I would have done this for you before."

She tried in vain to ignore the burning imprints left by his fingers on her throat as he successfully unfastened the stubborn ribbons. She tried to deny the tingling sensations alive on the surface of her skin as he slowly eased the cape from her shoulders. Now, with the cloak removed, she suddenly felt unbound and exposed. In her flimsy nightdress she was as naked to his gaze as if she were wearing nothing at all. Bending to retrieve what she had so foolishly discarded, she anxiously gauged the distance between the bunk and the door, praying that if she should spring from the bed now, she would be faster on her feet than his intoxicated condition would permit him to be.

As she moved, she heard her gown begin to tear, for part of the filmy skirt lay pinned beneath his unyielding weight. With a cry of frustration she tugged at the gown even as he roused himself again and grabbed her by the wrists.

"And here I thought you wanted me to hold you," he chided her, wrestling her onto her back and pinning her arms above her head.

Snarling, she writhed beneath him, her head thrashing from side to side as she fought once more to discourage his advances.

"I think you're carrying your protesting a bit too far, my sweet," he panted as he grappled with her. "One should always know precisely when just such an act grows tiresome and dulls the game."

Her shrill denial was silenced by a savage kiss. What a fool she had been, she chastised herself, what a naive fool. She was a child playing at being a woman, and she had succeeded only in ensnaring herself. But just as his lips began to explore the sensitive rim of her ear, another plan sprang into her desperate mind. She would play out his game, and once he had exhausted himself, she would finally make good her escape. And so she simply stopped struggling. She lay beneath his exploring touch, a docile creature, and willed her mind to ignore what was being visited upon her flesh, while she waited for him to wear himself out.

Janson's lips and hands were alive with glorious feeling. Wherever he laid his mouth, it was all sweetness and warmth, while beneath his caressing fingertips her skin was like gilded satin. He unfastened the tiny buttons on her nightdress, peeling the fine material away from her body as if he were peeling back the outer petals of a rose.

"My God, you're exquisite," he breathed, warming the valley between her breasts.

In her innocence, Sarina lay waiting patiently for his ardor to cool, but a sudden rush of air against her skin made her gasp. He had her gown undone, the bodice open to the waist and her breasts exposed and at his mercy. She whimpered as his mouth closed hungrily around one tender globe of flesh, and she arched her back, rising to meet the demands of his lapping tongue. A shudder of pleasure shook her body, and Sarina dug her fingers into his shoulders, but instead of the coolness of his robe, she felt the moist warmth of his skin and breathed in the alien scent of a man for the first time.

She looked into his eyes and lost herself. She was helpless and drowning, aching for a swift end to her delicious agony. He smoothed each curve and hollow of her body, following each swelling contour as he outlined her with tender fire. And then his hand came to rest on that most secret place from which all the strange new feelings were emanating. Sarina's breath caught in her throat, for here was where the flames were scorching her body and singeing her very soul.

He parted her legs then, using both his hands to gently separate them. She cried out in terror. Was she now to be pinned to this devil who was preparing to send her hurtling straight to eternal damnation?

Janson, his hunger now bordering on anguish, his need too great to be contained any longer, plunged inside her with a choking sob. He didn't understand why, when he had thought her to be as ready as he was, she was rearing up and attempting to buck him off. He was no plunderer, no despoiler; he had assumed her to be his more-than-eager partner by the time he had finally entered her. Confused, yet strained to bursting, he rode her with misgivings stunting his joyous ride.

Her attempts to push him away only brought him closer. She was pinned beneath him by his arms and legs, but it was her fear and her pain and her own need which truly bound her to him. With each thrust and parry of their warring bodies she felt herself being tugged down into a spiraling vortex, to be spun round and round, and then hurled upward again. And then, in one final stinging swell, she crested. She shattered into rainbow fragments, each one a crystal of reflected rapture, which slowly fused into a single glorious being once more.

All she could hear now was the slapping of the sea against the sides of the ship and the soft puffs of his even breathing. Smoky shadows wavered in the faltering lamplight and flung themselves across the bunk where she lay entwined in her lover's arms. Her body felt bruised, anointed by a strange and disquieting wetness, soothed and yet sore.

She turned her head to the wall, away from the sight of him, away from the dancing shadows, toward the darkness, where she and her blackened soul now belonged. A sob rose in her throat. She had proved herself to be no better than a common harlot, a daughter of darkness, a true child of Lucifer himself.

Seeing that he was safely asleep, she slid cautiously out of the relaxed circle of his arms. She stood for a moment on buttery legs, trembling from unaccustomed battle, before reaching for her discarded gown and cloak. As she hastily fastened the buttons on her nightdress, she heard him groan. She watched as he turned onto his side and flung out one arm as if to assure himself in sleep that she was still there. Ignoring the rest of the buttons, she threw on her cloak and slipped soundlessly from the cabin.

She found her way up to the deck again and leaned heavily against the ship's wooden railing. The moon was riding high, a full benevolent circle hung there among the stars, but as her eyes filled with tears, the moon and the stars dissolved into one hazy streak of shadowed silver. No man would marry her now. Her maidenhead had been stolen, her virtue lost. She thought of the innocent children she would soon be teaching and she wept for them as well as for herself. She was unclean now, unfit to instruct them in the ways of righteousness and good.

As she stood there seeking a refuge from her grief and her shame, a bracing slap from the howling wind began to dry her tears. Its cold breath then seemed to penetrate her body. It cooled her heart and chilled her soul and froze all that was soft and vulnerable within her. No longer would she be able to cloak herself in the protective ignorance of a child, for she had lost her first battle as a woman, and she could never again retreat into the sanctity of innocence.

As she drew her cape around her more securely, so she wrapped a newly gained strength around her aching heart. She could spend precious little time on mourning from now on. She would need all of her wits and all of her courage to prepare her for whatever awaited her in Shanghai. Firm in her resolve, she leaned closer to the rail, peering into the foam-capped ebony waves as if seeking a consoling reflection of herself. But there was none. Daughters of darkness left no reflection.

Janson stumbled onto the deck, certain that he would find her there. The satisfaction their coupling had granted his yearning body had been all too quickly tempered by the sight of her vanquished maidenhead staining his tumbled sheets. She had been, as she had protested, an innocent after all. Confusion and remorse warred within his pounding head, while both emotions were themselves overshadowed by a disquieting sense of relief at his discovery. On wobbly legs he battled the wind which rushed at him and held him back in his attempt to reach her. One pitch of the ship and she would be flung from her precarious perch and lost beneath the roiling surface of the sea.

"What the hell do you think you're doing?" he roared as he caught her roughly about the waist and pulled her away from the rail.

"Let go of me!"

"Is that any way to thank the man who's just saved your life?"

"My life didn't require saving," she retaliated.

"You obviously know nothing about ships, my angel. One healthy pitch and you'd have found yourself taking a rather cold bath."

In the moonlight her eyes were twin points of metallic gold, hard and cold, like the eyes of an animal fighting for its life. As he tried to steer her even farther away from the rail, she wrenched herself free and turned on him.

"Don't you dare touch me!" she cried. "The mark you've already left on me is one I'll wear for the rest of my life, and I'll never forgive you for that, Janson Carlyle, never!"

The wind whipped her hair into a golden frenzy and billowed her cloak like a great darkened wing behind her as she swept past him without another word.

"You know what the Chinese say, don't you?" he called
after her. "Save a life and you're forever responsible for
that life. So it seems I'm going to be responsible for you
from now on, whether you like it or not, Miss . . ."

He suddenly stopped. Hell, here he was her savior and
he didn't even know her name.

3

It was not the unusually violent pitching of the ship which confined Sarina to her cabin all the next day, but the combined burden of guilt and remorse, which cramped her belly and left little room for even the thought of food. Hunched over her Bible, she was unable to draw any comfort from its familiar passages, and the hands which kept turning the pages in the hopes of finding some solace there now seemed unworthy of even holding the holy book. But by the time the first scarlet rays of evening stained the sky, she could no longer deny the hunger which returned in earnest to claim her. With a dispirited sigh she set down the Bible on the wooden nightstand next to her narrow berth, smoothed out the creases in her rumpled gown, and made her way slowly toward the dining parlor.

She was not prepared to enter the room and find her customary table already occupied. At least not by Janson Carlyle. At the sight of him seated there, a tremulous pulsing began in her temples. Her legs seemed suddenly drained of blood, and for a moment she swayed unsteadily in the doorway. As any gentleman should, Janson swiftly rose and held out a chair for her, while she anxiously cast about for some other available table. There was none. Even Loo Wang had deserted her, for he was nowhere to be found.

Holding her chair with what Sarina considered to be mock deference, his mouth quirked in a lazy half-smile and one black eyebrow arched cockily, he seemed to be daring her to join him. The eyes of everyone else in the room were fixed on her now, smug with the satisfaction that their original assessment of her had been correct after all. In angry defiance Sarina squared her shoulders, raised her head proudly, and accepted the challenge being thrown down to her. Honoring Janson with her iciest smile, she sailed across the room toward him, and with a brief nod to acknowledge his gallantry, she settled herself on the hard straight-backed chair he was holding out for her. As he returned to his own seat, Sarina busied her trembling hands by opening her white linen napkin and draping it across her lap.

"I found my cabin especially confining tonight," he told her in a voice so low that she had to restrain herself from leaning forward to hear what he was saying. "And since you're the only passenger I've met on this trip so far, I thought you wouldn't mind sharing your table with me this evening."

"You flatter me," she returned coolly, "but I think you might have been a more welcome guest at one of the other tables."

"In other words, you don't approve of my own choice?"

She clamped her mouth tightly around her reply and stared up at the oil lamp suspended above their small table. She could not bear to look at him, for he was more shockingly handsome than she had remembered. He was informally attired in a full-sleeved white cambric shirt with a green silk cravat casually knotted at his throat, and his tan appeared more golden, his hair darker, and his eyes an hypnotically clear bottle green. Dropping her gaze, she found herself staring in fascination at the sprinkling of black hair on the backs of his hands as he toyed with the stem of his wineglass. All she could think of was how those same hands, so strong and yet so surprisingly gentle, had explored the secrets of her body and tumbled her ordered world around her in confusion.

"Do you really mind my being here, Miss Paige?" The deep thrust of his voice abruptly severed the silence between them.

"If given the opportunity, I would have chosen someone else for companionship, Mr. Carlyle," she tossed back at him with scornful emphasis on the "mister."

"Like your friend Loo Wang, for instance?"

Her eyes narrowed. "Do you know Mr. Loo?"

"Let's just say I know about him," he answered vaguely, taking a long sip of his wine. "Drink up, Miss Paige, this should really be a celebration, don't you think? After last night, you and I—"

"I'd prefer that you not talk about last night," she snapped.

"As you wish." He signaled one of the sailors on duty to refill his glass.

Sarina shifted about in her seat, feeling the need to cross her legs or to at least press the heel of her hand against that part of her which had been so cruelly violated, and which, at that very moment, was beginning to throb at the memory of that violation.

"Has my conversation spoiled your appetite or do you just not like the food?" he inquired, indicating her un-touched plate.

She glanced down at the plate as if noticing it there for the first time. Her stomach rebelled at the sight of the food. She decided to have some of the wine instead. As she slowly sipped at it, she watched Janson deftly slice a piece of the roast veal for himself and raise his fork to his mouth. Mesmerized, she saw how his lips closed around the meat and how his jaw worked as he began to chew it. Never before had the simple act of chewing seemed more suggestive or more profane.

She considered the contents of her own plate again. This time her stomach uncurled in a spasmodic growl, reminding her of how hungry she actually was. She reached for her fork. To her chagrin, it slipped out of her hand and clattered onto the floor. Heads turned. Her cheeks stung. The sound of that fork dropping onto the bare wooden floor echoed over and over again in her mind. She would have bent to retrieve the fallen piece of flatware had Janson not grabbed hold of her wrist.

"One of the sailors will bring you another one," he told her.

The mocking tone was gone from his voice, yet she still felt as if he were giving her a lesson in deportment. But he was as good as his word. The same young sailor who had filled Janson's wineglass a few moments earlier promptly appeared with a clean fork, which he slid into its properly allotted place in front of her.

"Thank you." She managed a polite smile for the boy, but she could not manage one for Janson.

The veal was tasteless, the potatoes cold, the peas and

lima beans shriveled and dry. She soon abandoned her attempts to eat and concentrated instead on a second glass of the wine.

"The captain tells me you're planning to teach at one of the American mission schools in Shanghai, Miss Paige." Once again he was intruding upon her thoughts.

"Yes, that's correct," was her forced reply.

"Aren't you a bit young to be traveling all this way alone?"

"The decision was mine to make, Mr. Carlyle, and in spite of my age, I'm quite capable of looking after myself."

Somehow his skeptical look implied otherwise, and she realized that by her own foolish actions the previous night she had already proved herself to be something of a liar. He must have divined her thoughts, for he suddenly reached out and placed his hand over hers. The warmth and the familiar pressure of his touch were almost more than she could bear.

"About last night," he said softly. "I was drunk and I mistook you for someone else. That is, I assumed you were someone you obviously aren't, and I want to apologize for that. If—"

"I don't know who you thought I was, Mr. Carlyle," she cut him off angrily as she pulled her hand away, "but some practiced apology on your part can never undo what you did in the name of drunkenness."

Remorse darkened his eyes for a moment, but when that moment had passed, stubborn pride had lightened them again.

"I offered you my apologies, Miss Paige, in good faith, and if you were anything like the lady you consider yourself to be, you'd know how a lady goes about accepting just such an apology." He drained the last of his wine and set down his glass. "There are too few hours in the day to waste even one of them on self-pity and regret. You'd better learn to let yesterday be yesterday, my dear, otherwise you'll have precious little place in your life for anything but mourning the past. It's a lesson I've learned all too well."

With that he flung his napkin onto the table and scraped back his chair. Again all heads turned in their direction. He snapped her a curt nod and then strode briskly from

the room, leaving a hum of excited conversation in his
wake.

Stunned by his verbal tirade, Sarina forced herself to
remain seated until she could collect what remained of her
scattered pride. Then she got up from the table, and with
as much dignity as she could manage, looking neither to
the left nor to the right of her, she walked to the door.
Once outside in the corridor again, she released a pent-up
sigh of relief and allowed her shoulders to sag. She found
her way back to her little cabin and collapsed on her bunk.
Only then was she finally able to stop shaking.

The days passed with agonizing slowness, one blending
monotonously into the next. Sarina was afraid of having
to endure another meal with Janson Carlyle, but he did
not appear in the dining parlor again. On her occasional
strolls around the deck, she would sometimes catch brief
glimpses of him at a distance, but when she did, she would
turn her back to him and concentrate instead on the
ballooning canvas and the snapping ropes and the spiny
lick of the wind in her face.

They were just three days out of Shanghai. Sarina and
Loo Wang were taking afternoon tea in the dining parlor
when the ship began to groan ominously. Without further
warning it lurched precariously to one side, spinning dishes
onto the floor and reducing them to porcelain splinters.
Sarina choked back a scream as her chair began to slide
across the room, while Loo Wang grabbed hold of the
table in time to prevent his own chair from sliding. And
then, just as suddenly as it had erupted, the turbulent
spasm gently subsided.

The lone sailor on duty in the dining parlor hastily
began cleaning up the broken dishes and righting the
toppled chairs. The two couples who had been sitting at
one of the other tables immediately used the lull to hasten
from the room, leaving Sarina and Loo Wang to begin a
fresh pot of tea by themselves.

"Have I ever told you about the festival being celebrated
in China this month, Miss Paige?" asked the kindly man as
he poured their tea.

"No," she replied somewhat hesitantly, still gripping the
sides of her seat as if bracing herself for another shock.

"May is the month for the Festival of the Dragon Boats,"

he told her. "To herald the start of the festivities, every family fastens large bundles made from artemesia leaves and sweet flag to the windows and doorposts of their houses. Then they leave their homes and spend many a joyous afternoon on the banks of a nearby lake or river simply watching the boat races. It requires thirty skilled men to row each of the fifty-foot boats, which are long and narrow and have bows carved in the shape of a fierce dragon painted in brilliant colors."

An oil lamp began to swing crazily overhead. The flame sputtered and then flared even brighter than before. A plate slid off one of the deserted tables and shattered as it hit the floor.

"The men row the boats using short, stout paddles," continued Loo Wang in a slightly louder voice. "A helmsman in the stern keeps them on course, while two men seated in the middle of the boat beat out the pace on a gong and a drum."

As Sarina set down her cup, she watched in horror as both the cup and the saucer slid off the table and onto the floor.

"When each race is over and the victors have been rewarded, cakes and spirits are passed around and—"

"I think we should return to our cabins, Mr. Loo," she interrupted him as she was struggling to get to her feet.

"Perhaps you are right," he conceded, pushing back his own chair and taking her by the arm. "We might do well, I think, to offer up a prayer to the goddess Ma Chu to ensure our safety." Although he was keeping his voice light, Sarina wondered if he were more frightened than he dared to admit.

They made their way down the narrow passage to their cabins, leaning up against the wall to keep from losing their balance. A sailor hurried past them dousing all of the oil lamps, and he cautioned them to keep their own lamps extinguished in the event of one of them breaking and causing a fire. This warning unnerved Sarina more than the erratic movements of the ship, and so when Loo Wang left her at her cabin, she was tempted to ask him to remain with her. But she resisted that impulse and groped her way toward her bunk in the dark all alone, flinging herself on the narrow berth and fumbling about in her mind for a prayer to give her some courage.

While time itself seemed to have been suspended, Sarina's
world, like some maddened dervish, spun and twisted and
twirled out of control. No longer content to rock the
Halcyon with the occasional spasm, the sea gods had begun
to unleash the full force of their fury on the hapless
vessel. The ship was lifted into the air and then thrown
down again, up and down, up and down, while all around
her the seething waves lashed and battered and tore at
her.

Clutching her stomach, emptied now of the day's two
meals and the tea she had shared with Loo Wang, Sarina
lay curled on her bunk in a weak, damp ball. Through
half-closed eyes she watched the walls of the cabin shimmering silver as they were emblazoned with flash after
flash of jagged lightning. What began as a growl of thunder in the distance crescendoed in a great rumbling crash
directly overhead, rattling the glass in the porthole and
causing her to clap her hands over her ears in an effort to
muffle the sound.

"*Our Father who art in heaven,*" she began to chant through
lips gone dry and stiff, turning to the one prayer she had
always turned to as a frightened child, "*hallowed be thy
name . . .*"

Had she embarked on this journey in God's own name
only to die? She could not believe her God capable of such
cruelty. She refused to believe He had set her on this
course if He had not intended her to see it through.

"*Give us this day our daily bread, and forgive us our trespasses
as we forgive those who trespass against us . . .*"

As she continued to pray, she began to wonder if God
even had time for the pleas of a fallen woman. She wondered too if at that very moment Loo Wang was offering
up his own prayers to his own gods in the hope of being
spared. Her terror mounted. Suddenly she could no longer
bear being alone. She pushed herself to her feet, desperate to flee the dark, stench-filled cabin which held her its
solitary prisoner. Starting forward, taking small, tottering
steps, she began stumbling toward the door.

In a searing blaze of lightning she caught a glimpse of a
virago staring back at her from the mirror hanging above
the washbasin. Her face was a strained white mask, her
hair a ghostly tangle of snarled curls, while her eyes,
smoldering like inky coals, were like the hollow sockets in

a death's-head. Stifling a scream, Sarina pulled open the door and staggered into the blackened corridor, now slick with brine.

Sloshing footsteps warned her that someone was approaching. She hastily flattened herself up against the wall to allow whoever it was to pass. A hand reached out and caught her full in the face.

"What the devil!" Janson Carlyle lost his balance and slammed into the wall. "Who is that?" he thundered.

Wincing from the pain of his unintentional assault, Sarina could only gasp out her name.

"I should have known," he grumbled, running his hands along the wall until he touched her huddled form. "Did I hurt you?"

In the dark she shook her head. "You startled me, that's all."

"I could say the same for you. Now, get back inside your cabin and grab hold of something strong unless you'd prefer to take a trip over the side."

No sooner were the words out of his mouth than the ship listed to one side, sending them both crashing to the floor. Sarina raised herself on her hands and knees, gagging as she spit out a mouthful of salty sea water. Janson stepped on the hem of her gown while he was struggling to get to his feet; then he reached for her hand. Her gown began to tear as he pulled her to her feet beside him, and Sarina was grateful for the darkness which hid her wretched state from him. She was all too conscious of the smell of her seasickness, conscious too of his disturbing closeness.

"Your cabin, I believe, Miss Paige." He kicked open the door and propelled her into the room just as the ship pitched again and threw them back onto the floor.

Sarina landed heavily on her stomach and cried out in pain. Winded, she fought to catch her breath, tugging at the air in great, desperate gulps. The engulfing darkness only frightened her more and made it impossible for her to find the air she needed.

"Don't breathe so quickly, you're only making it worse," Janson cautioned her, grasping her by the wrists and pulling her into a sitting position. "Try to take slow, even breaths. Slowly, slowly. That's better. Another one, now. A really deep breath. Good girl. Now another one."

She fought to do as he was telling her, and gradually

her heartbeats began to slow and each new breath became easier to draw than the last. When she was finally breathing normally again, he put his arms around her and cradled her against him. She wrapped her own arms about his neck and clung to him. He got up on one knee, and with her firmly braced against his chest, he carried her over to the bunk. But when he put her down, she refused to release him.

"I'm afraid," she whispered up to him. "I'm afraid to stay here by myself. Please stay with me awhile."

Without trusting himself to speak, he lay down beside her and drew her into his arms again. She filled the spaces he had tried to leave between them, much like a tiny animal burrowing into its shelter, and he knew, as she fitted herself to him, that he was lost.

"Please talk to me," she implored him, yearning for a gentle voice to soothe away her fears.

He ransacked his own troubled mind for the words to calm her. "Did you know that the Greek King of the Winds was called Aeolus?" he asked her softly.

She shook her head.

"Well, Aeolus had a daughter by the name of Halcyone, who, when she heard that her beloved husband had died, chose to drown herself rather than live without him. The gods took pity on them and turned the two of them into a pair of birds invested with the power to calm the seas."

"Is that why you named your ship the *Halcyon*?" she asked.

"Why else?" he smiled, smoothing a lock of damp hair back from her forehead.

His touch on her skin reawakened all the feelings she had been battling to overcome. With his face so close to hers, she had only to raise her head and she would be able to kiss him. Slowly, very slowly, she began to raise her head. She felt the warmth of his mouth and opened hers to receive him. The warmth dispelled the chill the fear had wrapped her in and enkindled her entire body. All around them raged the forces of death, yet in his arms and in his kiss lay the promise of life.

When he stripped away their dampened clothes, she was grateful. They were free. The dankness of the cabin enveloped her like a clammy fog, but his fingers drove the cold away again. She arched her back so that she could feel the splendid length of him against her, digging her nails into his scalp and locking them together in a fierce embrace.

He broke their embrace to explore her body, first with his mouth and then with his tongue. She cried out to him, bringing up her knees in defense against his newest assault on her. But where his mouth continued to caress and entice her, it was all warmth and wetness and weakening resistance. Her legs relaxed and parted, granting him access at last to her throbbing core.

She no longer fought the feelings eddying around her. They spun in ever-widening circles, growing deeper and stronger, until all of her seemed to be one tautly strung sensation. Giddy waves of wonderment coursed through her, and she rose and fell like the whitecaps on a storm-tossed sea. Unable to contain the exquisite agony any longer, she yearned to be released from her torment.

In the darkness she felt his face above hers again and she reached up to touch him. At his first tentative thrust, she rose and drew all of him inside her. His lips on hers were moist and full and ripe, and their tongues lashed and coiled one around the other. Where he led, she followed, and then, when she beckoned to him, he yielded and followed her.

He glided in and out of her with urgent fury, a piercing arc of fire welding them together. As she neared the pinnacle, where release lay in wait for her, Sarina longed to draw back and begin again. But it was not to be. All around her were the stars, and he set her out among those stars, where she lost herself in one glimmering burst of ecstasy.

In the indigo night, she was indigo. Gone was the golden aura, the delicate web of virgin purity. In her urgency, he had felt her hunger, and in that hunger he had felt himself being devoured. She was demanding of him what he had pledged no one would ever win from him—his life—and he ached to keep from her that which she fought to gain from him. Throwing back his head, Janson cried out his protest to the hovering blackness, but even as he did so, he released his final hold on himself.

Sarina, shuddering in the throes of her own return, grew rigid. The glorious heat of their union gave way to a frost so chilling that she began to shiver. Her tears fell in silence and dried as they fell, her arms dropped limply to her sides. She had offered herself, a willing suppliant, to what she had believed to be the promise of life, only to discover it to be a death of sorts after all. She now despised Janson Carlyle almost as much as she despised herself. Not only had she wantonly given herself to a man who cared nothing for her, but she had given herself to a man who, in his passion, had called out to someone else.

Someone named Hilary.

4

In the pearlescent glow of an ocean sunrise, the storm
burbled weakly and then finally died. Despite the sea's
welcome calmness, however, the turmoil within Sarina raged
on. She had feigned sleep, grateful when Janson had
stolen from her cabin sometime during the turbulent night,
leaving her to spend the remaining hours until morning
alone with her newer shame. Even now, as the duskiness
of her cabin warmed into the promise of a golden day, she
was still reliving each moment of his treacherous loving.

She knew they had been equally to blame for what had
happened between them. Janson Carlyle had been a man
driven only by lust, while she had permitted her fear to
propel her, with a woman's need for a man's strength, into
a passionate but loveless coupling. A woman. The word
stuck like a prickly brier to the walls of her mind. That she
had begun this journey with the eager innocence of a
child, only to see the child in her crushed by journey's
end, was lamentable indeed. But she knew, as she disentan-
gled herself from the twisted sheets and swung her legs
over the side of the bunk, that the time for lamenting was
past. She would do as Janson Carlyle himself had advised
her to do. She would learn how to set aside the regrets
born of yesterday's mistakes and direct all of her energies
to getting through, if not enjoying, today.

As she dressed, she found that in spite of her attempts
to deny it, her female vanity had been mortally stung by
Janson's calling out another woman's name as he spent
himself in her arms. Who was this Hilary? she wondered
as she pinned a thick coil of blond hair to the small nest of
curls already formed on top of her head. Was she very
beautiful? Releasing a number of smaller ringlets, she

arranged them in such a way that they softly framed her entire face. Was he betrothed to this Hilary? She pouted as she concentrated on freeing several more strands of hair to curl becomingly at the base of her neck.

Studying the severe lines of the simple pale yellow muslin gown she was wearing, she imagined that the mysterious Hilary's gowns would be cut from the finest silk, frothed with the most delicate lace and spangled with magnificent beads. Her undergarments would be made of sheerest lawn, all ruffled and frilled, and not sensibly plain like Sarina's. Her hats would be exotic pastel confections adorned by plumes and ribbons, and whenever she appeared out-of-doors in public, she would no doubt carry a parasol to shield her perfect skin from the rays of the sun and her modesty from the admiring glances of everyone she passed.

Annoyed that she should be indulging in such fanciful thoughts, Sarina picked up her brown wool shawl and hurried from the cabin, closing the door with a definitive bang to further emphasize the end of this conversation with herself. She started down the passageway, only to find her path temporarily blocked by Janson Carlyle, who was just closing the door to his own cabin.

Seeing her standing there, with her intricately bound hair and filmy flower-sprigged summer tea gown, made him smile. "Off to a garden party, Miss Paige?"

Sarina drew her shawl around her to defend herself against the heat of his appraising stare. "I thought I would take a walk on deck," she answered him coolly.

"With what you're wearing, I'd advise you to spend your time sitting in the dining parlor instead. The deck is still filthy because of last night's storm."

"Thank you for your concern, Mr. Carlyle," she managed through tightly clenched teeth, "but you needn't trouble yourself about my state of dress."

"How foolish of me," he smirked. "I forgot you were the one who could take care of herself. I apologize, Miss Paige."

Twin spots of color flamed in her cheeks. "Would you kindly step aside and let me pass!" she demanded.

"And deprive myself of such winsome company?"

"You may want *my* company, Mr. Carlyle, but did it ever occur to you that I might not want *yours?*"

"You didn't seem to feel that way last night," he returned, a hint of acid in his voice. "As I recall, you even begged me to stay with you."

"And did I forget to thank you for your solicitousness, Mr. Carlyle?" She decided to change tacks, and dimpled obligingly for him. "That was selfish of me, wasn't it? May I thank you properly now?"

Crooking a finger at him, she motioned for him to bend down. As he leaned toward her expectantly, she stepped quickly around him and, lifting her skirts high, tripped lightly up the stairs. Her satisfaction lasted only until she had reached the top step. Then the sound of his mocking laughter made her gnash her teeth in complete frustration. Once again it was he who had emerged victorious from yet another of their confrontations.

She did not see Janson again until the morning that the *Halcyon* sailed regally into Shanghai. Standing at the rail of the ship, with Loo Wang at her side, Sarina could barely contain her excitement, for here at last was the enchanted world he had so eloquently described to her. All around them the water was so thick with life that the harbor seemed to be covered completely by a jagged blanket bristling with boats of all sizes. Great three-masted junks predominated, their large square sails flapping in the gentle breeze as they moved among the smaller single-sailed sampans and narrow-bodied houseboats. As the clipper glided past these low, flat boats, Sarina noticed groups of small children at play on board all of them. Each of the boats was pushed forward by a man who stood at the bow using a long wooden pole, while the lone woman aboard was occupied either with preparing their noon meal or with spreading their wet clothing to dry over the boat's arched mat roof.

Lining the wharves were rows of low wooden warehouses, squat red-brick buildings and knots of ramshackle wood-and-paper shanties. The unloaded cargo from a number of recently arrived ships stood stacked on several of the crowded piers, while on others, groups of bare-chested men, both Western and Oriental, worked to fill the holds of those ships waiting to put out to sea. As Sarina's gaze slowly traveled upward, she could see, above the drab gray-brownness, a brilliant fringe of soft and welcome green. What she was viewing, she realized, were the trees and shrubs of the city's many residential avenues, for in between those patches of green nestled small, neat houses, square and white and gleaming. As the hills of the city climbed even higher, the expanse of green soon broadened. The houses grew larger and grander, and clay chimney pots rose in vertical profusion from dozens of peaked red-tile roofs. These, Loo Wang pointed out to her, were the great pillared homes of the wealthy.

She was scarcely aware of them docking. Only the gentle pressure of Loo Wang's hand on her arm alerted her to the fact that their luggage was being unloaded. She watched her three small bags being piled with the others on the dock below them with a mixture of anticipation and dread, for as surely as a new journey awaited her, another was quickly drawing to a close. Turning from the rail, she shielded her eyes from the stabbing white glare of the noonday sun. And then she saw him. A strange longing plucked at her heart and wedged a lump of painful regret high in her throat.

With the sun behind him, his hair was liquid silver, his features burnished bronze. Immaculately attired now in a fawn-colored frock coat, wearing an embroidered white waistcoat and white trousers, with a brown-and-white-striped cravat tied neatly below his proud square chin, he looked to all the world like the successful businessman, the ambitious entrepreneur. But Sarina saw only the majestic breadth of his shoulders, the strength in his arms as they lay folded across his chest, and the power in his thighs as he stood with legs set wide apart, his arrogant gaze trained solely on her.

Pinned beneath his unrelenting stare, she knew once more the dizzying effects of his power over her, and she damned him for being able to take what strength she had and reduce it to a yearning, aching need. Angry now, she turned her back on him and impatiently awaited her turn to disembark. She had no farewells for this man who had seized from her what any other man would have cherished, no good-byes for someone who could render her weak and mindless with a single piercing glance.

"Aren't you even going to say good-bye to me, Sarina?"

At his shocking use of her Christian name, Sarina whirled around to face him. She was prepared for anything but the troubled green eyes so solemnly regarding hers at that moment. Their surprising cloudiness unsettled her far more than his mocking voice had ever managed to do, and she found herself confused and suddenly tongue-tied.

"Well?" One dark brow lifted impudently and his voice was once again sharp. "Or do you really not want to say good-bye after all?"

This was the Janson Carlyle she recognized, the one for whom her claws were always ready. Haughtily Sarina raised her head and answered in a tone which surpassed his for coldness. "I'll say good-bye to you, Mr. Carlyle," she told him, "and gladly, too, I might add."

His head cocked to one side, he merely smiled. "Given some more time and another storm at sea, I might have changed your mind about that, my dear Miss Paige." With a polite bow he backed away from her, and hooking his thumbs into the pockets of his waistcoat, tossed out, "Until we meet again, then," before turning and walking away.

She was grateful for Loo Wang's steadying hand on her elbow as he guided her down the narrow wooden gangplank and onto the crowded pier. Her rapid heartbeats and trembling knees told her that from somewhere on the ship she had just left, a pair of deep green eyes were watching her. It was not the sun which scalded her back, but the strength of his burning gaze. Those were not the shouts of the dockworkers or the strident calls of the fruit-and-vegetable hawkers she was hearing, but the taunting sound of his laughter. With head held high and shoulders squared determinedly, Sarina vowed to relegate Janson Carlyle to the past, where he now belonged. Yet even as she walked with Loo Wang through the crush of the milling dockside throngs, a small insistent voice deep inside her kept repeating his name.

Janson watched as she walked down the gangplank, her head high, golden curls dancing at the nape of her neck below the simple gray straw bonnet she was wearing. She moved with a fluid grace which pulled at his heart and reminded him that each step she took was one more step out of his life. Deep in his chest, a tight throbbing began, and he absently massaged the rising ache with the palm of his hand.

"You all right, sir?" questioned the captain, who was standing next to him.

Startled, Janson glanced up and dropped his hand to his side. "I'm fine, Saunders," he assured the man, "just fine."

What had he done to drive her away from him the night of the storm? Had he been wrong in thinking she had given herself to him willingly, had, in fact, fairly begged him to make love to her? He set his mouth in a grim line. In spite of her sweet innocence, she had learned quickly enough how to manipulate a man to serve her own needs. There was something particularly treacherous about a woman exercising her wiles as she hid behind the mantle of righteous piety. To Janson, Sarina Paige and Hilary Woodthrop Gray were but two sides of the same tarnished coin.

He snorted aloud as he recalled the rash promise he had made to her that night up on deck. Savior indeed. It was he who needed saving from the capricious whims of duplicitous women. He would do well to follow his own best advice and put her far behind him. Yet, even as he scoured the pier for one more glimpse of her, he cursed himself for a fool and for wanting their time to come round again.

Sarina stood on the quay with Loo Wang at her side, watching as, one by one, the passengers from the *Halcyon* were bundled off into waiting carriages and driven away. Dabbing at her flushed, moist skin with a neatly pressed handkerchief already growing damp and limp, she gazed about her in increasing consternation for some sign of the short, round-bellied Dr. Townsend with his unmistakable thatch of snowy white hair.

"You really don't have to wait with me, Mr. Loo," she said, turning to the man who was patiently scanning the teeming docks on her behalf. "If Dr. Townsend doesn't come for me himself, he'll undoubtedly send someone else from the school in his place."

"It would be unthinkable of me to leave you here alone," replied the older man in his gentle voice. "I will wait, Miss Paige, and see that you are safely delivered into the hands of your Dr. Townsend."

"But you have a business appointment, don't you?" she persisted.

"I do"—he nodded—"but it will keep awhile longer."

In spite of her protestations to the contrary, she was grateful to have Loo Wang's company, for just as the minutes continued to chug slowly by, so her agitation continued to mount. Could Dr. Townsend have forgotten that she and her father had been due to arrive that morning aboard the *Halcyon*? Was it even possible that he had never received her father's letter and was at that very moment sitting down to lunch at the mission school on the Avenue of Filial Piety, completely oblivious of her presence in Shanghai?

"Missy Sarina Paige!"

Both Sarina and Loo Wang glanced up at the same time.

"Missy Paige! Missy Sarina Paige!"

A Chinese youth dressed in a sweat-streaked gray jacket and baggy gray trousers, a rumpled piece of paper fluttering in one hand, had just stepped from the gangplank of the *Halcyon* onto the pier and was heading in their direction.

"Thank heavens," sighed Sarina, raising her arm and waving her handkerchief at the young man still calling out her name.

He was short of breath and his round face was red and slick with sweat when he finally reached her side. "You Missy Paige?" he blurted out, and when she nodded, he said, "I am Ku Jen, gardener at mission school. Your father not come Shanghai?"

"My father is dead," Sarina told him, her voice faltering slightly.

"So sorry, missy," he murmured, lowering his dark eyes as a sign of respect.

Finding the moment an awkward one, Sarina quickly used it to introduce Ku Jen to Loo Wang and watched as the two men bowed in formal greeting to one another.

"Last week I promise Dr. Townsend I come today," explained the young gardener. "And so"—his gaze wavered—"I here now."

"And how is Dr. Townsend?" Sarina inquired. "It's been more than a year since I've seen him."

Again there was that slight shifting in Ku Jen's eyes. Puzzled by his hesitation, Sarina studied his face more closely. And as she did, gooseflesh traced a sudden chilling path down the length of her spine.

"Missy come long way," the young man finally mumbled, "and I very sorry, but Dr. Townsend dead."

Sarina gasped. The sun seemed to be flaring into a giant ball of white heat in front of her staring eyes.

"Oh, God, no," she whispered, shaking her head. "No, it can't be." A fearful numbness was beginning to spread through her entire body, while all around her the sun kept growing brighter and hotter.

"Mission school burned four days ago. Three women, five children flee Canton. One man return America."

She was only vaguely aware of Loo Wang's fingers biting into her upper arm and helping to keep her standing upright.

"You go Canton too, missy?" asked Ku Jen.

Loo Wang's pressure on her arm increased. Sarina tried to piece together some of her scattered thoughts, but she was unable to form a cohesive whole out of any of them.

"You return America, then?"

The young man seemed to be drifting farther and farther away from her, his figure growing smaller, his voice fainter.

"Miss Paige?"

Sarina stared bleakly at Loo Wang through eyes which were growing increasingly dimmer. She had been cast adrift upon an alien sea thousands of miles from everything safe and familiar, and set down among a hostile people to whom she was to have carried a message of peace and love. If there were those among them who had thought nothing of taking the life of a man as gentle and pious as Ezekiel Townsend, what would prevent them from taking her life as well?

Suddenly a great gray mantle fluttered down from the cloudless sky, obscuring the face of the sun and settling around her shoulders. Its gathering weight forced her to her knees. From there it was only a gentle slide to the ground.

She looked for the sun and wondered where it had gone. In the unfamiliar half-light she tried vainly to sit up, but when her world began to tip and tilt out of focus, she lay back and closed her eyes again. The next time she opened them, Loo Wang was bending over her.

Helping her to sit up, he first rearranged the silk cushions that were behind her and then handed her a delicate blue-figured white porcelain cup filled with a hauntingly fragrant green tea.

"Sip it slowly," he advised her, "so that you might more fully appreciate its special bouquet and beneficial soothing effects."

She did as he suggested, taking small sips of the scalding tea while gazing about at her strange surroundings. She was lying on a low silk divan in the corner of what appeared to be a vast warehouse. Great bolts of cloth were stacked neatly and according to color on wide wooden shelves reaching from the floor to the ceiling of the cavernous room. Low wooden tables scattered throughout the room were covered with similar bolts of cloth, some tightly rolled, others partially unbound and spilling like shimmering silken waves onto the floor.

"You chose a most fortunate location when you became indisposed, Miss Paige," said Loo Wang with a smile as he refilled her empty cup. "The man from whom I purchase my silk owns this very godown . . . pardon me, warehouse; so you see, it was a simple matter indeed to have you carried here."

Sarina was suddenly shy as she stared into the pale contents of her cup. "I'm most grateful to you, Mr. Loo, both for your continued kindness and for the kindness of your friend."

"It is the primary concern of every host to see that his honored guests are made as comfortable as possible, my dear young woman."

These words, spoken in soft, gently modulated tones from the doorway, possessed a quiet strength which permeated the entire room. Sarina looked up and immediately caught her breath. The man coming toward her seemed to be gliding rather than walking, for there were no feet visible beneath his magnificent floor-length crimson robe. Although of slender build, he gave the impression of a man of muscled hardness because of the proud set of his elegant head, his squared shoulders, and the rigid straightness of his back. Above his high, unlined forehead, his black hair was drawn into a long braided tail, and the top of his head was covered by a brimless round crimson hat.

As he drew nearer, Sarina could see that his robe was alive with great open-mouthed dragons elaborately embroidered in threads of blue, green, black, and gold onto the heavy crimson silk. Somewhere within the voluminous pointed sleeves of his gown were his hands, which, when he revealed them to her, were small and pale and pressed, palms together, in the formal Oriental gesture of greeting. He bowed low in front of her, and as he straightened up again his fathomless black eyes captured and held her golden ones. The smile which lit his unremarkable features and suffused his pale face with a gentle pinkness seemed then to insinuate itself around her own mouth, and Sarina found herself smiling back at him.

"Miss Paige," came Loo Wang's voice from what seemed to Sarina to be a great distance, "may I present your host, Wo Shue Kwen."

Once again the man bowed to her.

"I want to thank you, Mr. Wo," she murmured, aware of his eyes caressing her face as if committing her features to memory, "and I apologize for any inconvenience I might have caused you."

Wo Shue Kwen waved aside her apology with a regal flick of his wrist. "I trust you found the tea to your liking?" he inquired. "It is a tea grown and blended on the plantation bordering my own estate. Although my old friend Lao Hong Han still refuses to divulge all of the ingredients to me, he has admitted to using both jasmine flowers and rosehip petals in it."

"It did taste faintly of jasmine," Sarina remarked, pleased that whatever had been used in the tea had left her feeling so soothed and refreshed.

"Loo Wang has told me of the unfortunate predicament in which you now find yourself, Miss Paige," Wo Shue Kwen informed her in his gentle, lilting English. "You have already honored me by accepting my humble offering of a cup of tea, but you would do me an even greater honor by permitting me to assist you in this other matter as well."

"What could you possibly do to help me, Mr. Wo?" Sarina asked him.

"You were to have taught children at this mission school, were you not?"

As Sarina nodded her head, she was reminded once again of that terrible and senseless waste.

"Have you ever instructed children before in subjects other than your Bible?"

"In America," Sarina patiently explained, "I was responsible for teaching my students reading, English grammar and spelling, arithmetic, geography, and some history."

"I see." He steepled his fingers together in contemplation, and Sarina was fascinated by how delicate his hands were and how no hair grew along their smooth white backs. "I have three young daughters, Miss Paige, who would benefit greatly by a knowledge of the English language. Their mother knows some English because I taught it to her, but she has never chosen to pass on that knowledge to them. I have been dealing with the British and the Americans most of my life, and English seems as natural to me now as my own tongue. But I am a businessman, with little time for teaching English to children, especially girls."

Sarina was startled by his bluntness, and his condescending dismissal of his daughters took her slightly aback.

"Would you be willing to teach English to my daughters, Miss Paige?" Without giving her time to even begin considering his surprising offer, he elaborated. "You would live on my estate and you would be granted all the privileges usually granted the tutor of any landlord's children. You would instruct my daughters, as is customary, in the summerhouse on the estate, and as their tutor, you would be considered an honored member of our household. May I also add, Miss Paige, that should you decide to accept my offer, you will find me to be a generous and most appreciative employer."

Her head spinning, her body strangely languorous from the tea, Sarina forced herself to stand up and walk for a moment. Loo Wang had said nothing during her entire exchange with Wo Shue Kwen, but had merely stood in respectful silence in the corner of the room. Now as she glanced at him for some direction, his dark eyes seemed to be telling her that this was a decision she would have to reach on her own.

She wondered if, by some divine intervention, this was what had been intended for her all along. When she found herself standing beside one of the tables piled high with bolts of cloth, she reached out and absently began

stroking a panel of white silk which had been heavily
embroidered with tiny gold butterflies, gold roses, and twisting stems of golden leaves. The cloth seemed to dissolve
beneath her wandering fingers like sunlight on a trailing
willow branch.

She sensed him standing behind her even before she
turned around. Their eyes were level, and yet somehow
she felt dwarfed by him.

"Perhaps if we were to set a trial period of three months,
Miss Paige"—his voice encased her like a warming cloud—
"you would be less hesitant in your reply."

Once again she tried to think clearly, but his nearness
was robbing her of her ability to reason. She had no one
now, no comforting allies, and only the prospect of a
grisly death if she were to seek refuge at another doomed
mission school.

"Three months?" she repeated, and saw him nod his
head.

Standing so close to him, she noticed that his face was as
smooth and as free of hair as the backs of his hands. The
nostrils of his broad, flat nose, which might have been
considered weak on the face of another man, flared and
retracted as if pulsing with their own life force, and the
slender slash that was his mouth seemed capable of hardening and softening at will.

But it was in his ebony eyes that his true power lay,
there where the invisible fires fueling him dwelt the
strongest. In their inky depths glowed an elusive promise—
the promise of safety and shelter. It was in search of just
such a promise that she had flung herself so foolishly into
the arms of Janson Carlyle and found nothing but emptiness and pain.

Sarina swallowed hard, effectively thrusting Janson back
into her past again. Trusting what she saw in the eyes of
Wo Shue Kwen, she said simply, "I accept your gracious
offer, Mr. Wo, and I thank you with all my heart."

5

The seductive scent of jasmine wafted toward Sarina and she smiled as she inhaled its wonderful fragrance. It was as if she had just entered an enchanted bower bounded by lushly blooming flowers, twisting vines, and broad spreading trees. White lilies and pink lotus leaves floated across the surface of a tiny ornamental pond, and in the deepening flush of twilight Sarina was still able to see the occasional flash of a golden fishtail cutting the water. Bordering the pond was an intricate rockery, where dwarf green plants and shrubs were growing. Nests of pastel-colored flowers crept over each carefully placed rock and seeped in between each clump of spongy yellow moss.

"We call this inner courtyard *t'ien ching*, or heavenly well," explained Wo Shue Kwen as he led Sarina back up the three wide tiled steps and through the black iron gate into the gardens again. "Both the courtyard and the gardens are magnificent in the final hour of day—that is why I chose to show them to you first. There is time enough to view the house, for whether it is seen with the full light of the sun warming it or in the glow of a hundred oil lanterns, it remains for me equally dismal and dark."

Together they strolled the vast, well-tended grounds, which sloped and rose like so many small mountain ridges. Whether a grove of trees, a cluster of plump shrubs, or a flowering rockery, nothing had been allowed to grow of its own accord. Every bit of green had been artfully arranged and contrived by human hands, and although Sarina found the effects breathtaking, she was somehow disturbed by the artificiality of it all.

"As you can see," said Wo, encompassing the gardens with one grand sweep of his arms, "the gardens themselves open onto the world of nature. It is this miracle which replenishes us each time we emerge from behind the brick wall which surrounds our home and keeps us safe within. Only here, with nature, can true harmony and peace be found."

His voice was like a down pillow cushioning her from the ugliness of the world beyond those very gardens. Wrapping herself in the soft cocoon of his words, Sarina felt certain that here was where she too would find the elusive peace she was seeking. Here her bruised spirit would heal, and once the pain of the past had been vanquished, she would be restored, her faith strong again, her thoughts pure once more.

They crossed a narrow willow-patterned bridge which spanned a winding brook and followed a twisting path through a grove of flowering almond trees. Then they returned by way of another bridge, this one carved out of a thick wall of solid gray rock. It was growing dark by the time they approached the house, but some of the details of the sprawling two-story structure were still visible in the deepening dusk. Built entirely of white brick, each section of the house appeared to be covered by its own peaked red-tile roof, whose corners were adorned with the heads of ornately carved and painted dragons. Dark wood beams supported the eaves and provided a long, sheltered veranda for the main rooms on each floor. Sliding panels of heavily waxed white paper closed off each room from the common balcony, and although the panels retained the heat of the house, they also kept out the light. This, Wo Shue Kwen had explained to Sarina, was the reason the oil lanterns were kept burning at all times.

They paused for a moment in the courtyard, where several stone lanterns had already been lit, and as Sarina gazed around her at the beauty reflected in the tiny dancing flames, she clasped her hands together in a gesture of unabashed delight.

"To think that so many exquisite flowers could have existed all this time without my ever having known about them," she exclaimed.

Earthenware pots of brilliant green pomegranate buds, dwarf orange trees, and stately pink and fuchsia oleanders ringed the courtyard, while up the smooth white walls of the house climbed pink Chinese roses, purple wisteria, and yellow jasmine. She proudly named each one in turn, and Wo Shue Kwen favored her with a warm, approving smile.

"You possess a most retentive memory, Miss Paige, you are most fortunate. But come"—he motioned for her to follow him—"no doubt you are tired and will want to prepare yourself before the evening meal. It is then that I will be granted the opportunity of presenting you to the other members of the Wo household."

"And will that require much preparation?" she wondered aloud, more to herself than to him.

The sudden fierceness in his gaze took her by surprise.

"It is my approval which need concern you, my dear young woman, and not theirs. I am the father and the unquestioned authority in this household, something you will discover for yourself as you become better acquainted with our ways. You may find you disapprove of many of those ways; you may, perhaps, even attempt to change some of them. But know this, Sarina Paige, our customs have withstood the trials of many thousands of years, and like the Chinese people, our customs have endured."

She was spared the embarrassment of searching for an appropriate response to his rebuke by the sound of running footsteps coming toward them. A slender young man, shabbily dressed and glistening with sweat, pounded to a halt just feet from where Sarina and Wo Shue Kwen were standing. He was breathless and panting and as he bowed to Wo, Sarina watched the older man's face darken in anger.

"I see your loyalty still lies outside these walls, Chen," observed Wo with a bitter twist of a smile. "What is it that has detained you this time?"

"Forgive me, Father," the young man panted, "but the feeding of the silkworms required all of my attention today."

"And why was that, my son?"

"Yan-wu, the overseer, was taken ill this morning with a fever, and I was forced to do the work of two men. His wife, Na, is so heavy with child that she herself could scarcely walk or fill a basket with leaves." He paused to draw a breath. "I sent her back to their cottage early in the afternoon."

"But why?" demanded Wo. "In years past, Na, like the

other women, worked in the orchards until the moment
her child fell from her womb."

"But she is older now, Father, and frail."

"I will speak to Yan-wu tomorrow about his wife," Wo
declared.

"No, Father, please. He is sickly and she—"

"Enough!" Wo held up his hand to silence his son. "You
dishonor me each time you choose to differ with me. You
dishonor me by continuing to disobey me. But you bring
shame on both of us when you dare to humble me in the
presence of others."

The young man's troubled eyes shifted about as if seeking a place to hide.

Wo then turned to Sarina. "This young man who shames
me, both in manner and in dress, Miss Paige, is Wo Chen,
regrettably my only son."

Pressing his palms together, Wo Chen bowed to her
while his father concluded the introduction. Sarina's heart
ached for this handsome young man who was in such
obvious distress. Clothed in faded and baggy gray trousers
and a torn straw jacket, his scratched and dirty feet thrust
into a pair of battered leather clogs, he seemed more the
simple peasant than the only son of a wealthy landlord.

"You may leave us now, Chen," decreed his father with
an imperious wave of his hand, "so that you may present
yourself at the evening meal in attire befitting the son of
Wo."

"Yes, Father," he murmured, bowing once again and
stunning Sarina by his abrupt change in mood.

When he had gone, Wo led Sarina into the house. "Sons
are instructed early in the ways of filial piety," he told her
in a low voice. "The properly filial son willingly accepts
punishment if his father so decrees it, even if it may cause
him to bleed. Chen is like a spirited colt, testing his master's
patience and tugging at his bridle from time to time.
Although he strains beneath my guiding hand, he knows
that a father must rule his family as he would rule a
nation."

His eyes grew hard for a moment and his voice became
cold. "Did you know, Miss Paige, that a father is permitted
to order his own son put to death for disobeying him and
then go unpunished for such a deed?"

Appalled by what he was telling her, Sarina suddenly

doubted she would ever come to understand these people
and their strangely barbaric ways. Her tentative new peace
lay around her in shreds, dispersed, like the petals of a
flower before a harsh wind, by the words of the man
sweeping so majestically beside her. Just as she had learned
the names of the various flowers in the courtyard, so had
she begun to learn something far more vital. The word of
Wo Shue Kwen was law, and woe to anyone who broke it.

By the time they had reached the last closed door on the
second floor, Wo's dark mood had lifted. As he swung
open the door for her, he said, "Your troubled silence
distresses me,. Miss Paige, for I have caused you needless
concern. I humbly beg your forgiveness for failing to
fulfill my duty as your host." He motioned for her to
enter the room. "Please . . ." He bowed. "I trust you will
find this bedchamber to your liking. The only servants
who reside in this house are the personal maids of the
women, while the house slaves dwell, as do the peasants,
in cottages close by."

Was she to consider herself a servant, then? Sarina
wondered as she looked at her room for the first time.
Forgotten now was the altercation in the courtyard and
her resulting doubts about her own position within Wo
Shue Kwen's household, for not only was the room larger
than any bedroom she had ever seen, but it was also
more opulently appointed. She was overwhelmed by its
unique and exquisite artistry.

"I've never stood in a more beautiful room," she whispered to Wo as she began moving slowly about it, feeling
somehow that she was in a trance.

Lighted by four ornately carved brass lanterns, one hanging in each corner of the room, the white walls and ceiling
seemed to be pocked with tiny diamond-shaped shadows.
Against the far wall a wide bed was set low to the floor
and covered by a thick padded white quilt in a festive
pattern of blue irises and pink plum blossoms. Resting on
the floor at the head of the bed was the Chinese style of
pillow—a small rectangular bamboo frame with a deep
curve cut into the wood for one's neck. Involuntarily rubbing the base of her own neck, Sarina wondered if it
would be considered disrespectful to request a feather
pillow instead.

On either side of the bed stood a squat black-lacquered

wood table. The severity of the black was lessened by the gourd-shaped white porcelain vase filled with sprays of pink plum blossoms set on each table. Two intricately carved dark mahogany chairs, fitted with thick pink cushions, faced one another in front of the sliding panels leading onto the veranda, while along the opposite wall stretched a long, low carved mahogany dresser with brass drawer pulls. Near the door, where Wo was patiently waiting, hands lost within the sleeves of his robe, stood an elaborate mother-of-pearl and black-lacquered screen and a tall framed pier glass.

"You are pleased, Miss Paige?"

"Oh, yes," she breathed, meeting his amused look with a wide smile.

He accepted her smile with a slight inclination of his elegant head. Then he bowed to her and backed out of the doorway. "When the chime sounds, Miss Paige, it is to announce that the evening meal is about to begin. I will attend you in the guest hall then."

It seemed to Sarina that she had scarcely washed her hands and face and rearranged her hair before the dinner chime rang out. Hastily setting down her comb, she hurried from the room and scampered down the long hallway, fearful of being late and provoking Wo into yet another fit of pique.

"You descended the staircase like a frightened young hare, my dear Miss Paige." Wo's voice was gently chiding as he greeted her at the bottom of the stairs. "Have I put some terrible fear into you because of the words my son and I exchanged in the courtyard?"

"I—"

"My dear child, you are quivering." He touched her then for the first time, and Sarina jumped as his fingers grazed her shoulder. "There is no need for you to feel such fear," he said softly, soothingly, all the while increasing his gentle pressure on her shoulder.

The weight of his hand infused her skin with a strange warmth and her body with a returning strength, so that when he started down the dimly lit corridor toward the dining room, Sarina found herself walking calmly and confidently by his side. They stopped before a pair of carved mahogany doors and waited while two male servants clad in black pushed open the doors for them. Then they entered the room.

In the warmth of the lantern light, the embroidered silk tapestries covering the walls seemed encrusted with precious jewels. On a low mahogany base in each corner of the room stood a large blue-and-white-figured ginger jar, its lid removed, filled with sprigs of pink plum blossoms and long, arched mulberry branches which had been stripped of their small green leaves. There were five high-backed mahogany chairs drawn up to the rectangular black-lacquered dining table, and standing silently, at a discreet distance behind each chair, was a young male servant. Like the two servants at the door, they were all wearing loose black jackets with long sleeves, baggy black trousers caught at the ankle by thin strips of cloth, and soft black slippers.

Only when Wo jolted her to attention by announcing her name out loud did Sarina finally realize that three of the five places set at the table were already occupied. She followed after him on legs gone numb, to the foot of the massive table, where a small, shy woman was sitting with head bowed and eyes downcast.

"My honorable wife, Sua," said Wo as the woman inclined her head even farther and murmured something indistinct in Chinese. "She knows only the English I've taught her," he explained, "and is most ill-at-ease in the presence of strangers. But the words she uttered were welcoming you to our home."

The woman raised her head for a moment and Sarina used that moment to acknowledge her with a warm smile. There was a lovely serenity about Sua in spite of the plainness of her features. Her round, smooth face was heavily powdered and the two circles of rouge on her cheeks only seemed to broaden her undefined cheekbones, but there was a wonderful sweetness to the gentle set of her mouth. Her black hair was drawn into an elaborate series of knots and loops and adorned with tiny carved ivory flowers. Less flamboyant in her dress than her awesome husband, she was wearing a simple round-necked, long-sleeved robe in pale green silk, delicately embroidered with small white magnolia flowers and leaves of a deeper green.

"And this exquisite flower"—Wo's voice cut short Sarina's

overly long perusal of his wife—"is Li, my favored one."
Sarina found herself facing the young woman who was
seated directly across from a silent and watchful Chen,
dressed now in somber black. "The daughters born of my
union with Li—Liang, Hou, and Chui—are to be your
pupils, Miss Paige."

Stunned by Wo's revelation and by the look of undis-
guised contempt in the glacial black eyes of Wo Shue
Kwen's concubine, Sarina stared uncomfortably at the top
of the woman's head. Her glossy black hair had been
twisted and coiled in such a way that it seemed a plumed
black bird had settled there. A magnificent black bird
ablaze with diamonds.

Reluctantly she allowed her eyes to begin traveling
downward. Li appeared to be about thirty, and yet her
tiny figure was like that of a young girl. Only the thrust of
her surprisingly full bosom hinted at the voluptuousness
of a grown woman beneath her elaborate robes. Her pink
silk gown was intricately embroidered with turquoise and
silver cranes and silver leaves. The broad pink girdle which
bound her waist and emphasized its smallness was fastened by a large silver clasp in the shape of a crane as well.
Its head and tail were encrusted with diamonds and its
eyes were two small round turquoises. From her ears
swung heavy diamond pendants, and the ring she wore on
the index finger of her right hand held a turquoise as
large as a quail's egg. To Sarina's surprise, the nails on
both index fingers of the woman's small, pale hands were
encased in long gold sheaths.

But in spite of the spectacular beauty of her robes and
her jewels, it was in the perfectly carved features of her
lightly powdered white face that Li's astonishing beauty
lay. Beneath fine black brows her eyes, skillfully outlined
in black kohl, glittered like onyx beads. Her slender nose
was flared in proud disdain. Her rouged lips, the top one
cresting in high peaks, the bottom one full and ripe,
pouted above a gently rounded chin. Her cheekbones
were high and extended even higher by the subtle use of
red rouge, which lent the upward tilt of her magnificent
eyes a disturbingly feline cast. Sarina shuddered, imagining this sparkling creature scratching at her very soul with
her sharp golden claws.

When a sudden graceful smile lifted the corners of the

woman's shapely mouth, Sarina was more confused than
ever. "You are most welcome here, Miss Paige," came the
hushed voice in lilting English from those softly parted
lips. One tiny hand, its golden nail gleaming, indicated the
empty chair next to hers. "Would you be so kind as to seat
yourself here to my right?"

Sarina glanced uncertainly at Sua, thinking it her duty
to perform, but the woman's veiled eyes revealed nothing.
"Miss Paige?"

Wo nodded for her to follow his concubine's bidding,
stepping aside to allow one of the male servants to draw
out Sarina's chair for her. While Wo walked slowly to his
own place at the head of the table, Sarina looked over at
Chen. A muscle was jumping in his tightly clenched jaw.
But as soon as he became aware of her watching him, his
jaw relaxed and his face became an impassive mask again.
Sarina frowned and quickly looked away. Once Wo was
seated, Sua lifted a leather-topped hammer from the table
and struck the small brass gong set in front of her. The
doors opened and a procession of servants bearing laden
platters of food filed into the room.

There was no conversation during the meal itself, and
for this Sarina was grateful. She needed all of her concentration if she hoped to eat anything that evening. The
servants had placed each of the large platters of steamed
vegetables, meat, and fish in the middle of the table and
had then set down a small bowl of boiled white rice beside
each person's plate. Once the servants had withdrawn,
everyone but her had begun to eat.

Using a pair of foot-long ivory sticks, they expertly
plucked whatever they wanted from the center platters
and dropped the steaming bits of food onto their mounds
of rice. Then, bringing their bowls up to their lips, they
used their sticks again to deftly sweep the food into their
mouths, without so much as a single grain of rice falling
onto their laps.

Glancing uneasily about her, Sarina finally began poking at a large shrimp with the ends of her own ivory sticks.
Squeezing the chopsticks together, she managed to carry
the shrimp back to her bowl of rice, leaving only one small
drop of gravy behind on her plate. Hoping the others
were too absorbed in their own meal to notice her fumbling attempts to imitate them, she tried to scoop up the

shrimp along with some of the rice. The shrimp immediately slid back into the bowl. Biting her bottom lip in consternation, she bravely tried again. Several grains of rice splattered onto the gleaming black tabletop as, once more, the shrimp slipped out of her control.

"I think our young guest requires instruction in the proper use of the *kwai-tsz*." Although Li had spoken in a low voice, she had shattered the silence at the table as effectively as if she had screamed. "Here, my dear"—she gestured to a mortified Sarina with her thin, tapering fingers—"it is all a matter of balance."

Sarina struggled to place the smooth sticks between her fingers exactly as Li was showing her, and then, once she felt more confident, she practiced opening and closing them a number of times on her own.

"Excellent." All the time Li was smiling at her, her eyes were coyly fixed on Wo. "Your young tutor is a most apt pupil herself," she told him.

Wo merely acknowledged Li's remark with a slight nod of his head and raised his small porcelain wine cup in the air to indicate that it was empty. The young man standing in silent attendance behind the landlord's chair immediately lifted a large silver kettle from a heated brazier and filled Wo's cup with more of the hot rice wine known as *samshu*. Sarina timidly raised her own empty cup and then watched in amazement while hers was just as quickly refilled.

Dessert consisted of dried fruits and nuts, and Sarina fared far better with them once she was free to use her fingers instead of her chopsticks. The meal concluded with black tea, a far stronger blend than the green tea Wo had offered her that morning. As she sipped the slightly bitter brew, Sarina thought of how drastically the course of her carefully planned life had been altered in the span of just a single day.

While her attendant was helping her up from the table, Sarina noticed that both Sua and Li seemed to be leaning heavily on the arms of their own servants as they began walking slowly out of the room. As Li moved past her, she saw why. From beneath her elegant robes there peeped the tiniest pair of slippers she had ever seen. No more than three inches in length, made of pink silk, with narrow straps tied securely around Li's slender ankles, the entire slipper was tipped precariously forward on a high, slanted heel. The hobbled steps she was forced to take were as tiny as the feet burrowed deep inside those little slippers.

Sarina glanced down at her own feet. She had always considered them small, but now she felt peculiarly ungainly and awkward in comparison to the two Chinese women.

"Do not regret the size of your feet, Miss Paige," Chen spoke up once the women had left the room. "Bound from childhood, the feet of our women are so contorted that they spend their entire lives as cripples in continual pain. Here, such ugliness is considered beautiful."

"I fear my son pays even less respect to beauty than he does to his father," cut in Wo, addressing Sarina in a voice edged with steel. Then he trained a scathing look on his son. "I give thanks to the gods of our ancestors, my unworthy Chen, that none beyond these walls knows of the shame you have brought upon me and upon this house by your treacherous thoughts and deeds."

Chen's face, his features combining both his mother's gentleness and his father's strength, grew cloudy. "Am I forever to be denied a single thought which is my own, because it is contrary to the laws of our ancestors?" he demanded. "If I refuse to worship a maimed foot for its beauty, am I to be considered treacherous?"

"The foot of a woman is not maimed if it is bound," countered Wo, "but an object of beauty, more than worthy of the name 'lotus bud.' "

"Lotus bud," Chen scoffed. "If I were the humble lotus, I would weep to hear my name so defiled."

"Wo Chen!"

It was as if a sword had been sliced through the air above Chen's head, and he obediently fell silent. When Wo spoke again, it was in a voice quavering with emotion.

"Of the four sons your mother bore me, you alone remain to bear the noble name of Wo. Only you can bestow that name on a son of yours, and only those bearing the name of Wo can kneel in worship before the tablets of our honorable ancestors. As you know well, my disobedient son, without respectful worship, no man lives on in eternity once he is dead. I fear the death of the name of Wo more than I fear my own death. For if I am

not revered in life by my only son, how am I to be revered
when I myself have joined our ancestors?"

Sarina stood there speechless, waiting for Chen's response,
but the young man's face was again an unreadable mask,
with all visible traces of his anger gone. Bowing low, first
to his father and then to Sarina, he walked with quiet
dignity to the door.

"Where are you going?" Wo called after him.

"To the cottage of Yan-wu," came the stiff reply. "I am
hopeful that by now his fever will have broken."

"His fever is the concern of the physician who tends all
the peasants. It need not be yours."

As Chen turned around, a light flush of anger began
rising in his pale cheeks. "The health of every peasant *is*
my concern, Father, for they are bound to us as surely as
we are bound to them. If they were all to fall sick and
were unable to work, who would till the soil? Who would
tend the crops? Who would see to the feeding of your
precious silkworms? Would *you*, Father?"

For one ghastly moment Sarina was certain the two men
would come to blows, but that moment quickly passed.

"Go to your peasants, then," said Wo with controlled
anger in his voice, "for the gods know you are hardly
more than one yourself."

When Chen had gone, Wo took Sarina's arm and gave
her a weary smile. "Perhaps I unknowingly angered the
gods when I myself was a young man, and for that trans-
gression they have punished me by denying me more
sons. My concubines have borne only girls. Even my cherished Li has given birth twice to dead sons and three times
to healthy daughters." Leading Sarina into the hallway, he
said, "Although the women of this household have failed
to honor me with sons, they continue to favor me with
exquisite music. Come and you shall hear for yourself."

They entered a tiny room filled with clay pots of lush
green plants, where the only furnishings were two low-
backed cushioned chairs and a number of large brocade
pillows scattered about on the bare wood floor. The sliding paper panels leading out to the courtyard had been
left partly open, and a light breeze was drifting about the
room and rustling the leaves of the plants. Showing Sarina
to one of the chairs, Wo had just settled himself on a
cushion next to her when Sua and Li were led into the

room. As soon as both women were seated side by side on separate silk cushions, one of the servants handed them their small violin-shaped instruments. Once the women had tuned the instruments, instead of beginning to play, they simply laid them across their laps and waited.

A few minutes later the door opened and in floated a young girl wearing a loose gray jacket and a long pleated gray skirt; her unbound feet marked her as a servant. Li's face remained coolly impassive when the girl bowed politely to her, but Sua smiled warmly as she returned the girl's greeting, and some unspoken message passed hastily between them.

"That is Mei, personal maid to my wife," Wo told Sarina in an undertone. "With the sweetness of her voice, she has, on occasion, coaxed a tear from even the strongest of men."

Sarina wondered if he were speaking of himself at that moment, but just then Mei turned around and gave Sarina a clear view of her face, and she immediately forgot everything Wo had been telling her. She had never seen a beauty more ethereal, more delicate; beside Mei, Li seemed no more than a garish and overpainted distortion of true beauty.

Her thick, lustrous black hair had been braided into two heavy loops and pinned above her small, shapely ears. Her face bore no trace of even the faintest dusting of rice powder, and the blush suffusing her delicately curved cheeks was the result of nature and not artifice. Her small broad nose appeared even smaller because of her unusually large and expressive almond-shaped eyes, and her mouth, scarcely more than a sting of palest coral, widened into a glorious pink arc as she smiled and bowed to Sarina and to Wo.

Wo beckoned her over and introduced her to Sarina, who was taken aback when Mei greeted her in soft, gently cadenced English.

"I am very pleased to meet you, Miss Paige," she acknowledged with her sweet, open smile, "and I pray that the gods may bless your stay with us with much peace and contentment."

Charmed by the girl's beauty and guileless warmth, Sarina was certain that of the three women she had met thus far, in Mei she had found a friend. But Wo seemed perturbed.

All the time Mei had been speaking, he had been studying her with a guarded expression on his face. Now he said, "Perhaps I was overly hasty in engaging Miss Paige as a tutor, when it would seem that within the very walls of this house there dwells another whose English grows more proficient with each passing day."

The roses in Mei's cheeks deepened, and for a moment she appeared flustered, but she hastily recovered her composure and dropped her eyes respectfully, murmuring, "Master is most kind."

Then she backed away from them and went to take up her position in front of Sua and Li. Curious about their brief interchange, Sarina followed Wo's thoughtful gaze with her own, but a moment later her curiosity gave way to wonder. Sua and Li had begun plucking their instruments, filling the small room with a high-pitched melody of exotic sweetness. With her hands clasped together in front of her, Mei tilted her head back and closed her eyes. Then she began to sing.

She sang with such exquisite clarity that Sarina sat in her chair, tense and unblinking, her heart beating wildly in her chest. She knew none of the words, and yet the emotions alive in those words forced a lump of bittersweet longing into her throat. Mei was obviously singing of forbidden love, and Sarina began to ache with a strange, half-forgotten yearning.

A pair of strong arms were holding her in a stolen nocturnal embrace while a lean, muscled body curved against hers, bidding it to yield and follow. She tasted his mouth as it closed over hers and tingled as a rush of delicious feeling spun outward from where their bodies were joined together. With a firm shake of her head, she watched the images in her mind dissolve into fragments, but her golden eyes betrayed her. They were pooling with bright, unshed tears, mirroring the tears which had begun to spill in silvered paths down both of Mei's own upturned cheeks.

As Mei continued her singing, Sarina stole a covert glance at Wo. His eyes were closed and he appeared to have fallen asleep. Looking away again, she suddenly started, and sat straight up in her chair. Etched on one of the translucent white panels leading to the inner courtyard was the dark silhouette of a man. Straightening from a half-crouch, the figure appeared in the open doorway for but a moment. And in that moment, as if some force were beckoning to her, Mei opened her eyes. She turned her head, an imperceptible turn which only Sarina saw, and looking directly at the shadowed figure, she moved her head in the briefest of nods.

As the figure darted off, an icy prickle of fear slithered down the length of Sarina's spine. He had moved quickly, but not before she had recognized him.

It was Chen.

6

Exhausted by the events of the day, and only vaguely aware of no longer being lulled to sleep by the rocking of a ship at sea, Sarina slept soundly until morning. But as she drifted upward from that peaceful land of nothingness, she saw a girl, her black hair fluttering above her head like a giant black bird, running. She was running toward the shadowed figure who was waiting for her among the flowers, where the sun was a shimmering circle of crimson. As he opened his arms to her, they became the closing jaws of a fearsome dragon. The girl threw back her head and began to scream. But he silenced her screams with a scorching blast of fire from his nostrils, and the maddened eyes he turned on her changed from stormy black to a deep and brilliant green.

Sarina sat up in bed with a start, panting. It took her a moment to realize where she was and to discover that the heat she was feeling was not from a phantom dragon in a nightmare but from the strong sun glazing the waxed paper on the sliding door panels. And yet, as she stumbled from her bed and made her way across the floor, she still felt trapped by a pair of burning green eyes.

Sliding open one of the light panels, she sought to shake off the last vestiges of her dream by drawing in deep, comforting breaths of the fragrant morning air. But one image lingered still. Gazing down into the deserted courtyard, she could almost see him crouching there, that stealthy shadow figure, blending in with the darkness around him. She shivered as she turned away, wondering again what had passed between Chen, the landlord's only son, and Mei, his mother's exquisite young maid.

Both Wo Shue Kwen and Chen had eaten earlier, and

since Sua and Li were always served their morning meal in their private chambers, Sarina sat down to breakfast alone. She was just getting up from the table when Wo himself appeared in the doorway and beckoned to her.

"I trust you slept well, Miss Paige?" he inquired.

"Yes, I did, thank you," she replied. "I was very tired."

There was a briskness to him this morning, a contained restlessness which transmitted itself from him to her as his fingers closed around her arm. "I must leave now for the city," he explained, "but first, permit me to show you the summerhouse, for it is there that you will shortly be meeting my daughters."

A knot of nervous anticipation tightened inside her. "I'm certainly looking forward to meeting them," she said, masking her sudden apprehensiveness with a smile as she allowed him to steer her toward the back gardens.

Not far from the house, a small square white wooden structure with a peaked roof and winged corners sat nestled within a luxuriant floral border of pink and white azaleas. Shutters covered the building's many large windows, giving the place a forlorn and abandoned look, while its chipped and peeling paint attested to its long disuse.

"This is the summerhouse," explained Wo, preceding Sarina up six cracked white wood steps and unlocking the shuttered door. "In years past, it was used by my sons and their tutors, but as you can see for yourself"—he made a vague gesture with one hand—"this little room has long known only the dust and the lonely passage of the seasons."

Sarina noticed the same muscle beginning to jump in Wo's jaw as she had seen in Chen's, and as a look of pain creased his high brow, she could only guess at the bittersweet memories overtaking him then. Seeking to dispel his darkening mood, she hurried over to one of the windows.

"Let's open them, shall we?" she asked with forced lightness. "It wouldn't do to have my students stumbling about in the dark their very first day, now, would it?"

Visibly shaking himself, Wo deferred to her with a slight nod of his head. "How very sensible of you, Miss Paige," he smiled, "it would not do at all."

Together they opened all of the windows, flooding the room with radiant sunlight and banishing the painful shadows of the past.

"Who else is tutoring your daughters, Mr. Wo?" Sarina asked as she rubbed her hands together in an effort to remove some of the dust covering them.

He seemed surprised by her question. "They receive no tutoring at all, Miss Paige, except from their mother."

"I don't quite understand," she said with a frown.

"Li teaches our daughters all they must know if they are to one day become suitable wives and mothers themselves. They are taught the four virtues," he explained patiently, counting them off on his fingers as he continued, "modesty, docility, careful speech, and a submissive demeanor. They learn as well the three obediences, namely, that a daughter is dependent upon her father, that a wife is dependent upon her husband, and that a mother is dependent upon her son. They are also taught to weave and to embroider, to cook and to perform as a gracious hostess. You see, Miss Paige, we believe that a daughter is no more than a temporary adornment decorating the home of her father until it is time for her to embellish the home of her husband. An ancient sage expressed it most eloquently, I believe, when he said, 'A daughter is like a fine young bamboo springing up just outside your garden fence.' "

"But if you consider your daughters unworthy of an education, why did you hire me to teach them English?" Sarina demanded, greatly dismayed by what he had told her.

A veil seemed to descend over his eyes, making them dark and unfathomable and making Wo himself unreachable. "Perhaps it was no more than a simple conceit of mine that they learn something of the language." He shrugged. But his eyes began to lighten almost immediately, as did his voice. "However, if another exquisite flower, stricken as you were and in as dire a predicament as yours, had spoken French, then perhaps I would have chosen French for my daughters instead of English. Suffice it to say, my dear Miss Paige, that too seldom is one granted the honor of providing a happy solution to another's unhappy dilemma."

Then Wo had created a position for her because he had felt sorry for her! This flattered Sarina but also confounded her. Still, she knew that to press him further was futile. Wo Shue Kwen had provided her with the only answer he intended her to have. Recalling the children she could be teaching at any one of the many American or British mission schools, it distressed her to think that by being here instead of there she might be serving no useful purpose whatsoever, and that perhaps she herself was nothing but another temporary ornament decorating the house of Wo. Unhappily she considered the bright little room, with its high peaked ceiling and its bare walls and floor, where four small wood tables, each with its own low bench, still faced a larger rectangular table with a high-backed cushioned chair pushed up to it. How much different would a classroom have been in one of the mission schools? she wondered as her gaze fell on two stacks of faded blue-and-green-striped silk pillows standing in a corner of the room.

"Those were used by my sons," explained Wo in a distant voice, effectively ending the awkward silence between them. "Their instruction would commence at nine o'clock in the morning, and then at noon a light lunch would be brought to them here. After their meal, the children would sleep for an hour on those cushions or, as they grew older, simply recline on them and contemplate that which they had been taught during the morning. Their instruction would continue until four o'clock, at which time they would return to the house to bathe and ready themselves for the evening meal."

"And is that the schedule I should follow with the girls as well?" Sarina wanted to know, aware of the coolness which had crept into her voice.

If he had noticed her change of tone, nothing in his own voice revealed it. "That is to be entirely your own decision," he informed her. "No doubt you may find holding their attention a more difficult task than if they were boys, but if you are a skilled and patient tutor, you should overcome any obstacle they set before you. This is to be your domain, Miss Paige. Rule it well and you will be more than suitably rewarded for your efforts. And now I can no longer delay my departure, for many pressing matters await me in the city." He bowed to her and backed toward the door. "I will, however, order two of the house slaves sent immediately to clean away the years of dust from this room, so that all may be in readiness for my daughters." He bowed again. Then he left her there with the dust and the memories and her own troubled thoughts.

It was not long after the two young servants had completed their task that Sarina heard the sounds of high-pitched chatter coming from outside the summerhouse. A few minutes later three young girls were led into the room by an unsmiling and gray-garbed serving maid. This woman with the pale, grim face, Sarina knew, was the girls' *amah*, Lan-tai.

Despite the scant difference in their ages and in their height, all three girls were exquisite miniatures of the lovely Li. Their heavy black hair was cut in bangs and shaped like glossy caps to their small heads. They each wore identical pale peach silk jackets with matching trousers and soft little slippers, similar to the ones worn by Sua and Li. As they inched toward her, Sarina saw that the steps they took were tiny and hobbled, and resentment rose inside her at the sight of what she, like Chen, considered an unnecessary deformity. But she masked her emotions with a warm and welcoming smile, and as each girl bowed politely to her in turn, she bowed back.

"I am Sarina," she said slowly and clearly, pointing to her chest as she carefully enunciated each syllable. "Sa-ri-na."

"Sa-li-na," repeated the tallest of the three girls with a shy smile.

Sarina shook her head and said her name again. "Sa-ri-na."

Now all three girls attempted to repeat it for her. "Sa-li-na."

Sarina smiled and nodded her head. Salina. It would have to do for now, she decided. At least it was a beginning. She looked directly at the oldest of the girls while she pointed to her own chest again and said her name out loud one more time. Then she pointed to the girl, cocked her head to one side, and raised her eyebrows questioningly.

Without hesitation, the girl answered, "Liang."

"Liang." Sarina repeated the girl's name, and Liang proudly nodded.

When Sarina pointed to the girl standing next to Liang, she replied in a half-whisper, "Hou."

Sarina repeated her name and then made Hou say it again, but in a louder voice this time. When she was satisfied, she pointed to the shortest of the three and was rewarded with a shrill, "Chui."

This caused the other girls to giggle and cover their

mouths with their tiny white hands. The dour woman still standing behind them tapped each of them on the shoulder and sternly shook her head. The laughter stopped immediately. Sarina seized the moment. Looking at the woman, she pointed first to her and then to the door. The woman blinked, turned her head to consider the door, and did not move. Sarina again pointed to the door and made a praying gesture with her hands.

Liang seemed to sense what Sarina was attempting to do, because she turned to the hovering woman and addressed her in rapid Chinese. At first the woman hesitated, but when Liang spoke again, she nodded her head and finally bowed to the young girl. With an accusing glare at Sarina she bowed to her as well and then shuffled slowly out of the room. Sarina touched Liang on the shoulder and then carefully enunciated the words "Thank you."

Liang frowned. Sarina repeated the words and with a smile gave Liang a small bow. As Liang bowed back to her, out of her tiny rosebud mouth came a shy little "Tang u."

In spite of Wo's skepticism, Sarina followed the same schedule which had once been set down for his sons, and to her delight, she found his lovely daughters more than equal to the challenge. As the days passed, she also discovered that with each new English word the girls learned, she learned its equivalent in Chinese. She found this to be the easiest and most effective way of teaching her eager pupils. Each morning she would bring various items from the main house to the summerhouse—whether pieces of jewelry, articles of clothing, household utensils, or small objects of art—and point to each one in turn. After one of the girls had given her its name in Chinese, Sarina would repeat it in Chinese, then say it slowly in English, and the girls would repeat the procedure. Soon they were spending an hour each morning out in the back gardens, learning the names of the various trees and flowers and plants as well. Eleven-year-old Liang was proving to be the most enthusiastic of the three girls, and Sarina came to rely on her to infuse nine-year-old Hou and eight-year-old Chui with renewed enthusiasm whenever theirs began to wane.

The fullness of her days made Sarina deeply fatigued, but she was contented as she settled into bed each night. And yet, in the dark, with the sounds of the day hushed and stilled, she would be seized by a familiar gnawing restlessness which time seemed incapable of diminishing. It was as if a pair of hands were tugging at her from the inside, pulling her, fighting and resistant, backward; trapping her in time and making her remember all that she had been trying to forget. With the sliding panels open to the night air, she would lie in bed and watch as shadows drifted across the face of the moon. In those shadows she sometimes saw the shape of a ship being tossed about on the sea, while at other times she found two bodies there, twisting together as they played at loving.

In the sigh of the wind she would hear her name, whispered as he had whispered it. But then the wind would grow colder, its cry more shrill, and she would hear, not her name now, but that other name. Hi-la-ry. Hi-la-ry. And she would close her eyes and turn onto her side with her back to the moon and the wind and try to believe that one day the pain would disappear forever. But more often than not she would wake in the morning with loneliness chilling her soul and the heat of his green eyes searing her heart.

At four o'clock one afternoon, after returning the girls to the sullen and disapproving Lan-tai, Sarina set out on a walk about the grounds. Wandering through the vast mulberry orchard, she caught sight of Chen leaving one of the special wooden rearing houses where the silkworms were being bred. Calling out his name, she hurried toward him, eager to renew her acquaintance with the elusive young man she now saw only at dinner each evening. Chen seemed torn between wariness and pleasure as she drew nearer, but by the time she reached him, his face no longer registered either emotion. She marveled at his capacity to dissemble so easily, as once again she recalled his crouched and shadowed form and wondered at the dangerous deception in which he was involved.

"Your young charges have been dismissed for today, Miss Paige?" Chen asked with a faint smile as she fell into step beside him.

"And returned safely to Lan-tai who doesn't approve of me at all," she sighed.

Chen laughed. "Pay no attention to that poor old woman," he said. "She has approved of no one in the twenty-four years she has lived in this household. But she is an *amah* without equal, and the children she tends are for her the children she herself could never bear."

Sarina felt an immediate surge of sympathy for the woman, a tender concern which reminded her of the unfortunate peasants for whom Chen had shown a similar compassion, and she tried to remember their names.

"Na," she murmured, without realizing she had spoken aloud, "and Yan-wu." At Chen's startled look, she said, "How are they, Chen, the overseer and his wife?"

"To think that you should even remember them . . ." He smiled, gazing at her with eyes which seemed to be seeing her for the first time. "Yan-wu, I am pleased to tell you, has recovered fully, but Na is still of great concern to me. The child she will soon deliver will be her tenth, and I fear this child may claim her life. She has little strength left and she spends all her days inside their cottage, being tended by her eldest daughter. If my father were to learn of this, he would be most angry, for now there are two less hands than before to feed the silkworms."

"But if the woman is so sick, surely your father wouldn't object to her own daughter caring for her."

Chen's jaw tightened. "You do not know my father," he said tersely.

"Perhaps I know him better than you think," she argued. "Any man capable of showing compassion for a stranger such as myself is bound to feel an even greater concern for someone like Na who has worked for him for so many years."

Chen's eyes were guarded as he said, "Of what importance is a humble peasant, no matter how loyal, when the stranger is a beautiful young woman such as yourself, Miss Paige?"

Sarina was suddenly flustered. "Chen, I don't—"

"Do you not think it peculiar that my father, who so readily admits the uselessness of daughters, now insists that they learn English?" he cut her off, and Sarina's cheeks slowly began to burn. "Liang is already eleven years old, Miss Paige, and soon to be betrothed. In all her eleven years, my father has paid her little notice, and yet she and her two younger sisters are now being extended a privilege reserved only for sons. Why do you think that is?"

Her face was flaming, for his words were echoing her

own recent confusion, but she quickly rose to the defense of her employer. "You're insulting both of us by your insinuations, Chen," she admonished him. "You of all people should know how dangerous it is to even speak about your father in such a disrespectful way."

His handsome face closed and in the slight bow he gave her was his unspoken apology. "Have you ever been inside one of our rearing houses, Miss Paige?" he asked, his voice now flat and even.

Forcing herself to relax and put aside their disagreement, Sarina shook her head.

"Then come"—he grasped her lightly by the elbow— "let me show you the humble origins of the magnificent silk that even the imperial family have chosen above all other silks with which to make their robes."

He opened the door to one of the long windowless buildings and she walked ahead of him into the cool, dim interior. "It is said that many thousands of years ago the Empress Si-ling, wife of the Emperor Huang-ti, was the first to encourage the cultivation of the mulberry tree and the rearing of the silkworm," Chen explained. "She was a most remarkable woman who not only devoted much of her own time to the care of the worms but who was also credited with having invented the very loom which weaves the silk."

"Then why are women considered so unworthy," Sarina asked him, "when some have obviously contributed a great deal to your civilization?"

"That, Miss Paige"—he smiled ruefully—"is something for which I have no answer. It is both hypocritical and foolish, but as my esteemed father would no doubt argue, it is so because tradition has made it so."

They walked for a while in thoughtful silence through the vast rearing house, which was lined with floor-to-ceiling shelves, much like Wo's warehouse in Shanghai. But instead of bolts of silk cloth, the shelves held hundreds of flat wicker feeding trays where thousands of small black silkworms were hungrily devouring tiny fresh green mulberry leaves.

"The worms eat this way day and night for forty-two days," Chen said, "at which time they will have grown into plump white worms approximately three inches in length. During these forty-two days, the worms pass through four periods of deep sleep, each period lasting twenty-four hours. While they sleep, their skins crack open, and when they awaken, they shed their old skins and live on in their newer ones. It is after the fourth period of deep sleep that the worms begin their great and final feed."

"And then?" Sarina prodded him.

"By raising the foreparts of their bodies and waving them in the air from side to side," Chen continued, "the worms indicate that they are ready to spin their cocoons. We immediately place a number of fresh shrubs in the center of each shelf so that the worms may mount them and secure themselves to the branches. Then they begin to release the glutinous fiber from their bellies which they spin into their cocoons. After eight days, the bushes are removed and the cocoons picked off. They are then boiled in scalding water and dried with hot air to ensure that each small chrysalis has been suffocated." Sarina shuddered at this. "But this is a most essential step, Miss Paige," Chen told her. "Without it, the moth would emerge from the cocoon and break the silk thread. You see, the worm spins a cocoon in one continuous thread, much in the manner of a figure eight, and this thread is rendered unusable if it is broken."

"I see." Sarina nodded, feeling slightly sorry for the hapless silkworms.

"The cocoons are then shipped to the city in large cloth sacks, whereupon the cocoons are unraveled and wound onto drums. After that, they are reeled into spools of thread and then finally woven into silk cloth."

Chen's dark eyes were shining and his features were more animated than Sarina had ever seen them before. It was obvious to her that here on the land was indeed where Chen's love and devotion lay, something which boded poorly for the twenty-two-year-old son of a man whose own life was divided equally between the concerns of the city and the running of his estate, and who expected no less from his only heir. When they left the rearing house, Sarina found herself more afraid than ever for this independent young man, who, by his father's own admission, risked forfeiting his life for the sake of his independence.

That evening, as Sarina was preparing to dress for dinner, she was startled by a discreet knock on her door. Hastily tying the sash of her dressing gown, she padded barefoot to the door and opened it to find Wo Shue Kwen standing there. Before she could even begin to greet him, he brushed imperiously past her into the room. Midway across the floor, he stopped, turned around, and clapped his hands together twice.

To Sarina's astonishment, three young serving maids appeared in the doorway, bowed to her, and then slithered on soft slippered feet into her room. The first girl was carrying a pair of flat-heeled white satin slippers and what appeared to be various white silk undergarments. The second was holding a large black lacquer box, while the third carried a magnificent gown in her outstretched arms. Sarina gasped, recognizing the silk she had so admired that first day in Wo's Shanghai warehouse.

"I pray you will not consider me presumptuous, Miss Paige," Wo finally spoke, "but I had thought to surprise you." He pointed a finger at the young girl carrying the lacquer box and said, "This is Ing-han. She is to be your personal serving maid from now on." He spoke rapidly to the other two girls, who immediately laid the clothes they were carrying across the bed, bowed first to Wo and again to Sarina, and then hurried out of the room.

While Ing-han began emptying the lacquer box of its contents, Wo bent over the gown spread so carefully across Sarina's bed and leisurely traced its outline with his small, elegant fingers. Sarina followed his movements with her eyes, feeling somehow that it was her skin and not the gown he was caressing so tenderly.

"You have shown exquisite taste," he murmured as he continued to stroke the shimmering white silk. "This fabric was intended for a princess of the imperial family, but I sent her a bolt of silk so similar that she will never know a slight adjustment was made." His hand came to rest for a moment on the bodice of the robe. "You are so much a part of our household, Miss Paige, that I had hoped you might favor us by consenting to adopt our manner of dress from time to time. If you find this request a disagreeable one, you must not even consider it, but if you find it pleasing, I would be greatly honored, as would my family, to see you dressed as one of us."

Caught up in the tender web of his words, all Sarina could do was nod her head and agree. She was scarcely aware of him sweeping from the room before Ing-han was seating her in a chair before the pier glass so that she could observe each step of the elaborate grooming ritual. First, her thick golden hair was brushed back from her face, slicked into place with a transparent pomade, and then wound into a series of intricate knots and loops, which were securely pinned to her head. Then, using a large feathery puff, Ing-han patted a thin layer of white rice powder onto Sarina's face and neck. She smoothed red rouge made from safflower onto her cheeks and lips, and with a slender stick of black kohl emphasized the provocative slant of Sarina's golden eyes. Then Ing-han motioned for her to stand up. As she hastily complied, the young serving maid began to unfasten the sash of her dressing gown.

Unaccustomed to such attention and never having stood naked before a woman before, Sarina could barely contain her discomfiture. But as Ing-han worked to bind her in the special silk undergarments with efficient speed and an impassive expression on her pleasant young face, the shame Sarina felt slowly gave way to wonderment, and she watched spellbound as she was being transformed. She shivered as the cool silk of the floor-length robe closed around her body, encasing her in a translucent white whisper which was alive with gold butterflies and gold leaf-twined roses. When a broad girdle of gold silk was wrapped around her waist, Sarina sucked in her breath and held it, certain that to eat an entire meal would now be impossible.

Ing-han fastened the girdle with a large gold pin in the shape of a butterfly whose body and wings were encrusted with tiny diamonds and whose eyes were golden topazes. Next she clipped a pair of small matching earrings to Sarina's whitened ears and pinned ten more diamond-and-topaz butterflies at the base of several of the smooth gold loops of her hair. Then she bent to tie the satin straps of Sarina's slippers, leaving Sarina to stare wide-eyed at herself in the mirror. Ing-han rose at last and surveyed her creation with a small, contented smile. Bound by the gown and forced to take tiny, hobbled steps, Sarina gave the impression of floating above the floor with effortless grace as she moved closer to the pier glass.

"Oh, dear!" she whispered.

She was beautiful; a stunning golden vision. She touched

her cheek, as if to assure herself that the exaggerated features were indeed still hers. Would he know her now, she wondered, if his darker reflection were there in the glass beside her lighter one? She pressed a finger to her reddened lips and wondered, if his lips were to touch hers at that moment, would he even recognize them as hers? Lowering her gaze, she chastised herself for being such a fool. By now the arrogant blackguard, who should have been little more than a memory himself, had in all likelihood forgotten everything about her.

"You are even more exquisite than I had dared imagine," came the deep and reverent whisper beside her.

Shocked, she turned to face him, wondering how long he had been standing there. His face was close to hers, his warm breath fanning her cheeks as he said, "At last you have become the golden butterfly I knew you to be when I first saw you, lost in the innocence of sleep. You have bestowed on me a pleasure which simple words cannot express, but I pray that in time the gods in their wisdom may provide me with words more adequate."

With his hand guiding her small steps, Sarina drifted into the dining room and met the shock in the eyes of the three already seated there with a tremulous but radiant smile. When her eyes met Chen's, something flickered in their inky depths and disappeared. Her smile faltered as she watched him lower his head with that telltale muscle jumping in his jaw. As she took her place beside Li, she turned for a moment to look at her. A knot tightened in her chest. Gazing at the beautiful concubine, Sarina saw what she had never seen before in her masklike face.

She saw fear.

7

Under Wo Shue Kwen's benevolent tutelage, Sarina fluttered free of the cocoon woven for her by her well-meaning but overly protective father, to emerge fully aware of her own beauty for the first time. Returning to her room each afternoon, she would find yet another magnificent new gown, complete with shoes and appropriate jewels, carefully laid out on her bed, and Ing-han waiting patiently to dress her. She was, in turn, guilty and giddy with delight, a child long deprived, being suddenly and inexplicably pampered and spoiled. Gowned only in robes of icy white silk elaborately embroidered in gold, her jewels either diamonds, or topazes, or milky pearls, she would glide through each evening, a gilded lotus of Wo's own creating, warmed by the glow of pleasure on his face. And yet her triumph was a lonely one. Chen barely acknowledged her now; Sua was still little more than a pallid, pastel shadow hovering tentatively about; while Li observed her in frozen silence, the hatred and the fear gradually fusing behind her fathomless onyx eyes.

Before retiring each night, Sarina would stand before the pier glass in her bedroom, wearing only a simple lawn nightdress, her hair falling freely about her shoulders, her face cleansed, and examine her features for some sign of the changes she felt certain had already taken place within her soul. Was she being corrupted, she wondered, by her surprising delight in things material, when all her life she had been taught to shun them? Was her soul, already blackened by the act of fornication, now forever beyond redemption because of this newest excess? Without even referring to the Scriptures, she knew how strongly they would condemn her. And so one morning after a particularly troubled and sleepless night, she approached Wo in his study and tried to return his gifts to him.

He got up from his desk and went to her, his arms extended like a suppliant pleading humbly to be heard.

"A gift is a token of the soul of the giver, my dear Sarina," he said, dropping his voice as he used her Christian name for the first time. "If a gift is returned to the giver, it is like a small death to that part of the living soul which had hoped only to bring another pleasure."

"But I was raised in a far different world from yours," she protested, "where a gift is an act of kindness, a thoughtful gesture, a hand extended to someone in need. It is never a piece of clothing or a beautiful jewel. My father taught me of the importance of pure thought and action and that to yearn for possessions or to pay undue attention to one's person is proof of a weak spirit and an endangered soul."

Wo placed his hands lightly on her shoulders and his eyes burned into hers. "Perhaps your father, in his wisdom, only taught you this to protect you from those who might take advantage of your own rare and exquisite beauty. Should the rose bloom in the shade, denied the smile of the sun, simply because her beauty may bedevil some fool who gazes upon her? I think not, for in the shade the rose will surely die, and thus deny her beauty not only to a foolish few but also to everyone. Your beauty is a gift which has been bestowed on you by the generous gods, Sarina. Do not choose to wither in the shade of false modesty, my lovely lotus. You were created to bloom in the joyous brilliance of the sun."

Once again his words had the power to assuage her doubts and calm the turbulence within her, and so she bowed to his wishes and continued to dress each evening to please him.

One evening, as Wo was leading Sarina into the music room after dinner, a servant approached them and called Wo aside.

"You may begin without me tonight, my dear," he told Sarina as the servant hurried off. "It seems that a business acquaintance of mine is presently awaiting me in my study. Perhaps if we have concluded in time, I will bring him

with me to the music room, for he has long been devoted
to the songs of our lovely Mei."

Sarina's initial awkwardness at sitting alone while the
three women performed for her eased with each new song
Mei sang. Then, as always, she found herself transported.
Her eyes were closed, her head was resting against the
back of her chair when she finally heard Wo settling
himself on his cushions beside her. When he signaled an
end to the evening's music sometime later, she opened her
eyes, blinked them several times to clear her head, and
then rose dreamily to her feet. She tried to catch Mei's
eye, but the girl was staring past her, a smile of unabashed
delight lighting her face. And then, to Sarina's complete
astonishment, Mei gave a small, joyful cry and started
across the room.

Sarina turned to look after the girl, and her breath
caught in her throat. Her knees buckled. She was forced
to grab hold of her chair to keep her balance. The room
tipped crazily as the paralyzing weakness spread through
her limbs and numbed her mind. Not five feet from
where she was wavering stood a tall sun-bronzed figure
lifted from the pages of her memory book.

Janson Carlyle was no longer a dusky shadow relegated
to the safety of the past, but a devastatingly handsome
man there in the flesh, a man who was holding out his
arms to Mei as a father holds out his arms to his child.
Stunned, Sarina glanced over at Wo, but he seemed no
more than a silent observer himself, standing to one side,
arms folded across his chest, an amused smile playing
about the corners of his mouth.

Janson. Inwardly she whispered his name. Janson Carlyle and Wo Shue Kwen doing business together. She was
incredulous. Of all the estates near Shanghai, how often
had Janson been a guest in this one? Had he known she
would be there or had he been just as surprised as she
was? Forcing herself to meet the intense greenness of his
eyes, she was stung to find him studying her as though he
were looking through her and not actually seeing her at
all. Had he failed to recognize her, then, dressed as she
was, or had he already forgotten her?

Her cheeks blazing, she tore her gaze from his face and
allowed herself to travel the familiar length of him. He
was wearing a full-sleeved ivory linen shirt tucked into a

pair of gray nankeen breeches, and high black riding
boots. It was an outfit which accentuated his superb
masculinity. She chanced another look at his face and
found that he was still studying her. But whereas there
had been a disconcerting blankness in his eyes before, now
they were alive with a mocking lightness she knew all too
well.

Wo put an end to her ordeal by clapping a hand around
Janson's shoulder and saying, "Come, my friend, and meet
the exquisite blossom I have spoken about."

As Mei bowed and backed away respectfully from the two
men, Janson focused all of his attention on his host. "Miss
Paige and I have already had the pleasure of meeting," he
replied smoothly.

Bristling, Sarina pierced him with her haughtiest glare.

"You have met before?" Wo tensed, his eyes narrowing
into ebony slits.

"Indeed we have." Janson bowed over Sarina's hand
and raised it to his lips. Where his mouth was grazing her
flesh, a disquieting tingle was beginning. "Miss Paige and I
were fellow passengers aboard the *Halcyon* when she sailed
from San Francisco," Janson explained, releasing Sarina's
hand, whereupon it fell like a leaden weight to her side.

"I see." Although Wo seemed visibly to relax, he continued to scrutinize Sarina through half-veiled eyes.

"We shared a dinner table once," she coolly interposed.
"Nothing more."

Janson's mocking smile all but laid bare the lie in what
she had said, but all Wo could see was the flare of defiance in Sarina's golden eyes.

"Janson arrived only this afternoon from Hong Kong,"
said Wo, while Sarina struggled to concentrate on his
words. "He informs me that he has opened a trading
office there. I believe that my ambitious young friend
hopes to put an end to the most prosperous monopoly that
exists there now, controlled by the company of Jardine
and Matheson. Is this not correct, Janson?"

"I wouldn't go so far as to say that," he demurred. "You
know yourself there's still some cargo I refuse to handle."

"But if one mounts an offensive, my friend, one must
be prepared to fight with all the resources available to
him," countered Wo. "One day, Janson, even you may

condescend to dealing in items far more profitable than silk and tea or rhubarb and spices."

Janson's square jaw was taut as he said curtly, "Never, Kwen."

Wo allowed the matter to drop with a slight inclination of his head. Then in a silken voice he said, "Would you think me an ungracious host if I retire now to study the many papers you have brought me? Miss Paige will show you to one of the receiving rooms and see that you are served tea."

"I was hoping that you might excuse me," she hastily interjected. "I'm really very tired."

"But surely sleep can wait," suggested Wo. "We would not want our guest to think poorly of us or our hospitality."

"Kwen's right, Miss Paige." Janson's tone was taunting. "Besides, aren't you the least bit curious as to how I've been spending my time since we last saw each other?"

Sarina leveled her coldest stare at him. "How you spend your time, Mr. Carlyle, is of no interest to me whatsoever."

"Sarina!" Rebuke was sharp in Wo's voice. "I would be most obliged if you would take our guest into the receiving room and see that he is given some tea before he returns to the city."

Stung by his tone of voice, Sarina drew herself up proudly and stared at him for a moment before she finally relented and gave him a slight nod.

"Thank you, my dear." Wo patted her lightly on the hand and then turned to Janson. "And when can I expect to meet with you again, my friend?"

Janson shrugged. "Whenever you wish." For a moment his eyes rested on Sarina. "I might even become a regular visitor again, now that you've made such a tempting addition to your household."

"That would indeed be most gratifying." Wo nodded, his smile properly polite. "This young man is not the most sociable of creatures," he told Sarina. "He is always in too great a hurry. I think he must believe that to sink one's shoes too often upon the same mat of welcome is to leave an imprint impossible to erase." Turning to Janson again, he said, "My home is yours, my friend. Use it as you would your own. And remember that the hand offered to you in hospitality is not a claw to either entrap or imprison you."

"Thank you, Kwen, I'll remember that." Janson smiled, returning Wo's formal bow.

"And now, Miss Paige will see that you take some refreshment before you leave."

The room was small and lighted only by two hanging brass lanterns. Sarina and Janson faced each other in the middle of the room, both of them aware of the presence of the silent servant pouring them their tea. Sarina felt her body swaying, moving closer to his and then away again, even though she knew she was not moving at all. To think that he and Wo were business associates. To think that, in spite of his gallant boasts, she had never expected to see him again. And yet, here he stood, while the pull of his eyes reduced her to a fragile stem bowing before the will of a stronger wind.

Only when the servant had gone did Sarina motion for him to sit down. When she raised her cup of tea to her lips, her hand trembled. Angered by his effect on her, she closed both of her hands around the fragile gold-and-blue cup and forced herself to take a sip of the steaming brew. She swallowed hard, scalding her tongue and the back of her throat. Even her eyes were smarting as she hastily set her cup down on the low wooden tea stand which separated their two chairs.

"I never imagined that you could look more beautiful, Sarina," Janson told her in a voice which sent a wave of pleasure washing over her. "And yet Kwen's managed to change you into something just short of a goddess."

Coloring beneath his unexpected praise, she floundered for some reply. "I thought I would suffocate at first," she said with a nervous laugh, indicating the wide gold silk girdle binding her waist. "I assumed it would be impossible to eat or to even sit down, but I discovered I was wrong. Now I even enjoy dressing this way." An impish smile suddenly deepened the dimples in her cheeks as she added, "I *am* grateful for one thing, though."

"And what's that?"

"That I'm too old to have my feet bound."

He laughed at this, and she was grateful for his laughter, for it broke some of the tension between them and enabled her to relax somewhat. She watched him sipping his tea with the same fascination with which she had watched him eat his dinner that night aboard ship. She studied the large, strong hand grasping the delicate cup and shivered when she recalled how gently that same hand had once caressed her body. Each time he took a sip of his tea, with his head tipped back and his lips slightly parted, she could taste those lips, warm and demanding, as they closed over hers again. She looked down at his legs and felt their bruising pressure as once more they ground mercilessly into hers, coaxing from her a heat so intense that it flamed fiercer than any sun.

She squirmed uncomfortably in her chair as a tongue of fresh desire leaped upward inside her. Just then, the tip of Janson's tongue began to lazily skirt the golden rim of his teacup. Wide-eyed, she watched him tease the edge of the cup as boldly as he had once teased the nipples of her breasts. As if to place a barrier between his lips and her body, she reached for her cup of cooling tea and hastily brought it up to her mouth. But it was at that very moment that Janson chose to set his own cup down.

"Sarina?"

It was part question, part demand. He was both asking for her permission and declaring his intention to have his way with or without that permission. With her entire body engulfed by a sweeping flame and her mind still refusing to succumb to the sensation, she shook her head. She feared his power over her as much as she resented her defenselessness in the face of that power.

He was on his feet, pulling her roughly from her chair and into his arms. With diminishing strength she strove to break his hold on her. His mouth grazed her throat as she arched away from him, and his kiss was a torch to further ignite her flesh. He dug his fingers into the thick sweep of her hair and forced her head up closer to his. She caught her breath. The cup fell out of her relaxing fingers and was dashed to pieces on the floor. He moved to narrow the distance between his lips and hers. With a melting sigh she closed her eyes and offered him the mouth he had sought so long to claim.

"Missy hurt?"

The servant's cry of concern broke their embrace. Sarina stumbled from the enclosing warmth of Janson's arms into the cold and followed the servant's eyes down to the broken cup. Flustered, she simply gestured for him to leave. With his head respectfully bowed, he backed out of the room and closed the door again. Twisting her hands together nervously, Sarina refused to meet Janson's searching gaze. Instead she slid open the panels leading to the inner courtyard and stepped outside.

In the peace of the courtyard, she sought to restore some of her own, now shattered. Crickets chirped. A distant tree frog croaked. A shy breeze ruffled the leaves on the pomegranate plants and the dwarf orange trees and carried to her the lush fragrance of the lotus flowers afloat on the shimmering surface of the ornamental pond. Overhead, millions of sparkling stars had been carved out of the velvety sky, and as she heard him come up behind her, she almost wished his arms were enfolding her again instead of the indigo arms of night.

"The estate of Wo Shue Kwen is a far different place from that mission school in Shanghai, isn't it, Sarina?" The edge to his voice took her by surprise. "Could it be that the pious life wasn't really for you after all?"

"Just what do you mean by that?" she demanded, whirling around to face him.

"I thought I'd put it fairly clearly," he replied. "What happened to the properly pure young schoolteacher and her intentions of spreading God's word to the heathens of this world? Don't tell me you've actually succumbed to the very things you've always fought so hard to resist." One finger flicked disdainfully at the diamond-and-pearl earrings she was wearing, and she flinched, as much from his touch as from his words. "You had me convinced that your only concerns were righteousness and goodness, and above all, humility. What a hypocrite you've turned out to be, Miss Paige."

"How dare you speak to me that way!" she cried. "When I arrived in Shanghai, there *was* no mission school. There *was* no Dr. Townsend. But there was Wo Shue Kwen and three young girls for me to teach. I am not the world adventurer you are, Mr. Carlyle. For nineteen years my world was bounded by the state lines of Oregon, and most of what I ever learned was taught to me by my father." Her rising anger stained her cheeks scarlet and added venom to each one of her words. "How dare you preach to me! You who robbed me of a woman's most precious virtue. Did you actually believe me still fit to teach the word of God to innocents, considering my shame? At least on Wo's estate I'm teaching English, something I'm still fit to do."

"Sarina, I—"

"Don't touch me," she hissed, backing away from the hands she knew could shape her to his will if she weakened. "Don't speak to me about virtue and then do your best to make a mockery out of your own words. Play your twisted games with someone else, but not with me. Ever!"

As she saw the effect she was having on him, her anger began to cool and an icy calm crept into her voice. With eyebrows arched and eyes narrowing, she said, "I might even know of someone myself." She paused to allow his confusion to mount. "Yes, I believe I do. Perhaps you might consider playing your games with a woman whose name is . . ." Again she paused, one finger thoughtfully tapping against her chin. "Hilary?" she inquired sweetly. "Yes, that was her name. Hilary."

Janson gasped.

Sarina watched in satisfaction as he recoiled. With her catlike smile frozen on her face, she haughtily raised her chin in the air and turned her back to him. Above the sigh of the wind, she could hear his breathing, rapid and strangely labored, rasping harshly in her ears. How long they stood there, each trapped behind a climbing wall of pride, she could not be sure, but when she heard the sharp clacking of his boots against the stones, panic and remorse made her turn around and put out her hand to him.

But he had already stepped back inside the house, his strides long and purposeful as he crossed the floor of the receiving room. He closed the door behind him without so much as a backward glance, and Sarina, her lashes beaded with tears, trained her stricken gaze on the mocking face of the cloud-draped summer moon.

At first she sensed rather than saw the wavering shadow in the garden. What she had assumed was simply another oleander tree was not a tree at all. Before her astonished eyes, the shadow seemed to be peeling itself apart, splitting down the middle and separating into two distinct forms. No sooner had they separated than the two forms converged again, swaying together in the moon-dappled darkness for another moment before breaking apart once more. Each figure held out a hand to the other. The line formed by their touching hands lengthened as they began to move farther and farther away from one another. When they dropped their hands, it was like a band snapping, and the blackness rushed in to fill the widening space between them.

As the moon pushed aside a final curtain of cloud, the trees and grass were stained with its lambent silver light. A tender sprinkling of moondust glazed the departing figures, and Sarina clamped a hand over her mouth to silence her gasp of shock. With her heart hammering in her chest and her body moist with fear, she began backing toward the house and away from the fleeing lovers. Away from Chen and Mei.

Disjointed memories flooded her mind. Chen huddled in the courtyard. Mei's songs of thwarted love. Chen never once appearing in the music room. Mei speaking English, Chen obviously her secret tutor. Sarina staggered into the house, praying with each step she took that she had been the only witness to their folly and that she was the only one to know the truth about them.

From somewhere in the darkened house came the muted sound of a door softly closing.

8

With each stair she climbed, Sarina grew increasingly more convinced that the love Chen and Mei were sharing was a doomed love. Unlike the tragic Greek lovers Orpheus and Eurydice, both Mei *and* Chen would be trapped in a darkened netherworld. Carnal love between a master and a servant, she knew, had long been sanctioned by the Chinese, but for a master to take a servant, someone considered to be a "mean woman," as his wife lowered his status and the status of his descendants, and so was strictly forbidden.

Forbidden or not, there could never be any such marriage for Chen and Mei because the twenty-two-year-old Chen was already betrothed to Lao Kuer T'ai, the eldest daughter of Lao Hong Han, who owned the large tea farm bordering the Wo estate. It was simply a matter of time before the official date for their marriage was set. All Chen could hope to share with Mei was what his own father had been sharing with Li for twelve years—the love between a master and his concubine.

"Miss Paige."

His whisper nearly caused Sarina to miss her footing as she reached the landing. With the forefinger of one hand pressed to his lips, Chen was beckoning to her with the other. Catching hold of her by the elbow, he quickly steered her down the hall and into her bedroom.

"You know now?" he asked in a cautious undertone, and Sarina mutely nodded her head. "Just as the moonlight revealed a painful truth to your eyes, Miss Paige, so it revealed to me your presence as well."

"Are you here because you're afraid I might tell your father about what I saw?" she asked him, keeping her own voice low.

"I know that your loyalty must lie with him and not with me," he answered carefully, "but I am hopeful that you may still choose to keep our secret safe. I came here, Miss Paige, not to plead our cause with you, but to speak to you so that you would not think poorly of Mei."

"Think poorly of Mei?" repeated Sarina, startled by this, and yet somehow pleased that he would be so protective of the girl.

"She is a servant trained to submit to the will of her master in all matters. That is why you must know that she has never come to me as a servant obeying the wishes of her master, but freely and out of her love for me. As she loves me, so I too love her, and she remains untouched, Miss Paige, and pure."

So, their love was no carnal matter after all, no dusky passion which could be cooled by either daylight or reason.

"Do not be afraid for us, and more than that, do not pity us," he said. "We knew of all the obstacles before we even contemplated crossing that boundary which divides us."

"How long have you been meeting secretly?" she asked him.

"For two years now," Chen said, "Mei was but ten years old when she was sold by her family in Canton to my family as a kitchen slave. Her father was a poor farmer and Mei was the youngest of his twelve children. Although she was being trained to become one of the esteemed singsong maidens of her city, it was our household and not a tea-house in Canton which was blessed by her exquisite voice. I awoke each morning to her glorious singing, and the last sounds in my ears each night were the songs she sang for my parents in the music room. From a kitchen slave she rose to the position of parlor maid, and then last year she became the personal serving maid to my mother, an honor indeed for one so young, for Mei is now only eighteen."

Although she was deeply moved by what he was telling her, Sarina could not stop herself from blurting out, "But, Chen, you're betrothed to someone else."

His eyes dropped. "Knowing that I must follow my father's wishes and marry the woman he has chosen for me is an agony I endure all of my waking hours. Do you not think I know of the importance of such a proper marriage, so that our family can be maintained and our ancestors duly worshiped? And yet, while I must bend to this tradition as an obedient son, Miss Paige, my heart will continue to dwell with Mei, and it shall always."

"But if you love her, why won't you join us in the music room?" asked Sarina. "At least you could be close to her and listen to her singing."

"And how am I to remain seated in respectful silence while Mei sings of our own impossible love?" he demanded. "How am I to bear seeing the tears she sheds, knowing she will shed those tears again at our next parting? How am I to stop myself from wanting to take her in my arms and soothe her pain with promises I cannot keep? No, Miss Paige, to be so close to her would be to risk discovery."

Sarina collapsed onto a chair, suddenly weary. For a few minutes neither of them spoke, and then Chen approached Sarina and took hold of both her hands.

"Am I a fool to hope that our secret has been entrusted to one who merits our faith, Miss Paige?" he asked her.

Sarina shook her head. "No, Chen, you're not a fool. I give you my word that I'll keep your secret safe."

In gratitude he pressed a fervent kiss onto the back of each of her hands. "Bless you, my friend," he whispered in a thick voice. "Now I truly believe I may call you 'friend.' "

He had closed the door before Sarina was even aware of his leaving the room. Wearily she began to undress. Too tired to even cleanse her face of the rice powder and rouge, she fell into bed with an exhausted sigh and waited for sleep to erase all of the disturbing images still too sharply imprinted upon her mind.

She slept fitfully, rising and falling on the capricious tide of a discomforting dream. A large hand was pouring her out of a giant silver teapot into a gold-and-blue porcelain cup. All around her the celadon waves were gentle and playful, tempting her to dive beneath the tea's placid surface. But when she rose from one of her dives, she found that the wind had changed and that it had begun to whip the tops of the waves into frothy white peaks. Bubbles formed and burst in the air with tiny popping sounds. A wave washed over her head and she swallowed a mouthful of the tea. It was bitter and strong and it burned her tongue.

The tea continued to grow hotter. Soon it was boiling,

bubbling and hissing as if someone had banked a fire under it. Seething and steaming, the tea vapors rose higher, stinging her cheeks and causing her eyes to tear. As she struck out blindly, swimming with ever-weakening strokes, she suddenly felt someone there in the water beside her.

With the mist dimming her sight, she was unable to see the face of her companion, but the hands touching her shoulders were cool and strangely comforting. She shivered as those hands slid down along her arms and began to trace their way across the plains and valleys of her body. They molded her breasts with infinite gentleness and then smoothed a path across her belly down to where her legs were obediently parting. Half-ice, half-flame, she shuddered again and again as she was caught in the throes of a fiery chill.

A pair of wintry lips seared hers and a column of steam rose from their union. Together they slipped beneath the surface of the waves. Down, down, down they spiraled, turning slowly, around and around, as they tunneled through the darkening brew, a frosty shaft in a molten sea. She sighed as a blade of glimmering ice began to pierce her warmness, and spreading her arms in complete surrender, she allowed her soul to be severed in two.

She was wakened by an exquisite thrumming between her legs to the buttery spill of daylight aflame on her steaming skin. As the spasms gradually subsided, the gentle calm which pervaded her body made any movement virtually impossible. But her mind continued to work frantically. How dare he stride back into her life when she had thought him successfully forgotten? How dare he invade the privacy of her sleep and use her body in a dream as he had used it twice before? Pressing the palm of her hand over that sensitive place between her legs, she sought to comfort herself by the simple act of covering up that most precious part of herself which she felt had once again been so cruelly violated.

She had no appetite for breakfast that morning, and her attention wandered throughout the day. She felt a slight pang of guilt when she brought her young pupils back to Lan-tai at three o'clock instead of four, but most of her usual energy and patience had already been drained by her persistent and unhappy thoughts. She threw herself across her bed and simply lay there staring vacantly at the ceiling until Ing-han appeared in time to dress her for dinner.

She sat grimly at the table, using her chopsticks to toy with the solitary slice of roast pork resting on the cooling mound of rice in her bowl. She still had no appetite and she knew that if she even attempted to swallow that piece of meat, it would lodge in her throat and choke her. As the tedious meal wore on, she took small sips of her *samshu* and hoped no one would notice her obvious lassitude. On several occasions she caught Chen studying her with a worried frown, but as usual, neither of them spoke. When she felt Li staring at her as dessert was being served, she turned her head in answer to the woman's challenge, but the exquisite features beneath the powder and the kohl remained maddeningly impassive.

Immediately after dinner, Sarina asked to be excused.

"Are you feeling poorly?" inquired Wo as he followed her out of the dining room. "You ate none of your dinner."

"I know, I'm sorry," she apologized, "but I'm very tired and I haven't been hungry all day."

"Perhaps a tray sent later to your room?"

She shook her head. "All I need is some sleep."

"You did not sleep well last night?"

His questions were beginning to unsettle her. "I'm afraid I still haven't gotten used to the bamboo headrest," she hastily dissembled. "I was up most of the night because of a cramp in my neck."

His returning look was gently scolding. "Did I not urge you before to ask the servants for a feather cushion if you found the headrest uncomfortable?"

She grinned sheepishly. "I didn't want to admit I had been defeated by a simple headrest."

"You are to be commended for your persistence, Sarina"—he chuckled—"but I would rather you condescend to one small defeat and sleep in comfort than to sleep poorly because of stubbornness."

"I'll try it again tonight, and if I still sleep badly, I promise to ask for a down cushion in the morning."

"Good, then it is settled." He seemed pleased with himself as he escorted her to the foot of the stairs. "May the gods grant you the sleep you are seeking, my lovely lotus," he said.

But in spite of his prayer for her, Sarina lay in bed rigid

and sleepless. Dark shadows capered about the room, and
when she closed her eyes, they danced behind her lowered
lids as well. She saw each sinuous black fragment as a part
of Janson beckoning to her and enticing her, while holding out an elusive promise of fulfillment to her. Had he
stolen back into her life merely to torture her, to engage
her in some continuing shadow dance? Each time he succeeded in luring her closer, was he to adroitly step aside
again? If only he would stay away. Without him there to
intrude upon her days, she felt certain she could return
him once more to the safety of memory and find for
herself that special peace granted only by time and distance.

The hours of the night ground by all too slowly for her.
With fretful sighs she tossed and turned, tossed and
turned, searching for a comfortable place for her restless
body. But it was only when the first pink rays of morning
began to slant across the floor of her room that she finally
fell into a brief and brooding sleep.

At noon, while the girls were napping, Sarina left the
quiet summerhouse and sat down on the grass near the foot
of the steps. The sun was warm on her face and the perfume from the pink and white azaleas sweetened the
air. Her eyelids grew heavy as a languid peace stole over
her. Giving in to the spreading feeling, she curled up on
the grass with her head on her arms and closed her eyes.

A bothersome tickling made her wrinkle her nose. Thinking it was a fly, she absently swatted at it, but the tickling
continued. Cautiously she opened one eye. With a gasp of
surprise she angrily slapped away the hand trailing a long
blade of grass across her cheek.

"You looked so peaceful lying there that I almost hated
myself for disturbing you," said Janson with a wide grin,
"but now that you're awake, I don't hate myself at all."

"You haven't bothered to ask me how I feel about it,"
she grumbled as she struggled to sit up.

"Well, just how do you feel?"

"I don't think you'd care to hear."

"How do you manage it, Sarina?" he asked, settling
himself on the grass beside her. "Occidental by day, Oriental by night. Don't you ever get confused?"

"Of course not. I'm still the same person in spite of my
change of clothing."

"I wonder," he mused, nibbling on the blade of grass he had used to tease her.

"Do you really?" she retorted. As usual, she was rising to his casual baiting, but today he seemed lost in his own thoughts, with little interest in sparring with her. Recalling their recent argument and how he had left her so abruptly made her wonder why he had even sought her out again. Puzzled, she found herself staring at his profile, watching as the wind blew a lock of silvered hair across his forehead, while she resisted the impulse to reach up and brush it back into place. Instead, she busied her hands by tearing up a three-leaf clover and ripping off each of its small round petals.

"Do I make you nervous, Sarina?" asked Janson.

"Is that what you'd prefer to think?"

In answer to that, he simply threw back his head and laughed. How she loved the sound of his deep, throaty laughter and the tiny lines which fanned out from the corners of his eyes when he closed them, and the way his teeth flashed so whitely in his darkly handsome face. But she could not admit that to herself. At least not yet.

"Just why are you here, Mr. Carlyle?" she demanded crossly when she could no longer bear looking at him.

He sobered immediately. "Kwen and I have some business to attend to," he replied, "and I much prefer meeting him out here to going to his offices in the city." He stretched his arms above his head and drew in a deep breath of the fragrant air. "As much as I love the sea, Sarina, I could just as easily spend more of my time in the country. It has a special peace which the sea seldom has, and yet they both provide me with the kind of freedom a city can never give me." He shot her a quizzical look then. "Do you know what I'm talking about, Sarina, or are you now bound to this estate like the other women here?"

His question made her defensive again. "I'm not bound at all."

"There are more ways of being bound than simply having your feet bound, you know."

"And just what is that supposed to mean?"

"It means that it would be a shame if you chose to live the restricted kind of life Kwen's offering you."

"But he's broadened my life, not narrowed it," she argued.

"Has he really?" He looked skeptical. "Then he's shown you around his entire estate."

"No, he hasn't."

"But you've been back to the city again."

"No."

"You've met the families on the neighboring estates and—"

"No, I haven't!"

"So you teach his daughters English during the day," Janson declared hotly, "and then you dress the part of the pampered concubine to have dinner with his family and attend a music recital at night, and you tell me that you're not bound!"

"I am not bound!" She enunciated each word with crackling impatience. "Why are you always trying to provoke me?"

"Maybe it's just my way of keeping that spirit of yours alive."

"You have a clever answer for everything, don't you?" She was seething as she got to her knees, only to have him pull her back down again.

"I told you I was responsible for you, didn't I?"

"But I don't need you to protect me."

"No, you don't," he said fiercely. "You have Kwen now."

"Stop it!" she cried.

"Would you prefer it if I said nothing, then?" he growled, forcing her to lie flat in the grass. "Tell me what you'd prefer me to do, Sarina." He was leaning over her now, pinning her arms to her sides. "Would you prefer me to whisper instead? Or would you prefer it if I simply looked at you?" His breath warmed her cheeks as his face moved closer to hers and his eyes caressed her body as surely as if he were touching her with his hands. "Is this better, Sarina?" His voice was a husky whisper.

She closed her eyes and allowed his nearness to envelop her.

"Should I kiss you, Sarina?" he breathed. "Is that what you'd prefer?"

She could feel his mouth hovering just above hers. Her own lips parted, moist and expectant.

"Yes, I believe you would."

She was scarcely breathing now.

"But I have work to do and I've already taken up enough of your time."

Her eyes flew open. He was getting to his feet. Mortified, she lay there, her chest constricted with anger and shame. Again he had turned the tables on her, bent her to his will, and she, like a fool, had played the yearning maiden and followed where he had led. She sat up and brushed some of the grass from the skirt of her muslin gown. Was this his way of punishing her for the other night? she wondered, as once again she was treated to the sight of his proud back as he strode off, leaving her to rage after him in silent fury.

To Sarina's dismay, when she and Wo entered the dining room at the customary hour that evening, she found that Janson had been seated across from her usual place at the table. And then, to her chagrin, midway through the meal, Janson turned to Wo and asked if he could take Sarina for a walk through the grounds once the music recital was ended. Laying down her chopsticks with a clatter, Sarina threw Janson a withering look, which he neither met nor countered. She glanced quickly at Wo, observing his expressionless face with something akin to panic, certain that he would refuse Janson's request and half-hoping that he would.

There was a pucker of concern on Wo's forehead as he said, "Would you not then be returning to the city at a somewhat unsavory hour, my friend?"

"That doesn't concern me," replied Janson, giving Sarina an impudent wink. "The delightful company might be well worth whatever risk may be involved."

"I admit that the gardens are indeed lovely at night, but their beauty is far more readily appreciated during the day."

"Come, now, Kwen." Janson's tone was mildly reproachful. "Miss Paige already knows what the gardens look like during the day. But if it's *her* safety which concerns you now, I can assure you that she'll be safe enough with me."

"I do not doubt that she will be," Wo concurred with a tight smile.

Janson's black brows were arched in mock surprise. "You're not still concerned about *my* safety, are you, Kwen? Miss Paige looks harmless enough to me."

Sarina was now seething, but Janson's baiting seemed to have backed Wo into a most awkward corner. With a slight shrug of his shoulders, he extricated himself from the situation, saying, "With such persistence, my friend, I can well understand the success of your many business ventures. By all means, you may accompany Miss Paige about the grounds, but do not keep her too late. She has three most demanding reasons for receiving a full night of sleep."

Sarina glowered at him. Was she to have no say in their decision? Had either man asked her if she even wanted to go for a walk with Janson? Once again she felt herself being forced to accept his company against her will. She could only imagine what lay in wait for her beyond the confines of the house, out among the seductive shadows of the garden. She shifted about in her chair, her appetite gone, her thoughts uneasy, her body charged with a nervous expectancy, as though a thousand butterflies had been released inside her, their velvet wings beating frantically to be set free. And so it was with a tremor of apprehension that she grudgingly accepted Janson's arm as he led her from the music room sometime later.

Stone lanterns placed at regular intervals throughout the garden lit their way for them with tiny flickering nubs of flame. Against the inked smudge of night, small clusters of fireflies blinked in flashes of minuscule brilliance, while the stars, like celestial messengers, tapped out a heavenly code all their own. The damp grass was a sweet-scented carpet cushioning their steps, and Sarina was seized by the sudden impulse to strip off her white satin slippers and run barefoot through its spongy softness. Jasmine, borne on the ripples of the wind, wrapped her in a perfumed cloak and gradually soothed away some of the turbulence still churning inside her. And as they continued their walk, Sarina found it increasingly more difficult not to be enchanted by the night.

She stole a look at Janson's hard, chiseled profile and wondered if she would ever be able to fathom the man and his mercurial temperament. He caught her studying him, and she quickly looked away.

"You're scowling, Sarina," he remarked. "Couldn't you at least pretend to be enjoying yourself?"

"But I am," she protested.

"Don't you know that all Oriental women are trained to look pleased in spite of how they may really feel?" he continued as if she had never spoken. "I'm afraid you're not going to make a very successful concubine, my dear."

She bridled. "I have no intention of becoming a concubine."

Again he tossed her one of his skeptical looks. "Are you so sure about that?"

A finger of apprehension suddenly began to jab away at her.

"Of course, you'd also have to learn how to please a man," he went on, "but since you'd probably take to that part fairly easily, there may be hope for you after all."

In the dark she could feel the unwelcome rush of heat to her cheeks. "You are undoubtedly the most insolent man I've ever met," she told him.

"And have you met so many that you can actually make an honest comparison?" he teased.

She immediately stopped walking. "I'm getting cold," she lied. "I think I'd like to go back now, if you don't mind."

"Why should I mind?" he countered. "I'm free to take walks like this anytime I choose."

She refused to listen to any more of his caustic remarks. Hoisting up her long white robes, she started off in the opposite direction. A moment later, he caught up with her.

"Did you know that Kwen owns one of the largest estates in China?" he asked, as if nothing were amiss. "The original land was an imperial gift to one of his ancestors four hundred years ago, and each subsequent generation has simply added to it. You've chosen for yourself one of the wealthiest benefactors possible, Sarina, as well as one of the most powerful. But it's just that combination of wealth and power that makes a man like Kwen both an invaluable friend and a dangerous enemy."

"Why are you telling me this?" she snapped.

"So you'll know something about your protector."

"You're talking in riddles."

"No, I'm not," he insisted. "I'm just trying to warn you about him."

"Warn me?" she repeated incredulously. "About Wo

Shue Kwen? I don't need any of your warnings, Mr. Carlyle, because I have nothing to fear from a man who is kind and generous and loving, qualities you know nothing about. If I ever needed to be warned about anyone, I should have been warned about you!"

They had come to the gravel drive in front of the house, where Janson's horse was already saddled and waiting. He reached for the reins and then let them drop again. Turning to Sarina, he put his hands on her shoulders and pulled her toward him. "I know you don't believe me, Sarina," he said, "but I *am* concerned about you, and I want to see you safe, and not hurt."

She continued to stand rigid and unfeeling. Then he surprised her by lifting his hands from her shoulders and gently cupping her face with them. He bent forward so that his lips grazed the top of her head and followed the arch of each golden brow with his mouth before softly kissing the lids which veiled her golden eyes. She shivered in spite of herself when he kissed her cheeks, her nose, and her chin, and she waited impatiently for that moment when he would finally reach her mouth. He seemed to hesitate, drawing back so that he could look at her again. She held her breath. Her heartbeats quickened. And then, ever so slowly, his mouth closed tenderly over hers.

As their kiss deepened, he crushed her to him, his strong arms shaping her body to his. She threw her own arms about his neck and buried her fingers in the thickness of his hair. Hardness met softness, angles melted against curves, as each one gripped the other with a hunger equally matched, all teasing past. Over and over again he claimed her mouth with his, bruising her, branding her, driving her to grind herself against him in an effort to be even closer to him.

He broke their embrace with an abruptness which made her gasp. Even as she reached out for him, he was backing away from her. Grabbing hold of the reins, he flung himself into the saddle and put his boots to his horse's flanks. The horse's hooves clattered over the stones, sparking like flint on steel as they galloped down the drive. Soon, both horse and rider were blended into one black shadow by the night and lost from view.

Stunned, Sarina swayed uncertainly in the faltering

lamplight. Then with the tips of her fingers she retraced
the path his lips had taken only a moment before, a path
now wet and streaked with tears.

Wo stood at the window, his arms hanging limply at his
sides. In a face turned to stone, only his ebony eyes seemed
alive. A muscle twitched in his cheek. His jaw was still so
tightly clenched that even his teeth had begun to ache. As
soon as he relaxed the protesting muscles, his mouth
drooped into an unhappy scowl.

Li moved toward him on tiny hobbled feet. When she
unbound the sash of his robe, she felt him flinch, and his
body grew tense again. He was an ivory statue, frozen and
remote, and only the warmth of her fingers could restore
the life flow of blood to his cold flesh. As she patiently
caressed him, she murmured softly to him, using only
those words which would please and arouse him. When
she finally turned him around to face her, she could see
that, in spite of himself, he was beginning to respond to
her expert touch.

He stood there silently and permitted her to warm and
ready him. He failed to see her dropping to her knees at
his feet, for all he could see was the image of two figures
entwined together beneath the lamplight. She licked a
scorching path up from his toes to the tops of his hairless
thighs, wetting him, smoothing him, soothing him. Then,
moistening her own lips, she opened her mouth and drew
him inside.

He groaned. Leaning forward, he braced himself against
her shoulders. Using her tongue, she moved it in rhythmic circles around him, while he continued to grow. As he
stiffened and thickened, she drew him in deeper, lashing
at him faster and faster, with harder and stronger strokes.
Soon his fullness filled her mouth and stretched toward
the back of her throat. When she began to trace his anal
crevice with one long gold-tipped finger, she felt him
shudder and she knew that he was ready.

He tore himself from her mouth and pushed her roughly
to the floor. Before she could even spread her legs wider
to receive him, he had begun to thrust himself inside her.
As he plunged into her waiting warmth, he closed his
eyes, imagining a woman with golden skin and golden

hair opening up her golden thighs to him and welcoming him inside. He spent himself calling out her name, while he pledged both his seed and his love to her.

Pinned beneath his sagging weight, a mute witness to his cruel duplicity, Li turned her face away and wept.

9

Sarina was baffled by Janson's behavior following their walk in the garden, and even more confused by the attention he continued to pay her on his subsequent visits to the estate. And then, one Saturday morning, he arrived at the house and announced his intention of taking her into Shanghai with him.

"How very devious of you, Mr. Carlyle," she remarked coolly after he had cornered her in the front hall. "You know that Wo is in Yangchow for a few days, don't you?"

"Indeed I do, Miss Paige," he responded, matching her sarcasm with a bit of his own. "You don't think I'd expect him to let you out of his sight for an entire day if he were here, do you? Come on, Sarina, say yes. You can prove to me how independent you still are."

"Impetuousness can hardly be equated with independence," she sniffed.

"Words, words, words," he exclaimed impatiently. "Stop throwing them up as a defense for everything. I'd have thought you'd welcome the break in your routine. Aren't you at all interested in seeing something of Shanghai, or do you still feel that all you need to know of the world can be found here on this estate?"

"Do you consider a brief glimpse of Shanghai that much of a broadening experience?" she persisted, enjoying her ability to provoke a rise out of him.

"At least it's a start," he snapped, drumming his fingers on the banister. "Well, Sarina, what do you say?"

She wondered if she dared accept his invitation. Admittedly, she had felt an initial surge of excitement at the prospect of such a trip, but her more cautious self had immediately warned her against it. Would she be angering

Wo by leaving the estate in his absence? And what would Janson truly think of her if she did? She would be spending an entire day in his company, while he himself acted as both escort and chaperon. She suddenly dimpled. What a tweak on the nose of propriety that would be.

"Well?" Janson was squinting impatiently at his pocket watch. "Is it really that difficult a decision for you?"

She thought back to the challenge he had thrown down like a gauntlet to her that night in the garden. *There are more ways of being bound than simply having your feet bound,* he had said. She was most certainly not bound! And she would prove it to him. With a defiant toss of her head she said, "Wait for me here while I get my parasol."

It was just as she was nearing the head of the staircase, ruffled yellow parasol in hand, that she noticed Li standing in front of the door to her room. Her eyes were gleaming with a cold flame, as cold as the diamonds cascading from her ears. With a rustle of cream and yellow silk, she took several tiny steps forward and said, "In China it is most unseemly for a woman to venture from her home, Miss Paige."

"Those are your ways, Li," Sarina answered evenly, "not mine."

"You are employed in this household and accepted by its master as one of his esteemed family," continued the older woman, "and yet you would dare to dishonor him in this shameless way during his absence?"

"I'm doing nothing of the kind," Sarina retorted. "It's Saturday, and because I have no lessons today, the time is mine to do with as I choose."

"Then I suggest you choose to spend that time more wisely."

"Thank you for your advice, Li," replied Sarina, her voice tight, "but how I spend my time is none of your concern." And with that she snapped her parasol smartly under her arm and hurried back down the stairs to where Janson was waiting for her.

If he noticed the high color in her cheeks as he handed her up into his hired carriage, he made no mention of it, and once he was settled on the seat beside her, he turned to her, saying, "I thought we might stop at one of the oldest teahouses in Shanghai for tea at some point today." He slapped the pair of chestnut mares into a brisk trot

and waited for some response from Sarina. When none
was forthcoming, he said, "Does that idea hold any appeal
for you at all?"

But Sarina was staring straight ahead of her, her teeth
clenched, her mood souring, finding it impossible to be
civil right at that moment.

"If you think this outing is going to be that much of an
ordeal, I'll turn around right now, Sarina." Janson's voice
cut through the air like a whip, making her wince.

"I'm sorry," she offered lamely, hoping that her weak
attempt at an apologetic smile would appease him.

It did seem to mollify him somewhat, because after
casting another dark scowl in her direction, he proceeded
to ignore her completely. They lapsed into an awkward
silence and Sarina sought to distract herself by concentrat-
ing on the beauty of the passing landscape. As the sun
grew hotter, she opened her parasol to shield her face,
and as she did, she stole a sideways glance at Janson. Since
that night in the garden, he had never once tried to kiss
her again. In fact, ever since that night, he had been
treating her with all the respect and deference of an older
brother or guardian. Guardian! Sarina nibbled thoughtfully on her bottom lip. Janson Carlyle was obviously intent on keeping his foolhardy promise to her after all, a
promise she now realized she wished he had never made.
She did not want him for a guardian!

What role would she prefer him to play, she asked
herself, when he was so unpredictable? He could be gentle
and laughing one moment and then brooding or angry
the next. When he was provoked, as he had been earlier,
his voice would resemble an ominous roll of thunder, his
movements streaks of summer lightning. And then, just as
quickly as they had come, the clouds would lift, his expression would clear, and his mood would lighten again. She
glanced at him once more and frowned. He was an impossible man, she decided, and deserved to play no role in
her life whatsoever.

They had reached the outskirts of the city now, where
the streets, many of them lined with newly installed gas
lamps, were still as poor as the rutted roads of the
countryside. Impassable during the rainy season, they were
for the moment dry and hard, with granite chips and bits
of broken brick from the underlying roadbed poking up

through the dirt. Janson handled the team easily, guiding the carriage safely between all the other carriages and past the many rickshas and sedan chairs streaming through the open gates of the city.

The city itself was a joyous burst of noise and color. As they rode on, the pitted roads gave way to streets paved with irregular stone slabs. There were no sidewalks, and the houses and shops were packed so tightly together that all the air seemed to have been squeezed out of the place to make room for them. A group of coolies ambled alongside the carriage, each carrying a large wicker basket of rice, while from the opposite direction came two young men bearing wooden buckets of water, crying out "Hay ho! High ho!" as they went by. An elderly lantern seller, his brass lanterns swinging from both ends of the long pole he was balancing on one shoulder, smiled up at Sarina and nodded toward his wares. Although she returned his smile, it was with an apologetic shake of her head.

Wherever space permitted, rickety wooden stalls had been set up in front of many of the busy shops. At one there was a traveling tinker, at another a wandering physician, at still another a money changer with a pair of brass scales on the table before him. Sarina counted a spectacle maker, a barber, a cook, and a fortune-teller before the carriage turned the corner.

A group of blind beggars immediately caught her attention. Four of them, each holding on to one of the other's ragged clothes, were shuffling single file along the street. A lump rose in Sarina's throat as she watched them wandering from shop to shop, their arms outstretched and pleading. There were fewer shops on this particular street. All of them were large and well-constructed. Most of them were two stories tall, with square ornamented roofs, overhanging tile eaves, and windowsills lined with pots of blooming azaleas, pinks, and roses.

The road began to broaden, the buildings thinned, and soon the raucous street noise all but disappeared completely. Sarina was aware of a brilliant wash of blue sky for the first time. Janson nudged her with his elbow, indicating the harbor to her right, where hundreds of ships' masts were slicing into the clear blue of that welcome expanse of sky. To her left stretched a line of large, imposing brick homes with beautifully tended lawns, artfully pruned trees, and intricately designed rock gardens.

"This is the Bund, Sarina," Janson told her as they continued down the wide tree-shaded avenue. "Not long ago it was simply a huge ditch filled with garbage and littered with wooden sheds and squatters' shanties."

Fascinated, she looked eagerly about her. There were very few Orientals, she noticed, except for the ricksha drivers and the sedan-chair-bearers. The couples being drawn in open carriages like theirs and strolling along the avenue were obviously Europeans and Americans, and all were fashionably and expensively attired. Some of the men were dressed in British naval uniforms, others wore immaculate white suits, and all of the women carried lace-edged silk parasols to complement the richly flounced pastel-colored gowns they were wearing.

"You're causing quite a few heads to turn, my dear," noted Janson in the stuffy guardian voice she had come to detest.

She merely smiled at his remark and felt a mild surge of satisfaction when she saw him scowl. Then she realized he was not scowling at her at all. Turning her head, she saw that a middle-aged man with thinning sandy-colored hair and a bristling mustache was seated in the open carriage keeping pace with theirs and staring at her frankly and unabashedly. With an impatient flick of his wrists Janson slapped their horses into a faster gait, pulling ahead of the offending carriage. To Sarina's delight, the man winked broadly at her and raised one of his gloved hands in a farewell salute.

In an effort to avoid any possible unpleasantness arising from the incident, Sarina hastily caught hold of Janson's sleeve, and pointing to the building they were passing, asked him what it was.

"That's the Chinese customhouse," he grumbled.

"And the one beside it?"

"I don't know."

"Oh." She sat back in her seat again, prepared to allow him to fume for a while in silence, when he surprised her by suddenly shaking off his blackening mood.

"Do you see that small red brick building standing next to the tall gray stone one?" he asked her. When she nodded,

he said, "That's the Shanghai office of the Carlyle Trading Company."

"Do I detect a note of pride in your voice, Mr. Carlyle?"
she gently teased him.

But he treated her remark in an offhand way, saying,
"It's already too small for our needs. Right now I'm looking for a larger building and several more warehouses.
And if our business continues to expand, before I sail for
home this time next year I should be looking for even
larger quarters."

Sarina tried to keep from smiling. Next year. Perhaps
during that time she would be able to convince him that
she was not a child in need of two guardians, but a woman
. . . She stopped herself from going any further. She was
indeed a woman. Even her mirror attested to that. Her
breasts had begun to display a new fullness of late, and
her skin seemed to glow with a translucent clarity she had
never noticed before. Deep inside, she felt ripe and round
and strangely contented.

"Would you like to share your secret with me?" asked
Janson.

"What secret?"

"The one you're obviously enjoying so much it's making
you grin."

"But then, if I told you, it wouldn't be a secret anymore,
would it?" she replied, her smile widening.

"No, I guess not." He shrugged, hunching over the
reins again.

Her smile turned into a pout. Janson never played her
games for very long. He always gave up too easily, as
though he were already bored and thinking about something else. He reminded her of a hummingbird condemned
to live in perpetual flight or die. On those rare occasions
when he *did* relax, it was never long before he grew
restless again, as if he were responding to some inner
alarm only he could hear.

"You're really off on a cloud, aren't you?"

Sarina started guiltily. "I beg your pardon?"

"I was just asking you if you were going to miss me."

Her hands tightened around the wooden handle of her
parasol. "Miss you?"

"When I leave for Hong Kong."

"But I thought you intended to stay here for another year."

He shook his head. "I'll probably return to Shanghai once or twice, but I'll be spending most of my time in Hong Kong."

Sarina quickly turned her face away, wishing for the first time that she were more like the Oriental women he had teased her about. Then she would have been more adept at masking her feelings.

"On my last trip to Hong Kong I opened a temporary office and rented a few warehouses," Janson went on. "Now I have to find a building to house my permanent offices. I also have to hire more staff, rent some more warehouses, meet with the local merchants and farmers, arrange for berths down on the waterfront for my ships, and so on. All that takes time, Sarina, and as much as I despise being trapped in one place for so long, I have no choice. I'm the only one who can do it."

Suddenly she no longer had any interest in what she was seeing. A strange emptiness was beginning to fill her. It began in the pit of her stomach and fanned outward until it had spread through her entire body. She could barely feel the handle of her parasol anymore. Even her toes were numb. A wave of nausea spiraled upward from her aching belly, and she swallowed hard, praying to God not to let her be sick. In spite of the heat of the day, she felt cold inside, cold and dead.

The carriage jolted to a halt and she nearly fell out of her seat. Janson put out a hand to steady her and then motioned for her to turn around. Grimly she did as she was told. What she saw was a small pagoda-shaped building with a high peaked roof of pale green tile and stucco walls painted a warm shade of apricot. Its tiny windows were framed by white shutters, and the ledges of the windows were lined with pale green clay pots filled with white azaleas. As Janson led her up to the front door, Sarina smiled when she saw the intricately detailed dragon painted across it, with the large brass door handle lodged squarely in the middle of one of its brilliant red eyes.

The interior of the little teahouse was painted apricot as well, but out of the harsh glare of the sun the effect was far more pleasing and restful. All of the small round tables were covered by trailing pale green cotton cloths and the chairs drawn up to them were fitted with plump green-and-apricot cotton cushions. In the center of each table was a deep white porcelain dish filled with melon seeds and peanuts and a second dish holding a short white wax candle banked with plum blossoms and mulberry leaves.

Groups of Chinese men were sitting at several of the tables sipping cups of tea and cracking open melon seeds with their teeth. While most of them were chatting quietly among themselves, some were simply leaning back in their chairs and puffing on long bamboo pipes or dozing behind their news sheets. One man, perched on a low cushioned stool near the door, was even busily working at his abacus. He raised his head for a moment to gaze curiously at Sarina as she followed Janson to one of the few empty tables, and then returned to his counting.

As soon as they were seated, a young girl dressed in a pale green quilted silk jacket and a long apricot pleated silk skirt appeared at their table with a white porcelain teapot. Setting down two small white cups, she poured Sarina and Janson their tea, then bowed to each of them and backed away from the table. Sarina stiffened as the girl's eyes met and held Janson's for a moment longer than necessary. Was it her imagination or had they just greeted one another as two people who were something more than complete strangers? The girl was lovely, Sarina admitted to herself, and the look passing between them had been a look exchanged by a beautiful woman and a handsome man, not a serving girl and a customer.

"You've obviously been in here before," she observed somewhat caustically after the girl had gone.

"I come in here quite often," he answered matter-of-factly, pushing back his chair and stretching his long legs out in front of him.

Was she imagining it again, or was he continuing to stare after the girl? Sarina began to chew on the inside of her cheek.

"I like this place because it's quiet," said Janson, taking a sip of his tea. "No women." He winked at her. "Most of the other teahouses in Shanghai are filled with chattering, gossiping American and European women who always manage to make a man feel like a fool for being there instead of in a bar."

"But I don't see any Chinese women in here either," commented Sarina as she glanced about her.

"You never cease to amaze me, my dear." Now Janson was using his pompous teacher's voice, and Sarina gritted her teeth. "Life on Kwen's estate is no different from life inside the meanest hovel in this country. Whether their feet are bound or not, all Chinese women are bound to their homes and to their husbands, just as Sua and Li are bound to Kwen. Only the occasional concubine has the chance to break with tradition for a while." He gave her a pointed look. "The concubine of a mandarin," he said. "As one of China's highest officials, he needs a hostess to travel with him. Whenever he's posted to some distant region, while his wife stays home and tends to her ancestor worshiping, it's his concubine who goes with him." He took several quick sips of his tea. "So if you ever decide to become a full-time concubine, Sarina, choose a mandarin, not a landlord."

Sarina slammed her cup down on the table. "I find your vile insinuations insulting and cruel," she stormed, her eyes alive with coppery sparks. "Wo Shue Kwen calls you his friend to your face. What do you think he would call you if he knew how you were talking about him behind his back?"

"No doubt he'd consider me his enemy, and you, my sweet, his most devoted and ardent champion." Janson's smile was nasty. "What loyalty, Sarina, what complete devotion, and spoken with such vehemence, too."

"Yes, I'm loyal to Wo," she argued back, "*and* devoted. Why shouldn't I be?"

"Why indeed?" he challenged her. "Do I detect something other than a simple defense of your employer in your tone, Sarina? Could it be that you're a little bit in love with Wo Shue Kwen?"

She was rendered speechless by his remark. For a moment she just sat in her chair, opening and closing her hands, as if she were gripping something and then just as quickly dropping it again.

"In love with him?" The question exploded from her lips. "How can you presume such a thing! Because of your own warped mind, you can twist the most innocent gesture into treachery and the mildest statement into blasphemy. There's something evil inside you, Janson Carlyle, something rotting whatever may have been decent and kind in you. My father taught me to have compassion for people who were sick or lame, and somehow I think you're both sick *and* lame. I pity you, Janson, I truly do."

Janson's face was darkening. "Save your pity for someone else, Sarina, and save all of your Christian forgiveness for Wo Shue Kwen, not me. He needs it. I don't."

"Then if you hold him in such contempt," she retaliated, "why are you doing business with him?"

"Because he has the finest silk in China."

"So you're nothing but a self-serving hypocrite," she hissed.

"And you, my dear Sarina," he thundered, "are a blind little fool!"

Heads were turning. Sarina's cheeks were beginning to sting. She raised a trembling hand to her face as if to cool a climbing fever with her touch, but the fever climbed even higher. With studied dignity she pushed back her chair and stood up.

"Please take me home now," she said in a tight, angry voice.

"It will be a pleasure." Janson downed the last of his tea, tossed a handful of silver coins onto the table, and followed her outside.

They rode back to the estate in stony silence. Janson's jaw was drawn into a hard, uncompromising line and Sarina's was just as stubbornly set. As soon as they pulled up to the front gates of the house, Sarina scrambled down from the carriage by herself. She was just about to open the gate when she realized that she had left her parasol behind.

"My parasol," she snapped to Janson, holding out her hand.

He bent to retrieve it from the floor of the carriage, but instead of giving it to her, he held it in the air slightly out of reach.

"Knowing why you're being loyal is one thing, Sarina," he told her, "but being loyal out of ignorance or blind trust is something far different."

"What are you hinting at now?" she demanded, straining to reach the handle of her elusive parasol. "Why can't you say exactly what you mean?"

"Because I'm still not sure you'd want to hear what I have to say."

She was suddenly seized by the same feeling of dread she had experienced when she had walked into her father's bedroom on that last morning.

"Sarina . . ." His green eyes were pleading with her to look at him. "Sarina, Kwen is a corrupter," he said.

"What do you mean?" she whispered, as the feeling began to spread.

"For God's sake, what do you think I mean!"

"Please don't raise your voice to me."

"I'm sorry," he apologized, "but you're making this very difficult."

"You initiated it," she reminded him.

"All right, then," he capitulated. Fixing her with his steely gaze, he said, "Silk probably accounts for the smallest part of Kwen's enormous wealth. Most of his fortune comes from the poppies he grows."

"Poppies?" Sarina was confused.

"Your benevolent employer grows poppies for their opium, Sarina, and he supplies most of China, all of Hong Kong and Hawaii, as well as several western American states with the illegal drug. He knows I won't ship the opium for him, so he uses Jardine and Matheson instead."

Sarina began backing away from the carriage.

"Not only that, but he also provides some of the most . . ."

Sarina heard nothing more. She had clapped her hands over her ears to block out the sound of his voice. She backed into the gate and slumped against it, too weak to move. Then, with fingers too numb to release the catch on the gate, she was finally able to grab hold of the ring on the large dragon-shaped iron door knocker. A rush of prickly heat swept over her, her vision blurred, and she began sinking slowly to her knees.

The last thing she saw before she fainted was the snarling grin on the face of the iron dragon.

10

"Sarina?"

At first she thought it was Janson calling her name, for in the wavering grayness all she could see was the faint outline of a man's face.

"Sarina?"

She weakly tore away the strands of mist still dimming her sight, but when she was finally able to see him clearly, she cried out in alarm and struggled to sit up.

"Lie down, Sarina," urged Wo Shue Kwen as he gently pushed her back again. "Now, lie still until you are fully recovered."

An apprehensive shudder shook her body at the sound of his voice, and suddenly the fingers gripping her arm were not fingers at all, but the coils of a snake. Staring intently into his face, she strained to find some trace of evil there which would prove that what Janson had said about him was true. But there *was* no evil in Wo's face, only compassion. And a look of such tender concern that it tore Sarina's heart in two.

Surely Janson had lied about this man who was holding a cup of hot tea to her lips and coaxing her to drink all of it. How could he possibly be a corrupter? she wondered, leaning forward while he plumped up the down cushions he himself had decided should replace her bamboo headrest. If anyone was a corrupter and a despoiler, it was Janson Carlyle.

"I presume you had no meal at noon," said Wo, and Sarina shook her head. With a scowl of disapproval he reached for the covered bowl which one of the servants had brought in with the tea. "*Congee,*" he explained, spooning some of the thick white rice cereal into her mouth.

Remembering how often her father had fed her hot oatmeal made her smile. "I haven't eaten cereal since I was a child," she confided to him shyly.

"But you are very much *my* child now, Sarina," he told her, "and as with a child of my own blood, I will see to it that you are always most lovingly tended."

Hearing him speak that way suddenly intensified her own turmoil, as once again she tried to reconcile what she believed about him with what Janson had told her about him.

"There is something troubling you deeply, Sarina," Wo remarked as he set aside the empty bowl. "Perhaps if you shared your thoughts with me, it might bring you some comfort."

As she continued to struggle with her doubts, she knew that according to Chinese custom, what she was about to ask was something even his own wife was forbidden to ask him.

"Is it true . . . ?" Her voice faltered and she had to begin again. "Is it true that you grow poppies and that you sell the opium from them all over the world?" There. It was out. Refusing to meet his eyes, she stared down at her tightly clasped hands and waited.

He sat at the edge of her bed for another moment without saying a word. Then he got up and walked over to the window. With his back still turned to her, he said in a very quiet voice, "Yes, Sarina, I do."

She squeezed her eyes shut as the pain of his betrayal shot through her and she realized how much she had wanted him to deny what Janson had accused him of.

"For many hundreds of years now, we in China have called opium 'God's own medicine,'" explained Wo in his carefully modulated voice. "It is not only the most powerful reliever of pain we have ever known, but it is also capable of producing the most tranquil of slumbers. Used with care, it is a source of comfort to anyone who is suffering intolerable pain, whether it be of the body or of the mind. It is used by the esteemed emperor himself and by the most humble of peasants; and mighty or meek, all who know of the powers of the poppy are in awe of such powers." Turning to face her at last, he asked, "Was it Janson Carlyle who told you of this, Sarina?"

"Yes." She nodded, still staring bleakly at her hands.

"I see." He folded his arms across his chest and tucked his hands up inside the voluminous sleeves of his turquoise-and-gold silk robe. "My friend Janson is a most confounding young man," he said with a wry smile, "for like so many of your countrymen, he is not above seeking a release from pain through the drinking of harsh spirits." He gave his head a rueful shake. "How simple a matter it is to condone that which is familiar and to condemn that which is not. But then, perhaps you of the West consider yourselves a more virtuous people than we. In China, I know very few men who would not gladly deny such false virtue for a moment's surcease from pain." Coming to stand by her bed again, he tipped up her face so that he could look into her troubled eyes. "I wonder, my lovely young lotus, what choice you would make if ever that choice were yours."

He left her then to grapple with her thoughts alone. The shock of Janson's revelation had been blunted by Wo's frank admission, an honor she again realized no Chinese woman would ever have been accorded. She had found some truths in his argument which not only allayed some of her own fears but also made a mockery out of Janson's sudden display of righteous indignation.

"Let him who is without guilt cast the first stone." Sarina thought of those words from the Scriptures, and something hardened inside of her. Once again Janson Carlyle had proven himself to be exactly what she had thought him to be. A hypocrite. For in spite of his own excesses, he had chosen to cast a first stone anyway.

One week later, just as Sarina was returning from the summerhouse with her young charges in tow, the door to the study opened and Wo emerged, followed closely by Janson himself. Sarina tried to urge the girls up the stairs more quickly, but her attempts were foiled by their tiny bound feet. She was trapped. When Wo called out to her, she had no choice but to join them.

With her head erect, her back straight, and her hands clenched by her sides, she walked stiffly over to Wo, her eyes never once straying to the tall grim-faced figure standing next to him. Then, as if by some prearranged agreement, Wo gave Janson a light slap on the back before returning to his study and closing the door, leaving Sarina to stare after him in astonishment.

"Would you like to go for a walk?" asked Janson in a formal voice she had never hear him use before.

"No, thank you," she replied curtly, heading for the stairs again.

He caught hold of her arm. "Then just come outside with me for a moment."

She wrenched her arm free. "I've already been outside."

"All right, then." He shrugged. "I suppose I'll just have to find some way to change your mind."

She screamed as he picked her up in his arms and carried her out of the house and down the drive. Then he set her down. Her lightly pinned hair had come loose and was now being tossed about by the late-afternoon breeze. Her face was flushed, her breathing ragged as, angry and resentful, she lashed out at him with doubled fists.

It took him only a moment to catch both of her wrists in one of his large strong hands. Then he used his other hand to stroke her cheek, as if she were a wild beast he was attempting to gentle and tame.

"I prefer you this way, Sarina," he told her, his own breathing slightly jagged. "Now you're like the woman your name implies. A sea siren, with her hair released to the wind, not pinned and glued into place, and her face coloring naturally instead of being painted to look real." He slowly wound a lock of her golden hair around his index finger. "I pity the man who loses his heart to you, my lovely sea siren. Not only will he be losing his heart, but he'll probably be losing his soul to you as well."

Sarina cautioned her pounding heart not to listen to the sweet words tumbling from his lips. He was not to be trusted, this changeable man, this hypocrite, for whom words, whether false or true, bitter or sweet, came all too easily. And so while he continued to talk to her and to touch her hair, she hardened her resolve to put him behind her once and for all.

"I'm sailing for Hong Kong tomorrow," he said.

In spite of herself, her heart skipped a beat.

"That's why I wanted to speak to you, to tell you—"

"Good-bye?" she hastily supplied. "How thoughtful of you."

"I also wanted to explain to you about the other day. I wanted to—"

"Apologize for leaving me where Wo could find me?"

"It wasn't like that at all. I carried you as far as—"

"As you can see for yourself," she cut him off again, "I'm fully recovered. Now I must get back to the house."

"Sarina, please."

She tugged herself free and started up the drive.

"Sarina!"

She waited for the crunching sound of his boots coming after her, but as she continued walking, all she could hear was the rhythmic click of her own low-heeled shoes on the gravel. Reaching the front door, she paused for a moment, one part of her determined to march straight into the house without looking back, the other part yearning to stop and turn around. He was leaving, she reminded herself. What purpose would it serve to look back at him one last time? Her mind made up, she pushed open the front door and went inside.

But there was something terribly final in the way the wind snatched the door from her hands and slammed it shut behind her.

As the days passed, Sarina found it increasingly more difficult to get out of bed in the morning. She would waken with nausea high in her throat and her stomach churning violently. Once the nausea was quelled, she was so weak that the only way she was able to swing her legs over the side of her bed was if she held on to one of the lacquer tables. And then every step she took as she moved about the room was taken with feet which seemed weighted with lead. Brushing her hair exhausted her, and fastening the tiny buttons on her summer gowns was soon more than she could manage by herself.

She had lost all appetite for breakfast, and even when she forced herself to take a few sips of tepid green tea, she felt as if she were about to bring it back up again. She staggered through each day like a sleepwalker, dozing on the grass outside the summerhouse when her charges took their nap, and waking only when Liang came outside to wake her up. After the girls were returned to Lan-tai at four, Sarina would collapse on her own bed and sleep until Ing-han came to dress her for dinner.

Dinner itself was a protracted torture now. No sooner had she smelled the meat on the table than a threatening ripple of nausea would seize her again. Sitting stiffly in her chair, her hands gripping the sides of the cushioned seat, she would draw in deep, steadying breaths of air and pray not to humiliate herself by being sick in front of everyone.

She was both surprised and relieved that Wo never mentioned Janson Carlyle by name again, and given her own distressing condition, she herself had little time to dwell on the bittersweet memory of him. But where she forgot, her dreams remembered. They still summoned him up for her, a green-eyed presence, burnished by the sun, so warm, so close; and when she sometimes woke to find her pillow damp with tears, she felt betrayed by the ally she thought she had found in sleep.

One afternoon she was shaken awake, not by Ing-han, but by Wo. Startled to find him there, she rubbed her eyes with the heels of her hands to clear away the last vestiges of her heavy sleep.

"Forgive me for disturbing you, my dear Sarina, but I had hoped to persuade you to leave your bed for a while and accompany me to the rearing houses. We have already begun to boil and dry the cocoons of the silkworms, and I thought you might care to view this most interesting process."

She gave him a wan smile. "I'd like that very much," she told him, "but I don't think I have the strength to walk that far."

He dismissed her misgivings with a wave of his hand. "I have already ordered a sedan chair for Li. I will simply have a second brought round for you."

He must have noticed her surprise, for he hastily explained, "My cherished Li seems particularly fascinated by the boiling of the cocoons. It has long been a yearly custom for her to be brought to the rearing houses whenever the process is about to begin. Come," he urged her. "I will help you."

The sedan chair was simply a large bamboo box with two long poles running through it, painted black and fitted with brilliant blue silk side draperies. As soon as Sarina was comfortably seated inside, four servants hoisted the poles onto their shoulders and the box was lifted into the air. While they made their way slowly through the gardens, Wo walked alongside them, keeping his anxious gaze trained on Sarina as she fought to stay awake.

Li was already seated on a low mahogany stool inside the rearing house when Sarina and Wo arrived. If the woman was displeased by Sarina's being there, nothing in her expression revealed it. Dressed in a peacock-blue silk jacket and long pleated skirt, her hair, ears, wrists, and fingers ablaze with sapphires and turquoises, she seemed strangely out of place beside the roughly dressed peasants.

Above one of the caldrons of boiling water, Sarina's eyes met Chen's. Although he nodded politely to her and smiled, she could still see traces of sadness in his face, a sadness which had been there ever since Na, the peasant woman, had died with her child the week before. She returned his smile and would have gone over to him had he not looked away and begun to empty the wicker basket full of plump gray cocoons he was holding into the steaming caldron. Recalling what he had once told her about the process, she felt a returning queasiness in her stomach, and she wondered why she had ever permitted herself to be lured away from her bed and the sleep she still craved.

"You appear distressed, Miss Paige." It was Li, speaking to her in her clear, honeyed voice. "Not all of the worms are condemned to die," she purred. "Many are saved and allowed to emerge as moths. In time, they will reproduce, their eggs will hatch into larvae, and the process will continue. You must learn to consider these simple creatures as mere sacrifices, my dear, to creatures of a higher order who must be properly attired."

Sarina heard Chen clearing his throat. "Did you know, Miss Paige," he interjected, "that it requires approximately one hundred and forty pounds of cocoons to yield one hundred and twenty pounds of raw silk?"

Sarina turned to him with a wobbly smile. "No," she murmured, wiping a thickening film of perspiration from her forehead. "No, I didn't." The vapors filling the room were making her dizzy and the smell of the boiling cocoons was causing her stomach to heave again.

"Are you ill, Sarina?" Wo hurried over to her and pressed his palm to her damp forehead. "You seem feverish."

She brushed his hand away. "I think I'll just step outside

for a few minutes, if you don't mind. I'll feel much better as soon as I've gotten some fresh air," she assured him.

Once she was outside, she slumped against the side of the building and closed her eyes. She massaged her cramping stomach in slow circular movements until the spasms gradually eased; then she started off in search of her sedan chair. Wo would have to forgive her, but she simply had to get some more sleep. She caught sight of the house servants resting beneath one of the spreading mulberry trees, and she began weaving an unsteady path in their direction.

"Missy!"

She glanced up just as she collided with a young peasant carrying a large copper kettle filled with boiling water. The scalding liquid splashed onto her gown and feet and Sarina began to scream. Her flesh ignited, flaring into tissues of living flame. She crumpled to the ground, and the young man, his face white with terror, began backing away from her. Dropping the kettle with a hollow clatter, he broke into a run and quickly disappeared among the mulberry trees.

In her agony, Sarina clasped her swelling ankles with both hands and began rocking back and forth on the ground.

"Help me," she whimpered, gazing up through pain-filled eyes at the figure that had appeared in the doorway of the rearing house. "Help me, please."

But Li simply stood where she was, with her arms folded across her chest and a smile of sweet satisfaction on her perfectly painted face.

"Help me!" Sarina called, one hand stretching out to the silent figure. "Help . . ."

Her voice trailed off as her world dimmed and faded into blackness.

She woke to a strange, pungent smell all around her. As she began to retch, Wo held her head over a large porcelain basin, and when she was done, he sponged off her face and gave her some cool water to drink.

"What you are smelling is the paste our physician, Qi Ting-fang, used to coat your burns," Wo told her, wringing out a fresh cloth and draping it over her forehead. "Your feet are bandaged now, Sarina, and it is Qi's orders

that you do not attempt to rise until the flesh has begun to
heal. So you see"—his tone turned playful—"you will now
have more than ample time for the sleep of which you
seem so fond of late."

Sarina grimaced. The throbbing in her feet seemed to
have spread throughout her entire body. Even her head
was pounding with the same steady, pulsing rhythm. She
licked her dry lips and thought of how Janson would be
laughing at her now for having her feet truly bound at
last. Her mouth twisted into a bitter smile. She closed her
eyes to dispel the image of him, but behind her darkened
lids writhed another image. Once again she saw Li standing in that doorway and smiling in cruel indifference at
her terrible pain.

"I have some tea for you, Sarina," came Wo's distant
voice. "It will help you to sleep now."

As she took her first sip of the tea, she found it similar
to the fragrant jasmine-scented tea Wo had offered her
that day in his warehouse in Shanghai. She took another
sip and then another, and when the cup was empty, she
obediently drained a second cup and then lay back again
with a contented sigh.

Although her head was resting on her feather pillow, it
was as if she were being cushioned by a feathery cloud
instead. She could scarcely feel the pain now. She was
leaving her body and floating. Floating above the pain,
drifting high above her scalded flesh and her aching
stomach. Even her mind was being bathed by a gentle
wash of forgetfulness. Now she was weightless, her flesh
dissolving so that she could flutter free among the clouds,
nothing more than a wisp of cloud herself.

Wo bent over and kissed her lightly on the mouth. "You
will sleep the most exalted of sleeps now, my treasured
flower," he crooned, stepping back from the bed. "Forgive
me, Sarina, but the choice was never yours to make."

Taking the pot of opium-laced tea with him, he slipped
out of the room and quietly closed the door.

11

It was ten days before Qi Ting-fang permitted Sarina to return to the summerhouse and the three young girls anxiously awaiting the resumption of their lessons. Although her feet were still lightly bandaged, she felt very little pain. What *did* pain her was knowing that the young man who had accidentally scalded her had received twenty strokes of the lash for what he had done. Each time she thought of his punishment, she found herself wishing that the treacherous Li had been the one to suffer the sting of that lash instead.

To her delight, Chen stopped by at noon to visit with her, something he had done each day of her confinement. But today as they sat together on the grass while her charges napped inside the summerhouse, Sarina could see that the young man was deeply troubled. There was a strange hopelessness about him. It was there in his forced smile, in the uncharacteristic stoop of his shoulders, and in the frenetic movements of his hands as he picked apart an azalea blossom and scattered its pink petals to the wind. When he began to rip apart a second flower, Sarina took the tattered sprig away from him.

"What is it, Chen?" she asked him. "What's wrong?"

He pressed the tips of his fingers to his temples as if to contain whatever it was that was bothering him.

"Chen?"

His face contorted in pain. "My father . . ." His voice cracked. "My father has begun to speak of the date for my marriage." He closed his eyes and Sarina saw tears beginning to bead his stiff black lashes. "I am in despair," he whispered, "terrible despair. I have not seen Kuer T'ai since I was a child, and yet, on the day we marry, I will be

124

expected to welcome this stranger into my home as my wife. I am to permit her to worship at the tablets of my ancestors and I am to take her to my bed." He opened his eyes then and the tears coursed slowly down his cheeks. "Did you know, my friend, that in China a woman is considered to be of greater importance as a daughter-in-law than as a wife? And all because she is the one who tends the sacrifices to her husband's parents and to his ancestors. She enters the home of her husband and she becomes the bridge both to his forebears and to his descendants. But what of the bridge between herself and her husband? Is it to be built solely on responsibility, on duty, and on tradition? What, then, of love?" he sobbed. "What becomes of love?"

He buried his face in his hands and tears welled up in Sarina's own eyes at the sight of such despair.

"My poor Chen," she murmured, "my poor, dear friend. Although I still can't understand many of your complicated ways, what I *can* understand is your unhappiness." She lifted his head and forced him to meet her eyes. "Listen to me," she said. "Even if you have to marry Lao Kuer T'ai, you don't have to stop loving Mei. She can still live in your house, she can even bear your children, she—"

"As my chosen one, yes," he retorted bitterly. "My concubine." He spit the word out at her. "In most households, the concubine is considered to be nothing more than a servant, one who must suffer the indignity of tending to the needs of the wife. No, my friend, Mei will never serve a wife of mine or live in a home where she and I should dwell together and be served by others."

"Have you ever asked Mei if she would consent to being your concubine?"

"I do not have to ask her. I know what she would say, for her pride is as great as mine."

"But if you're wrong?" she persisted. "What if she preferred living in your house as your concubine to having to live without you?"

Chen turned his head away so that Sarina was unable to read the expression on his face.

She quickly pressed her advantage. "You seem to be forgetting that not all concubines are treated like servants, Chen. Not all concubines are powerless."

"Ah, yes," he sniffed disdainfully, "the beauteous Li.

She is one of the very few who have effectively usurped the powers of the wife, bewitching my father and casting my mother into the shadows." He shook his head sorrowfully. "Mei is not Li, my friend, nor could she ever be." Wiping his eyes with the backs of his hands, he got slowly to his feet. For the next few minutes he prowled restlessly about the garden before coming back to where Sarina was still sitting and putting his hands on her shoulders.

"Sarina, my friend," he began uncertainly, "may I ask one more favor of you?"

It was with mounting trepidation that she nodded her head.

"Would you allow me to have the key to the summer-house each day?"

Sarina gasped.

"Please, my friend, the time which remains to us grows shorter with each day that passes. If I am soon to wed a woman I will never love, let me leave the woman I do love with something far sweeter than kisses stolen in the darkness. Let me love her as only a man who truly loves her can, and perhaps the memories of our moments together will enable us to more easily endure the empty years which lie ahead for us."

"But if your father ever found out . . ."

"We would meet at night for an hour, no more, as we do now," he whispered urgently, "and each afternoon you could leave the key for me." Glancing about for a suitable hiding place, he indicated a large flat white rock speckled with moss at the base of the pink azalea bush not far from where she was sitting. "Hide it there, and I will simply put it back again each night before I return to the house."

The risks were great for all of them, and yet, as she looked at Chen's tormented face, Sarina could not bring herself to deny the young lovers what brief time was left to them. Instead of Chen and Mei, she saw two other lovers, their bodies locked together, rising and falling as a ship rose and fell on an angry sea. Two lovers clinging to one another and to the sweet promise of life, while the threat of death raged around them. Stolen moments were all she had ever been permitted to know; stolen moments were perhaps all Chen and Mei could hope for now.

"All right, Chen," she told him, "I'll leave the key."

He fell to his knees in front of her and kissed her

solemnly on each cheek. "By this gesture, my friend, I
have sworn a debt to you which can be repaid only with
my life."

"No, Chen, no," she gasped, horrified by what was im-
plicit in his vow.

"I swear it before you and before the gods of my
ancestors," he pledged fiercely before he rose to his feet
and pulled her after him.

That night, as she lay in bed, Sarina thought of Chen
and Mei entwined in each other's arms inside the darkened summerhouse. She tried to imagine which of the
striped silk cushions they were lying on as they explored
the wonders of one another's bodies, and what promises
they would make as they consummated their hopeless
love. Hugging her pillow to her chest, she finally fell into
a shallow and dream-filled sleep, waking several times
during the night, still clutching her pillow as if it were a
lover; until she woke one final time, with the opal sheen
of dawn, to find her pillow lying on the floor beside her
bed.

Several days later, Ing-han was stricken with a summer
fever and Sua generously offered Sarina the services of
Mei until Ing-han was well again. It was with a mixture of
anticipation and apprehension that she waited in her
room for Mei to appear that evening, for she had not
spoken to Chen alone since the afternoon she had begun
leaving the small brass key to the summerhouse under the
moss-covered stone. When she heard the light knock at
the door, she opened it cautiously, bracing herself for her
first private encounter with the girl for whom Chen was
willing to risk so much.

She was startled to find Wo standing there instead.

"Mei has not yet arrived?" was all he said as he quickly
scanned the room. "Good." He hastily closed the door. "I
have brought you someone, my dear Sarina, who will keep
you safe from harm. For it would seem that I have been
failing to protect you as I should."

She followed his eyes down to her feet, where the skin
was puckered and red and still in the process of healing.
Pressing something cold and hard into the palm of her
hand, Wo said, "Her name is Ji Hsi. She is the goddess

who is the protector of young women, and she will protect you as no mere mortal can."

Sarina opened her hand and looked down at a tiny statue of a beautiful Chinese woman which had been carved out of deep green jade and stood only two inches tall. Her elaborate headdress and long sashed robe were encrusted with hundreds of tiny diamonds, and her eyes were two brilliant red rubies.

"She's exquisite," acknowledged Sarina, "but do you really believe I need such protection?"

"One can always benefit from the protection of the gods," he stated, taking back the statue and laying her facedown in his own palm. "Here," he instructed Sarina, stroking the statue with his thumb, "rub her back as I am doing so that it may warm the jade and release her mystical powers."

As Sarina watched him stroking the goddess's smooth green back, she felt as if he were caressing her back instead. Glancing up at his face, she found that his eyes had begun to glow like ebony stones and that his ivory skin had been tinged with rose. It was as though his entire body were being warmed by a magical heat he himself was releasing from inside the tiny jade goddess. When she tried to look away, he held her there with his eyes, trapping her between his penetrating gaze and his moving fingers until she was incapable of any movement whatsoever.

The gentle rapping at the door jolted Sarina from her trancelike state.

"Forgive me," blurted out Mei in Chinese as she stood uncertainly in the doorway. "I will return later."

"Come in, come in, little one." Wo beckoned with an easy smile. "Miss Paige has been most anxiously awaiting your arrival." He glided over to one of the lacquer tables next to Sarina's bed and gently laid the statue down.

"Now I will leave you to perhaps even surpass the artfulness of Ing-han," he said graciously to the young serving girl, who acknowledged his remark with a deep bow. Wo smiled at Sarina and then swept grandly from the room, leaving Mei to close the door behind him.

No sooner had she shut the door than the impassive mask she was trained to wear fell away and a joyous smile illuminated each perfectly carved feature of her lovely face. With her almond-shaped eyes bright with tears, Mei clasped Sarina's hands in hers and pressed a reverent kiss onto each one of her fingers.

"Words cannot convey to you my boundless thanks," murmured the girl in her lilting English. "You are risking much to bring joy to two people who are but strangers to you."

"Mei . . ." Sarina gave her head a warning shake. "You mustn't talk about it. Not here." Too many silent feet could move stealthily past her door and overhear them.

But the young serving girl would not be deterred. "Chen has told me of how he calls you 'friend,' " she said, "but I shall call you flesh of my flesh: my sister. And for the life you have given to me, I, like Chen, pledge mine to you in return."

Once again Sarina felt she was being pledged something far too precious for such a small act of kindness.

"I have sworn this before Chen and before the gods," the girl continued, "and now I have sworn it before you." She kissed Sarina on both cheeks and then slipped the mask back into place again. "As I have vowed always to serve you, my sister, how may I serve you now?"

Hastily recovering her composure, Sarina pointed toward her closet and with forced gaiety said, "You can help me decide which gown to wear tonight."

Mei began to arrange Sarina's hair, and while she curled and pinned each golden ringlet into place, she sang. Sarina closed her eyes, allowing the sweetness of each melody to lift her up and out of her skin, so that she was soon drifting in a gentler place, suspended above all feeling. It was while she was standing in front of the pier glass, watching as Mei wrapped her in her silk undergarments, that she noticed the slight distension of her belly for the first time. Frowning, she rubbed her hand over the slight swelling, unaware of Mei's dark eyes following her movements.

"You did not know?" whispered Mei as their eyes met in the mirror.

"Know?" she repeated, her frown deepening.

Mei's eyes dropped. "That . . ." She hesitated. "That you are with child?"

Sarina winced at the sudden pain knifing through her. With child. Yes, she knew. And yet she had not really known. Or perhaps she had simply chosen not to know.

Her time of month had come and gone twice since her arrival in Shanghai, something she had naively attributed to the adjustments her body had been forced to make to a new climate, new food, and a new way of life. And yet it seemed that her monthly flow had been stanched, not by her new life, but by some brief encounter in her old life. Tears sprang to her eyes. She doubled her fists in helpless rage. Janson Carlyle had done far more than bruise her feelings and scar her soul after all. He had implanted her with his seed. She would never be free of him now. Although he himself was gone from her life, the life she was carrying inside her would remind her of him for as long as she lived.

Mei's hands on Sarina's face were cool and soothing as she wiped away her falling tears. "Then you too have known love, just as I have," she exclaimed, her eyes shining.

"Love!" The word wedged itself in Sarina's throat. She shook her head. "No, Mei, it was *not* love."

Some of the light faded from Mei's eyes. "I had hoped that perhaps the handsome master Carlyle—"

"No!" Sarina cried. Desperately she foraged about for a convincing lie, something that would satisfy everyone when the time came for them to know. "No, Mei," she repeated, "Janson Carlyle has never been anything but an acquaintance of mine. I . . . I was abused on board ship by a sailor whose face I can't even recall anymore. He . . . he was drunk. He trapped me in my cabin and . . . You see, I was traveling alone, and—"

Mei threw her arms around Sarina and hugged her tightly. "My poor sister," she moaned. "How cruel that you should know of the evil side of love before you could know its sweet and gentle side. But even as his face has already faded from your memory, so will this terrible act fade as well. You are beautiful and pure, my sister, and the child you carry will be beautiful and pure. And one day, when you are blessed with a sweet and gentle love, you will know only the joy of that love and remember none of the pain of that one evil moment."

Sarina was swallowing air in deep, heaving gulps. Did Ing-han know? And Wo? Did he suspect? Terrified, she seized Mei by the shoulders. "Promise me, Mei," she pleaded, "that you'll tell no one about this. Swear it to me!"

The girl nodded her head. "I will tell no one. I swear it before you and before the gods."

Sarina whirled around to face the tiny jeweled figurine standing on the table beside her bed. Ji Hsi. One of the gods. One more guardian too late to protect her. As she gazed at the statue, the little jade goddess, her blood-red eyes ignited by a blazing garnet ray from the setting sun, glared back at her.

12

On the day Ing-han was to return to her duties, Sarina woke with a feeling of impending doom sitting like a weight on her chest. As skillful and obliging as she was, Ing-han was not someone to be trusted. No sooner would the serving girl realize that Sarina was pregnant than the entire staff would know about it as well. The servants in the Wo household, as in all wealthy Chinese households, thrived on the tales told about their masters, and Sarina was certain that the truth of her condition would provide them with untold hours of malicious delight.

She had still not told Wo about her condition, nor did she intend to. In only two more weeks her three-month trial period would be ending, and when she informed him of her decision to return to America, he would have no cause to suspect the real reason behind it. She dreaded his finding out and dismissing her because he considered her unworthy of continuing to teach his young daughters after the loving kindness he had shown her. Nor could she risk the possibility of his sharing what he knew with the one man who would guess the truth, the one man she had vowed must never know the truth.

The morning was as bleak as her mood. Gray clouds tumbled across a faded blue sky, staining the trees and the grass with the leaden hue of approaching autumn. It was Saturday and so there would be no lessons today to occupy her mind. Instead of going downstairs for breakfast, Sarina chose to remain upstairs in her room. Slumped in a chair, with one hand resting on her softly rounded belly and the other absently stroking the tiny jade statue of Ji Hsi, she dismally contemplated her future and the future of her unborn child.

With her three months' wages she could book her passage back to San Francisco and still have sufficient funds to see her safely resettled in Oregon City. Here her plan faltered. Would she be able to convince those in her father's former parish that she had been married and widowed in the few short months since their departure? She began chewing anxiously on her bottom lip as she discarded that plan in favor of remaining in San Francisco instead. Angry at herself for even considering such an idea, she gave her head an impatient shake and began all over again.

"Sarina, did you not hear me knocking?"

Wo was already halfway across the floor by the time Sarina realized she was no longer alone. With a guilty start she took her hand away from her stomach and hastily began patting at her hair. Dressed in a royal-blue silk robe over which he had added a sleeveless maroon quilted vest, his head covered by a maroon silk cap, Wo appeared ready to leave the house.

"Put on a warm cloak," he told her, "and come with me."

"Why?" Suddenly wary, she tightened her grip on the little statue.

"My intention is to take you for a carriage ride."

"Where are we going?"

"That, my inquisitive Sarina, is to be a surprise." He smiled.

In spite of her initial hesitation, her interest was piqued. For the moment at least, she could set aside her worries while she tried to imagine just what his surprise would be. Tucking the jade statue into one of the pockets of her morning dress, she went to fetch her cloak.

To her dismay, the road they were taking was the road leading into the city. As she settled back in her seat, she tried gamely to enjoy the ride, but thoughts of a previous journey along that same road skipped like irksome pebbles across her mind. She turned her head to keep Wo from seeing the tears springing to her eyes. Tugged backward in time by the persuasive pull of memory, she suddenly began to shiver. Wo hastily tucked a large silk lap quilt around her in an effort to make her more comfortable, but she continued to shake in spite of the quilt. Her shivering, she knew, had nothing at all to do with the weather. It grew out of the cold buried deep inside her.

* * *

Li turned from the window and gazed thoughtfully at the tumbled bed. Less than an hour had passed since he had gotten up from that bed, wiped himself clean of their passion, and left her lying there alone. When she had risen some moments later, it was in time to see him handing the golden one up into his carriage. Tapping one of her gold-tipped fingers against her small white front teeth, Li pondered what had to be done.

It did not take her long to decide. After summoning a sedan chair, she made her way slowly down the stairs to the front hall, where two house servants were waiting to lift her into the chair. They draped a quilted silk blanket across her lap and closed the silk side draperies against the morning chill. With her mouth set in a resolute line, she stoically endured the bumpy ride over the rutted, twisted paths which led to the tiny village of Da-po.

When they reached the village, she ordered the sedan-bearers to stop in front of a ramshackle wood building whose peaked red tile roof was badly chipped and broken. The whitewash splattered unevenly over its ancient walls was mottled with age and stained by the ravages of too many rainy seasons. Of the nine steps leading up to the sagging front door, only two remained intact, while the other seven were merely lumps of disintegrating stone.

Leaning on the shoulder of one of the sedan-bearers, Li picked her way cautiously up the steps and into the darkened building. An elderly man with a drooping white mustache and straggly beard and a snow-white queue trailing down the length of his stooped back shuffled out of a shadowed corner to greet her. She told him why she had come and he led her to the back of the room, where a large bronze statue sat on a long, low wooden altar. At the foot of the statue burned a censer of incense, its heavy smoke clouding the air and filling Li's nostrils with the rich scent of sandalwood.

Kneeling before the statue, Li pressed the palms of her hands together and held them close to her chest in the traditional gesture of greeting.

"Banish the evil spirit which has come unbidden into our home," she said. "Drive her from our midst, I beseech you."

Bowing to the statue three times, she repeated her re-

quest again, and then she added, "If you grant me my
wish, I will honor you with a thank offering of savory
duck, sweet pork, and tender chicken."

From the deep pocket of her scarlet robes she withdrew
a small black lacquered box. She removed the lid and used
it to collect some of the ashes from the burned incense.
Once she had emptied them into the box, she signaled the
elderly temple keeper to bring her the packet of thin
yellow paper strips he was holding. She selected twelve
papers in all, six of them stamped with the head of a dog,
six with the head of a buffalo, and paid for the charms
with a silver *tael*. Then she placed all but one of the strips
of paper inside a small bronze vessel with two elaborately
carved handles. Holding a lighted candle to the strip still
in her hand, she watched it catch fire before dropping it
into the bronze vessel, where it immediately ignited the
rest of the paper.

Once the paper strips had been reduced to ashes, she
poured some of them into the small black box and then
replaced the lid. Pushing herself to her feet, she allowed
the temple keeper to return her to her waiting sedan
chair. All the way back to the estate, she kept the small
black box clutched tightly in her hand. A pinch of the
ashes stirred into the golden one's tea each morning would
release the potent powers of the charm. When the ashes
were gone, the golden one would be gone, and all would
be as it was before.

"But I don't need any new gowns," protested Sarina,
her eyes wide as she surveyed the small cluttered shop
with its shelves lined with rolled bolts of fabric and its
counters covered by round wicker baskets filled with as-
sorted buttons, beads, and fanciful trims.

"Whatever you are wearing now is suitable only for the
months of summer," explained Wo in placating tones,
"but autumn is approaching, and you will require robes of
a heavier cloth, in a darker shade than white, as well as
many quilted outer garments."

"Young miss more beautiful than Wo Shue Kwen say,"
remarked Chiang Tan, the proprietor of the shop, in her
stilted English. Wearing a mauve-and-white embroidered
silk jacket over a long pleated mauve silk skirt, the woman
was an exquisite example of her own renowned handiwork.

Not only did her shop make all of Sarina's clothes, but she was reputed to dress many of the members of the imperial court as well. Fingering Sarina's long brown cloak with something akin to disdain, she nonetheless managed to smile warmly at her as she gestured toward one of the curtained rooms at the rear of the shop. "If young miss come, she will be most pleased by cloth Chiang Tan show her."

But Sarina stood her ground and refused to move. The woman expected to take her measurements for these new clothes. How was she to submit herself to such an ordeal, knowing that Chiang Tan's expert eyes would miss nothing? If only Wo had given her some inkling as to where they were going, she could have pleaded fatigue, illness, anything rather than having to face certain discovery.

"You have appeared most downcast of late, Sarina," declared Wo, a hint of reproach in his voice. "My thought was only to bring some pleasure to you by this visit to the woman who has so artfully clothed you." He spread his hands open in a gesture of defeat. "If I have presumed too much, for this I most humbly apologize."

"Please don't think I'm ungrateful," she said, "but you've already been far too generous to me. As you know, I've always led a simple life, and because my needs were few, they were always satisfied. If you continue to fill my head with grand notions and even grander dreams, how am I ever going to be satisfied again once I return to that life?"

"You still speak with the innocence of your father's child, Sarina," he scolded her. "Have you learned nothing from what I have taught you? You are an exquisite jewel to be mounted in only the most opulent of settings, to be displayed and to be adored. You need never consider a return to a simple life again. There are no notions too grand, no dreams too great that they cannot be realized. You have but to ask, and anything you desire can and will be yours."

For one moment she hurled an unspoken challenge at him. He could clothe her in magnificent gowns and encase her in splendid jewels, but could he provide her with a father for her unborn child? Could he give her child a name other than the name "bastard"? Could he grant her the shelter she still sought from a pair of probing green

eyes which found her out no matter where she was, and
turned her strength to weakness and her resolve to longing?

"I'm the tutor to your daughters, Wo," she told him in a
frosty voice which she had never used with him before, "I
am not your concubine."

She thought he might strike her for her insolence. Chiang
Tan's dark eyes were wide and frightened as her hands
flew to her throat. But Wo's face betrayed nothing. He
simply continued to gaze at her. And then he took her
completely by surprise by releasing a rumble of rolling
laughter from deep in his chest.

"You are indeed a spirited delight, my lovely lotus," he
choked out, patting her on the cheek. "Your pride, even
as you protest your humility, is a flame which kindles both
your glorious eyes and your most glorious spirit." Clasping her face in his hands, he pressed a tender kiss onto
her forehead. "No, my dear Sarina, you are not my
concubine. You are my own cherished child. Now, do
your father's bidding and please him as he has sought
only to please you. Let Chiang Tan clothe you as is fitting
for a daughter of the house of Wo to be clothed."

Sarina wondered at which point she had lost her battle
with him. Neither of her tactics had succeeded, and somehow all she had managed to do was entrap herself. Dimly
she watched as Chiang Tan parted a pair of mauve silk
curtains to reveal a cubicle covered in the same mauve
silk and whose only furnishing was a large unframed oval
mirror hanging on a heavy brass chain against one wall.
Each time the woman reached for the fastenings on Sarina's
cloak, Sarina brushed the woman's hands away. Finally
she blurted out, "We're in a terrible rush, and it would
save a great deal of time if we simply selected the fabrics
for my gowns without bothering to take any new measurements. I'm certain they're still the same."

Just as she was beginning to wonder how much of what
she had said had been understood by the little woman,
Chiang Tan gave her head a definitive shake. "Winter
gown not same as summer gown," she insisted. "Need new
measure. Need different measure for coat, for cape, for
vest."

Again the small pale fingers reached for the closings on
her cloak, and again Sarina protested. "I'm really quite
cold. Couldn't we—?"

"Why have no fabrics been brought in to you?" called Wo from the other side of the curtain. "Are you having some difficulty, Sarina?"

Sarina and Chiang Tan exchanged glances.

"I will speak with Master Wo," the woman declared.

"Sarina?"

"Wait, please," whispered Sarina, grabbing hold of the woman's arm. "We're just taking my measurements now," she called back to Wo. Only when she heard him grumble something in inaudible Chinese did she finally relax her grip on Chiang Tan's arm.

Perhaps if she sucked in her stomach and held her breath, the woman would assume that she had simply put on weight and think nothing more of it. But her breasts. They were so much larger now. The brown cloak fell to the floor and Sarina blinked back a rush of nervous tears. When Chiang Tan began working on the tiny buttons on the front of her gown, Sarina straightened her back and prepared herself for drawing in her stomach and as deep a breath as she possibly could. With her dress open to just below her waist, she was seized by a sudden terrible panic. Grappling with the woman's swiftly moving hands, she tried to gather the front of her gown together again.

"I . . . I'm sorry," she stammered, "but I'm so cold, and your fingers were—"

Her words were abruptly cut off as the curtains were ripped aside and a glowering Wo Shue Kwen swept into the cubicle. "I demand to know what the matter is!" he bellowed.

A timorous Chiang Tan backed away from Sarina, who was still desperately trying to cover herself. But from the stunned expression on Wo's face she could see that it was too late. She watched him shove Chiang Tan out of the room, and then she braced herself for his attack.

"So this was the reason for your modesty," he murmured, his eyes fastened on the telltale swelling of her breasts.

She covered herself with her hands, but he brushed them away and placed the flat of his own warm hand on her distended belly. In his eyes was a look of such wonderment and joy that for a moment Sarina forgot her shame while she stared at the transported Wo in stunned disbelief.

"You are soon to be blessed with the most precious of life's joys, my lotus," he said in an awed and gentle voice, "the most sacred of trusts bestowed upon a woman by the beneficent gods." His eyes searched hers and what he found in their troubled depths made his own eyes cloud over. "But you are feeling none of this joy, are you, my sweet Sarina?"

She shook her head as she summoned up her courage to tell him the lie she had hoped never to use again. "This was not a choice I made, but one which was made for me," she said, surprised at how calm her voice sounded. "I was taken against my will aboard ship by a sailor who forced his way into my cabin."

"And no punishment was meted out to the offender?" demanded Wo.

"I didn't tell anyone about it," she admitted. "I was frightened and terribly ashamed."

"But did you not inform our friend Janson Carlyle?" he persisted.

Steeling herself, Sarina answered, "As I told you before, we had dinner together once. That scarcely made him a friend of mine in whom I could confide." Squaring her shoulders, she raised her head proudly and directed a level gaze at the pensive Wo. "I had hoped to keep this from you, but now that you know, instead of leaving in two weeks as I'd intended, I'm fully prepared to leave the estate immediately."

"Leave?" he echoed.

"I plan to return home to America."

"But you have made China your home," he protested.

She stared down at the floor. "I'm unfit to teach your daughters now."

"Because the seed of life was sown against your will within your womb?" he questioned, putting out his hands and drawing her toward him. "Whether by choice or by force, you have become the vessel for this sacred life entrusted to your keeping. You are to be cherished because of it, not turned away as if you were in disgrace. No, Sarina, you will set aside all foolish thoughts of leaving. I will not hear of it. The family of Wo Shue Kwen is your family now, and as the father of that family, I offer you its love and its shelter."

"But what about the others?" she whispered.

"I am the law which governs my household, as well you know. No one will dare to question me."

She had been prepared for any response but this. Shaken
and deeply moved, she rested her head on his shoulder
while he tenderly stroked her hair. Her body was drained,
weak with relief, and as his arms tightened around her,
she sagged against him. Perhaps she had been wrong not
to have confided in him. Perhaps with Wo she truly *had*
found a home.

Although it was Wo who cushioned her with his body
and with his gentle, soothing words on the return journey
to the estate, it was the name of another man which Sarina
kept hearing in the steady clip-clop, clip-clop of the horses'
hooves. Jan-son. Jan-son. Jan-son. Jan-son. His name rico-
cheted through her mind, twisting and turning as it followed the convoluted passageways within her brain. Jan-son.
Jan-son. Jan-son. Jan-son. Would her child have his black
hair or his green eyes? she wondered. Would its face be
her face or his? Even after the years had dulled the pain
and dimmed his image, would she still look at his child
and be condemned to remember him?

The carriage lurched to one side and Sarina was thrown
heavily against the door. Her hand fluttered protectively
to her belly. Cursing under his breath, Wo pounded on
the roof with his fist and ordered the driver to stop the
carriage. Then he flung open the door and stepped down
into the roadway.

With her hand still resting on her belly, Sarina sighed
and closed her eyes. For the first time since she had
realized the truth, she knew a sudden inexplicable surge
of happiness. This tiny life growing within her was as
much hers as it was his; more, in fact, because it was her
body which would shelter and nourish it, her body which
would one day bring it out into the world. Her jaw tightened stubbornly. No, she decided, this child was hers and
hers alone. Janson Carlyle had relinquished his claim to
this child on the very night it had been conceived.

Just then Wo climbed back into the carriage and slammed
the door shut. Sarina sat up with a start. "What was the
matter?" she asked him.

"That fool," snarled Wo, gnashing his teeth in ill-
concealed fury. "But have no fear, I have ordered him
suitably punished."

"Who?"

"That insolent fool of a peasant," he snapped. "How

dare he lead his ox cart down the middle of the road and refuse to make way for our carriage!"

"And he's going to be punished?"

"He shall receive fifty strokes of the lash."

"For not allowing the carriage to pass?" She was incredulous.

He patted her hand with an air of condescension which suddenly rankled. "Do not wear such a pained expression, my lovely Sarina," he chided her. "It is the law, and he must be punished for breaking that law."

Pulling her hand away, she turned and stared stonily out of the window. Was this the man she wanted to be her protector? Once again her brush with peace had been all too fleeting. Once again she found herself plunging headlong into doubt.

13

The first pains woke her shortly before dawn. She lay on her back, breathing heavily, her body tensed and waiting. It was impossible. The baby was not due for another month. She gasped as another pain slashed through her. Grabbing one of her pillows, she held it up to her face to muffle her cries each time a fresh pain struck. It was too early and the pains were still too far apart for her to rouse anyone just yet.

With her face turned toward the sliding balcony doors she watched as the pearlescent haze of another January morning lightened the sky. The pains had intensified, knifing through her now at regular intervals. Reaching over to her bedside table, she struck the small brass gong Wo had placed there for her three times, and then fell back onto the soaked and rumpled sheets to wait.

A few minutes later the door opened and Wo appeared, followed by Sua and Mei. As soon as Wo saw Sarina's stricken face, he sent Mei to fetch Qi Ting-fang and Ya-lin, the midwife. He then drew up a chair beside the bed for Sua, while he went to stand at the foot of the bed.

"Breathe so," Sua instructed Sarina, drawing a deep breath and then releasing it in short, staccato puffs. As she repeated the procedure, Sarina, caught in the throes of another contraction, tried to imitate her. "Good." The older woman smiled. "Better breathe so."

Following Sua's advice helped to lessen the severity of her contractions, but Sarina was terrified of the pain becoming so intense that she would lose consciousness. Arching her back, she strained to smother another rising scream. She must not faint, she counseled herself over and over again. She must not lose control, and in her agony, in her weakness, call out his name.

Once again she checked a scream as she tried valiantly to breathe the way Sua had shown her. Perspiration streamed from her forehead and into her eyes. She bit down hard on her bottom lip and moaned. Perhaps she was wrong. Perhaps if she shouted out his name, Wo would punish him as he had punished the peasant for scalding her and the ox-cart driver for failing to move his cart out of the way of their carriage. No. She thrashed her head from side to side. She intended to punish Janson Carlyle herself—by the very act of saying and doing nothing at all.

"Qi is here now, Sarina," she heard Wo say, "and Ya-lin as well. You will now be in the most capable of hands."

His words brought her little comfort, because all she was aware of now was the excruciating pain. It had even assumed a shape for her, that of a dancing gnome, a spindly long-armed elf with a saucy smile and skinny fingers which poked and jabbed at her. The more she writhed and squirmed, the wider the gnome's smile became. He danced about on her belly, in and out of sight, and as he danced, he poked away at her with fingers of sharpened steel.

As she slipped in and out of awareness, she began to pray. She began praying for a son. A son whom she would call Thomas-John, after her beloved father. A sob rose in her throat and she did nothing to hold it back. She pushed the gnome aside and conjured up for herself the image of her father. Together they strolled the distant hills of home, bristling with laurel and verbena, sweet gale and blue wild flag. She saw the glimmer of the Willamette River as it wound its way past dense forests of pine and cedar, where thousands of deer and elk, bobcats and grizzly bears, cougars and timber wolves still lived without fear of the hunter's gun. She heard the sound of St. Clement's bells summoning her father's parishioners to Sunday-morning services and heard the laughter of the children as they bounded down the steps when Sunday school was out.

"Sarina, you must help us," called Wo from somewhere deep in the mist which surrounded her. "Please, Sarina, you must help."

She tried to find him, to ask him how she was supposed

to help, but the fog was growing thicker. She was lost. As
she stumbled blindly toward his fading voice, white tentacles of mist stretched out to hold her back.

"Push, Sarina, push!"

She could hear his voice again, clearly for a moment,
and then it seemed to fragment and disintegrate. Make
the pain stop, she shrieked, only to hear it echoing back to
her from inside her own head. Please, dear God in heaven,
make it stop. . . .

The smoke filled her throat and trickled down into her
lungs. She coughed and the pain flared again. Another
cloud of acrid sweetness enveloped her and she opened
her mouth to draw some of it inside. This time she did not
cough. Again and again she inhaled the strange scented
smoke, and as she felt it begin to dissolve the bonds of her
pain, she felt herself beginning to float upward toward a
welcoming sky of clearest blue.

In the sun's buttered sweetness she saw his face. Rimmed
with gold, the silver in his hair gleamed with a brilliance
matched only by the green of his eyes. She drifted toward
him with tantalizing slowness on the wings of a cloud. He
waved to her, urging her to come to him quickly, but her
stubborn cloud craft refused to be hurried. Holding up a
shiny gold watch, he pointed to it, showing her that there
was very little time left and that soon there would be none
at all.

She used her hands to scoop at the reluctant air in a
frantic attempt to propel her vaporous craft along more
swiftly, but still it moved too slowly. Once again he pointed
to his watch and twice he called her name. A sparkling
shaft of sunlight struck the watch full in the face, and the
intensity of its reflection forced her to close her eyes or be
blinded by its aura.

When she opened her eyes again, she saw him drifting
backward. She stretched out her hand to him, but he
drifted farther and farther away from her. He called out
to her until his voice was no more than an echo within her
own mind. Reaching for him with both arms now, pleading with him to return, she threw back her head and
screamed out his name: *"Janson!"*

*   *   *

She wakened slowly. Her throat was parched and sore, and when she passed her tongue over her dry lips, her tongue was dry as well. She moaned softly to herself as she tried in vain to wet her lips and soothe her burning throat. A moment later, several drops of cool water splattered onto her face, and a gentle finger smoothed the welcome moisture over her mouth, bringing her some relief.

She stirred, suddenly aware of a strange hollowness inside her. She dragged a leaden arm across the covers and touched her belly. Gone was the hard, thrusting mound. It was now no more than a small, softening pouch. Her baby. Her son! She strained to hear the sounds of a child crying, to smell the sweetness of newborn flesh, to feel its tiny body, warm and moist, pressed up against hers, and a hungry mouth closing around one swollen breast. Touching her breasts and feeling their ripe fullness, she reached up eagerly for her child.

"Sarina?"

Her arms fell to her sides. Turning toward the voice, she slowly opened her eyes. She blinked and quickly closed them again. The next time she opened them, she saw that he was swaddled in sunlight, and once again she reached up for her child.

"Sarina."

He was saying her name in a voice which pulled at her heart. He settled himself on the bed and touched her cheek with the palm of his hand. "My delicate lotus," he murmured over and over again, while he continued to stroke her face.

"My baby," she whispered. "Where is my baby?"

"Your child ..." he began, and then stopped. She watched his throat working, swallowing once, then swallowing again, and terror threatened to close her own throat. "Sarina, there was no life in the child we pulled from your womb. My precious blossom, your child is dead."

"No!" The scream ripped the lining from her soul. "No, no, no, no, no!" She lashed out at him, scratching and clawing, straining to force him to deny what he had just said. Even as he was struggling to control her, she continued to fight him, spitting and screaming, thrusting herself at him, using her exhausted body as a last desperate weapon. "Bring me my child! I want my child! Why won't you bring me my child?" she shrieked, her voice growing stronger as her body grew weaker.

"Sarina, please." He finally caught hold of her flailing hands and pinned them to her sides.

"I want to see my child," she whimpered, twisting her head away from the cruel silver glare of the sun. Only a few hours had passed since the pains had begun, and yet they had already taken her child away from her. "Dear God," she moaned, "where is my baby?"

"Sarina," he whispered hoarsely, "your child was buried last night."

"Last night!" she cried. "It isn't possible." How could an entire day have slipped out of her grasp? An entire day during which she had given birth to and lost a child. "No"—she shook her head—"it isn't possible. It simply isn't possible."

"You must sleep now, Sarina," Wo told her. "With sleep, the wounds of your body and of your spirit will begin their healing."

"I don't want to sleep," she sobbed. "I want to see my baby. Please take me to see my baby."

"When you are strong again," he promised, "I will take you to your child."

He released her hands just long enough to reach down for the long wooden pipe he had been heating on the small brazier on the floor. "Here, my sweet Sarina." He placed the stem of the pipe between her lips. "Soon you will again be sleeping the sleep of endless reverie."

As she drew the familiar acrid sweetness into her lungs, Sarina finally realized how one entire day had been lost for her. She inhaled a second time and waited for the blissful healing she knew would come. Wo had been right after all. She sighed as her eyelids drooped. There *was* no evil in the poppy, only good.

Suddenly she pushed the pipe away and tried to focus on Wo's wavering face. "Tell me . . ." she whispered up to him. "Was it a boy?"

He nodded. "Yes, it was a boy."

"A boy," she repeated, her voice growing weaker. Prickly with pain, she reached for the pipe again and tugged on it in deep, hungry gulps.

Wo bent close to her ear so that she could hear him. "As

you have already borne one son, my beautiful Sarina, so you shall one day bear others."

Her recovery was slow. Although Qi assured her that her body was nearly completely healed, he explained to a worried Wo that the wound inflicted upon her spirit would take a far longer time to heal. Once she was allowed to leave her bed, Sarina spent each day sitting in a chair, holding her statue of Ji Hsi and staring blankly out at the countryside. Clouds like great smudges of coal dirtied the somber face of the wintry sky, and even the occasional shaft of sunlight splitting the gloom did little to brighten the blackness of the days for her.

She spoke to no one but Mei, who came to her room every evening before dinner to sing for her. It seemed that where Sarina had been cursed by her God, Mei, on the other hand, had been blessed by hers. Twice the day of Chen's marriage to Lao Kuer T'ai had been agreed upon, and twice it had been set aside—once because Kuer T'ai had been stricken with a near-fatal spotted fever, and more recently, because of a blight affecting much of China's priceless tea crop. As a shrewd businessman, Wo was patiently awaiting the arrival of spring to determine the condition of Lao Hong Han's newly planted tea before agreeing on a new date for his son's marriage.

As the evening wore on, Sarina would begin to doze in her chair. Her sleep was fitful and alive with phantoms, and she would wake every few minutes to the sounds of a baby crying. Her eyes would dart anxiously about the room, examining every shadow and searching each darkened corner for some trace of the crying child. But there never was one. Near midnight, Wo would find her slumped in her chair, her face streaked with tears, too exhausted to even stand. Only his gentle urging gave her the strength to walk the few steps back to her bed, and only a cup of fragrant green tea lightly laced with opium provided her with the peaceful sleep she sought but could no longer find on her own.

There was a hint of softness in the air which convinced Sarina that spring was coming at last. Although it was only the middle of February, the grass beneath her feet seemed greener and spongier, and whenever she peered closely at the potted plants in the courtyard she could see clusters of new flowers dotted there among the leaves. The sun rose earlier and set later, and instead of its silvered half-light bleaching the blue from the sky, it was now tingeing it the color of a clear aquamarine.

It was Saturday, and Sarina had promised herself that on Monday she would resume her teaching in the summer-house. The girls had gone without their lessons for over a month, and they needed her to improve their English as much as she needed them to keep her distracted. Instead of still spending her days locked away in her room, Sarina had begun to divide her time between walking the grounds and standing in front of the tiny stone marker in the Wo family graveyard.

Set in a small clearing surrounded by flowering plum trees, it was the one place she could go whenever she needed to be near the child she had carried for eight months, but whom she had never even held, if just for a moment. Here, in the privacy of the clearing, away from Wo's watchful eyes, away from the unspoken sympathy on the faces of everyone else around her, she would talk to her dead son and call him Thomas-John and tell him about the man for whom he had been named. Standing there so close to him and spending time with him was the only way she knew of one day being able to say good-bye to him forever.

Now, as she made her way from the burial ground back to the house, she caught sight of Wo standing in the courtyard with what appeared to be one of her quilted cloaks folded over his arm. As if urging her to hurry, he held up the heavy topaz-colored silk cloak and waved it in the air like a great jewel-toned flag. She was out of breath by the time she reached him.

"Is something wrong?" she gasped.

"Not at all." A slight smile tugged at the corners of his mouth. "I was merely attempting some artifice of my own to bring back the roses to your cheeks." Bending closer to her, he pretended to be scrutinizing her very carefully. Then, with a satisfied nod of his head, he said, "I am pleased to note that I have succeeded in my task.

For the first time in more than a month, Sarina found herself smiling.

"I am leaving for the city now," he announced as he

draped the cloak around her shoulders. "And you, my dear Sarina, will be accompanying me."

She immediately shrank away from him, fumbling inside the pocket of her gown for the little jade goddess and anxiously beginning to stroke her back.

"It is time, Sarina"—his voice was stern—"time for you to live as a young woman again, instead of the withering husk you seem content to be now."

"That isn't fair!" she cried.

"Is it unfair of me to prefer you to laugh rather than weep, to see you walking with the spring of youth in your step rather than with the stoop of an aged crone, to want you to live with those who still live, and not squander your precious life among those who are dead?"

She felt her knees giving way beneath the blows of his words. Yet, even as she was weakening, she felt something stir inside her, and she began to fight, to strike back at what she knew to be the truth. Janson Carlyle was gone from her life just as her son was gone from her. She had been fittingly punished for her sins, having exchanged the life of her child for her wanton abandonment of her father's pious ways. Her eyes began to glow with a defiant gold flame, its fire deepened by the shimmering topaz of her cloak. Throwing back her shoulders, she proudly lifted her head to meet Wo's approving gaze.

"Perhaps you're right," she conceded. "Perhaps it *is* time, after all."

With an exasperated sigh Li slammed the last of the drawers shut and straightened up again. It was obvious that the golden one still carried the jade goddess with her everywhere. She hobbled to the door and cautiously opened it. After peering into the corridor to make certain that it was deserted, she slipped from the room and silently closed the door behind her.

The charms had failed. Twice now she had returned to the temple in Da-po for more charms, but the golden one still stubbornly refused to submit to their power. If only she could destroy the statue. Without Ji Hsi's protection, the golden one would be vanquished. Li considered with baleful eyes the empty black box she was holding. She had used the last of the ashes that morning. There was nothing she could do now but wait and pray to the gods for patience.

*   *   *

"I believe you will find this teahouse far more agreeable than my offices," said Wo to Sarina as the carriage slowed and finally halted. "While you rest and take some refreshment, I will conclude my business, and then within the hour I will return to take some tea myself."

As he helped her down from the carriage, Sarina stumbled and grabbed hold of his arm for support. A sudden chill penetrated her in spite of her warm cloak as, once again, the weakness returned to her knees.

"Whatever is the matter?" asked Wo as she slumped against him.

What little color there was in her face was quickly being drained away as she stared openmouthed at the fanciful dragon with the glittering red eyes painted on the teahouse door.

"Sarina?"

She gave her head a shake as if to clear it, and resolutely lifted her chin. "I'm sorry . . ." She smiled at Wo, patting the hand still tightly clasping her arm. "I was just startled by the painting on the door."

Wo chuckled as he pulled the door open for her. "It is rather a fearsome sight, is it not, but quite harmless, I would think."

Several men glanced up from their tea as Sarina followed Wo to a table, but she coolly ignored their lingering stares.

"You will be comfortable here?" inquired Wo solicitously when Sarina was seated in a quiet corner of the room.

"Yes," she assured him in spite of the rapid beating of her heart, "I'll be fine here."

"I will return within the hour, then." Bowing formally to her, he turned and swept majestically through the room, his long scarlet-and-black silk robes swishing softly behind him.

Sarina sat rigidly in her chair with the jade statue of Ji Hsi on her lap and nervously stroked the figurine's cool, smooth back. As her fingers gradually began to warm the stone, the stone returned some of the heat to her own cold skin. She sipped her tea slowly, savoring its welcome warmth inside her, while she continued to caress the tiny jade goddess. By the time she started another cup of tea, she was calm enough to release her hold on the statue and help herself to some of the peanuts and melon seeds she had never had the opportunity of tasting on her previous visit.

Leaning back in her chair as she munched a second handful of peanuts, she slowly scanned the familiar room. It was just as she remembered it—the flickering candles bathing the apricot walls in a soft glow, some of the old men puffing on their long pipes, one working at his abacus, another dozing behind his news sheet. She wondered if that young serving girl were still here, as she released a small, contented sigh and picked up her teacup again. Just as she was about to take a final sip of her tea, she suddenly paused. Eyes widening, she sat up straight in her chair and stared.

Was it possible? There in the far corner? The cup nearly slipped out of her hand, and she put it back on the table with a soft thud. She clutched at her throat, unable to draw a full breath. A fist of steel was closing around her lungs and squeezing all the air out of them.

She half-rose and then just as quickly sat down again. Her legs had stubbornly refused to support her weight. She glanced over toward the corner again. He was talking to a woman whose back was turned to her, affording Sarina only a glimpse of a small plumed ivory bonnet rakishly perched atop a cloud of hair as black as a raven's wing. Still trembling, her breath coming in short, hacking gasps, Sarina used all of her will to push herself to her feet. Her heart sank when she heard a light clink as the jade statue slid from her lap and dropped onto the wood floor.

With her heart fluttering wildly, she bent down and retrieved the fallen statue. Dusting it off, she let out a gasp of dismay. One of Ji Hsi's ruby eyes had fallen out! Torn between searching for the missing stone and escaping before he noticed her standing there, Sarina frantically chose the latter. Starting for the door, she bumped into a table and was forced to mumble a hasty apology to the three men who glared up at her accusingly. She lurched against another table in her headlong plunge for the door, upsetting a full pot of tea and drawing a chattering protest from every other nearby table.

It seemed as if the entire tearoom were erupting in

protest as Sarina pushed her way past a startled serving
girl in her bid to reach the front door, which was now only
a few feet away from her. Half-falling against it in relief,
she began wrestling with the handle. It was then that she
heard it. Above the chatter and the clanking of the cups,
above the scraping of chairs and the click of the abacus,
she heard Janson Carlyle calling her name.

   She forcefully pulled down on the door handle. Pushing
the door open with a triumphant cry, she bolted into the
street.

14

Janson slowly surveyed the street again, wondering which of the many rickshas and carriages for hire had been the one to spirit her away so quickly. He frowned as he dug his hands into the pockets of his trousers, and for the second time that day he cursed himself roundly for being such a fool. Across the street, four young British sailors were going into a tavern, and he gazed after them enviously. Right now he could certainly use something a bit stronger than the tea he had been drinking before he had decided to chase after an elusive golden-haired shadow.

His scowl deepened. Janson had always considered himself to be a fairly sensible man, and yet his reaction to seeing Sarina Paige in the teahouse had been just as senseless as his response an hour earlier to the sudden reappearance in his life of Hilary Woodthrop Gray. Just when he had considered her safely relegated to his past, by the simple act of crossing the floor of his office she had effectively laid siege to that small part of him which had still not completely forgotten her. Had the white heat flaming through him at the sight of her been shock or desire? he asked himself again as he stared after another passing carriage. Whatever it was, when he had risen to greet her, ignoring her upturned mouth in favor of placing a light kiss on her cheek, he had been grateful for the distance afforded them by the full skirt of the ivory-and-blue-striped velvet gown she was wearing.

Trust Hilary, he had found himself thinking, to have chosen a fabric to match the cobalt blue of her eyes, and then to have heightened their dramatic intensity by wearing clusters of brilliant blue sapphires on her ears and around her neck. Freeing his own eyes from the pull of hers, he had followed the slender column of her patrician nose down to her mouth, that lascivious splash of red whose luscious softness had once served as a welcoming cushion for his; and he damned himself for being a man, whose weakness lay in his body's yearning response to a pair of parting lips and the promise they held.

The office had begun to close in on him then. Before either of them could speak, he had taken her by the hand and pulled her after him into the street, where he immediately located an empty ricksha and helped her into it. Only in a public place would he be safe from the grinding heat in his groin and the hypnotic tug of her nearness.

"I've made a mistake" were the first words she uttered after their tea had been set down in front of them.

He had clamped both of his hands around his cup and said nothing.

"I married Prescott because I was afraid," she continued, her voice like a rush of cool wind stirring his sleeping memory. "I miss you, Janson, and I want you to take me back."

The hands gripping the scorching teacup could just as easily have been closing around her throat. She had left him in order to marry someone else, and now she wanted him to excuse her for having made a mistake and take her back! Why? Did she believe that because he had safely passed the age of thirty he was no longer as much of a risk as he had been? Or had she learned of his growing trading empire and decided that being the rich widow of a young man was just as appealing as being the rich widow of an older one?

"Janson?" One of her small jeweled hands had reached for his, and he had hastily picked up his cup. "Don't you have anything to say?"

"Sure." He nodded, finally taking a sip of his tea. "What brings you to Shanghai?"

Her eyebrows lifted in mild surprise. "My husband is here to buy porcelain and jade," she answered tightly. "Janson, I—"

"And he's interested in using the Carlyle line to ship his merchandise back to America?"

"Why do you say that?"

He shrugged. "I simply assumed that was the reason for your coming to see me."

She lowered her voice to a conspiratorial whisper. "I've just told you why I came to see you."

He had leaned back in his chair and hooked his thumbs over the waistband of his trousers. "Oh, yes, you said something about your leaving your husband and my taking you back again."

"I said nothing about leaving my husband," she returned stiffly.

"I see." He had tipped his chair back even farther.

She leaned across the table toward him and her voice took on a note of urgency. "I've been stopping by your office for nearly a week now, hoping that you'd return from Hong Kong before we had to sail back to San Francisco. I had to see you, Janson. I had to make you understand—"

"Just what *am* I supposed to understand?" he demanded. "You say you won't leave your husband, but seeing as how I'm still alive and well, you figure you can have on the side what you—"

"Stop it!" she cried. "How can you be so crude!"

"Crude?" He had sat up straight and thrust his face into hers. "Put it in whatever fancy terms you like, Hilary, but the meaning is still the same."

"For God's sake, lower your voice," she hissed, glancing uneasily around them.

He had thought of everything he could have said to her then, all the hurtful things he had stored away for just such a possible confrontation. He thought of how he had once wanted to reduce her to a weeping knot of raw pain and then leave her to bleed alone, just as she had once left him. But as he had sat there looking at her, he had felt the anger slowly draining out of him, until all that was left was a peculiar kind of emptiness. It was as though he were no longer sitting with her, but observing her instead from a great height, from someplace outside himself.

As he watched her toying nervously with her broad gold wedding band, he was suddenly reminded of a pair of golden eyes. Eyes alight with bronze sparks. Eyes capable of searing the heart of a man and piercing his carefully protected soul. A moon-kissed angel created for promises, with a tender heart made for bruising and a trusting spirit ripe for betrayal. He was hardening his jaw, setting his mouth in a line of grim determination, when Hilary cut into his thoughts.

"Janson, please say something. Talk to me!"

Were those actually tears he was seeing in her sapphire eyes, or a flickering illusion due to the wavering flame of the candle?

"I never meant to hurt you, Janson, but you know the kind of position our affair had placed me in."

Suddenly all he could hear was his own sharp intake of breath. All the time he had been thinking about Sarina, she had been sitting at a table just across the room from where he was sitting. He started to get up and then quickly changed his mind. But now *she* was standing. He watched as she bent down to pick up something she had obviously dropped.

"Janson, what's the matter with you?" Hilary's voice was pulling at him again. "Are you all right?"

Sarina was leaving. He pushed out his chair and stood up.

Hilary's fingers were coiled tightly around his wrist, holding him back. "Janson, where are you going?"

As he had worked to pry himself free of her, he had shouted out Sarina's name.

The only explanation Sarina offered Wo for her breathless arrival at his office was that she had felt ill and had preferred not to remain in the teahouse alone. He brought his meeting with the two representatives of Jardine and Matheson to a hasty close and immediately summoned his carriage. During the entire return journey to the estate, Sarina sat with her head resting on Wo's shoulder and one of his arms draped protectively around her, feeling a wonderful relief at being shielded and comforted by this man who had already begun to supplant her own beloved father in her affections.

"Perhaps you were correct after all, my lotus," said Wo in a solemn voice as he helped her down from the carriage. "Forgive me if I was perhaps too hasty in my wish to see you returned to your former self."

"I know you meant well," she told him, "and I'm grateful for your concern, more than you can possibly imagine."

Seeing how distressed he was, she hastily discarded the idea of telling him about Ji Hsi's lost ruby eye. Instead she chose to plant a tender kiss on one of his smooth, pale cheeks.

"That was to thank you for all of your kindness," she murmured, suddenly feeling shy because of her impetuous behavior.

But Wo was beaming as he said, "To be rewarded in such a pleasing manner for being wrong makes one ponder the reward for being correct."

That made her smile.

"Will you come inside now?" he asked.

"I thought I might take another walk," she said, but noticing the returning flicker of doubt in his eyes, she quickly added, "just for a few minutes, I promise."

She headed straight for the clearing again. She desperately needed to be close to her son, to tell him about his father for the first time, and to feel the healing only another visit to his grave could bring her. Crouching before the little gray marker, she rested one hand on the cold, hard stone, wishing it would grow warm beneath her touch the way the tiny jade goddess did. Tears welled up in her eyes as she pressed her other hand against her throbbing forehead.

"Forgive me, Thomas-John," she whispered, "but I despise him. I hate the man who would have been your father."

She hated him for leaving her alone with his seed to carry. Perhaps if her child had been conceived in love instead of through lust, and nurtured with joy rather than shame, he might have lived. She hated him for being in Shanghai and for sitting with another of his willing partners where he had once sat with her. But most of all, she hated him for calling out her name and making her remember the sound of his voice.

After a while Sarina dried her eyes and made her way slowly back to the house. The sky was darkening. Evening had released its dusky curtain and it was falling gently to the ground. As she approached the house, its windows aglow with honeyed lantern light, she saw it as a refuge from all the unpleasantness which lay beyond its brick walls and its iron gates. Wo had told her that it was beyond those very gates, outside with nature, that one could find the truest form of peace. She had believed him once, but now she was no longer sure.

Looking down at her little jade statue, with its one flashing ruby eye and one dull green socket, Sarina felt sad. As if to comfort the tiny goddess for the injury she had sustained, she began to stroke her face, feeling the stone growing warm again in spite of the indignity of her half-blinded state. Suddenly Sarina stiffened. She whirled around, expecting to find someone standing behind her. But there was no one there. Slipping the little figurine into the pocket of her gown, she hastily opened the gate to the inner courtyard.

It swung shut with a reassuring clang, making her feel safe again.

She awoke with a start in the middle of the night. Turning onto her side, she raised her head and listened. Was it her own breathing she was hearing, or was someone there in the dark with her? It was a moonless night, black and impenetrable, without even a single shadow stretching its way along the walls or ceiling of her room. She had been trying to sleep without the help of the jasmine tea for over a week now, but she was still having trouble sleeping soundly through the night.

She cocked her head to the other side as she strained to catch the sounds of an intruder. But she knew there *was* no intruder, just as there had been no child crying each time she woke up in the night during those early weeks after Thomas-John's death. Lying down again, she burrowed deeper beneath the quilted coverlet and was soon fast asleep.

In the morning she dressed quickly and returned to her bedside table for the little jade statue. Her hand froze in midair. Her heart began to race. The hackles stood up on the back of her neck. Someone had been in her room after all.

Both of Ji Hsi's ruby eyes were missing now.

15

Janson had stayed away from the estate for one week. Now, as Kwen escorted him out to the summerhouse, he was beginning to regret having made the trip out from the city when their business had already been successfully concluded. It made him feel uncomfortably obvious. There was an aloofness in the landlord's manner which led Janson to suspect that Sarina had told him what she had learned about him and from whom. No matter, he decided, if that was the reason for Kwen's distance, there was nothing he could do about it. Kwen's friendship was not what he was after right now.

Sarina followed Wo down the stairs of the summerhouse, only to pause before her foot touched the bottom step. How dare he show his face there again! How dare he present himself to her and have the temerity to even look penitent! Only Wo's firm hand on her arm prevented her from turning around and climbing back up the stairs again.

"Hello, Sarina," said Janson in a strangely toneless voice.

"Mr. Carlyle." She acknowledged him with a curt nod of her head.

He was formally dressed in a dark green frock coat and fawn-colored trousers, but the high, straight standing collar of his white shirt appeared to be choking him, and this brought a smile to her lips.

"You're looking well," he told her. Beneath the lightly draped coral-and-white dotted-muslin gown her body seemed fuller, more womanly.

"And you," she replied coolly, "have you been ill?" There was a wicked gleam in her eyes as she said it, and Wo glanced over at her sharply.

"I . . . ah, no," he stammered, feeling like a fool. "No, I've been fine."

She said nothing, she simply waited, while her pulse finally began to slow and the silence between them grew.

"How are your students?" Janson fumbled for something to say, aware of Kwen's shrewd gaze trained on him again. "Are they learning English or are you learning Chinese?"

"A bit of both, I'd say, wouldn't you?" Sarina smiled at the man who was still standing on the step beside her.

"It is the wise teacher who learns from his pupils" was Wo's enigmatic reply.

Janson's temper was rising. He stared pointedly at Kwen and was satisfied only when the older man released his hold on Sarina's arm and came down the last of the summerhouse's sagging white steps.

"If you will both excuse me," Wo said, bowing to Sarina and then sweeping off in the direction of the house without even bowing to Janson.

Sarina stared after him in surprise. She had never seen him treat Janson as rudely before, and she wondered if her long-forgotten discussion with Wo had adversely affected what had once been a most cordial relationship between the two men. She began to worry at her bottom lip, seesawing back and forth between indifference and curiosity as to the reason for Janson's being so obviously slighted.

"Sarina, I have to talk to you." Janson touched her arm, and she jumped.

"I don't think I care to hear anything you have to say."

In spite of her hostility, he plunged on. "I managed to get my operation in Hong Kong running much faster than I'd anticipated," he said, "so I'm returning to San Francisco tomorrow."

Her heart skittered and sank inside her. "Your comings and goings are of little interest to me," she told him.

"At one time I could have sworn just the opposite was true."

"Then you're obviously not the perceptive man you thought you were."

"Or perhaps time simply has a way of changing things."

"Perhaps." She shrugged.

"Don't you even want to know why I came out here today?" he persisted.

"I can't imagine," she returned archly. "You already have all the cargo you could possibly want waiting for you in Shanghai."

"Don't be vulgar, Sarina," he snapped. "It doesn't suit you."

"And lecturing others doesn't suit you! You undoubtedly treat your ships more respectfully than you treat people."

"At least I work for an honest wage, Sarina, and everything I've built, I've built myself. I've never had to sell either my principles or myself to get what I've wanted."

"So we come back to that again, do we!" She glared down at him, her hands on her hips. "You're still accusing me of being Wo's witless plaything, something to be picked up and discarded according to his whims. Well, I'd suggest you look to yourself, Mr. Carlyle, before you begin accusing others so freely."

"I can see that time hasn't really changed anything at all," he snarled. "You're still defending him."

"If that was what you came all this way to tell me, then we have nothing more to discuss," she declared. "Now, if you'll excuse me, my girls will be waking up from their naps in another few minutes."

"Sarina, wait!" He pulled her down off the step and onto the grass. "Dammit, Sarina, that wasn't what I wanted to tell you."

"Then would you like to explain just why you're here, or would you prefer me to guess?"

He raked his fingers through his hair while he squinted up at the canary globe of the sun and wondered why he was putting himself through such a painful ordeal. Then, before he could think better of it and stop himself, he said, "The woman with me at the teahouse the other day was just a friend of mine, someone I used to know in San Francisco."

For one giddy moment Sarina's heart lifted and soared, only to come plunging back down again. "I don't really care who she is," she replied haughtily, "and I certainly don't know why you're even telling me about her."

"I just wanted you to know about her in case she was the

reason for your running out of the place the way you did."

"My God!" Her head shot up proudly. "Your presumptuousness actually surpasses your rudeness."

In his growing impatience Janson began tugging at the high stiff collar of his shirt. This was even worse than he had imagined it would be.

"I've thought about you a lot during these last few months, Sarina." His eyes were hooded as he stole a covert glance at her. "I even found myself worrying about you, wondering what kind of mischief you were getting into without my being here to protect you."

The stiffness was beginning to go out of her spine. His words were effectively thawing some of the numbness she had known for so long, opening her up to a feeling she had never thought to feel again.

"As I've told you before, there isn't much room in my life for sharing, Sarina, not when there are still so many things I want to do before . . ." His voice trailed off. He cleared his throat. "But I *do* have time for moments. Not promises," he hastily added, "because I can't live comfortably with restrictions and pulls on my time, draining away my energy, so that bits of me are going one way, while pieces of me are going another. But I *do* have time for moments."

"I don't think I understand," she whispered, aware of a returning ache deep inside her, where no ache should ever have been felt again.

"You're in my blood, dammit!" he cried, grabbing her roughly by the shoulders and shaking her. "I wake up in the morning and you're what I see when I open my eyes. You're at the table with me when I eat, you walk beside me on the street, you're there at every meeting I have with people whose faces I can't even remember now. You're the last thing I see when I close my eyes at night." He crushed her to him and pressed his lips hard against her temple. "I want you, Sarina," he breathed. "God, how I want you!"

She lost herself in his embrace, arching her back to mold her body to each of his muscled curves. With her fingers buried deep in his hair, she stood on tiptoe, thrilling to the way her breasts flattened and spread against his hard, broad chest. The ache inside her was both soothed and inflamed by the growing hardness he thrust almost savagely against her. Yielding to its insistent pressure, she felt her body opening and softening, spreading itself before him.

And then, suddenly, the heat evaporated. As the specter of their dead son rose between them, it cooled the sun of her renewed passion, and a biting chill swept over her once more.

"No," she moaned, twisting away from him and out of the reach of his arms. "Not again, never again. As always, your words are sweet and your kisses are practiced, but you're still using them against me."

"Sarina, please." He tried vainly to catch hold of her again. "Sarina, it isn't true."

Sparks of molten bronze were leaping from her eyes. "Did you really think I'd consent to being your whore?" she hissed.

"Sarina!"

"You'll make love to me when it pleases you, and you'll travel the world whenever *that* pleases you, and then, when you come back for those moments you talked about, you'll expect me to be waiting for you, your eager and grateful partner. Well, I'm sorry"—she shook her head as her bottom lip began to quiver—"but you'd better look elsewhere for what you want." Tears of bitter anguish welled up in her eyes. "And please, please just leave me alone."

"Am I supposed to leave you to Kwen, Sarina?" he hurled back at her. "Do you expect him to offer you what you think you want?"

"He's been a father to me," she whispered hoarsely. "He's shielded me, protected me—"

"I'll protect you!"

Her laugh was scornful. "You have too many others to protect already."

"There *are* no others."

Sarina raised a skeptical eyebrow.

"I told you, she means nothing to me. Hilary and her husband are . . ."

Hilary! The name froze the tears pooling in her eyes. She began backing away from him, revulsion curdling whatever remained of her feelings. Hilary! The full impact of that name slammed into her and forced the air out of her throat in one long agonized gasp.

"Sarina . . ." He was advancing on her as she continued to retreat. "Sail with me tomorrow. Come back to San Francisco with me."

"No."

"We'll have time together, I promise."

"Until you leave again."

"If I can be satisfied with some time rather than none at all, why can't you?"

"Because I'm not you!" she shouted. "Because what you're offering me is only half of a life."

"What *do* you want, then?" Janson thundered. "A meek little clerk chained to his safe position in someone else's company, and shackled to you and to the passel of children you'll give him? Is that what you want, the safety and security that come with sameness? Well, if it is, perhaps you're right, I'd better leave you alone, because you'll find no clerk and no children in the life I'm offering you."

In her anguish and confusion she wanted to strike back at him. She wanted to hurt him by telling him what she had sworn never to tell him. That he had already fathered a child and that he had failed at that just as he failed at being decent and kind and loving. But she held herself back. She simply clamped her mouth shut around her pain and said nothing.

"I'll ask you once more, Sarina," he said in a calmer voice, watching her start up the steps of the summerhouse again. "Sail with me tomorrow."

With her head held high, she lifted her skirts and took another step.

"I'll be sailing aboard the *Coriander*. We leave at eight, on the morning tide."

She reached the top step and pulled the door open.

"I'll wait for you, Sarina," he called after her. "Tell me that you'll be there, and I'll wait."

She took a deep breath and then she closed the door.

She stood on the balcony, shivering in the dampness. The stars hung in the sable sky with such precision were the same stars the men aboard the *Coriander* would soon be using to chart their course across the Pacific. Her hands tightened around the wooden balustrade. Perhaps with three thousand miles separating her from Janson Carlyle, distance would accomplish what time had so far been unable to do—it would finally enable her to forget him.

She closed her eyes and saw herself dissolving again in his embrace. She touched the throbbing temple where his lips had burned his fierce declaration into her skin. *I want you,* he had said. *I want you.* She tore her hand away and gave her head an angry shake. Yes, he wanted her, the way any man wants to possess without being possessed himself.

Her shoulders began to sag. She peered into the blackness for a glimpse of the sleeping summerhouse. Were Chen and Mei in there now, making love or simply holding on to each other? Tilting her head to one side, she wrapped her arms around herself and tried to imagine Janson there holding her instead. How she envied Chen and Mei for being brave enough to settle for the sweetness of their stolen times together. She sighed, a low, dispirited sigh. Was she wrong? Had Janson been right? Were a few moments together better than an entire lifetime spent apart?

Panic seized her, but then it just as quickly subsided. She let her arms drop. Her head came up proudly again. She squared her shoulders and set her jaw in a firm, hard line. She and Janson Carlyle were not like Chen and Mei at all. Never once had Janson spoken to her of love.

"Sarina?"

She spun around, shocked to find Wo standing there, wearing only a quilted silk dressing robe and padded slippers.

"The light beneath your door alarmed me," he explained. "I was concerned that you might be ill."

Sarina tightened the sash on her own dressing gown and stepped back inside the room.

"Then you couldn't sleep either?" she asked him.

He made a vague gesture with his hands. "You would be wiser to concern yourself with your own poor sleep and not mine," he said, not unkindly, "for it is now past three o'clock."

There was a light rap at the door and one of the kitchen slaves entered carrying a black lacquer tray with a porcelain teapot and two porcelain cups on it.

"Now perhaps we will both be permitted the blessed release of sleep," proclaimed Wo as he waved the servant away.

While Sarina closed the doors to the balcony, Wo poured their tea and then settled himself in a chair. Sarina took the cup he offered her and sat down in the chair facing him. Raising the cup to her lips, she was disappointed to discover that it was not the jasmine-scented tea but the kind they drank at dinner every night. She glanced up at Wo and found him studying her with an unfathomable look in his dark eyes. When he began to drink his own tea, she hastily took a sip of hers, anxious not to offend him after he had been so thoughtful.

As she drained her cup, she was suddenly struck by the intensity of her disappointment a moment earlier. Had she become so dependent on the jasmine tea that she was now incapable of falling asleep without it? Was Wo aware of her shameful need? Was this his way of helping to wean her from her dependency? She was frowning as she allowed him to refill her cup.

"It grieves me to see you saddened this way, my delicate blossom." Wo's voice was so low that Sarina had to lean forward to hear him. "It would seem that your visit with Janson Carlyle has distressed you most severely."

Her answering laugh had a hollow ring to it. "Mr. Carlyle won't be distressing me anymore. He's sailing for America in the morning."

"Ah, this, then, is the reason for your great distress, my lotus."

She shook her head and the room tipped and then righted itself again. "He even had the audacity to suggest I return to San Francisco with him."

Wo's fingers were steepled together as he continued to watch her carefully. "And you refused?"

She nodded, and her head wobbled unsteadily. "I refused." Blinking her eyes, she tried to clear her blurring vision.

Wo was smiling. "I fear our friend Janson is not the most fortunate of suitors. But then, it is a rare man who can properly serve both his prideful ambition and those he professes to care deeply for."

Sarina set down her empty cup and tried to stand up. The room was now pitching the way the *Halcyon* had pitched and tossed the night of that violent storm. She put out a hand to steady herself, and stumbled against Wo's chair.

"I . . . I don't feel . . ."

Wo caught her easily as she fell forward into his arms.

"It is a rare man indeed, my most precious of all delights," he murmured as he carried her to her bed. "You are most fortunate, my joy, to have been blessed with just such a man."

He stroked the long golden hair fanning across her pillow like a silken cape, and then, tenderly, reverently, he kissed each of the delicate features of her face.

"Sleep, my lotus, and when you wake again, your past will be but a distant memory; for it is in your future that your fulfillment and your glory lie."

For a moment Sarina thought it was morning. But when she opened her eyes to find Ing-han bending over her, she sat bolt upright in bed and stared disbelievingly at her serving maid.

"Is it time for dinner?" she asked in halting Chinese, and Ing-han nodded, pointing to the gown she had laid out at the foot of the bed.

Sarina pressed her fingertips to the sides of her head, massaging her temples, which seemed to be pounding with the memory of some forgotten pain. And then she remembered. The tea. Wo had obviously drugged her tea so that she would be able to sleep. She choked back a cry of dismay when she realized that she had slept away the entire day. A familiar emptiness began to spread through her then, filling all the cavities of her body and seeping into her bloodstream to numb the rest of her.

"He's gone," she said dully, only vaguely aware of Ing-han's puzzled frown. "Janson's finally gone."

"Missy, look, please!"

She responded slowly to the excitement in her serving maid's voice, but when she did, her mouth fell open in astonishment. Ing-han was pointing to a gown she had never seen before, nor had it been made out of any of the fabric she had chosen at Chiang Tan's shop in Shanghai. Curious now, Sarina leaned forward on the bed, stretching out her hand to touch the exquisite robe, which shim-

mered in the lantern light as if it were encrusted with
thousands of tiny colored stones.

It was a glorious sunburst of yellow silk, heavily embroidered with red pomegranates, gold marigolds, and broad,
flat green lotus leaves. The silk sash to bind her waist was
yellow, as was the pair of low-heeled silk slippers, and the
jewels Wo had selected to complement the extraordinary
gown were artfully fashioned clusters of ruby, topaz, and
emerald flowers. As Sarina stared at the gown, stroking its
silken coolness, her initial reaction of stunned surprise
began to give way to something more disturbing and almost sinister—foreboding.

Sarina knew what each color and symbol stood for, and
suddenly their meaning took on a greater significance for
her than ever before. Yellow represented the earth; the
pomegranate signified abundance; the lotus stood for
summer; the marigold, the flower of ten thousand years,
meant eternal youth. She began plucking anxiously at the
quilted coverlet as her trepidation continued to mount.
Was she imagining it or had Wo sent her a message with
this newest gown?

Janson Carlyle was gone. Was it possible that Wo had
not only helped her to fall asleep, but that he had also
made certain she would *stay* asleep? Sarina's pulse suddenly began to race. Had Wo been afraid of her changing
her mind and sailing with Janson after all? The pounding
in her head was worsening, not from the aftereffects of
her drugged sleep, but from a terrifying new awareness.
Prodded by a bolt of electric fear, she sprang from the
bed, her eyes wide, her mouth working in frantic silence.

The gown was a veritable fertility robe!

She had proved herself capable of bearing sons, and Wo
Shue Kwen wanted more sons. Sarina's heart was beating
so rapidly that she could feel it slamming into the walls of
her chest. Tears flooded her eyes. What if Janson had
been right about Wo and his intentions for her? But Wo
had been a father to her. What if . . . ?

Her eyes flew to her bedside table. Even before she
looked, she knew what she would find. Ji Hsi was gone.

Janson slammed the near-empty bottle down on his
desk and pushed himself to his feet. Sunsets on the ocean
had always excited him in the past. He loved their glorious

clash of colors, of scarlet and turquoise, violet and orange,
ocher and pink. To him a sunset was a battle of supremacy between bold primaries and tender pastels, with victory never predictable, never the same twice. But tonight
he had seen none of the majestic beauty in the setting of
the sun. All he had seen was a descending rush of blackness which was better suited to his own black despair.

She had kept her word. She hadn't come. And yet, like
a fool, he had waited. One hour and then two. Until the
captain had come to warn him that they were losing the
tide. He had continued to wait, nonetheless, so certain was
he of her changing her mind and sailing with him. When
the captain came to him a second time, he was forced to
give him permission to cast off. He had then closeted
himself in his cabin to work his way slowly through as
many bottles of gin as it took to render him unconscious.

What a fool he had been to think that she would choose
him over Wo Shue Kwen. He picked up the bottle, took a
deep swallow of the gin, and carried the bottle over to the
porthole with him. He put out a hand to brace himself as
his legs threatened to give way beneath him, and raised
the bottle to his lips again.

He heard the door opening. Spinning around, he nearly
lost his balance. Using the wall to support his weight, he
leaned up against it with his back and squinted at the
figure moving toward him in the half-darkness of the
cabin. Moonlight seemed to be trapped in her gown and
in her hair as she glided across the floor. She was ivory,
gilded with gold and suffused by a pure golden light. His
heart began to pound. She had changed her mind. She
had come after all!

Her name died on his lips.

What he had taken to be her golden hair was not her
hair at all, but the hood of her gold satin cape which she
was now pulling back from her face. The lantern light
deepened the pitchy blackness of her hair and set indigo
sparks flashing in the blue of her eyes.

"Didn't you know that Prescott had booked us passage
aboard your ship, Janson?" came the husky voice he had
counted on never hearing again. "Don't you think it was
rather considerate of him?"

She moved closer to him, until she was an indistinct blur

of gold and black and defiant blue before his swimming eyes.

"He's asleep, Janson," she purred, one silken hand caressing the roughness of his unshaved cheek. "Older men retire early and leave their wives to their own designs. Do you think that's foolish of them, Janson, or wonderfully convenient?"

It was the gin, he told himself. It was the gin and not her nearness which was forcing the blood up to his face and into his groin and down into his trembling legs. He had told her no that day in the teahouse and he would tell her no now. He flattened himself against the wall, both arms flung out to support his shaking body as the fire inside him burned brighter and hotter and threatened to rage out of control.

She swayed against him, just enough to brush the tips of her thrusting breasts across his chest and to leave a stinging path of prickly heat behind. He groaned and turned his head to the side, feeling the bite of the rough plank wall against his skin. The imprint of her mouth on the side of his neck blazed like a brand. Each touch of her lips on his throat pushed his howl of protest deeper and deeper inside him and forced his tortured urgency closer to the surface.

With a snarling cry he flung the bottle away from him and caught her around the waist. Forcing her back, he buried his face, his lips, and his teeth inside the swelling crest of her bosom. Then he picked her up in his arms and carried her to his bed, drawing her down on top of him, while he kept his mouth fastened to her breasts. She gently freed herself from his hungry mouth and raised herself until she was able to reach the oil lamp on the table beside them. She turned down the wick, and the light sputtered and died.

As the cabin was plunged into benevolent darkness, the devil's temptress with his angel's face lowered her lips to his.

16

There were times over the next few weeks when Sarina was convinced that she had imagined everything—Wo's having drugged her tea that night, the significance of the gown he had given her, and the reason for the disappearance of the jade goddess, Ji Hsi. Nothing in Wo's behavior or manner suggested that anything had changed since that night, or would, in fact, ever change. If he were curious as to why she had never worn the elaborate yellow robes, he concealed it well; if he were aware of her suspicions, he gave no such indication; and because she was convinced it was he who, for reasons of his own, had taken back the statue, she never mentioned its disappearance to him. To her surprise and relief, he remained as kindly and solicitous toward her as ever, which led her to believe that her suspicions had been unfounded and, as such, were unworthy of further consideration.

One afternoon, when she was placing the brass key to the summerhouse under the flat moss-speckled stone, she was startled to find a piece of paper lying there. For a moment her mouth went dry and her hands began to tremble. Unfolding the note, she saw that it was from Chen, asking her to please come to the summerhouse at midnight. Not daring to take the note with her, she hastily put it back under the rock again along with the little key. As she walked slowly, pensively, through the gardens toward the main house, she knew that it would take all of her patience and will to wait out the eight remaining hours until midnight.

Five minutes before the designated hour, Sarina drew on a deep blue silk cloak and tugged the hood up over her head, hoping that by wearing it she would blend in more easily with the inky shadows of the night. If she encountered any member of the Wo household up and about, she would simply explain that she was having difficulty sleeping again and that she had hoped to tire herself out by taking a brisk stroll about the grounds. But the house was dark and still as she stole furtively down the stairs and out into the courtyard.

She was dismayed by the fullness of the April moon as it rode high in the clear black sky and cut a glittering swath through the rustling oleanders and flowering plum trees. She picked a cautious path through the gardens, hovering close to each shadowed place and scampering, with her breath sucked in, through every errant shaft of moonlight marking her way. So familiar during the day, the small white building, rising like a ghostly citadel above a cloud of pink and white blossoms, seemed alien to her now as she neared it. She paused for just a moment, then lifted her skirts and tiptoed hurriedly up the steps.

Even before she could knock, Chen swung the door open and beckoned her inside. Moonlight spilled in even squares across the floor and up the walls and illuminated the seated figure of Mei as she sat cross-legged on the first of three silk cushions which had been placed beside one another on the bare wood floor. Chen led Sarina over to the far cushion, while he settled himself on the one in the middle. As she pushed back her hood and shook out her hair, she was struck by the hushed and seductive peace of the little room. Awake while the world around it was sleeping, the summerhouse was a far different place from the noisy schoolroom she knew during the day. Gazing thoughtfully at the cushions, she began to wonder. A shadow strode arrogantly across the field of her memory and she angrily blinked it away.

"We both thank you for risking much to come here tonight, my friend," said Chen as he rested a hand protectively on Mei's knee. The girl smiled and covered his larger hand with her small one. "We believed the three of us should share together what I have to say."

Sarina swallowed hard and braced herself.

"Soon Mei and I will no longer have need of the summerhouse," he told her, "and you will no longer be in peril as you have been these many months."

Sarina was stunned. With wistful regret she saw them

finally putting an end to an affair whose future held only separation and heartache for them.

"Mei and I will be leaving shortly for Canton."

Sarina gasped.

"We will marry there and I will purchase a small farm close to the farm of Mei's father."

"But you can't," exclaimed Sarina. "Your father could have you put to death if you did."

"And risk the end of the noble line of Wo?" scoffed Chen. "No, my friend, in spite of his threats, my father would not suffer my death so easily, knowing that it would also mean the death of his most illustrious name. I believe he would prefer to see that name sullied before he would consent to seeing it extinguished forever."

"Mei, you mustn't allow him to do this," she implored the girl, who had been watching Chen in reverent silence. "Surely you wouldn't want him to place himself in such jeopardy."

But the face she turned to Sarina was suffused with the radiance of her love, and when she spoke, even her voice was anointed by that love. "Chen is my love and my master, and I will do his bidding in this as in all other things."

"Chen, please, don't do this." Sarina grabbed hold of his arm and gave it a sharp tug. "Please."

"To leave is the only way for me to live in harmony with myself and at peace with my soul," he declared. "I have lived all my life with a love of the land, a love I will carry within me whether I myself am a landlord or a simple farmer. Although my father has schooled me in the ways of business, they are ways I care nothing for." He looked down at her anguished face and smiled, a sad and rueful smile. "I am too simple a man to be the son of the exalted Wo Shue Kwen, my friend, and for this I feel pity for my father, for we have failed one another equally."

Sarina released her hold on his arm and folded her hands in her lap. In a tremulous voice she said, "I'm afraid for you, Chen. I'm terribly afraid for both of you."

"Once before I begged you not to fear for us," he told her gently. "Now once again we have chosen the only path our hearts will permit us to choose."

"When will you be leaving?"

"On the first day of the Festival of the Dragon Boats,"

he said. "It is a time of great celebration and safer for one
to travel while each family is occupied by many days of
festivities."

Sarina's shoulders slumped. The festival would begin in
another three weeks. With a sudden jolt she realized that
in just three weeks an entire year would have passed since
she had sat in the dining parlor of the *Halcyon* and heard
a kindly silk merchant named Loo Wang describe the
Festival of the Dragon Boats to her, while the dishes
crashed onto the floor and the oil lamps swung crazily
overhead and the ship pitched and tossed in an angry sea.

Chen touched her shoulder, and she looked up to find
him already standing.

"Come, my friend." He put out his hands and tugged
her to her feet. "It is time we returned to the house, for
your sake as well as ours."

Sarina arranged the hood of her cape over her hair
again. "When do you intend to tell your father?" she
asked.

"I will not tell him at all," he said firmly. "By my absence he will know that I am gone. Once we are married
and we have begun our new life together, I will inform
him of the deed, which cannot then be undone." He
cupped Sarina's face gently in his hands. "Will you not
attempt to set aside your fears, my dear and loyal friend,"
he pleaded, "so that you may be pleased for us?"

Sarina laughed wryly as she shook her head. "I *am*
pleased, Chen, but I'll stop being afraid only when the
three weeks have passed and you're safely away from
here."

Mei stepped in then and put her arms around Sarina.
"May the gods bless you one day with a love as sweet as
the love they have bestowed upon us, my sister." In her
eyes was a pointed message meant only for Sarina to see.
"You will visit with us one day, will you not? We will have
a simple home, but it will be finer than the home of Wo
Shue Kwen, because the fullness of love will be inside it."

Sarina caressed Mei's lustrous black hair with her fingertips and nodded. "One day," she agreed, acknowledging
both of the girl's tender wishes. She hugged the girl close.
"And I'll pray for you, Mei," she said fiercely. "I'll pray
for you and Chen just as you've prayed for me."

They went back down the steps one by one, slipping

through the grounds in turn, darting in and out of the
shadows until they were safely inside the house again. By
the time Sarina closed the door of her bedroom, she was
glazed with perspiration and her gown was clinging uncomfortably to every line of her body. As she stripped off
her cloak and tossed it onto the bed, her eyes fell on the
nearest of the two lacquered bedside tables. Near where
the jade statue had always stood rested her father's
leatherbound Bible.

She approached it cautiously, warily, like a repentant
sinner returning to church for the first time after a long
absence. Picking it up and feeling its familiar weight in
her hands, she sat down on the edge of the bed and rested
the Bible in her lap. She needed comfort tonight. She
needed solace and reassurance and she needed a prayer to
keep Chen and Mei safe.

And so, for the first time since the death of her son,
Sarina opened the Bible and returned to God for His
loving help.

For the first time in the many years she had spent with
him, Li blessed Kwen for his violent outburst of ill temper.
If he had not cursed her for failing to bring him to
completion, when she had used all of her many skills to
satisfy him, and ordered her to return to her own
bedchamber, she would never have borne witness to the
treachery of the golden one. Nor would she have ever
learned of the duplicity of Kwen's own son. Li smiled. She
had done well to destroy the statue. Where the charms
had failed, *she* would triumph.

By her own hand, the golden one had sown the seed of
her own downfall.

It was shortly after sunrise that the sound of a woman
screaming shook Sarina awake. Jumping out of bed, she
tied her dressing gown around her and ran barefoot from
the room. She careened down the stairs, still groggy with
sleep, and when she reached the front hall, she was brought
up short by what she saw. It seemed as if a funeral procession were making its way through the open door of Wo's
study.

Wo came first, his eyes dull, his face ashen with despair,
aged cruelly overnight by some malevolent unseen hand.

He was followed by Chen, whose head was bowed as he shuffled slowly between two of the stout male servants who guarded the estate. Behind them trailed a weeping Mei, her hands covering her face, stumbling and half-falling and being hoisted to her feet again by another of the guards. Sua, her eyes red-rimmed and swollen, her white cheeks streaked with tears, hobbled after Mei, leaning heavily on the arm of one of the house slaves. Last was Li. Of all of them, only Li was walking with her head high and her back straight, floating with haughty disdain behind the others, who were bent over by the weight of their grief.

"What's wrong?" Sarina called out to Wo, who appeared not to have seen her standing there. "Please, tell me what's happened."

She caught hold of his arm, only to have him brush her hand away as if she were a troublesome bramble snagging the sleeve of his robe. Li released a peal of triumphant laughter which pierced the deathly silence and drained the blood out of Sarina's veins, to congeal in a solid, frozen lump in the pit of her stomach. In mounting horror she stared at Wo, certain that the gaze he was now training on her was as fearsome as the gaze of the Lord when he had transformed Lot's treacherous wife into a pillar of salt. As Sarina began backing away from him, she felt herself shrinking, disintegrating into grains of lifeless sand. *They know,* her numbed heart thudded. *They know.*

"Since you have been a participant in this perfidy, my dear Sarina"—his carefully measured speech seethed with contained fury—"you may witness for yourself how a father deals with a treacherous son."

He clapped his hands and another guard appeared and seized Sarina by the wrist. The procession started forward again. Although she fought to loosen the fingers of steel clamped so tightly around her flesh, her battle was a futile one. She found herself being dragged after the others through the back gardens and up to the steps of the summerhouse. The little building seemed so innocent now, she thought, bathed by the shy pink blush of early morning. Innocent and yet treacherous.

Twisting around, she gazed back at the main house, scanning the closed balcony doors, looking, searching. Her eyes met Li's, and in their glowing depths lay the answer she was seeking. Hatred rose like a bilious wave in Sarina's throat. With a howl of rage she nearly lunged at the woman, but was held back painfully by the male servant keeping her prisoner.

"Turn around, Sarina!" Wo's voice cut through the air to seek her out. "See how we punish a son who defies his father by fornicating with a servant whom he intends to take as his wife."

Through half-veiled eyes she forced herself to look at Chen. His hands had been tied with a length of rope to the wooden banister of the summerhouse, and his jacket removed, baring his pale back to the cool morning air. While one of the guards remained at his side, with his legs spread, his arms folded across his chest, and his dark gaze never leaving Chen's half-naked form, the other guard had stepped back a few paces and was unwinding a long strip of leather which had been tightly coiled around a thick bamboo handle. Sarina heard Mei's low, muffled sobbing and she squeezed her eyes shut, wishing she could also cover her ears to block completely what she knew was coming.

"Open your eyes, Sarina!" barked Wo.

This was not her Wo, she told herself. This was not the man who had tended her, protected her, and nurtured her; the man who had loved her as only a father can love his own child; the man whom she had loved as a father in return.

"Do as I command you, Sarina!"

This was the Wo Janson had warned her about. The unscrupulous trader who dealt in opium; the arrogant landlord who punished ox-cart drivers; the proud and vengeful father who had it in his power to put his own son to death.

"Sarina, open your eyes and look at him!"

This was the Wo she had refused to see, the Wo who lived side by side with the only Wo she had wanted him to be.

"Sarina!"

Her head snapped back as her captor grabbed a handful of her long hair and gave it a vicious tug. She yelped in pain and her eyes flew open. The crack of the lash against Chen's back made her scream again, but her cry of protest was overwhelmed by Chen's shriek of agony. He cried out just that once. With each subsequent sting of the whip across his back, he either moaned or grunted, but he proudly refused to submit to the pain or to his father. And Sarina seemed to absorb each stroke of the lash herself, wincing with each new crackle of leather against skin, while she longed to strike out at Chen's fickle gods for finally abandoning him.

"One hundred!" announced Wo as the guard, breathing heavily and running with sweat, allowed the lash to fall to his side.

Sarina stared bleakly at Chen sprawled against the railing of the summerhouse. The rope was cut and he dropped to the ground. His back was a bloodied pool of pulpy flesh and Sarina turned her head away.

"Carry him to the house," Wo barked, "and send for Qi Ting-fang."

The two guards, one holding Chen under the arms, the other grasping him by the ankles, lifted him into the air and started off for the house. As they passed Sarina, she looked down into the contorted face of her friend and saw his eyes roll upward and then close. She silently thanked God, for Chen had mercifully passed out.

Wo then turned to Mei, who was huddled on the ground. Her eyes were closed and she was rocking back and forth, her arms wrapped around her knees, and keening softly.

"You have shamed the house of Wo," he charged, signaling for her to be lifted to her feet. She wavered in front of him, head bowed and eyes downcast. "You have taken the trust of your honorable mistress and befouled that trust by behaving in a manner befitting the most common harlot. By your own foolish action have you chosen your own destiny, my foolish young Mei. You will be taken from this house this very morning and never permitted to return. I am banishing you from our midst forever, to be bound into service at a brothel—the brothel of Madam Blue. Let those who hunger after you hereafter pay for the favors you so generously bestowed upon my unworthy son."

"No!" Sarina screamed, straining to break free of the guard's determined hold on her. "You can't do that! No!"

"Take her away!" ordered Wo.

"No, please, dear God, no!" Sarina bucked and kicked at her captor, who was now holding tightly on to her other wrist. "Mei!" she screamed as the weeping girl was dragged away. Mei turned her head and their eyes met and held in one last tortured farewell.

Revulsion and contempt writhed inside Sarina as Wo approached her and cupped her chin in his hands. Each time he tried to hold her head still, she angrily turned her face away, lashing her head back and forth in her attempt to keep his hands away from her skin. She had never known such hatred before. She had never thought herself capable of such rage. In her mounting anger, she knew that if her hands were free and she was holding a weapon in those hands, she would not hesitate to use it on the man standing before her. A man who was no less than the Son of Lucifer himself.

"Listen to me, my treacherous Sarina," Wo hissed, his face only inches from hers. "I have dispatched a messenger to the house of Lao Hong Han, asking that the marriage between my unworthy son and his daughter Kuer T'ai take place two weeks from this very morning. It is regretful that we must wait so long to witness the happy union of these two young people, but it will take this time for Chen's wounds to begin to heal. Then we will at last be welcoming another honored member to our household." He seized her face roughly in both hands and twisted her head around so that she was forced to look directly at him. "As for you, my deceitful blossom"—he smiled, a smile which snaked across his face and lightened the darkness of his eyes—"you have only begun to serve the house of Wo."

Sarina's throat was parched, her mouth dry, and yet she longed to form a wad of spittle and hurl it into his hateful face. Proudly, she squared her shoulders and stared unflinching into his eyes.

"You, my golden lotus, have proven yourself capable of bearing that which the gods have too long denied me."

She felt the breath being sucked out of her body. Her lips quivered. Her legs began to tremble.

"Once the festivities of the marriage feast are ended, there will be another celebration." He traced the outline of her mouth with the tip of his index finger, and Sarina flinched. "It is then that I will bestow upon you the most exalted honor a man can bestow upon a woman. You will become my favored one, my sweet Sarina, and you shall bear me sons."

Sarina did not move, nor did she speak. She simply stood where she was, while half of her shriveled and died and the other half detached itself from her body and floated upward to a higher plateau, where there was freedom from all feeling. When she heard the shrill scream, she thought it was hers, but she followed Wo's eyes and turned just in time to see Li's face crumple into a horrible grimace of pain and anger.

17

The gates of her floral prison had swung shut. Sarina was trapped, a gilded butterfly, with the determination but not the strength to break through its bars and fly free. Like a pendulum, her moods swung from bleak despair to rage and then back again. Over and over she castigated herself for having been lulled into complacency by nothing more than wishful thinking, when her own instincts had warned her that all was not right. She rattled the bars of her prison each time she cursed herself for refusing to believe Janson Carlyle, for choosing Wo's proven protection to the uncertainty Janson had held out to her, and for allowing him to sail without her, leaving her stranded.

Wo had betrayed her, and for this she would never forgive him. He had taken her trust and her love and corrupted them, turning them back to her as a weapon honed solely out of lust. The thought of his pale, hairless hands touching her skin, his lips pressed against her mouth, and his body thrusting into hers was so repugnant to her that at times she feared she might be driven to end her life rather than to suffer the humiliation of being his concubine. Concubine! The word itself was a lance piercing her skull, skewering her insides, and forcing the bile up into her throat, where it remained lodged in a bitter, choking lump.

In her disgust and hatred for the man she could easily have called father, she refused to speak to him or wear any of the clothes he had given her. To protest his treachery, she took every robe, cloak, pair of shoes, and piece of jewelry and piled them into a huge glittering heap in front of his bedroom door and returned to wear-

ing only the few simple gowns she had brought with her
from Oregon.

After Wo's shocking declaration in front of the summerhouse that morning, Li refused to leave her room, and so
it was a grim and troubled threesome who sat down to
dinner in the evenings. Sarina ate sparingly. She sniffed
suspiciously at all of her food and steadfastly refused to
drink tea again. As one day followed another, the air of
tense expectancy heightened, pressing down upon the house
like a stifling blanket, until Sarina knew that unless she
escaped, she would suffocate and die.

In spite of the elaborate preparations for the marriage
of Chen and Lao Kuer T'ai, Sarina doubted that the
wedding would ever take place. Although Chen's back was
slowly beginning to heal, he refused to hasten the healing
process in any way. Lying on his stomach in bed in resolute silence, he refused all food and drink and spoke to no
one. He kept his face turned toward the wall, and although his eyes were open, they were vacant and staring.

Five days after his terrible lashing, Sarina rose with the
first mauve sweep of dawn and went downstairs. She
made her way to the large room at the rear of the house
where the altar and the tablets of the Wo family ancestors
were kept. It was here that Sua could be found, as she
could be found every morning, fulfilling her duties as Wo
Shue Kwen's obedient wife by paying homage to all those
who had come before him.

As soon as Sarina entered the darkened room, her nostrils were filled with the rich scent of sandalwood. In the
glow of the lighted candles she could just make out the
tiny form of Sua, who was kneeling before a long wooden
altar on which a number of intricately carved wooden
tablets stood. Burning before each tablet was a thin white
candle and a slender gray stick of incense. In the shallow
niches carved out of the walls rested even more tablets.
It was inside these wooden tablets, inscribed with the names
of the deceased of four generations, that the Chinese
believed the spirits of their ancestors dwelt.

Sarina knelt beside the praying woman and touched her
lightly on the sleeve of her pale blue robe. Although Sua
turned her head to acknowledge Sarina's presence, her
mouth continued to work in silent supplication. Sarina
waited patiently while Sua prayed, with her eyes closed

and her hands folded in her lap as she swayed back and forth.

A few minutes later, Sua ended her prayers by stretching her arms out in front of her and touching her head to the floor. Then she straightened again, pressed her palms together, and held her hands to her chest and bowed twice to the tablets on the altar. Sitting back on her heels, she finally turned to Sarina with a gentle smile. But in spite of her smile, her eyes were pained and sadness was etched in deep lines beneath her dark eyes.

"I have come about Chen," said Sarina, interspersing her English with the Chinese words she knew. A cloud drifted across the woman's face as Sarina continued, "He's going to die if he doesn't begin to eat soon. Surely Wo wouldn't want his only son to die. If he did, he would have put him to death for disobeying him instead of having him lashed."

She waited for Sua to respond to what she had said, but the older woman simply sat there with a blank expression on her pale face.

"Couldn't you go to Chen and try to convince him to eat?" Sarina asked.

After what seemed to be an eternity, Sua solemnly shook her head.

"But you're his mother!"

"He son of Wo," came the halting reply.

"But his father doesn't want him to die," insisted Sarina. "He wants him to marry Lao Kuer T'ai and give you grandchildren who will honor you and continue the mighty name of Wo."

Sua shifted about on the floor and refused to meet Sarina's gaze.

"Do you want your only son to die?" she demanded.

"If Chen die, it will of gods."

Sarina began plucking at the hem of her skirt as her agitation mounted. "If you won't go to Chen, would you speak with Wo?" she persisted. "Would you ask him to bring Mei back to live in the house again? Sua . . ." She gently tugged on the long sleeve of the woman's robe. "Your son will die if Mei is not brought back to him." *Forgive me, Chen,* she whispered to herself. *Forgive me for interfering, but I can't sit by helplessly and watch you die.*

Sua slowly raised her head, and although her expression was still the same as before, her voice was firmer as she said, "It written if hen rule at morning, family end. Wo rule, Sua follow Wo."

It was senseless to pursue it any further. The sight of Sua's downcast eyes and humble demeanor caused Sarina to grind her teeth in frustration. How she deplored the customs of this country, which emptied a woman's mind of all thought except to serve and to obey! As she got to her feet and forced herself to bow respectfully to Sua, she found it difficult to contain her contempt for the woman who refused to help keep her own son alive. She burst from the cloying and oppressive bleakness of the shrine into a welcome stream of yellow sunlight, much like a swimmer breaking through the water's surface, grateful to breathe the air again.

Her clothes reeked of incense. The scent of sandalwood was clinging so tenaciously to her hair and skin that she decided to return to her room and change her gown. To her chagrin, Wo was standing at the foot of the stairs. She tried to work her way around him, but he grabbed hold of her arm and forced her back down the steps again. She turned her face away and refused to look at him.

"Am I to be denied the sweetness of your voice forever, my lotus?" he inquired, his own voice silken and smooth.

When she continued to ignore him, he said, "I have been most patient these past days, Sarina, but even the most patient of men grows weary with time." His grip tightened on her arm. "You would speak to me if I commanded you to speak, my stubborn one, but I would much prefer you to comply to my simple request of your own desire."

Sarina tossed her head in defiance of him and continued to stare straight ahead of her.

"A veil of silence has descended like a cloud upon the house of Wo." He sighed. "The tender voice of Mei has been stilled, my cherished Li refuses me entry, my unworthy son speaks to no one, and you, my most precious of treasures, deny me all of your golden sweetness." He traced a line from her throat down to the full curve of her bosom with his thumb, and she shuddered in revulsion. "I have been made lonely by those I have treasured most. I think perhaps I will set aside all thoughts of ceremonies, my lotus, and raise you to that most honored of states this very evening. With your golden beauty to hallow my bedchamber, I will most assuredly be spared any further loneliness."

"Never!" Her denial was wrung from her stubborn lips in spite of her attempts to remain still, but she could no longer tolerate him touching her. "Never, do you hear me!" she snarled. "I'd die first."

He laughed at her for that. "To die without knowing the ecstasy of love is a waste indeed, my treasure. Once I have shown you such love, you will never be so foolish as to prefer death to me again."

She lashed out at him then with her free hand, straining to claw at his face. But he caught her arm before she could reach him and slammed her up against the wall, pinning her there with the weight of his body, while he wedged one knee in between her legs.

"So my rose is one with many hidden thorns," he growled, panting slightly from their tussle. "You would do well to sheathe your thorns, Sarina, and use them only in those moments when I too may more fully use them to further both my pleasure and yours."

She was repelled by what he was saying to her, his intentions perverse and vile, and she knew that she would have to speak to him if she had any hope of staying the inevitable awhile longer.

"Just what do you want?" she hurled at him from between clenched teeth.

"Civility," he tossed back at her. "I demand that you speak to me as though I were more than the air you cannot see."

"And if I speak to you, will you leave me alone?"

His eyebrows lifted. "You would exact a price so high for as simple a demand as mine?"

At the dangerous sparking in her eyes, he smiled, a devious slant of a smile. "I will agree to temper my impatience and await the designated time," he said, "but I have a second most simple request." Before she could protest, he hurried on. "Time grows short, and because there has been much for me to do here, I have been unable to attend to several most important matters in the city. Tomorrow you will accompany me into the city and you will proceed to the shop of Chiang Tan to select for yourself robes suitable for a wedding of the son of Wo."

"I can wear one of the gowns I already have," she muttered.

"After you have discarded them in such obvious displeasure?" He smirked. "No, my lotus, you will dress as I say you will dress, or there will be no bargain between us at all."

She suddenly realized how foolish she would be to protest further. The seed of an idea was taking hold within her mind. Her heart lifted. This visit to Chiang Tan might provide her with the opportunity she had been waiting for.

"All right," she capitulated, carefully masking her growing excitement, while she forced herself to give him a faint smile. "I'll do as you say."

"You give me immeasurable happiness by your assent, my golden one." Wo smiled. He placed a chaste kiss on each of her cheeks and then backed away from her.

Grateful to be free of his bruising weight at last, she began to massage her sore arms, but no sooner had he disappeared inside his study than she wet the tips of her fingers and scrubbed at her cheeks to erase the imprint of his mouth from her skin. At the sudden tinkle of brittle laughter above her, she glanced up to see Li standing at the head of the stairs, with one small hand resting on the banister for support.

"You accept his kisses with a smile upon your face," the cool voice drifted down to her, "and when he shows you his back, you wipe them in contempt from your skin. You must learn to better mask your innermost feelings, my innocent Miss Paige, or by your own actions will you destroy all you have hoped to attain."

Sarina charged up the stairs, her cheeks flaming, her eyes blazing. When she reached the landing, she thrust her face into Li's and drew some satisfaction from the way the woman blinked her eyes uncertainly and then took a tiny step backward.

"Don't you dare suggest that I ever wanted to take your place!" She was seething now. "I came here as the tutor to your three daughters, and that was how I had intended it to remain. It was Wo Shue Kwen who decided otherwise, not I."

For a moment Li appeared to be scrutinizing Sarina, as if taking her measure for herself.

"It is true that you would choose to deny him what he most desires?" she asked somewhat incredulously. "You would refuse to accept the privilege of being his favored one?"

"I was never taught to consider it a privilege to be some man's whore," Sarina returned, her voice frosting over as she faced the woman who had always treated her as if she were her mortal enemy.

But Li did not appear to have been slighted or at all insulted by what Sarina had said. Her face was closed, the expression in her kohl-rimmed eyes unreadable. She did, however, begin to tap her long red-lacquered nails against the banister in a most unsettling way.

"Since you are not one of us, you cannot know of the honor bestowed upon a woman when she is the favored of all her master's concubines," Li said in a subdued voice. "Only the ignorant would call a chosen one whore."

Her nails were clicking faster now, and Sarina was baffled by the woman's sudden nervousness, especially when she glanced up and down the hallway several times as if to assure herself that they were not being observed. Then she startled Sarina even more by whispering, "Come with me to my bedchamber."

"What—?"

"Do not question. Come with me."

As the tiny figure in the flowing lavender robes began to hobble down the corridor, a puzzled and curious Sarina trailed after her. The woman closed the door to her room and held one gold-tipped index finger up to her lips for silence. Sarina obliged her by quickly nodding her head, and then she waited, her hands clasped tensely in front of her.

"Are you prepared to leave this house and never return?" asked Li in a stealthy undertone.

Stunned, Sarina could scarcely believe what she was hearing.

"Are you?"

"Yes," she barely managed to blurt out, as suspicion and hope began churning inside her.

"You have funds for passage?"

Sarina nodded. "I have all of my earnings."

"That is good."

"Are you going to help me?" Sarina whispered, her heartbeats quickening.

The woman shook her head. "I would be banished."

Sarina's rising hopes faltered and began to plunge earthward. "Then why are you asking me these questions?"

Li stared directly into Sarina's eyes. "You are certain you have no wish to remain as the favored one of Wo?"

"Yes, I'm certain," Sarina answered, beginning to grow testy.

"You will swear before your God that you will leave?"

"I swear!"

The woman put her hands together and took a deep, steadying breath. "Then I am prepared to sweeten your leaving, Miss Paige," she said quietly. "If any doubt remains as to the wisdom of the choice you have made, what I tell you now will forever end all such doubt."

Sarina waited, her mouth dry, her hands clenched expectantly.

"Your son is alive."

Sarina took an unsteady step backward as her hands flew to her mouth. Her hold on the floor and on the very ground itself seemed to be slipping from her grasp. She saw Li as a wavering blur of black and lavender, with indistinct slashes of scarlet where her cheeks and lips should have been. She reached out for the doorjamb for support and sagged against the wall as her knees gave way.

Your son is alive. Over and over Li's mouth formed those blessed words in her mind and sent them singing through her body. Your son is alive. Was it possible? Was it true? Sarina tried to catch her breath and think clearly, but clear thought was all but impossible now. Her son was alive!

Through a radiant haze she heard Li saying, "Wo thinks none knows of his treachery, but he is mistaken. For thirteen years I have shared the pipe with him, just as I have shared his bed, and the power of the pipe in loosening one's tongue is greater than the power of any man, even one as mighty as Wo Shue Kwen. Your son is now the son of a British family whose name is Deane. They live in Hong Kong."

Sarina's lips began to move as if they were no longer

connected to the rest of her body. "Wo gave my son away?"

"Lewis Deane is a trusted employee of Wo," Li told her. "First he was manager of the trading offices in Shanghai; now he manages the offices in Hong Kong. Wo sorely misses him, and Anne, his wife, is a sickly woman and cannot bear her husband children."

"And so he gave them my son," Sarina whispered as a dread numbness began to replace the surge of joy she had felt just a moment before. "He told me my son was dead, when all the time he was alive and living in someone else's house. Why? Why in the name of God would he do such an evil thing?"

"Why?" Li repeated contemptuously. "He wanted no memory from your past to cloud your sight when he took you for his chosen one. He wanted sons of his own flesh to bear his exalted name, not the son of another."

"Then why not simply kill him instead?" Sarina demanded bitterly.

"Wo Shue Kwen gives life," came the caustic reply, "he does not take it. Like his honorable ancestors before him, he reveres all life. He would not dishonor his name or the names of his ancestors by daring to take the life of another."

Her son was alive! Sarina thought of all the hours, all the days she had spent talking to the son she had believed lay buried beneath that small stone marker. How Wo must have laughed at her. She thought of all the times he had comforted her and poured her cup after cup of jasmine-scented tea to help her escape the pain he himself had inflicted on her. She wanted to scream! She wanted to run out of the room and down the stairs to his study, screaming that she knew the truth now and that nothing would stop her from finding her son. She wanted him to know how much she despised him and how she would spend the rest of her life praying that one day he would be punished for all the ways he had shown just how much he revered all life.

"You must go now," Li hissed, pulling Sarina back from her rampaging thoughts.

Her numbed fingers pushed down on the brass door handle and released the catch. She was halfway out the door when Li whispered urgently, "Think carefully but with haste, Miss Paige, for the net of time is swiftly gathering."

And with that she closed the door with a muted click.

18

"I am prepared to see you carried on a litter to your wedding, my most unworthy son," bellowed Wo, "and once this union is sanctified, you may then die of your own stubbornness if you so choose. The lands of Wo and Lao will be joined, and I will live to have many sons more worthy of the name I bear than you."

The door to Chen's room slammed shut and Sarina hastily closed her own door and crept back to bed. She lay down again and tried to gather up the broken strands of the thoughts which Wo's blistering attack on his son had hopelessly scattered. Turning her head toward the open balcony doors, she sighed. The joyous news which had set even the roots of her hair tingling was already being tempered by doubt.

Had Li told her the truth when she had said that her son was alive, or was it merely another of her treacherous schemes to discredit her before Wo? Was she hoping that she would fail in her attempt to escape and so anger Wo by her continuing disrespect that it might provoke him into punishing her severely or even putting her to death? Sarina turned onto her side and stared bleakly at the wall. If she *did* succeed in locating her son in Hong Kong, how would she go about getting him back? Without proof that he was hers, how was she to walk into the home of strangers and announce that she was the mother of the child they were raising as their own? They would undoubtedly contact Wo and she would have gained nothing.

But if by some bold stroke of good fortune her son *were* returned to her, then what? Should she carry on with her original intentions and return to Oregon as a widow? And what about Janson Carlyle, the unsuspecting father of a

four-month-old boy? In spite of her attempts to convince
herself otherwise, a gnawing guilt kept reminding her that
if their son were indeed alive, Janson had a right to know.

She flicked at her doubts as though they were troublesome gnats, but, persistent, they returned to bother her
just the same. She flipped over onto her back and followed the progress of a sinuous shadow as it streaked in a
wavering path across the ceiling. She had no answers to
any of her questions now, and she knew that if she continued to look for them, she would become paralyzed, incapable of any action whatsoever. She sighed again and turned
onto her stomach and closed her eyes. But she remained
awake, tossing fitfully for the rest of the night.

With all of her precious coins wrapped inside a small
square of white silk which she had knotted and tucked
into her brown silk reticule, Sarina sat stiffly on the leather
seat beside Wo in the open carriage. Each clip-clop, clip-
clop of the horses' hooves was like an added heartbeat
throbbing inside her chest and yet another troubled thought
rattling about inside her head. Wo was grim-faced and
distracted, sitting with his head against the seat and his
eyes closed, varying expressions of anger and grief, determination and even resignation warring for supremacy over
his usually placid features. The sight of him so obviously
distraught, unusual though it was, brought her little
pleasure, but being spared the unbearable necessity of
having to talk to him did.

When the carriage drew up to Chiang Tan's little shop,
Wo seemed unaware of their even having stopped. Sarina
allowed the driver to hand her down and then watched in
mild surprise as he rapped on the door of the shop and
waited until Chiang Tan herself appeared. The woman
bowed to Sarina and then to Wo, who was now sitting up
in his seat with his eyes trained somewhat uncertainly on
Sarina.

"If there were fewer matters requiring my attention, my
dear, I would assist you in your selections," he said in a
voice strangely flat and toneless. "I must, however, leave
you in the capable hands of Chiang Tan instead." He
signaled to the driver. "I will return for you in three
hours."

As Sarina gazed after the departing carriage, she silently thanked him. While Sua and Li remained bound to the estate and received shopkeepers like Chiang Tan with a great fuss and flourish, she was still being permitted the freedom granted to an outsider—the very freedom which would enable her to effect her escape. Still, when she turned to Chiang Tan with a forced but amiable smile, she felt somewhat like a prisoner who has just been handed over to her jailer.

She was surprised to find the shop filled with chattering women, many of them Americans like herself, who were obviously here to outfit themselves for the just-beginning social season. While some of the women were busily unwinding various bolts of cloth and others were attempting to match appropriate trims to the fabrics they had already selected, all of them seemed to be anxiously competing for the attention of the diminutive Chiang Tan. Sarina smiled to herself, knowing that the overcrowded shop could only work to her advantage. When Chiang Tan led her to one of the small curtained rooms ahead of several women who had expected to be next, she listened to their grumbles of disapproval with mounting satisfaction.

She stood in the cubicle in her simple brown-and-yellow daisy-sprigged muslin gown as bolt after bolt of exquisitely embroidered silk was brought in to her, and feigned great interest in each of them. With practiced ease Chiang Tan would unwind several yards of the silk and drape it expertly across Sarina's shoulder and then stand back while Sarina examined the effect with a thoughtful frown of concentration. Then she would shake her head with a regretful sigh and wait for Chiang Tan to fetch several more bolts for her to consider. With carefully disguised delight she observed the poor woman's growing impatience with her.

"Missy need three gown," she said, her voice faintly pleading. "How you find three if no like cloth?"

Sarina rewarded her concern with a wide-eyed look of simple innocence. "This is a very special occasion," she told her quietly. "I would dishonor the house of Wo if I chose hastily."

The woman mumbled something under her breath and bent to pick up some of the bolts of silk from the floor, saying, "Excuse, please, look for others."

Each time the woman left the room, it took longer for her to return again. Finally Sarina decided that the game had gone on long enough. She peeked out from between the drawn curtains and met the hostile stares of two middle-aged American women, their personal maids standing behind them laden with bolts of cloth, obviously waiting for her room. As soon as she saw Chiang Tan entering one of the other cubicles, Sarina hastily slipped out of hers and headed for the door. Turning around for just a moment, she barely managed to suppress a laugh when she saw the two women rushing toward her vacated room, elbowing each other out of the way.

It was a brief ricksha ride to the red-brick building on the Bund, expanded now as Janson had planned, to include the smaller one-story red-brick building next to it. She paid the driver and approached the office of the Carlyle Trading Company with a mixture of anticipation and dread. When she pushed open the door, she imagined him standing behind it and sweeping her a deep bow as he welcomed her inside. But there was no one standing there to welcome her when she walked in. There was only a large room with whitewashed walls hung with maps, and five young Oriental men working behind cluttered wooden desks.

With her back straight and her head held high, she banished her ridiculous notions from her mind and walked over to the young man seated at the desk nearest her. Yet, even as she waited for him to look up and acknowledge her there, she found herself wondering which of the offices opening off that main room was reserved for Janson.

"Yes, please?" The young man was looking up at her now with a cordial smile on his smooth, bland face.

"Could you please tell me when your next ship will be leaving for Hong Kong?" she inquired, wondering if her voice sounded as shaky to him as it did to her.

"Moment, please, I see." He nodded obligingly.

From among the various ledgers and papers scattered across the top of his desk he located a wide, flat black-bound book and snapped it open. One long, slim finger traced its way slowly down the first narrow column of neat script on the left-hand page and then followed the same procedure on the right-hand page. With each name he passed over, Sarina's stomach took another downward turn.

Had she actually believed one would be leaving that same afternoon? she asked herself. As unlikely as that was, she knew that if a ship *were* leaving for Hong Kong that afternoon, she was prepared to board that ship with only the clothes she was wearing, without her father's precious Bible and without even saying good-bye to Chen.

The finger stopped at last and the young man looked up again with a smile. "Three day," he told her. "*Jade Star* sail Hong Kong twelve noon."

"Three days," she repeated. She would have to return to the estate after all, and then she would have to find some way of getting back to the city again.

"Does the ship take passengers?" she asked.

"Oh, yes, *Jade Star* most comfortable ship. Very new," he said proudly. "Very fast."

Sarina began to untie the strings of her reticule. "Please book a cabin for me, then."

He opened the drawer and pulled out several small sheets of printed white paper. "Name, please?"

She hesitated just for a moment. "Mrs. Thomas," she replied. "Mrs. John Thomas."

With her ticket tucked safely away inside her purse, Sarina returned to Chiang Tan's shop armed with an appropriate explanation for her disappearance. But she need not have worried. When she arrived back at the shop, she noticed that Chiang Tan had been too busy to even realize she was gone.

It was knowing that she had to carry on as if nothing were any different that made the waiting so difficult. And what saddened her most was knowing that she would be unable to say good-bye properly to the three young girls who had been such an important part of her life for nearly one year. And yet, she reasoned, how could she explain to them that she had to leave them because she had a child of her own to care for now? She could only hope that when they learned she had left without telling them, they would not think too unkindly of her.

The evening before her scheduled departure, she slipped into Chen's room one last time. The changes in him tore at her heart and brought a gush of hot tears to her eyes. With his back covered by a square of fine white cotton cloth and his features tinged with gray, he provided a ghoulish contrast to the crimson-quilted coverlet with its cheerful pattern of large yellow chrysanthemums that he was lying on. His handsomeness was slowly being devoured by starvation and grief. His cheeks were sunken and his small, broad nose seemed to rise like a beacon from a weathered and decaying landscape.

"Oh, Chen," she murmured as she crouched beside his bed. "What have you allowed them to do to you in the name of love?"

She touched his cheek, a cheek which felt like a dry and withered leaf, and she bent closer to his ear to speak to him.

"I've come to say good-bye to you, Chen," she whispered. "I'm leaving, just as you would have left if the gods had been kinder to you." She swiped at the tears sliding down her cheeks. "I . . . I'm leaving tomorrow, Chen."

She smoothed his lank black hair with her hand and felt how dry and warm his forehead was.

"Chen, my dearest friend, you can't die," she pleaded. "You mustn't die. Please fight to stay alive. You have to live for your sake and for Mei's. In love, there can never be a true parting, because it's not like death. Death is final, Chen, one never returns after death. But as long as you're alive, there's always the chance that one day, by the will of the gods, you and Mei will find each other again. Please, Chen, please live!"

The unseeing eyes blinked. The lips which had refused to utter a single sound began to move. "Sarina." It was a hoarse whisper rising from the chasm of death.

She brushed the hair back from her face and pressed her ear close to his mouth.

"Go with the smile of the gods warm on your back, my dearest friend, and do not mourn for me. I have loved as few are permitted to love, and I am content now to die."

"You can't," she sobbed, longing to take him by the shoulders and shake him. "You must live, Chen, you must!"

He weakly shook his head. "It is you who must live now, Sarina, for only when there is love is there life." A cough broke off his words, but a moment later he continued. "Go to him whom you have spurned and share with him what you once permitted two strangers to share. Love him, Sarina, as he most assuredly loves you."

Sarina gasped. What was he saying? Her head began to

reel. He was delirious, she decided. A fever was obviously affecting his mind. Love? There *was* no love for her to share with Janson Carlyle, and there never had been. But like Mei, had Chen suspected all along exactly what *had* been there between Janson Carlyle and herself? And Wo? He must have suspected too, and played them both for fools. Suddenly Sarina felt something stir inside her. Had she, then, been the biggest fool of all?

Setting aside her own conflicted emotions, she seized Chen's face with both hands. "Listen to me, Chen. If you want me to live by your command, then you must agree to live by mine." He tried to turn his head away, but she held him fast. "I want you to live, do you hear me? I want you to live for the woman who's waiting to become your wife and for the children who will bear your name and worship you after you're gone. But most of all I want you to outlive those who used your love against you and separated you from that love, so that one day you can find a way to be together again."

A choking sob escaped him then. He closed his eyes and allowed the tears to flow unchecked down his sunken cheeks. Weakly he raised his arms and clasped them around Sarina's neck. She pressed her face against his and gently stroked his head while he wept, willing some of her own strength and her own life to enter his frail and ravaged body and return him from the encroaching shades to the shores of light again.

When he seemed to have fallen asleep, she kissed him tenderly on the forehead and whispered one last good-bye to him. With a leaden heart she trudged from his room and cautiously approached Li's bedchamber farther along the deserted corridor. Li opened the door almost immediately. She still refused to come downstairs, and so she was dressed only in her lavender dressing robe. But her face was carefully powdered and rouged and her black hair, although unadorned, was intricately arranged. Her kohl-lined eyes narrowed suspiciously for an instant as she studied Sarina's solemn face.

"I need a sleeping potion" was all Sarina said before she turned on her heel and walked back down the corridor again.

*　　*　　*

The *Jade Star* was sailing in another four hours. Sarina winced as she tightened the broad silk sash around her stomach and felt her father's Bible dig deeper into her tender flesh. She wore only a pair of lawn pantaloons under her full-skirted gown this morning, having discarded her corset and crinolettes in favor of being able to breathe. Draping her brown wool shawl over her shoulders, she carefully arranged its trailing ends so that they completely covered the slight bulge beneath her brown-and-white-striped muslin gown, and slipped the ropes of her brown silk reticule over her wrist. In spite of her determination not to allow herself a moment's backward longing, she weakened in her resolve and slid the balcony panels open for a final glimpse of the inner courtyard and the flowering back gardens. Then she looked around her bedroom one more time.

She swept down the staircase and headed for Wo's study, while the sharp corners of the Bible jabbed away at her stomach and the tops of her thighs. With each determined step she took, she hoped she wasn't grimacing from the discomfort of carrying such a heavy book strapped to her body. Was the bulge at all visible? Was she trembling, but unaware of it? Were her eyes inordinately bright? Did her purse appear to be weighted down as it dangled from her wrist? The palms of her hands were clammy as she knocked on the door of the study and then opened it to stand in the protective shadows just inside the doorway.

Wo glanced up from his desk and scowled. "You are dressed for an outing," he said. "Are there to be no lessons today?"

She gave him a helpless smile. "If there are, then I'm afraid none of my gowns will be ready in time for the wedding. As you well know, Chiang Tan is as demanding of her clients as she is of her staff, and because time is so short, she asked me to return to her shop today to have the robes fitted."

"Why does she not simply bring them here when she brings the robes for Sua and Li?" he demanded.

Sarina felt the room beginning to tilt in front of her. "Unfortunately, Chiang Tan won't be bringing the robes here at all," she lied smoothly. "One of her women will be coming here instead. She asked me to explain to you that because the season is beginning in the city, it's impossible for her to leave the shop for an entire day."

"She would dare to choose the wives of some American merchants over the women of Wo Shue Kwen?" he blustered, half-rising from his seat. "Agh!" he spit, sitting down hard in his chair again. "I have no patience for such frivolous matters today." He rubbed at his eyes with both hands and sighed. "If Lao Hong Han should learn of the state of my unworthy son, there will be no marriage, and you will have no need of such robes."

For a moment he seemed to be vacillating. Then he clapped his hands together twice and waited impatiently for one of the male servants to appear in the doorway.

"Fetch my carriage," he commanded, "and send for Shi-duo."

Sarina had been prepared for this, and she did not flinch.

"Shi-duo will accompany you," said Wo, waving her away with an imperious flick of his wrist and returning to the papers before him.

Sarina remained in the doorway for just another moment. She took one long, final look at him—at the set of his features, the tilt of his head, the strength in his shoulders as he hunched over his papers. Firm in her resolve, with his face and body imprinted upon her memory, she closed the study door, secure in the knowledge that if all went well, she would never see him again.

As she crossed the front hall, she glanced up at the head of the stairs at the figure she had known would be there. Li was standing there proudly, resplendent in robes of emerald-green silk richly embroidered with blue irises and white peonies, with emeralds set in her hair, swinging from her ears, and flashing at her wrists and on her fingers, prepared to resume her rightful place once more. Sarina approached the foot of the staircase and waited. Li glanced cautiously around her and then sent a small black silk pouch sailing through the air to land at Sarina's feet. Sarina hastily tucked the tiny sack into her reticule and looked up at Li again. To her astonishment, the woman was bowing to her. In spite of the pressure of her father's Bible as she bent forward, Sarina returned her former enemy's gesture with a deep bow of her own. For them it was their first formal greeting and their last farewell.

Shi-duo was the servant who had stood next to Chen when he had been flogged that day. Now he was sitting beside Sarina in stolid silence, with his arms folded across his chest and his black eyes staring straight ahead of him. Sarina, breathing in shallow and irregular gasps, both from nervous anticipation and from the edges of the Bible cutting into her, busied her shaking hands by stroking the small purse settled in her lap as if she were stroking the fur of a cat. When the carriage finally halted before the familiar shop, Shi-duo helped her down and then settled himself in one of the two wicker chairs on the narrow porch in front of the shop.

"Why missy here?" exclaimed a startled Chiang Tan as she paused in her helping of a customer. "Change mind?"

Sarina dismissed the presumption with a wave of her hand. "I thought I would choose the silk for two more gowns," she declared grandly, her eyes covetously sweeping the well-stocked shelves.

"A pleasure." Chiang Tan smiled, bowing to her. "Great pleasure."

It was with smug satisfaction that Sarina noted the bristling impatience on the face of the young American woman whom Chiang Tan had been serving.

"Please don't let me interrupt you," she said as she breezed over to one of the brimming shelves. "After all the difficulty I had the other day, I'd much rather you tended to your other clients until I'm certain about my choices."

"Very good, missy." The woman nodded, returning to the bolt of pale gray silk she had started to unroll before Sarina came in.

Sarina worked her way through numerous bolts of cloth, smiling at Chiang Tan each time their eyes met, relieved when she could relax in her charade whenever the woman disappeared into one of the curtained rooms to the rear of the shop. After a while Sarina asked for a cup of tea, as well as one for Shi-duo. No sooner had Chiang Tan brought her the tea than she went off with another customer. Sarina tugged the little pouch from her purse, and turning her back to the room, emptied the contents of the sack into one of the cups. Her heart was beating wildly as one trembling finger stirred the scalding tea to make certain the powder was mixed and that no traces remained on the

sides of the cup. Then she tucked the black pouch away
and pulled the strings to close her reticule again.

"Tea?" She smiled benignly at the grim-faced servant,
whose dark eyes seemed even darker by virtue of the
somber black jacket and trousers he was wearing.

He accepted the cup without hesitation, nodding to her
with his eyes respectfully downcast. She waited until he
had taken his first sip of the tea before stepping back
inside the shop. She sifted aimlessly through several baskets of buttons and satin trimmings and waited. Her forehead was soon beaded with perspiration and the back of
her gown was starting to stick to her skin. She wiped at
her forehead with one end of her shawl and pretended to
be absorbed in examining a bolt of glimmering gold silk
embroidered with scarlet poppies and silver pussywillows
when Chiang Tan came back into the room.

"Missy like?" she inquired.

Sarina jumped. "Y-yes," she stammered. "No . . . I mean,
it's too bright." She vaguely pointed to the scarlet poppies
and shook her head.

Chiang Tan pursed her lips. "Missy no like tea?" She
nodded at Sarina's full cup.

"It's cold now, I'm sorry." She laughed nervously. "I was
so busy looking at the silk that I forgot about it. Could I
trouble you for a fresh cup?"

"No trouble," said the woman. "A pleasure." She bowed
and took the cup with her to the rear of the shop.

Sarina used that moment to slip outside again. Scarcely
daring to look, she could see that Shi-duo was slumped
forward in his chair, with his head resting against his
chest, looking for all the world as if he had simply gotten
bored and fallen asleep. It had worked! The empty cup
lay tipped on its side next to his wicker chair. Sarina
hastily righted the cup, and then, without another backward glance, she ran into the street and signaled to the
young ricksha driver leaning against the building beside
Chiang Tan's shop. He helped her up into the tilting
bamboo seat, picked up the two long bamboo poles at-
tached to the seat, and started off down the street at a
brisk pace.

When they reached the harbor, Sarina was breathless
and filmed with perspiration, feeling as if she, and not the
boy, had run all that way. She pressed a coin into his hand

and stepped onto the wooden planks of the pier. She heard none of the hawkers' cries and saw none of the cluttered stalls clogging the streets of the waterfront. All she could hear was the joyful thumping of her heart; all she could see was the name *Jade Star* printed in bold white letters across the dark wooden hull of the sleek clipper riding at anchor just ahead of her. She moved slowly toward the ship with a sense of having walked that way many times before. But it had been only once before, and that had been a year ago. She allowed several couples to board ahead of her, while she held back, turning around again for a final glimpse of the harbor.

All the emotions she had managed to keep in check bubbled perilously close to the surface as her eyes swept the waterfront, grazed the trees lining the Bund, and continued upward to the grand pillared houses and flowering shrubs nestled on the crest of the hill. She lowered her gaze and trained it on a distant estate she could no longer see, an estate where mulberry leaves were being fed to the silkworms, where three young girls were awaiting the return of their tutor, and where preparations were under way for a wedding which might never be. She thought of Chen and her heart missed a beat. Of all the hearts she had left beating there, she knew that only one of them would now be lifting with joy.

She turned, and with her head held high, vowed to put the pain of the recent past behind her. When she walked on board the *Jade Star*, all she was thinking of was the future and the son she was setting out to reclaim.

19

Fragrant harbor. That was what the words Hong Kong meant. But there was nothing fragrant about the street outside Sarina's hotel. The capital city of Victoria was divided into eastern and western sections by Queen's Road, and the run-down Waverley Hotel was wedged into a kind of no-man's-land between the two of them. On one side sprawled Chinatown, with its dilapidated wooden shacks and shanties, bedraggled shops and stalls, poor sanitation and air laden with the smells of cooking, rotting food, and too many unwashed bodies crammed into too small a space. On the other side of Queen's Road lay official Victoria, where the privileged Westerners lived—a clean, open residential area with wide avenues, elegant homes, fine shops, and a number of private social clubs.

As soon as she walked down the hotel steps into the crowded street, Sarina immediately regretted having inhaled such a deep breath of the sodden air. It was as foul in the morning as it had been the previous afternoon, when she had chosen the Waverley as her residence for the duration of her stay in Hong Kong. Because the small hotel had no dining facilities, she purchased a bowl of *congee* from one of the vendors on the street and sat down on one of the hotel steps to eat the lukewarm rice cereal.

Her hunger satisfied for the moment, she set off determinedly, threading her way through the teeming streets, as she headed for the British sector, which lay just beyond the posh Hong Kong Club. Above her there was laundry hanging from rope lines strung across the narrow alleyways and fluttering limply in the feeble breeze. Ahead of her, groups of ragtag women were on their knees scrubbing the pitted streets while they expertly dodged the men and women and shouting children hurrying by. All around her, craftsmen worked busily at their open-air stalls—some carving either ivory or wood or stone, several making paper lanterns, others painting china or decorating paper fans. Fruit stalls offered the curious passersby mangoes, melons, papayas, guavas, and litchis. Adjoining stalls displayed cucumbers, spinach, lotus roots, eggplants, and bamboo shoots. Sarina's mouth began to water, but she quickly turned away from the tempting sight. Fruits and vegetables were precious treats she could ill afford.

When she turned onto Queen's Road, it was just two short blocks to the main post office, an imposing two-story white stone building with three wide stone pillars rising to a triangular pediment above a pair of freshly painted white doors. Sarina stopped for a moment to pat her simply arranged hair into place and to smooth the skirt of her striped muslin gown before proceeding up the broad stone steps. It was only when she stepped into the shaded coolness of the post office, with its wood ceiling fans stirring the air about, that she realized just how hot and humid the streets had been.

A middle-aged man with an angular face and balding head, with a manner more befitting a butler than a postal clerk, swept up to the marble counter and peered curiously at her.

Not in the least intimidated by the man's attitude, Sarina said, "I'd like the address of Lewis Deane, please."

"Certainly, madam," he replied, moving slowly back to his desk and opening a worn-looking book bound in navy-blue leather. After perusing it for a moment, he scribbled something on a slip of paper, closed the book, and returned to the counter. "There you are, madam," he announced brusquely, pushing the paper toward her. "Number eighteen Casuarina Road."

Sarina's hands were trembling as she tucked the paper into her reticule and drew the strings closed again. "Could you please tell me how to get there?" she inquired.

He shot her a scathing look. "I hardly imagine you'll find anyone at home, madam."

"Why not?" Sarina felt a momentary twinge of panic.

"The rainy season, of course, madam. Very few families remain in Hong Kong during the summer." He wrinkled his nose disdainfully. "Far too dangerous, madam, what with the heat and the dampness and the possibility of some foul pestilence spreading up this way from the wretched harbor front."

Although somewhat discouraged, Sarina refused to be dissuaded. "I appreciate your concern," she said, "but I'd still like to know how to get to Casuarina Road, if you don't mind."

"Very well, madam." His tone suggested that he had already washed his hands of her, but he gave her the directions nonetheless.

She thanked him with an equal measure of frostiness in her own voice and left. No sooner had she closed the door of the post office behind her than she was enveloped by a cloud of moist, tepid air. Following his instructions, she began her slow climb up Palm Tree Way, one of the city's many ladder streets, so called because they rose in steeply graded steps from the harbor to the highest part of the island, called the Peak, stopping every now and then to catch her breath. As she dabbed continually at her skin with a white linen handkerchief, she could see why the more fortunate residents of the island abandoned the city during the summer months. The combination of the heat and the rain-soaked air was truly unbearable.

Forcing her tired feet to take her up the last few steps, she was relieved to find herself on a broad tree-lined street called Banyan, which she knew would lead her directly onto Casuarina. It was cooler here, the great leafed trees along the road not only affording her shade from the occasional stabs of brilliant sunlight but also providing her with a welcome hint of a fresh breeze as well. While the Peak was reserved for the wealthiest British and American families, this residential area contained the homes of the comfortable middle class, men like Lewis Deane himself. Set behind rows of neatly clipped box hedges among well-tended green lawns and flowerbeds planted with geometric precision, the houses were so similar that it was difficult to tell one from the other.

Number eighteen Casuarina was a house like most of the other houses—a white stucco two-story dwelling with a peaked red tile roof tucked away behind a box hedge and comfortably banked by frothy clusters of fuchsia and pink azalea bushes. A flagstone path led up to a front door, painted the same slate gray as the window shutters, which were closed against the damp heat of the day.

As Sarina stood there staring at the house, she was besieged by a rush of warring emotions—hope and despair, excitement and dread, joyful certainty and terrible doubt. All the questions she had refused to consider before lest they immobilize her came together now in one great maddened clash inside her head. What was she going to say to the people inside that house? She took an unsteady step forward and then stopped. What if the clerk in the post office had been right? She shook the grim possibility from her thoughts and took several more steps up the walk. What if Li had lied to her and the child inside that house was not hers at all? She tottered uncertainly on the top step and pressed a trembling fist to her mouth, while she garnered the strength she needed to take those final few steps and then lift the brass door knocker.

To her, the slamming sound of brass on brass shattered the calm of the entire neighborhood. The door was answered by a young Chinese houseboy wearing a long-sleeved white cotton jacket and white trousers and a pair of soft black slippers.

"Yes, please?" He gazed inquiringly up at her.

"Is Mrs. Deane at home?" she asked in as even a voice as she could manage.

She found herself staring at him incredulously as he shook his head. "Missy Deane in England."

A deep pit opened up inside her, and Sarina felt herself sliding down into it. She gripped the sides of the door-frame to keep from losing her balance.

"Visit family in Sussex," he continued. "Not come home many month. Wait for summer end."

The clerk had been right after all. Sarina blinked back the onrush of tears to her eyes. She lacked the funds to follow the woman to England, yet, if she did, what guarantee would she have of Anne Deane's even being there when she arrived? What if she left for the Continent or decided to return to Hong Kong earlier than planned?

"Missy ill?"

Sarina shook her head. "No . . ." Her voice wavered. "I'm not ill."

Part of her stubbornly refused to believe him. She strained to catch him in a lie, to hear the crying of a child or to see a child's playthings scattered about on the floor of the darkened hall behind him.

"Is Mr. Deane in Hong Kong, then?" she asked hopefully.

Again the boy shook his head. "He in Europe. Much work."

"And will be returning with Mrs. Deane?"

In spite of his polite nod, he appeared most anxious to close the door.

"And their son?" she persisted, thrusting her foot out to keep the door open awhile longer.

He seemed surprised at her question. "He with Missy Deane. Excuse, please."

She stepped back finally, watching as the door closed in her face and slammed shut on her hopes. For a few minutes all she could do was stare at that grim gray door. The longer she stared at it, the more of a challenge it became. It was an obstacle she was determined to surmount. If her son did in fact live behind that door, nothing and no one would keep her from breaking it down to get to him. She turned and strode back down the flagstone path. Her mind was made up. She would remain in Hong Kong until the Deanes returned, and then she would confront them. She would fight them for her son, and she would win.

The weeks dragged by with tedious monotony, while her money disappeared with alarming speed. She had bought two muslin gowns from an inexpensive ready-to-wear shop near the harbor, and a second pair of shoes when her only pair was worn through, and these purchases had seriously depleted her funds. She was now eating *congee* for her lunch and then waiting until as late in the evening as possible before buying some soup or fish stew from one of the merchants on the street. By ten o'clock, most of them were tired and anxious to return to their homes, and the wilted vegetables and bruised fruit she was often able to buy at reduced prices would serve as her breakfast.

Despite her meager wardrobe and her skimpy meals, it was the weather she found most demoralizing. When it was not raining, the damp heat seemed to be a living thing, breathing foul fumes into her lungs, while it sucked whatever freshness there might have been out of the air, to leave it feeling like a malodorous sponge. Its smell lived in the sheets on her bed, in the walls of her room and in her clothes. Mildew sprang up on the bedposts and on the mirror, and one morning she awoke to find a spongy gray fungus beginning to grow on the floor near the door. The hotel keeper advised her to use carbolic acid to keep the mildew under control, and her room was soon reeking of the noxious fumes given off by the acid.

The monotony of her days, coupled with her anxious state of mind, conspired to make sleep an elusive entity she pursued with mounting frustration. She would lie on her damp and lumpy mattress at night and look at her three soiled gowns hanging from the rope she had strung across her room in an effort to keep them dry and free of mildew, and she would long to feel against her skin again the silken coolness of the exquisite robes she had once worn. Gazing at the pathetic fruits and vegetables in the chipped porcelain bowl on top of her bureau, she would try to recall each separate taste of the many exotic foods she had come to enjoy. And instead of the dank stench of her shabby little room, she would imagine she could smell the jasmine again, drifting toward her on the wings of a breeze.

As her horde of silver coins dwindled dangerously low, Sarina began to despair. She would have to find some way to support herself if she intended to wait until the fall, when the Deanes were to return. Perhaps there was a mission school on the island, or some family requiring the services of a tutor or nanny. She considered her three worn gowns, and her heart sank. No one would hire her if she presented herself in such shoddy attire. And yet, to spend her precious funds on an elegant ensemble without even the prospect of gainful employment seemed a rather foolhardy thing to do. As she had done with her problem of the mildew, she decided one night to take her latest concern to the hotel keeper, an aging American who had given up the life of a sailor ten years before to run the Waverley Hotel for the failed son of a prominent British family, who was living out his dissolute life on a pension and in obscurity in one of the hotel's larger rooms.

He squinted up at her from his chair behind the counter in the dim lobby of the hotel, pushed his spectacles farther up on his bulbous nose, and chewed thoughtfully on the stem of his battered pipe while she shifted from one foot to the other and waited.

"A job, you say?" He scratched the top of his head, where a few gray hairs could still be found. "I think you'd better be thinkin' about goin' back home instead, young lady. Ain't many jobs round here for the likes of you."

"Surely you must know of a mission school on the island," she prodded him.

He shook his head. "This ain't China, missy," he said. "Ain't a one I know about."

"Then perhaps I could work as a governess or a nanny for some British or American family."

"Sure you could," he agreed. "Come September, you can have your pick, but right now there ain't a family around worth talkin' to."

She finally drew herself up stiffly and announced in a clear, firm voice, "All right, then, I'll look for work at one of the taverns near the harbor or in one of the shops—"

His coarse laugh drowned out the rest of her words. "Before you go gettin' as desperate as that, whyn't you try some place you can make a whole lot of money for darned little work? Heck, you might even like it."

"And where might that be?" she inquired coolly, resenting the way he seemed to be making fun of her now.

"There's plenty of them places for a gal lookin' to make herself quick money," he said, "but I think you're more special than most. Only the best for you, right?"

She was studying him now through narrowed eyes.

"I know a place they'd go crazy for someone with hair like yours. Yessir, missy, you take yourself down to Dragon Flower Street."

"Dragon Flower Street?"

"Yes, ma'am, you can't miss the place, but if you do, just ask. Everybody knows about Madam Blue."

She reeled backward as if she had just been shot. Her eyes were wide, her mouth open, as she absorbed the full impact of the name he had just thrown out so casually to her. Madam Blue! All the time she had been assuming the brothel was in Shanghai, Mei was right there in Hong Kong.

"You all right, young lady?" He was gaping at her, his pipe dangling precariously from his bottom lip. "Hey, if I hurt your feelin's I sure as heck didn't mean to. Hey, now, don't you go runnin' off like that, I said I was sorry!"

Sarina dashed out the door and down the steps, ignoring the awkward apologies he shouted after her. What he was saying now no longer mattered, it was what he had said before that really counted. She laughed out loud and drew a number of curious stares from some of the fruit vendors hurrying past her. For the first time in so many dismal weeks, she could smile again, if only at the irony of it all. Mei was in Hong Kong! She glanced about her excitedly, wondering which was the way to the house on Dragon Flower Street. And then suddenly she sobered. This was hardly an ordinary social call she was planning to make. How exactly *did* one go about paying a visit to a brothel?

Her footsteps slowed. She kicked at a pebble lying on the road with the toe of her shoe, followed after it, and then kicked it again. It was nighttime. From what little she knew of houses of ill repute, nighttime was when the women worked. She frowned. It was impossible to imagine her sweet and lovely Mei being paid to make love to one strange man after another, when her young body deserved to know only the body of the man who had risked his life to love her. Thinking about it brought all of her bittersweet memories sweeping back again, storming the wall she had erected over the past weeks to keep them safely at bay. She wiped at her eyes with the heel of her hand and turned back in the direction of the hotel again. She would wait until morning, and then she would ask the way to the house of Madam Blue.

She had just passed a cabaret, where a singsong girl was entertaining the customers, when she suddenly stopped short. How could it be? It was Shi-duo! Shi-duo and the servant who had flogged Chen one hundred times. Both men appeared to be drunk, for as they were stumbling into the cabaret, Shi-duo slammed into the doorjamb and his companion had to steady him with one arm to keep him on his feet. In spite of the heat of the night, Sarina began to shiver uncontrollably.

She backed away from the cabaret, then turned and ran all the way back to the hotel. She slammed the door to her room and leaned up against it, panting and running with perspiration. What a fool she had been to think she could escape so easily! She had been so preoccupied with waiting out the time until the Deanes returned that she had given little thought to Wo's pursuing her.

Had Wo suspected Li's complicity in her disappearance and found a way of forcing her to tell him where she was? Could Wo even be there in Hong Kong himself? A spasm of sick fear nearly doubled her over. To think that she had successfully escaped from the estate, only to run the risk of being found and returned to him. There would be no escaping a second time, of that she was certain.

As her heartbeats slowed and her breathing became more regular, she tried to think more clearly. Wo had offices in Hong Kong. Perhaps the presence of his two servants on the island had nothing whatsoever to do with her. That possibility brought her a moment's relief, but no more. There could be others on the island with them, men she would not even recognize. She could pass any one of them on the street and never know it. But they would most assuredly know her. She crossed the floor and stared glumly out of her open window onto the street below. Gone now were all thoughts of gainful employment; what she needed now was a place to hide.

She lay down on her bed fully clothed and gazed up at the limp gowns hanging like two headless women from the rope above her head. She put her hands around her throat, felt the life pulsing there, and shuddered at how easily that life could be squeezed out of her. Reaching over to the nightstand, she picked up her father's Bible and hugged it to her chest. She turned onto her side, brought her knees up to her chest, and closed her eyes.

In the morning she would locate Mei and ask the girl to help her find a place to hide. Mei would help her—she had given her her word; they were sisters. Mei would find a place where she would be safe until . . . until . . .

She fell asleep with the name of her son on her lips.

The three-story structure stood on a street like all the other streets in Chinatown. Among the twisted wooden houses, crammed up against one another in jumbled confusion, the large stucco building, with its freshly white-washed walls and peaked roof of perfectly matched red clay tiles, looked strangely out of place. The shutters were painted a brilliant blue, and against the splotchy drabness of the other buildings it seemed as if a part of the summer

sky had been trapped inside those shutters. Heavy draperies were drawn across the windows, and as Sarina climbed
the steps to the wide stone stoop, mindful of the curious
looks of a number of passing hawkers, she noticed that the
curtains were the same shade of blue as the shutters.

A well-dressed young man, obviously British, opened
the door just as she was about to raise the brass knocker,
and nearly slammed into her on his way out. His face was
flushed and he was nervously tugging at his striped silk
cravat. When he caught Sarina staring after him, he paused,
pulled off his broad-brimmed white straw hat, and bowed
stiffly to her.

"Terribly sorry," he muttered, jamming his hat back on
his head again and continuing down the steps to the
discreetly curtained enclosed carriage which had just drawn
up to the curb.

Sarina giggled, wondering whose betrothed or errant
husband she had embarrassed by witnessing his hasty departure from a brothel at six o'clock in the morning. In
his nervousness, he had failed to close the front door
properly, and Sarina immediately took advantage of his
oversight. Opening the door, she stepped into a large tiled
foyer and then into the main hall of the house, which
opened onto several small receiving rooms. As her eyes
gradually became accustomed to the light, she sucked in
her breath and then released it very, very slowly.

It seemed as if the entire house had been painted by a
celestial cerulean brush, giving her the sensation of floating weightless in a cloudless sky. The walls were all hung
in blue silk, and cascading ropes of blue porcelain beads
served to divide one room from another. Ornate brass
wall sconces topped with small blue silk shades bathed the
rooms in a delicate azure glow. Groupings of low blue silk
sofas and wide blue silk armchairs, together with square
white lacquered tables and blue-and-white woven silk rugs,
were artfully placed about each room. Standing on many
of the lacquered tables were blue gourd-shaped porcelain
vases holding arrangements of gray pussywillows, yellow
roses, and pinks, the only pastel departure from the stark
blue-and-whiteness of the place.

And pervading the entire house was a sense of calm. Of
peace. No street sounds penetrated its walls, no unruly
clamor begged entry from the world outside. It seemed to

hang suspended in a protected space all its own, holding out a promise of peace and tranquillity to anyone who entered and wished to escape forever from the bonds of a crueler earth.

"Are you looking for someone?"

Sarina spun around at the sound of a woman's clipped tones behind her. Standing there in the doorway was a startlingly beautiful girl wearing a high-necked blue sheath of a gown that melted along each curve of her slender but voluptuous body. Her thick auburn hair was drawn up into a fanciful confection of curls and adorned with blue silk flowers, and the lids of her frosty gray eyes were painted to match the blue of her gown.

"Are you certain you've come to the right place, then?" the girl inquired, her pale eyes sweeping Sarina's worn and soiled muslin gown.

"This *is* the house of Madam Blue, isn't it?" Sarina asked, bristling under the girl's scrutiny.

"It is."

"Is there a girl named Mei here?"

Suddenly the other girl's eyes narrowed. What had merely been curiosity before was now obviously suspicion.

"Please, if she's here," Sarina hurried on, "would you tell her that Sarina is asking for her."

"Sarina?" the girl repeated as her expression shifted again. "Yes"—she nodded solemnly—"Mei is here."

"Would you take me to her, then?" Sarina exclaimed excitedly.

The girl hesitated. "I don't think I would see her right now if I were you," she said. "I'm afraid she may have a bit of difficulty recognizing you at the moment."

"I don't understand."

"She's not very well, you see. She spends all of her time locked away in her room, dreaming, as it were." She made a helpless fluttering gesture with her hands. "You see, Sarina, your friend Mei is addicted to opium."

She recoiled. "Oh, God, no, not Mei."

"That was how I knew your name," the girl explained. "Although Mei has spoken to no one since the day she first arrived, her room adjoins mine, and when she smokes one of her pipes, she dreams and calls out the names of those with whom she was obviously close before she came

here. She has repeatedly called out your name, as well as
the name of someone called Chen."

"You must let me see her," Sarina insisted. "She'll recognize me, I know she will."

"I think perhaps I should waken Madam Blue and—"

"No!" Sarina stood firm. "I want to see her now. If you
won't take me to her now, then I'll find her by myself."

The girl gave in with a shrug of her shoulders. "Very
well, then, follow me."

They climbed a curving mahogany staircase to the second floor, turning left down a corridor hung in the same
blue silk as the rooms downstairs and lighted by the same
blue-shaded oil lamps. There were a number of blue doors
on either side of the corridor. The girl stopped at the last
one on the right, knocked twice, and then opened the
door and motioned for Sarina to go in. As soon as she
entered the room, she was assailed by the stale, bittersweet
odor of opium.

The heavy blue silk draperies were drawn against the
intrusion of the morning, the only light coming from the
small brass oil lamp burning on the white lacquered bedside table, on which an empty opium pipe and a stylet
were resting. Like the rooms downstairs, Mei's bedroom
was hung in blue silk, the two armchairs set in front of the
windows were covered in the same silk, and the low, wide
bed upon which Mei's emaciated form was lying was fitted
with a thick blue quilted coverlet.

At the sight of the girl who was lost within the folds of
her blue silk dressing gown, Sarina's chest constricted in
pity. The figure on the bed was a fleshless image of the
Mei she had known, the girl whose sweet voice had banished the ghosts from so many of Sarina's nights, whose
gentle presence had been such a soothing comfort to her.
Kneeling beside the bed, Sarina began to gently stroke the
matted braid of hair lying across Mei's sunken cheek and
hanging limply over one shoulder. Deep in her sleep, Mei
reached up and scratched her cheek, as if to ease the itch
of some imagined insect's sting.

"Mei," Sarina called to her. "Mei, wake up, it's Sarina.
Sarina's here to see you."

The figure on the bed suddenly twitched. She moistened her lips with the tip of her tongue and then began to
snore softly.

"Mei." Sarina gave her a light shake. "Wake up, Mei. It's Sarina."

After shaking her several more times and calling her name, Sarina got to her feet and went to draw the curtains. From the bed came the sounds of a grumbled protest as the warmth of the morning's brightness spilled across the blueness of the secluded room. Sarina hurried back to the bed and again shook Mei by the shoulders, shoulders so thin and bony that she was afraid she might break them if she shook her too hard.

The sooty lashes fluttered and Mei slowly opened her eyes, revealing dark purple smudges beneath her almond-shaped eyes, whose whites were tinged with yellow and crisscrossed by tiny red blood vessels as fine as a spider's web. She pushed herself onto one elbow and squinted up at Sarina as if she had never seen her before. Sarina bent down, cupped Mei's chin in her hand, and brought the girl's face closer to hers.

"Mei, it's Sarina," she said, speaking slowly and clearly, trying to penetrate the protective shroud the girl had wrapped around her fragile frame. "Look at me, Mei, and remember. It's Sarina."

"Sarina," she repeated dully in a voice raspy from sleep and from prolonged use of the opium pipe. "Sarina . . ." She smiled, a disturbingly vacant smile, as if she were seeing her friend in a drug-induced dream.

"Mei, look at me!" Sarina demanded, her voice hard and firm. "I'm here with you now, Mei. Open your eyes again and look at me!"

Suddenly the translucent veil obscuring her vision seemed to lift. Mei began to blink her eyes, while at the same time she released a cry of joy and flung her arms around Sarina's neck. Great heaving sobs racked her body as she buried her head against Sarina's chest, and Sarina, with her own arms locked around Mei's narrow back, held her tightly until her crying stopped.

"Sarina, my sister," murmured Mei, "you have come for me. Chen has sent you for me, as I knew in my heart he would."

Sarina swallowed the truth and shook her head. "Soon, Mei," she told her. "He'll be sending for you very soon, I promise."

But Mei suddenly pulled away from her to sit cross-legged on the bed. She dabbed at her eyes with the sash which bound her dressing gown, and then, in a voice scarcely more than a whisper, she said, "Have you come here to tell me that Chen is dead, Sarina?"

"No, Mei, no." Sarina vehemently denied what could very well be the truth by now. "When I left the estate, he was ill, but he was still alive. Do you hear me, he was still alive!"

"But you are here in Hong Kong," the girl persisted. "Why are you here, my sister, if not to bring me news of Chen?"

"I ran away," Sarina said. "Wo Shue Kwen intended to put me in Li's place so that I might bear him sons. I ran away, but because there's something I must do before I return to America again, I'll have to stay in Hong Kong for a while. But I need your help, Mei. I believe Wo's men are looking for me, and I've come to ask you if you can help me find a place to hide."

"You will not speak of this thing you must do?" she questioned Sarina gently. But when she shook her head, Mei simply smiled in silent understanding. "Then I will not speak of it again."

"And you'll swear never to reveal to anyone who I am or where I came from?"

"As I swore my life to you, so I now swear this too. We are all strangers in this house, my sister, with pasts none will reveal."

She rose unsteadily from the bed and held out one shaking hand to Sarina. "Come," she said. "I will take you now to Madam Blue."

Sarina took hold of Mei's hand. "Will she know of someplace I can hide?" she asked.

Something akin to amusement flickered for a moment in Mei's dull ebony eyes. "Oh, yes"—she nodded—"she will know of a place. She will hide you where none can find you, my sister. She will hide you among us here."

20

Before Sarina could recover from her shock, she was being ushered into the elegant blue bedchamber of the woman who ran one of the most famous and luxurious brothels in the Orient. She stared in fascination as a figure dressed all in blue hobbled toward her on tiny blue-slippered feet. Her ivory skin beneath its carefully applied rice powder had a golden cast to it, and her delicate features combined the most perfect parts of the Asian and the European. Coal-black hair, startlingly lit by a narrow streak of white beginning above her right temple, was drawn back from her face into three braided loops fixed into place by three large diamond pins in the shape of plumed birds. The high-collared, short-sleeved blue silk gown that clung to her slender body was heavily embroidered with silver and had a deep slash daringly cut to the knee up either side of its narrow skirt.

As the woman drew nearer, Sarina found herself staring down into the most breathtakingly beautiful blue eyes she had ever seen. They were the blue of the sky on a cloudless day, the very blue that had been washed over the entire house. When the woman pressed the palms of her hands together and held them against her chest, Sarina noticed that they were trembling violently, that the joints of her fingers were enlarged and red, and that the fingers themselves were slightly twisted. As she bowed to Sarina in greeting, she seemed to be having some difficulty straightening up again, but if she were in pain, nothing in her serene expression or her magnificent jewellike eyes revealed it.

While Mei conferred in a muffled undertone with Madam Blue, the woman's eyes remained fixed on Sarina. She shifted uncomfortably from one foot to the other, ashamed of her shabby attire in the presence of such elegance, but unlike the girl she had met downstairs, there was no condescension in the woman's frank gaze. When Mei had finished speaking, Madam Blue nodded her head several times and then dismissed the girl with a gentle wave of her wrist. Mei bowed first to Madam Blue and then to Sarina and hurried out of the room, leaving the two women alone.

"Mei tells me that you are in flight and in need of shelter," said Madam Blue in a throaty voice tinged with a slight British accent.

Sarina was momentarily stunned by the woman's impeccable English, but she managed to recover quickly enough to nod her head, adding, "I'm also running short of funds, and so I'd gladly work—as long as it would be in a safe place." She hoped that Mei had said nothing to Madam Blue about her staying there.

"Please . . ." The woman indicated one of two blue silk armchairs on either side of an elaborately carved ivory tea stand, and Sarina sank gratefully into the deep, comfortable cushion. Madam Blue perched stiffly on the edge of hers, and Sarina's heart went out to the woman, who was obviously in great pain despite her seemingly ageless beauty.

"Let me ease your troubled mind, my dear, by assuring you that I know nothing about you or why you are in fear for your life, and that is how it shall remain unless you yourself should choose to enlighten me. As Mei has no doubt told you, this is a house of closely guarded pasts."

Sarina sighed. It seemed that Mei had spoken to Madam Blue about her staying there after all.

"I know no more about the girls who pass through these doors than they know about me," the woman continued, "and that has afforded me a comfort so often denied others for nearly thirty years now. Most have entered this house of their own choosing. When others have been referred to me by various agents throughout the world, the names of the agents are the only names I know, since most of the girls here choose fanciful names for themselves as a further safeguard to their own precious pasts."

This was said with a tinge of bitterness, and not for the first time did Sarina find herself wondering about the past of the mysterious Madam Blue and the real name behind the one she had picked for herself thirty years ago.

"Then you don't know who sent Mei to you?" Sarina asked, and was greatly relieved when the woman shook her head.

"All I know is that she was sent here by an agent in Shanghai, and that is all I care to know."

"I see." Sarina nodded and pushed no further.

"Do not think me rude, my dear, if I ask if you have ever been inside a house such as this one before."

Sarina cleared her throat. "No," she said somewhat indignantly, "no, of course I haven't. Why would you ask me that?"

The woman laughed, a husky bubble of laughter. "I asked simply because you are like someone treading on the shell of a quail's egg, both cautious and curious as to what lies inside that egg. Please do not be embarrassed by my forthrightness, my dear. A woman of your obvious breeding would have little reason to suspect that she might one day find herself in such a house. I myself led a most protected life, and I would have been appalled had anyone dared suggest that the path of my life would lead me here. But"—she smiled and encompassed the room with a wide, open sweep of her arms—"in thirty years I have become accustomed to what I am."

Sarina felt a sudden surge of warmth for this frank and enigmatic beauty, and with a mischievous twinkle in her eye she said, "Tell me, Madam Blue, what would you have done if your eyes had been black?"

Again she was treated to that wonderful bubble of throaty laughter. "My dear, to have draped this house in the crepe of mourning might have proved to be the most fiendishly unique contrast to the celebration of life which my exquisite girls so lovingly provide."

As Sarina joined in Madam Blue's exuberant laughter, she suddenly believed that in this unlikeliest of women she might have found an ally and a friend.

But when the laughter subsided, Madam Blue's face and voice grew serious again. "As you have no doubt observed, I am not as well as I would choose to be." She held out her hands, and Sarina again saw how misshapen they were. "As my hands are becoming more twisted, so my body is becoming twisted as well. It is growing increasingly difficult for me to walk up and down the stairs, and it is almost impossible for me to get up from my bed without assistance." Although her eyes held an impish gleam in them now, her mouth was cynical in its set. "Rather an inconvenience for a woman in my profession, would you not agree?"

Sarina's cheeks grew warm at the obvious implication in Madam Blue's words.

"My dear, would you be willing to consider a trade of sorts?" the woman startled her by asking.

"A trade?"

"Yes." Gripping the arms of her chair, Madam Blue leaned closer to Sarina. "Would you consider working here and acting as hostess in my place?"

Sarina gulped.

"You would act as hostess, nothing more—that I can promise you. With a black peruke of human hair, the appropriate *maquillage*, and gowns, a lifetime friend could approach you and never know it was you. So you see, my dear, you would have the ideal disguise as well as the ideal hiding place."

"I don't know." Sarina shifted uncomfortably in her chair.

"By your agreeing to such an arrangement, you would be helping me as well," the woman said softly. "You see, my dear, there are sixteen beautiful young women here, for whom I bear a certain responsibility. Because of my condition, the word has begun to spread that the house of Madam Blue is one of sickness, and poorly run because of it. Houses undeserving of our superior reputation are beginning to surpass us and are now threatening our very existence." She looked down at her crippled hands, and her face was grim. "I have fought against my infirmity a long time now, and perhaps my stubbornness has done irrevocable damage to those who depend on me. But then, perhaps your timely arrival was ordained by the gods themselves. Who is to say?" Her look was now beseeching. "Would you not agree to this, then, for both our sakes, although I realize that as a stranger, you owe me nothing."

"Before I even consider your offer," Sarina said, "could you tell me about Mei? Has she . . . ?" She hesitated. "Has she slept with many men since she came here?"

The woman shook her head. "No," she answered quietly, "Mei has slept with no one."

"But I assumed that would be the only reason for your keeping a girl here."

"Many years ago I learned that to bend with a capricious wind is far better than to be broken because of prideful arrogance," was her gentle reply. "Mei was sent to me a broken spirit, and I could not find it in my heart to put her to work in the position intended for her. I had hoped that with the passage of time she would heal, but I was wrong. To ease her torment, I permitted, even encouraged her to use the pipe, but now I am afraid she refuses to part with it. I believe that without the release the pipe provides, she would take her life."

"And yet you're still keeping her here?" Sarina persisted.

The woman's eyes grew distant, as if she were reaching back into her own shrouded past for some elusive memory. "There are times in the lives of us all when we do, not what we might want to do, but what we have perhaps been destined to do. When we extend a hand in love to someone whose need is greater than our own, we are rewarded many times over. And who is to say when we ourselves may one day have need of a gentle hand extended to us in our own moments of need. You see, my dear, the girls who have made their home with me are the daughters I myself have never borne, and I love them as any mother would love the children of her own body."

Sarina was staggered, humbled by the love pouring from the woman's heart. It was at that moment that she willingly put her fate in the trembling hands of Madam Blue.

It was with little regret that Sarina abandoned the brutal squalor of the world she had been inhabiting to step inside a silken world of muted sounds and heightened sensations spun against the soothing blue of a cloudless sky. The only bedchamber available to her was on the third floor of the house, but when she approached Janella, the British girl she had met that first day, and asked if they might exchange rooms so that she could be next to Mei, the girl readily agreed. While her gowns and wigs were being made for her, Sarina borrowed one of the other girls' gowns and one of Madam Blue's wigs and observed the woman in her role as hostess each evening. She soon learned to speak in a voice scarcely above a whisper, with her eyes properly downcast and her head bowed slightly. Most of their callers were wealthy Englishmen and Americans, with only a handful of Chinese mandarins and businessmen, and although most of them spoke some English, Madam Blue took the precaution of teaching Sarina some essential Chinese phrases nonetheless.

Madam Blue was a patient teacher, and the girls, although secretive about their own pasts, eagerly supplied Sarina with bits of gossip about each of their regular callers. Of the sixteen girls, excluding Mei, five were Oriental, four British, three French, two American, one Italian, and one Spanish. As the others had all chosen exotic names for themselves, so Sarina finally chose one for herself: Dragon Flower, after the street outside the house she saw as her haven from the clamorous world beyond its tranquil blue walls.

On the afternoon her clothes were finally ready, Madam Blue walked Sarina slowly through the house one last time and reiterated what she had explained to her so many times before.

"The house is open each day but Sunday, in order that the girls may have an entire day to themselves. We open our doors each evening at eight o'clock and lock them precisely at one. In this way we have successfully discouraged the gentlemen who prefer to call at their convenience in the early hours of the morning."

They entered the last of the three receiving rooms, and Madam Blue stopped for a moment to rest. "No man, no matter how respected a patron he is, is ever permitted upstairs unaccompanied. You will see to it that this rule is adhered to at all times, my dear Dragon Flower, in order to avoid one of my ubiquitous servants from forcibly ejecting the unfortunate caller and causing undue embarrassment to all concerned."

Sarina thought of the six surly-looking Oriental men she had been introduced to that first day and shuddered. They appeared only too capable of snapping even the burliest man's neck with very little effort and no compunction whatsoever.

They came to the last room on the ground floor, which was lushly draped in blue silk to resemble a small tent. There was no furniture in the room, only a number of large plump blue silk cushions scattered about on the blue-and-white woven silk rug, and several small copper braziers in the center of the room. This was the opium parlor.

"As you know, some of our callers prefer to spend all of their time here, while others choose first to enjoy the pipe before they proceed upstairs," Madam Blue explained.

Sarina finally worked up the courage to ask, "If a man smokes the pipe first, won't he simply fall asleep before he can even go upstairs?"

"Some men will, my dear, but there are those who use the opium either as a stimulant or to delay the moment of their release, thus enabling them to prolong their lovemaking."

Sarina felt a slight tingling inside her. She could see Janson there among the cushions, with his long legs stretched out in front of him, tugging on the pipe, inhaling the acrid smoke into his lungs and then releasing it again through his nostrils. He would float, as she herself had floated, high above the earth, and there among the stars they would find one another again. She would meld her body to his and share the glory of his loving, which the magic in the pipe would prolong for them forever.

"Come, my dear"—the gentle voice tugged her back to earth again—"it is time for you to dress."

When she stood in her elaborate disguise for the first time, she realized that the transformation of Sarina Paige begun by Wo Shue Kwen had now been completed by Madam Blue. She was no longer either Sarina Paige or Wo's coveted gilded lotus; she was truly only Dragon Flower now.

It was almost impossible to determine her exact height due to the full black wig, which was drawn up into an intricate arrangement of braided curls, and the pair of wedged blue silk slippers she wore tied securely around her ankles with narrow blue silk ribbons. The blue silk gown, or *cheongsam*, molding itself to her body, was heavily embroidered with tiny white jasmine flowers, and like Madam Blue's gowns, it had a high collar, short sleeves, and a slit cut to the knee up either side of its long, narrow skirt. Seeing her body so boldly defined brought a stain of modesty to her face. Try as she could to convince herself that this was nothing but a masquerade, she still saw herself as a tool of the devil—Cleopatra flaunting herself before Caesar; Delilah tempting Samson; Salome enticing Herod. She recalled Wo's words to her with a rueful smile: she was still very much her own father's child, the pious minister's daughter.

Her face was a masterful blend of rice powder, rouge, and black kohl, and her nails were lacquered in a red polish painfully reminiscent of the color Li had worn. A paste made from ground kohl and saffron oil was applied to her pale lashes to make them as black as the twin arcs which were now her eyebrows. Her lids were painted as Janella's had been, with a blue powder mixed with water, extending up to her darkened brows. Lined in black kohl and narrowed as Madam Blue had taught her, her golden eyes darkened to a rich mahogany lightly flecked with bronze. Lost within her glittering setting, Sarina looked to be the perfect blending of East and West, just as Madam Blue herself was, a mysterious and exotic Eurasian whose true identity was impossible to discern.

"You are magnificent, my dear Dragon Flower," breathed the older woman, tears filling her eyes as she stepped back to admire Sarina. "Truly magnificent."

It was an opinion shared by each of the men who stepped through the front door into the foyer that evening and found her there instead of Madam Blue. She watched in veiled amusement as their looks of bewilderment were immediately replaced by approval and then by a flattering proposition, which she politely declined. Her effect on the men was observed by the rest of the girls with something less than amusement. As soon as one of them noticed any of her regular callers lingering too long in the foyer, she hurriedly approached him and whisked him away with her. More often than not, he would turn around for another long look at Sarina, a look she quickly learned to ignore.

As the evening progressed, she realized that not all of the callers were interested in being paired with one of the girls. Some of them spent the entire evening in the opium parlor, reclining on the silk cushions and smoking several pipes by themselves. Many preferred to gamble at various games of chance in the first receiving room, while a number of others chose the second room, where they could sip either sherry or *samshu* and listen to Ariadne and Felicity sing selections from the light operas of the irreverent British humorists Gilbert and Sullivan.

It was four o'clock in the morning by the time Sarina crawled into bed. Her back ached and her feet were tender and sore from standing for so many hours in her new wedged shoes. But even as she lay there with her cramping feet, she was smiling to herself. Like a delighted child after a marvelous birthday celebration, she counted and recounted each of her small triumphs during the evening as if they were precious gifts. It was going to work, she told herself happily; she would be safe here after all.

The colors outside her window were changing. In the tiny garden behind the house, the orchid trees had lost their fresh greenness, the azaleas were limp and faded, and the roses were withering. Gold chrysanthemums replaced the yellow roses in the blue porcelain vases throughout the house, while mauve asters replaced the sweet-smelling pinks. Sarina's twenty-first birthday was on September 2, only weeks away, and for her, time was moving too swiftly and yet not quickly enough.

Like the other occupants of the house on Dragon Flower Street, she slept during the day, usually waking at one in the afternoon. Occasionally she would draw on a light silk cloak, pull the hood up over her head, and take a walk through the congested, clamorous streets of Chinatown. Sometimes she would simply sit in a wicker rocker in the secluded back garden and watch the colors drain from the afternoon sky into a pool of inky night. And once a week she would climb into a hired carriage and drive past number eighteen Casuarina Road in the hopes of finding the Deanes home at last. But there was never any sign of renewed life in the shuttered house, and she dared not inquire as to their whereabouts, for fear of the Chinese houseboy's having been warned by Wo's men to contact them should she ever appear again. She could not risk arriving at the house one time to be confronted, not by either Lewis or Anne Deane, but by Wo Shue Kwen instead.

She could not bring herself to confide in Madam Blue, in spite of the woman's obvious affection for her and her own admiration and growing love for the woman. Nor could she entrust her secret to Mei, so afraid was she of the pipe loosening Mei's tongue and her inadvertently betraying the very person she had sworn to protect. And so she kept her precious secret hidden, concealing it as successfully as she was concealing herself, beneath her mask of white, her gown of blue, and her veil of silence.

Until the morning she woke up screaming. Pitched from sleep by the nettled sting of a nightmare, her body was trembling, her fists were clenched, and her heart was hammering against the walls of her rib cage with painful fury. In sleep, death had closed its bloodless fingers around the throat of her child, and she had felt it in her own body, as surely as if death had been squeezing her own life out of her.

The door opened and Mei staggered into the room, her dressing gown hanging open, a smoking pipe dangling from her fingers. She stumbled over to the bed and draped one arm protectively around Sarina's shoulders.

"I heard you call out," she said. "What is wrong, my sister?"

"I had a terrible dream," panted Sarina, still short of breath and clutching at her throat. "Oh, God, I felt . . . he was dead and I . . . it was as if I were dead and he . . ."

"Who was dead?"

"My ch . . . my f-father." The truth had nearly slipped past her, but she had checked herself in time. "He was lying there, and I felt as if I couldn't breathe, and . . ."

"Here." Mei was offering her the pipe. "It will banish the demon which has frightened you."

"No." Sarina pushed the pipe away. "I can't."

"But it will grant you the peace you seek."

"No, Mei," she moaned, thinking of all the times she had tried to convince her to give up the pipe and failed. "I can't, Mei. Look at what it's done to you."

"I too have my demons, Sarina," the girl said bitterly, "and I cannot live without the sleep of endless reverie the pipe provides me."

The sleep of endless reverie. How well Sarina remembered that exquisite feeling of weightlessness, of nothingness. And peace. Above all, peace.

"One puff, my sister, perhaps even two," coaxed Mei. "It will ease your pain and banish the demon." She pressed the pipe to Sarina's stubborn lips. "Breathe deeply of the pipe, my sister, and know its power as it fills your body with the softness of a cloud."

Sarina inhaled and coughed sharply as she swallowed some of the harsh white smoke. The second puff was easier, and the third easier still. Just this once, she promised herself, just enough to get her back to sleep again. Soon the familiar sweet nothingness began flooding through her, emptying the channels of 'her body of the pain and the fear and replacing them with a delicious, all-pervading calm. She sighed and closed her eyes. A soft pink cloud, born of the rays of the rising sun and the vapors of another damp summer morning, lifted her up and floated her off toward blessed oblivion.

The next time a nightmare woke her, she expected to find Mei there in the room with her, and the pipe warm and ready. But she was disappointed to find that she was alone, that the room was gray with the encroaching bleakness of autumn, and that, try as she might, she was unable to get back to sleep again. That evening, her performance as hostess was erratic for the first time. Each time the peace of her slumber was shattered by her brutal dreams, she would totter through that evening in an exhausted daze, collapsing with fatigue at four in the morning, desperate for the release of sleep, but unable to achieve it.

It was when she woke up one morning, breathless from running after the boy who always seemed to run faster and farther than she could, that she stole into Mei's bedchamber and finished the pipe she had left burning before she had fallen asleep herself. After that, Sarina kept a pipe of her own on the table next to her bed. It was there only in case the dreams returned, she told herself. But as the dreams persisted with alarming regularity, she altered her routine. She began to smoke a full pipe of opium each morning before she got into bed. That way she could be certain the dreams would not return at all. And for ten days her sleep was blissfully undisturbed.

As a test to prove to herself that she could fall asleep again without resorting to the pipe, she went to bed that morning without it. She woke up several times before finally giving up and climbing out of bed before noon. To her dismay, she found that her mouth was dry and that her nose was clogged with mucus. It was not long before she was sneezing fitfully. She was restless all through the day and she could barely swallow a mouthful of food without feeling nauseated. Returning to her room to lie down before getting dressed for the evening, she was suddenly seized by a griping pain in her stomach. She lay down on her bed and turned onto her side, bringing her legs up to her chin, and waited for the spasms to subside.

A little while later, there was a discreet knock on the door and Madam Blue hobbled slowly into the room. "You are not well?" she asked Sarina, who was fighting back a groan as a new pain hurtled through her.

"I'm just a little tired, that's all."

"You ate nothing today, and now I notice that you are shivering."

"I think I might have a slight fever."

"You have no fever," the woman snapped. "You are suffering the effects of one who has become dependent on the pipe and is attempting to go without it."

Sarina was incredulous. "But I've used it for such a short time!"

"Ten days is not a short time, my dear Dragon Flower."

"But it isn't possible!" she cried. "This wasn't the first time I've ever used the pipe."

"And just how many times have you smoked the pipe?"

"Only a few times," admitted Sarina, gasping as the pains began to intensify.

"I see." Madam Blue's eyes were cold and hard. "To use the pipe once or twice is to escape the ill effects you are suffering now."

"B-but it d-doesn't s-seem p-p-possible," protested Sarina through chattering teeth. The cramps were nearly intolerable now. Propping herself up on one elbow, she reached across the bedside table, where her little pipe and the stylet were lying, nearly knocking over the covered oil lamp in her effort to pick up one of the tiny fresh plugs of opium she kept in a small porcelain bowl.

"No, Sarina," the woman barked. "Put it back!"

"I c-c-can't," Sarina whimpered, shaking her head to hold back her tears. She pressed the opium onto the tip of the stylet. "I need it to stop the pain."

"Stop yourself now before it is too late," Madam Blue pleaded. "If you are afraid, I will remain with you and help you to resist. Please, Sarina, do as I say."

"Forgive me," she sobbed, raising the stylet and holding it over the lighted flame of the lamp, "but I can't bear the pain. I have to stop the pain."

With an unhappy sigh, Madam Blue turned and hobbled out of the room, leaving Sarina to her pipe and to her dreams.

She saw his green eyes before she saw the rest of his face. He walked toward her in the thickening fog, and she smiled at him and waved. He raised his arm to wave back at her, but then he seemed to change his mind, and he pointed an angry finger at her instead. He pointed to the billowing cloud, which she had mistaken for fog, wrapped around her like a cloak, and started backing away from her.

She called his name and hurried after him, but the cloud was now weaving itself around her, spinning its gossamer lightness into an ever-tightening cocoon of silken threads, pinning her arms to her sides and locking her legs together so that she could no longer pursue him. As the milky strands grew tighter, binding themselves around her throat, all she could do was gasp out his name. When the cocoon closed over her eyes, she woke up to find her face pressed deep into her mattress and his name a bitter aftertaste on her tongue.

Mei sat in the hired carriage with the sealed letter resting in her lap and instructed the driver to take her to the post office on Queen's Road. Her hands were trembling and her head ached, but her mind was clear. Once the letter was safely dispatched, she returned to the house and made her way slowly up the stairs to her room. Her body craved the pipe, and because she had successfully accomplished what she had set out to do, the pipe would now be her reward.

On the other side of the wall she heard Sarina calling out in the throes of a dream, and tears welled up in Mei's luminous black eyes.

"Soon, Sarina," she murmured as she settled herself on her bed. "Very soon, my sister, when you call out to him, he will be here to answer you."

With a sigh of contentment, she reached for her pipe.

21

Janson slammed his fist down on top of his desk and took some pleasure from the bolt of pain shooting up his arm. Each time he reread Mei's letter his reaction was the same—outrage and frustration. When the ship lurched suddenly, nearly throwing him to the floor, he directed his anger at the captain, the ship, and even the sea itself by repeatedly hammering his fist against the desk until his strength was gone. Rubbing his bruised flesh, he glared up at the oil lamp swinging madly above his head and blinked back the threat of angry tears rushing to his eyes.

"Damn, damn, damn!" He tossed the letter aside and began restlessly pacing off the floor of the small cabin. "You were more of a fool than I was, Sarina, to have let me sail without you. Dammit, Sarina, I'll kill him! I'll kill him for what he's done to you."

As he prowled the cabin, his eyes came back again and again to the piece of paper lying on his desk. Mei's child-like scrawl had revealed only that Wo had wanted Sarina to replace Li as his favored one and that she had fled to Hong Kong, joining Mei at the house of Madam Blue. What baffled him was Mei's being at the brothel in the first place and Sarina's choosing to go to Hong Kong rather than returning home to America. But what stung the most was that single heart-stopping word: opium.

"I was supposed to be protecting you," he continued, combing his fingers through his hair in his agitation. "And all the time you kept insisting you didn't need my protection. Ha! What a stubborn, headstrong child you were, Sarina Paige. I should never have listened to you."

Child? He had to laugh at that. Sarina Paige was no child. The image his mind kindled for him had an exquisite face, with golden eyes and wind-tossed golden hair, a smile with an impish set to it, and a gloriously curved body sheathed in shimmering white silk. The heat that still scourged him so mercilessly in his dreams, defeating him in his efforts to forget her, caught him in its fiery fingers now and slowly stroked him into yearning arousal.

He threw himself onto his bunk, and as he lay there cursing himself for his weakness, he suddenly thought of his brother, Garrett, whom he had come to bless for his perceptiveness. Garrett, the frightened one, the careful one, who had listened to his older brother, the bold adventurer and taker of risks, and then had dared to call him a cautious fool. Perhaps it had been the word "cautious" which had rankled most. Cautious! Within a year he had expanded their trading interests to include not only Hong Kong but also Colombia, and Garrett had dared to call him cautious! But he had known exactly what Garrett meant by it.

He turned down the lamp and was grateful for the soothing darkness. Rubbing his eyes with the tips of his fingers, cooling down their burning lids, he felt someone there on the bunk beside him. He put out a tentative hand and felt only the darkness. Sarina. Hilary. Each taken once on a bed of his in a sea-tossed cabin, which was different and yet the same as the one in which he was lying now. Hilary had been taken once in brutal defiance of Sarina's abandonment of him, and then thrust from his bed and from his life forever.

"Sarina . . ." He whispered her name out loud and banished the memory of that other one for all times. Clenching his fist, he shook it savagely in the face of the God he could not see. "Please, let me get there in time," he prayed. "Just let me be in time."

The carriage traveled slowly down Banyan and turned onto Casuarina for the second go-round of the block that afternoon. Sarina pulled the hood of her blue cape lower over her eyes and leaned forward in her seat, peering intently out of the window. This was the third time this week that she had returned to the area after finding the slate-gray shutters on the white stucco house thrown open at last. A chill October wind rattled the carriage door and shook the clear glass pane, which was becoming fogged from Sarina's rapid breathing. With her hands clasped tightly in her lap, she was preparing herself for yet another disappointing afternoon, when suddenly she sat straight up in her seat. "Slow down, driver!" she called, rapping sharply on the roof with her knuckles.

She caught her breath and held it. Tears glazed her eyes at the sight of the high, covered pram being wheeled onto the sidewalk from the familiar flagstone path by a tall, thin woman in a long hooded rose wool cape. Sarina pressed her fist to her mouth and felt the tears plopping onto her skin and trickling through her clenched fingers. "At last," she whispered to herself, "at long, long last."

As the carriage passed the woman, Sarina turned around in her seat for a better look at her. She had the gaunt, shadowed face of the chronic invalid, and although her nose was being stained red by the wind, her cheeks remained waxen and pale. In spite of her warm cloak, she appeared to be shivering, and as she bent her head forward a bit more, her hood slid farther back from her face to reveal thin, pale ginger-colored hair.

Sarina hastily instructed the driver to turn the corner and to wait for her in the middle of the block; then she climbed down from the carriage and started walking very slowly back up the street again. It was several minutes before the woman and the pram finally rounded the corner. With her head still lowered against the wind, she seemed oblivious to Sarina until they nearly collided with each other. The woman glanced up with an apologetic smile and tried to maneuver the pram out of Sarina's way. "What a beastly day," she exclaimed as she struggled with the heavy carriage.

"Never mind," Sarina quickly assured her. "There's more than enough room."

"Thank you, my dear," the woman sighed, obviously lacking the strength to do more than what she had already done. "I've not quite gotten used to this contraption, I'm afraid. Our nursemaid is far better at it than I am."

But Sarina scarcely heard a word she was saying as she stared dry-mouthed at the hood of the pram. "May I?" she inquired.

"Yes, yes, of course," answered the woman, stepping aside to enable Sarina to take her place.

She peered into the carriage and her heart seemed to

forget how to beat. Wreathed in a cloud of soft golden curls was the face which still haunted her nightly dreams. Her intake of breath was lost in the howl of the wind as a pair of deep green eyes opened and gazed up at her in curious surprise. The world seemed to slide away from her. All she could see was the face of Janson Carlyle on the face of this boy. There could be no mistaking whose child he was. He was theirs, Janson's and hers. Li had told her the truth after all.

"I'm afraid I really should be taking him back now," came the quavering voice from somewhere behind her. "Please, my dear, it's frightfully cold, and he mustn't catch a chill."

"I'm sorry," apologized Sarina as she backed away from the carriage on legs she could no longer feel. Watching the pale, bony fingers of some stranger straightening the blanket which covered her own son was a torment almost too great to contain. It was all Sarina could do not to push that stranger aside and scoop up her child and run with him as fast and as far as she possibly could.

"Are you not well, my dear?" The voice was so sweet, so genuinely concerned, and the pale brown eyes so gentle, that Sarina was torn by guilt and longing.

"It's just the cold," she smiled, stealing another look at her beloved child. "Tell me . . ." She held the woman back for a moment. "Have you lived here long?"

"Three years now," she replied breathlessly as she fought to turn the pram around.

"I've just arrived in Victoria," explained Sarina, "and my husband, who's presently at sea, left me with the task of finding a house for us. Would you know if there are any for sale around here?"

The woman shook her head. "I'm afraid not. You see, we've only just returned from Europe ourselves. Now, if you'll please excuse me . . ."

Once again Sarina put out her hand and stopped the poor woman. "Could you tell me your son's name?" she asked.

"Michael Steven," came the tight reply from between lips beginning to turn blue.

"Michael Steven." Sarina slowly repeated the name to herself. Michael Steven. There would be no calling him

Thomas-John now. "He's a very handsome child," she said softly.

The woman's pale face suddenly glowed with a radiance which made her plain features almost beautiful. "Yes"— she nodded—"we have indeed been blessed, my husband and I, just as you and your own husband will no doubt be blessed one day." With a firm push she got the pram rolling again. "If your quest for the proper house should bring you this way again, do stop by for tea, won't you?" she called back over her shoulder. "It's number eighteen Casuarina Road and the name is Deane. Anne Deane."

"Thank you," returned Sarina with forced gaiety. "Perhaps I will."

She stood there in the cold, looking after the departing pram with a terrible hollowness inside her where feeling should have been, and an empty place in her arms which his closeness should have filled. But at least she knew that Michael Steven Deane was in fact her own precious child. And not only had she established a believable excuse for being in the area again, but she had also received an invitation to tea from the woman who was now his mother.

As she walked slowly back to the waiting carriage, she found, to her surprise, that the wind seemed less fierce than before and the air not quite so cold. By the time she was settled inside the carriage again, some of the feeling was beginning to return to her body and to her limbs. In fact, she was beginning to feel warm, a giddy and exultant kind of warmth. She laughed out loud, clapping her hands over her mouth as her smile widened and her laughter deepened.

What a ninny she was! She had every reason to rejoice now. Her son was alive! His name was Michael Steven, not Thomas-John, and he lived with a family called Deane instead of with her, but he was still her child, flesh born of her flesh. And now that she had found him again, nothing would stop her from seeing him; nothing would keep her from sharing whatever she could of his life. She would have to be content with that for now, because some of him was better than none of him, which was what she had been forced to endure for ten lonely months. But she knew that she would not be content with the arrangement for long. It was only a matter of time before she would find a way to get all of him back again.

*   *   *

She slept until noon, buoyed by only half of a pipe and one long, continuous dream filled with the glorious face of her son. Then, for the first time in several weeks, she joined Madam Blue in her bedchamber for lunch. The older woman took all of her meals in her room now and seldom walked about the house anymore without the aid of a silver-topped carved-ivory stick. It grieved Sarina to see the woman's beauty beginning to fade and to watch as she grimaced in pain when she thought no one was observing her.

"You seem in far better spirits today than you have been in some time," commented Madam Blue with an approving smile as Sarina poured them each a cup of tea. "Even your appetite has improved." She noted the second slice of roast pork on Sarina's plate. "Could it be that one of our callers has finally succeeded in turning our stubborn Dragon Flower's head?"

Sarina made a face. "Hardly," she scowled. "Dragon Flower is nothing but an act, as you well know. She doesn't exist."

"Neither does Sarina, I fear," the woman sighed as she sipped at her tea. "Whether Sarina or Dragon Flower, what matters is that you, my dear, have revived the waning interest in the house of Madam Blue, and for this I am most humbly grateful." The expression changed in her eyes as she continued to scrutinize Sarina's face very carefully. "However, in spite of your protestations to the contrary, you are a woman, my dear, and a very beautiful woman at that. You would indeed be a fool if you continued to waste those precious gifts which the gods have so generously bestowed upon you."

"I don't consider refusing to sleep with a man for payment a waste of these so-called gifts," replied Sarina more harshly than she had intended. "I'm afraid the price I would have to pay would be far greater than theirs."

"I believe that you are speaking not only about those who might pay for your favors, but about all men equally. Will there be no man, then, who will free you from the prison you have chosen to make of your heart, my dear Sarina? It would seem that you are both jailer and prisoner, and as such, you will be very lonely indeed."

Sarina tightened her jaw. "If I am, it isn't because I chose it to be that way."

"Then you have permitted your heart to be bound to a memory?" asked the woman.

Sarina stared up at the ceiling and said nothing.

"The truth is oftentimes as great a healer as the passage of time itself," continued Madam Blue. "Would you not prefer to loosen the bonds of that memory by sharing it with one who cares deeply about you? I see you are already shaking your head. Perhaps you might think about it awhile before deciding so hastily. Come, come, my dear, do not allow my words to drive you away. They are spoken with love, just as any mother would speak to her own child with love."

"I know." Sarina gave her a grateful smile; then she set her plate down and went over to the woman and wrapped her arms around her. "You're more of a mother to me than anyone else has ever been," she told her, "but please be patient with me. Sharing confidences with another person is still quite difficult for me to do."

The older woman patted Sarina's hand reassuringly and planted a gentle kiss on her forehead. "I will be patient, my dear, for I learned long ago that to be otherwise is both foolish and futile."

Sarina finished her tea and then returned to her own room for her cloak. She located a carriage for hire a block from the house and settled back in the seat for the familiar climb up to Casuarina Road. The day was milder than the previous day, with only a slight breeze stirring the leaves on the eucalyptus and banyan trees lining the streets they passed as they left the waterfront far below them. She tried to caution herself against being too greedy, that she would be wiser if she spaced her visits further apart. But caution was something she refused to consider today. She had to see him again, if only to prove that he was neither a figment of her imagination nor a product of the pipe.

She sat with her fist to her mouth and her forehead pressed against the glass of the carriage when they drove past the Deane house for the second time. She was becoming more and more discouraged as they turned back onto Banyan again. What if something had happened to him? What if he had gotten sick because she had detained Anne

Deane for those extra minutes in the windy cold? She
considered calling on the woman and accepting her invitation for tea, but she immediately dismissed the idea as
foolhardy and impetuous. Then, just as they were passing
the tiny tree-shaded park on Banyan again, Sarina spotted
the pram.

Instead of Anne Deane pushing it today, it was being
pushed by a short, somewhat plump young girl with the
creamy complexion of the British countryside. Her light
brown hair was drawn up into a soft swirl on top of her
head and her round cheeks and pert nose were faintly
pinkened by the cool air. Her cherry-red cloak was a
cheerful splash of color against the drabness of the gray
afternoon, and as Sarina alighted from the carriage and
followed the girl into the park, she suddenly felt like
humming.

No sooner had the girl seated herself on one of the wide
stone benches, with one hand gently rocking the carriage,
than Sarina strolled casually up to her. "Would you mind
if I sat down?" she inquired politely. "There seem to be so
few people about today."

" 'Course not, mum." The girl bobbed her head and
patted the space beside her. "I always like a bit o' comp'ny
meself, and Lord knows the little one 'ere's a mite young
fer me to be chattin' with."

"How old is he?" asked Sarina, knowing full well what
the answer would be.

" 'E'd be ten months now, 'e would, and quite the looker,
too, eh, mum? 'E's goin' to be breakin' 'is fair share o'
'earts one day."

Just like his father, Sarina thought bitterly as she gazed
down at the handsome face of her sleeping child. The
lashes curved so delicately across his cheeks were as black
as Janson's own lashes, as black as his brows, as black as
the hair between the strands of silver.

"You 'ave little ones, mum?" The question, asked so
innocently, took Sarina by surprise.

"We hope to have children one day," she answered
vaguely.

"This is ever so nice a place fer little ones, mum," the
girl confided cheerfully. She glanced about for a moment,
and then, dropping her voice, she said, "My mistress Deane
now, she couldn't 'ave no little ones 'erself. This little one's

a foundlin', the poor soul, but 'e's a lucky one, 'avin' a ma
to give 'im more love than 'is own ma saw fit to give 'im.
You see, mum, little Michael's about all my mistress Deane
lives fer now. So 'e's blessed, 'e is, with folks like my
mistress and the mister to love 'im."

The girl's vehement declaration clawed at Sarina's heart.
Blessed. The exact word Anne Deane herself had used.
There would be no getting him back now, of that she was
certain. Michael Steven was Anne Deane's life. He was
supposedly a foundling whose own mother had abandoned him, leaving him for strangers to love instead. She
stared at her son in growing despair, and the longer she
looked at him, the more she wanted to touch him.

She ached to know each curve of his little body and to
discover all those secret ticklish places which would make
him giggle. She wanted to smell that special sweetness
which lives only in the skin of babies. She longed to feel
his small fingers exploring her face, tugging at her hair,
and closing around one of her own fingers with a grip so
tight that nothing could ever break it and separate them
again. Without realizing what she was doing, she was bending over the carriage and reaching out for her child.

" 'Ere, now, mum, you'll be wakin' 'im up if you do
that."

She felt the girl's hand on her shoulder, tugging her
back.

"Once 'e's up, it's near impossible to get 'im back to
sleep again. 'E's a stubborn one, our little Michael, 'e's got
a mind o' 'is own, awright."

Just like his father. Sarina slumped against the back of
the bench and heaved a long, low sigh. What had she been
thinking of? Perhaps it was better this way, never knowing
how he would feel in her arms. For if she held him once,
how could she not want to hold him again? And again.
And again. How could she touch him once and not spend
the rest of her life remembering that moment and being
enslaved to it, just as she was already enslaved to a memory?

She rose abruptly and gave the girl a forced smile. "I
think I'd better be off now, Miss . . ."

"Greer. Lucy Greer."

"Lucy." Sarina nodded. "Thank you for your company."

Lucy Greer bobbed her head again. "I do 'ope I'll 'ave
your comp'ny again soon, mum." She was still smiling

broadly when Sarina drew her cloak around her with a
flourish and swept hurriedly out of the park.

She took several short tugs on the pipe to calm her raw
nerves and blunt the edges of her pain before she dressed
and went downstairs that evening. Without the soothing
comfort afforded her by the opium, she would have simply remained in her room and wept. With it, she was able
to move about with ease, speaking softly and graciously,
and flirt with practiced grace with each of the men who
came in as the night progressed.

"Now, I'd say I've just found me something I like,"
drawled a deep voice from the doorway as the tall, broad-
shouldered young American ducked his head to step into
the foyer. Sweeping off his Stetson, he combed his fingers
through his thick brown curls and, with his brown eyes
twinkling, said, "You're just about the purdiest thing I've
seen so far today, Miss Dragon Flower."

It was a game they had been playing every night for the
past week.

"Am I, Mr. Galvan?" Sarina smiled as she bowed to him
in greeting.

"You sure are, Miss Dragon Flower."

"You flatter me, Mr. Galvan, as always." She signaled to
one of the parlor maids to take his hat. "Poker, Mr. Galvan?"

"Why, sure, Miss Dragon Flower." He nodded, tucking
her arm through his and allowing her to lead the way into
the first receiving room.

She was aware of Tung-tsu, the servant assigned to
oversee the gaming parlor, watching them intently. With
an imperceptible shake of her head she indicated to him
that she could deal with Wesley Galvan on her own.

"If I win tonight, Miss Dragon Flower"—the young man
bent to whisper in her ear—"you think I'll finally have
enough money to buy some time with you?"

"I'm afraid I would still have to refuse you, Mr. Galvan,"
she told him, patting his arm in a placating way.

"All right, Miss Dragon Flower," he conceded with a
good-natured grin, "but one of these days I just might
change that stubborn little mind of yours. You'll wish me
luck in any case, now, won't you?"

"Good luck, Mr. Galvan," she obliged him, before she
returned to the foyer in time to greet the three British

naval officers who amused her by always arriving together
and then leaving together after precisely two hours.

It was nearly one o'clock. The slight fluttering inside
her reminded her that it would still be several more hours
before she could retire to her room to the blissful release
of the pipe. Stifling a yawn, she was considering locking
the door a few minutes earlier than usual when the sound
of footsteps bounding up the stairs changed her mind.
She groaned inwardly. All the girls were occupied, and so
it would be left to her to entertain this final caller if he
chose to wait until one of them was free.

Pressing a smile of welcome onto her face, she prepared
herself to be polite this last time.

"Just made it, didn't I?"

The voice froze her to the spot.

"Is she still such a stickler for her one-o'clock curfew?"
That mocking tone was still there. "I've never seen you
before." Now the voice sounded confused. "Where's Madam
Blue?"

Discovering that he was no stranger to Madam Blue's
chilled some of the liquid heat surging through her body.
Her eyes, fixed firmly on the tips of his black boots,
traveled slowly up the legs of his dove-gray trousers, past
the tails of his long charcoal-gray frock coat, up to the
white brocade waistcoat, and then stopped abruptly at the
large gray pearl stickpin in the middle of his gray-and-
white-striped cravat.

With her head still bowed, she said in a breathy whisper,
"I am Dragon Flower, your hostess." Even with her eyes
lowered, she could still feel the persuasive pull of his gaze,
and she fought against it just as she fought to maintain
her composure.

"And Madam Blue?"

"She is asleep in her bedchamber. If you wish, I will
ring for her."

"No, wait."

The touch of his hand on her wrist drove a fiery stake
through her groin.

"I'm really looking for someone else. Her name is Sarina."

Her sharp intake of breath took them both by surprise.

"You know her, then?"

She could scarcely hear him above the loud pounding of
her heart. He had come looking for her! But how had he

known where to find her? No one even knew about him
here except . . . Mei! Could Mei have sent for him?

"I asked you if you knew her." His voice was growing
impatient and his grip on her wrist was tightening.

"No." She shook her head, wondering what had made
her lie, wondering at the game she was now playing. "I do
not know her." And neither, so it seemed, did he. A flush
of triumph spread through her when she realized that
even *he* had failed to recognize her.

"Then take me to see Madam Blue." His voice was still
harsh, but he released his hold on her.

She could feel the stinging imprint of his hand as if it
were still encircling her wrist when she motioned for him
to follow her. She was aware of his gaze searing her back,
roaming the length of her, as her hips undulated sugges-
tively in her tight-fitting blue *cheongsam*. Tiny flickers of
heat seemed to be darting from his eyes to her legs each
time they flashed through the slits in her gown when she
began walking slowly up the winding staircase ahead of
him.

The cool silk rustling against her body grew warmer
with each step she took as she led him down the corridor,
not to the room of the sleeping Madam Blue, but to her
own room instead. When she reached for the brass door
handle, he brushed her hand away. "Allow me," he offered gallantly.

He leaned across her to open the door, and where his
chest was grazing her shoulder there flared a treacherous
tongue of fire. She showed him into the room and then
closed the door and leaned up against it.

"What kind of a joke is this?" he demanded, wheeling
around to face her again after viewing the empty bed.

"Is Madam Blue not too old for a man of your tender
years?" she murmured, arching her back invitingly and
watching his eyes devour her thrusting breasts. "Does
Dragon Flower not please you?"

"Yes, I'd say Dragon Flower might please me," he growled
as he caught hold of her arms and gave them a hard
squeeze, "but only after she's taken me to Madam Blue."

"You are hurting Dragon Flower," she pouted.

"I'll hurt Dragon Flower even more if she—"

"And if I take you to this person you were asking for?"
she challenged him coyly.

"So you *do* know Sarina!"

She nodded her head. She was growing tired of the game, and his cruel grip on her bare arms would leave bruises she could ill afford. "First you must let Dragon Flower go," she told him.

His arms dropped to his sides. "All right. Now, where is she?"

Without another word, Sarina swept off her wig. With a shake of her head, she released her own hair to spill about her shoulders in a tumbled cascade of silvered gold. Then, with a tinkle of victorious laughter, she simply said, "She's standing right in front of you."

22

"Sarina!"

He took a step back as he gasped out her name.

She squared her chin and raised her head to finally meet his eyes. In their verdant depths she saw amazement gradually being tempered by a returning flicker of sardonic humor.

"For such an innocent, you've certainly learned to master the role of the temptress quickly enough, my dear Miss Paige," he commented wryly.

She treated him to a wintry smile. "Wasn't that the part you said I'd find the easiest?"

"Occasionally one prefers to be proved wrong," he replied stiffly.

"Oh, I'd say you've been proved wrong more than just occasionally, *Mister* Carlyle."

Suddenly his hand snaked out, and for a moment she thought he was going to strike her, but he startled her by simply reaching for one long curling tendril of her hair and wrapping it slowly around his index finger. As he wound it tighter, he began gently but forcefully drawing her toward him. She swayed and tried to hold her ground, but it was either yield to him or suffer the pain of her hair being tugged out at the roots.

"Don't you have a more appropriate greeting for someone who's just sailed across an entire ocean to see if it's true what men on two continents are saying about the mysterious Dragon Flower?" His voice was low and mocking, his eyes trained seductively on her mouth, and she felt her lips parting and growing moist under his hypnotic gaze.

"Don't," she quavered.

"Is that what Dragon Flower says to all the men she takes upstairs to her bedroom?"

Sarina's rising mortification deepened the stain of the rouge high on her cheeks.

"Dragon Flower has no clever reply?"

Their lips were now a breath apart. She closed her eyes to break his hold on her, to destroy the power which lived in his remarkable eyes. She tried to turn her face away, but his grip on her hair would not allow it. Her starving senses craved the completion only his nearness could provide. Yet in his presence she was a wound still not quite healed, vulnerable and open to further scarring.

"Sarina?" It was a puzzled whisper now.

She chose to risk the pain, and strained to turn her face away. His lips grazed her throat, and she arched her neck and bit down gently on her bottom lip. "Please, I have to go back downstairs," she whimpered, blinking back the tears that were now stinging her eyelids.

"Isn't my company good enough for you?" he snarled. "Or are you afraid I might not be able to afford you?"

"Let go of me, you—"

The crushing weight of his mouth on hers silenced her. Relinquishing his savage hold on her hair, he clasped her face with both hands and pressed her up against the wall. While he lashed her mouth with his tongue, he thrust his body at her, in anger, out of despair and with a painful, yearning need. Sarina suffered the assault on her flesh in stunned silence, too shocked to either retaliate or respond.

There was a sharp rap on the door. Janson froze. There was a second knock, and he stumbled away from Sarina and turned his back to her. She waited another moment to catch her breath before calling out, "Who is it?"

"It is Tung-tsu, missy."

She frowned, wondering if something could have happened downstairs.

"One moment, Tung-tsu," she called again as she worked quickly to gather her tousled hair into the wig that she retrieved from the floor. A hasty glance in the mirror confirmed the worst. Her rice powder was streaked, the rouge was gone from her lips, and several of the braided curls on her wig had come loose. With no time to change into another of her many ornate headpieces, she hastily pinned up the untidiest of the curls and then hurried over to the door. Opening it just enough for her to see him without Tung-tsu's being able to see into the room, she apologized for having kept him waiting.

With his face as impassive as always and his dark eyes betraying no emotion whatsoever, he simply bowed to her and handed her a sealed white envelope. She recognized it as coming from the writing desk in the third receiving room.

"This from master Galvan," he said. "He wait in parlor for reply."

She tore open the envelope, and when she unfolded the enclosed piece of paper, a number of British pound notes fluttered to the floor. She ignored the money, which Tung-tsu immediately bent down to collect, and hastily scanned the brief message.

"How's this for a start?" Wesley Galvan had written in script as brash and as bold as his manner. "Say yes, Miss Dragon Flower, and I'll go back to the tables and whip the hide off the rest of them suckers."

The young Texan's persistence coaxed a semblance of a smile onto her strained face, but she took the money Tung-tsu was holding out to her, tucked it back inside the writing paper, folded it, and then slid it into the envelope again.

"Please tell Mr. Galvan that the answer is still no," she instructed the servant, "but tell him thank you."

"Very good, missy." He bowed to her again and hurried off down the hall.

She continued to stand there holding the door open while she debated whether or not to return downstairs.

Janson made the decision for her by coming up behind her and slamming the door shut. Leaning his back against it, he dug his thumbs into the pockets of his waistcoat and studied her with a contemptuous sneer on his face. "Would you mind telling me the difference between what you're doing here and what you would have been doing for Kwen?" he asked her.

"It isn't what you think," she snapped back at him.

"Don't tell me that you now prefer several men at a time to just one."

She refused to dignify his remark with an answer, and so she simply remained silent.

With a sigh of frustration Janson said, "I wish to hell I could read what's hidden inside that beautiful head of yours, Sarina. Maybe then we wouldn't be at each other's throats all the time."

She glared at him through narrowed eyes. "But then I'd have to know what you're keeping hidden from me, wouldn't I?"

"I suppose that would be a fair assumption," he said, pushing himself away from the door. "But then, who said anything about being fair? I want some answers from you, Sarina, and I'm not about to play tit for tat to get them. Why are you here?" he demanded. "Why are you in Hong Kong, and how the hell did you get to Madam Blue?"

She gave her head a defiant shake. "I could ask you exactly the same thing, you know."

"No games, Sarina!" he barked. "I want the truth."

"And so do I!"

"All right, then, I'll tell you." He shoved his hands into the pockets of his trousers and sauntered over toward the windows. With his back turned to her he said, "I'm here because Mei sent me a letter telling me about Kwen's intentions for you and that you had left the estate and were here with her at Madam Blue's."

She felt her body beginning to sway. "Is that true?" she murmured. A tiny spasm clutched at her stomach, and she was hard pressed to know whether it was from the shock of what he had just told her or from her need for the pipe again. "You came because of me?"

He turned to look at her, and a teasing grin cut across his handsome face. "Well, let's just say this was one of the stops I had to make anyway. I have offices in Hong Kong, remember?"

She looked down at the floor, feeling strangely deflated. "I remember," she answered tonelessly.

"I believe it's your turn, my dear Dragon Flower." One black eyebrow was lifted expectantly.

"You already know why I left Shanghai," she said, stalling for time while she scrambled about for a plausible lie.

"Why Hong Kong? Why not simply return home?"

She shrugged. "I really have no home anymore. It hardly mattered where I went."

"But you chose Hong Kong," he persisted.

She concentrated on the space just above his head as she

decided to answer him with an abbreviated version of the truth. "I had only one opportunity to escape, and Wo provided me with it by insisting that I accompany him into the city one day. The only ship leaving that same afternoon was one bound for Hong Kong, so the choice of destination wasn't mine to make. While I was waiting for a ship sailing to America, I ran low of funds and decided to look for work, but I was nearly seen by two of Wo's men. I was afraid of their finding me and returning me to Wo, so I came here. Madam Blue needed a hostess, and I needed a place to hide."

"And that's it?"

Meeting his skeptical gaze with a steely gaze of her own, she said, "Do you think your paltry explanation deserves anything more? You asked me your question and I gave you my answer, so now that I've satisfied your curiosity, I'd appreciate it if you'd leave." She swept over to the door and held it open for him. "Now!"

"I still have too many questions which—"

"But I have no more answers," she cut him off sharply.

"I'm not leaving here until I get them."

"I'll call for Tung-tsu," she warned him.

He strode angrily across the room and batted the door out of her hand again. With an outraged cry she lunged for the door handle, but he stepped in front of it and hauled her into his arms. As she struggled to break free, a violent shudder rippled through her, followed by a flush of moist, angry heat.

"You're hoping I'll leave, aren't you, Sarina, so that you can be alone with your goddamned opium!" His words lashed out in fury at her and made her turn her head away. "If you're wondering how I know about it, Mei told me that too."

She closed her eyes, gulping back a defeated sob, but she thanked God that she had never told Mei about her son. At least she had been wise enough to keep that one precious secret all to herself.

"Why, Sarina?" He was shaking her by the shoulders now. "Why opium? Did Kwen give it to you? Did he, dammit? Answer me!"

"I was scalded by boiling water once and he gave it to me then to deaden the pain," she improvised.

"And now?"

"I don't sleep well. I have terrible nightmares, and the opium helps me to sleep."

"So would a glass of port or brandy," he ground out impatiently, "but you wouldn't become addicted to either one of them. Oh, Sarina," he whispered, pressing her head to his chest. "Sarina, let me help you. Let me help you sleep without the opium."

Against the curve of his shoulder, her laugh was harsh. "And how do you intend to do that?" she asked him. "Do you have the power to change the dreams for me?"

In answer to that he cupped her face in his hands, and his eyes grew tender. "I really don't think you're supposed to be crying with all that rice powder on your face," he said. "You're quite a sight now, you know."

"Thank you," she sniffed, her eyes going to his soiled coat. He followed her gaze and then burst out laughing.

All of the fight drained out of her as his deep, familiar laughter filled the room and filled up the lonely spaces still reserved for him inside her. Still smiling, he crooked a finger under her chin, and tilting her face up to his, he lightly brushed his lips back and forth across her mouth several times. Then he kissed her. A gentle, sweet, and unhurried caress, which she answered, cautiously and tentatively at first, and then with increasing ardor. She twined her arms about his neck and deepened their kiss, while his arms slid hungrily around her back, driving her soft, relenting body up against his hard, relentless one.

When he broke their kiss, it was to trace the contours of her face with his mouth until he was burrowing in the gentle curve of her neck and shoulder, teasing a series of warm, shivering twinges from her. He kissed the lobe of her ear and then used his tongue to trace its sensitive rim. Gooseflesh rose all along her arms, and her nipples tensed and stiffened. With one arm he bent her back, while his fingers unfastened the tiny side buttons on her gown, exposing inch by inch the golden translucence of her ivory skin. Then he followed the pathway with his lips and tongue.

She moaned as his fingers closed around one breast, gently stroking the silken globe in tender circles until he reached its peaked and throbbing nipple. When his lips closed around that darkened nub of hardened flesh, she shuddered, and a glorious heat rose and fell in rhythmic

waves all around her. Her body limp, all the strength gone
from her legs, she was alive with thousands of tiny, tingling sensations.

He followed the swell of her hip, down her silk-encased
thigh to where the deep slash in her gown exposed one
slender, shapely leg. The warmth of his palm bruised the
coolness of her skin as he traced his way back up her
thigh, the gown riding higher and higher behind his exploring hand. She whimpered, catching her breath in a
sudden ecstatic gasp as he gently cupped her warm
moistness, kneading it softly and tenderly at first, then
growing more insistent as she grew warmer and moister.

A loud crushing thump against the door broke them
apart. No sooner had they moved out of the way than the
door flew open and two men toppled to the floor inside
her room. One of them was Wesley Galvan; the other was
Tung-tsu. With one hand clutching the open bodice of
her gown, Sarina stepped back just as Galvan struggled
to his feet and then bent down to level a punch at
Tung-tsu's face. She screamed as she heard the sound of
bone crunching and buried her face in Janson's chest.

A moment later she felt herself being wrenched out of
Janson's arms, but Wesley Galvan's flushed grin of triumph
was short-lived. His smile twisted into a grimace of pain as
Tung-tsu rammed him from behind with the top of his
head. Both men tumbled to the floor again. Blood spurted
from a cut on Galvan's upper lip, but it was a mere trickle
compared with the bloody stream gushing from Tung-
tsu's broken nose.

As Galvan's fingers closed around the smaller man's
throat, Sarina heard the cocking of a pistol and Janson's
cold voice saying, "I hate to break up a good fight,
gentlemen, but my patience is just about worn out."

Both men froze. Wesley Galvan recovered first, taking
advantage of the lull to backhand a slap across Tung-tsu's
pulpy face. Sarina screamed again. Before either man
could react, Janson was down on one knee, the barrel of
his pistol pressed against Galvan's right temple. "I don't
like to repeat myself," he said calmly. "Now, get up and
get the hell out of here. Right now."

The big man pushed Tung-tsu away from him like a
bull shaking off a fly and staggered to his feet. Janson
gave Tung-tsu a hand up and the young man stumbled

from the room, with one hand clapped to his bleeding nose. Wesley Galvan raked his fingers through his curly hair and trained a now sheepish grin on Sarina and at the pistol still pointed at him.

"I guess I couldn't figger out no other way to get myself some time with you, Miss Dragon Flower," he told her as he backed out of the room. "But I can see you ain't been lonely." He shot Janson an envious glance.

Janson responded by kicking the door shut behind him.

Fumbling with the buttons on her gown, Sarina made her way on shaky legs over to her bedside table. She heard Janson locking the door as she fitted a small molasses-colored plug of opium to the end of her stylet and held it over the flame of the lighted oil lamp. Just as the ball was beginning to roast, Janson spun her around and knocked the stylet out of her hand and onto the floor. Sarina's angry fingers reached out to scratch at his face.

"I think we've had all the fighting we need for one night," he told her as he held her off.

"Leave me alone," she snarled. "This is my room and I want you out of here."

"And have you falling prey to every lumbering ox who feels like barging in here?" He clucked his tongue at her. "Heavens, Sarina, even with her door locked, a girl can never be too safe."

"We have guards to tend to those matters."

"Oh, yes, the guards," he nodded. "I saw an example of how effective they can be just a moment ago."

"You bastard," she sputtered, "you can still manage to twist everything around, can't you?"

"I told you I wanted to help you, dammit!"

"I don't need your help!"

"The hell you don't."

"The hell I do!"

He dropped her hands. "My God, I think I liked you better as a pious schoolteacher, Sarina. You're sounding more and more like a sailor every day."

She ignored his comment and knelt to pick up her metal stylet, but the tip of his boot came down hard on the little instrument, making it impossible for her to move it.

"Sarina." His voice was gentle again. "Sarina, let me help you. Let me stay here with you and show you that

you won't need the opium to get you through the night.
Let me help you, Sarina, please."

She slowly straightened up again. He pulled her into his
arms and removed her black wig, running his fingers
through the shimmering spill of her hair as it tumbled
about her like a golden cape.

"Let me hold you," he murmured, his lips pressed to
her forehead. "I'll keep the dreams away, Sarina, and I'll
help you with the pain."

She raised her head to look at him, and in his answering
gaze she knew that perhaps she should trust him, at least
with this one small part of herself. But she continued to
vacillate, dreading the pain, dreading even more the prospect of his seeing her brought so low.

"I'm afraid," she finally admitted to him.

"I know," he told her, beginning to unfasten the buttons
on her gown again, "but I'll be here with you."

Clad only in her thin silk chemise now, she began to
shiver, as much from the cool night air on her skin as
from her growing need for her pipe. He lowered the
window and came back to the bed to pull the quilted
coverlet over her, and then he began to take off his own
clothes. In the golden glow of the oil lamp, his skin was
the color of burnished bronze, still stained from the summer sun. The hardness of his muscles was softened by the
light, silky covering of black hair on his arms and legs and
by the thick tangle of black-and-silver hair matting his
chest. She closed her eyes against the ache of desire rising
up in her and moved as close to the far end of the bed as
she could. But when he climbed in beside her, he drew
her back to him, circling her shoulders with one arm and
forcing her head down onto his chest.

She was shivering uncontrollably now, in spite of the
coverlet and the heat from his body. "Janson . . ." She
said his name out loud, still not convinced that he was
there in bed with her, instead of where he usually was,
obscured by the mists of her nightly dreams. "Janson."
She whispered it into his chest, feeling the beating of his
heart against her mouth.

"I'm here, Sarina," he answered her. "I'm here."

Her stomach was beginning to cramp. She gritted her
teeth and tried not to cry out, but her resistance weakened
with each fresh onslaught of pain. She sneezed once, and

although she attempted to block each subsequent sneeze, she was soon sneezing so violently that it was all she could do just to catch her breath. As the pains in her stomach worsened, she doubled herself into a ball, but that brought her very little relief. Janson turned her over onto her back and began to massage her stomach. Over and over, round and round, his hands stroked and warmed her flesh, coaxing some of the knots out of her and bringing her a temporary peace.

"J-Janson," she called up to him through the red web of pain blurring her sight. "T-talk to me. P-p-please t-talk to m-m-me."

He brushed back a damp strand of hair from her forehead and smiled. "Would it make you feel better to know that I'm not going to be dealing with Kwen anymore?" he asked her. "When we docked yesterday, one of my men delivered a message to his office here, telling him that the Carlyle Trading Company is no longer interested in transacting any further business with him."

Her pain was momentarily replaced by shock. "B-but you said his silk was the f-finest in China."

"It is," he agreed, "but with a little luck I'll eventually find other silk to equal his. I've been turning down a number of excellent silk growers these last few years, some of whom were willing to pay double what I was charging Kwen, which was still less than what Jardine and Matheson charge. Don't worry about me, Sarina, this was something I should have done a long time ago. The only one I feel sorry for is Lewis Deane, because he'll probably have to bear the brunt of Kwen's rage when he finds out about this."

At the mention of Lewis Deane's name, Sarina winced. A sharp spear of agony lanced her with its needle-sharp blade, and the wavering vision of Deane's sickly wife wheeling the pram with her very own son inside brought a whimpering sob of protest to her lips. She quickly turned onto her side and burrowed as close to Janson as she could, relieved when she felt both his arms tightening around her back again.

"It's your turn now, Sarina," he said to her some moments later, "I want you to tell me about Mei."

And so in halting tones she told him, swearing him to secrecy as she did.

"God, what a fool Chen was," he groaned. "How could either of them have thought they could get away with it?"

"I d-don't even know if Chen's still alive," she whispered, her heart turning over at the memory of that ashen face and those vacant eyes.

"Those poor innocent fools," he muttered again, "both of them."

Sarina wanted to ask him if he considered them fools because they had dared to defy Wo or because they had fallen in love. But she knew it was a question she would never ask. The pains were easing, the shivering subsiding as he continued to hold her, and so she threw one leg across his and turned her head to look up at the shadows undulating on the ceiling. After a few minutes she began to yawn.

"Are you getting sleepy?" he asked her while he lay there studying her profile. He tenderly traced a line down the middle of her forehead, along her slim nose, over the fullness of her lips, and down across her gently pointed chin.

As if already in a dream, she turned her head and their mouths touched. She nipped at his bottom lip with her teeth, giving him dozens of tiny love bites followed by several light, soothing sweeps with the tip of her tongue. He moaned, and although she was pleased with his response, she knew that she was beginning to drift away from him. Her eyelids were growing heavy. She blinked, fighting hard to keep them open. She wanted to explore more than his mouth, more than the sweet welcome of his tongue as it met hers. Her eyelids fluttered closed again. She was loosening her hold on him, releasing her grip on the very nearness of him.

Against her will, she who had once craved sleep so desperately lost her first battle to fight it off. And so she slept.

23

"To you, Sarina, and to one very successful week," Janson said proudly, raising his snifter of brandy and clinking it against hers.

She accepted his toast with an impish smile and took a deep swallow of her drink. Not only was she touched by his thoughtful gesture, but she too was proud of herself. As well she should be, she reminded herself, remembering the torture of those first few nights while Janson had patiently weaned her off the pipe.

"I think it's only fair that you share in one half of this toast," she told him, a hint of shyness in her voice as she faltered slightly meeting his direct gaze. To think that for seven nights he had held her in his arms, their bodies becoming as familiar to one another as they themselves had become, and never once had he attempted to take advantage of her weakness or their closeness by making love to her. As she took another sip of her brandy, she realized, to her complete surprise, that she was now disappointed rather than relieved by his gentlemanly behavior.

"This is supposed to be a celebration," he chided her. "Why so glum?"

After another swallow of brandy, she felt exceedingly bold. With an impudent toss of her head and forced gaiety in her voice she said, "Now that you consider me one of your successful patients, Dr. Carlyle, I suppose I'll just have to get used to sleeping all by myself again."

He cocked one eyebrow at her. "Why, Dragon Flower, I'm shocked. Is there an indecent proposition lurking behind that statement of yours?"

She blushed at her own boldness and got up from her chair and went to stand by the window.

"Why, I do believe there is," he said, going after her. Setting his glass down on the bedside table, he took hers out of her hand and put it down next to his. "Sarina?" He turned her around to face him and wrapped his arms around her.

She snuggled close to him, her head resting on his chest, her own arms circling his broad, strong back, breathing in the familiar scent of him and wishing they could stand that way, just holding on to each other, forever.

"Sarina?" he asked softly, his mouth buried deep in her hair. "Sarina, who's Michael?"

The moment froze and shattered.

"M-Michael?" she stammered, hearing her heart's frantic pounding in her ears.

"You called out in your sleep to someone named Michael several times this past week." He tipped up her chin to look into her eyes, and his were mischievous. "Do I have a rival named Michael?"

She dimpled and lowered her gaze. The shock of his saying Michael's name was beginning to pass, and in as light a tone as she could manage, she replied, "Would you be jealous if you did?"

"Jealous?" he repeated. "I'm surprised it was only Michael. I was expecting David and William and John and—"

She took a playful swipe at his shoulder. "You're avoiding my question, Janson."

"But then, my sweet, so are you," he returned, giving her a brief peck on the nose. "Ladies first."

Would any answer of hers solicit a truthful response from him? she wondered as she considered what to say to him. *Michael is the name of your son, Janson*, was the only answer he deserved, and yet it was the one answer she would never be able to give him. To think that they were the parents of a child they would never know, never share together, never . . . She quickly stopped herself.

"Michael was the name of my twin brother," she finally told him, staring over his shoulder at the far wall. "He died of diphtheria when we were fourteen."

"Oh, Sarina, I'm sorry." He crushed her against him, one hand pressing her head deep into his chest. "I'm so very sorry."

Forgive me, Janson, she whispered to herself. *Forgive me for lying to you*. But in a way, it *was* the truth. Michael

Steven *was* dead for her, for both of them. And as with a
twin, it was as though half of her had actually died along
with him. Suddenly she could no longer bear being as
close to Janson as she was. She broke away from his
embrace, snatched the crystal decanter from the bedside
table, and poured a small amount of brandy into her
snifter. Her hands were trembling as she lifted it to her
mouth.

"You're not going to turn into a drunk now, are you?"
Janson teased her as she downed the brandy in one burning gulp. "I only suggested you keep it there in case you
couldn't sleep, and it's hardly time for bed now." As he
was speaking, he snapped open his pocket watch and
frowned. "As a matter of fact, it's nearly two," he said. "I
have an appointment at two-thirty, so I'd better leave right
away." He gave her a light kiss on the mouth. "I'll see you
as usual around ten tonight."

He was halfway across the floor when her voice stopped
him. "I'm still waiting for your answer, Janson."

For a moment he appeared confused; then he grinned
at her and winked. "Jealous, Sarina? Now, what do *you*
think?"

He waved gaily at her and left her standing there fuming.
With a frustrated shriek she hurled her glass at the closed
door, and when she heard it smash into pieces, she felt a
bit better.

She waited another fifteen minutes and then threw on
her long blue cloak and drew the hood up over her head.
Hurrying from the house, she walked for two blocks before spotting an empty carriage and hailing it. The route
was so tediously familiar to her now that she leaned back
in the seat and closed her eyes. It was a game she had
started to play with herself: she would keep her eyes
closed, gauging the distance they traveled, until she could
sense they were approaching the Deanes' house. Then
and only then would she open her eyes again and look.
She was becoming so accomplished at it that now as she
opened her eyes they were just coming up to the white
stucco house with the slate-gray window shutters and the
narrow flagstone path.

She adjusted her hood and sat up tensely in her seat.
This was her fourth trip up the hill this week, and on each
previous visit there had been no sign of the pram and no

sign of either Anne Deane or Lucy Greer being out and about. A light rain was beginning to fall, and Sarina despaired of seeing them today in such foul weather. As they swung past the deserted park on Banyan, Sarina began drumming her fingers impatiently against the windowpane. She chewed away on her bottom lip as they passed the house a second time and then a third. When they turned off Banyan and approached the house a fourth time, she finally made up her mind. In spite of the possible risk involved, she would accept Anne Deane's invitation for tea. She simply had to see her son again.

Suddenly her eyes widened. Another carriage had just drawn up to the curb in front of the Deanes' house. Sarina's hand flew to her throat. A man dressed in a dark gray frock coat and trousers, carrying a small black bag, had stepped down from the coach and was striding briskly up the flagstone path. A doctor! Was Michael Steven ill? Had something happened to him? Was that why there had been no pram all week?

Sarina instructed the driver to pull ahead of the other carriage and to wait at the corner of Casuarina and Acacia. Then she turned around in her seat and stared intently out of the window while she waited herself. She had counted five carriages going past before the one she was looking for finally headed their way. Flinging open her door, she stepped into the street, and as the coach drew nearer, she waved frantically at the driver to stop. He obligingly sawed back on the reins, and the carriage halted with a bucking lurch. She rapped on the glass and the man inside threw open the door with a great display of irritation. But at the sight of her beautiful face draped in the blue silk cape, gazing up at him so pleadingly, his scowl was immediately replaced by an appreciative smile.

"Forgive me for inconveniencing you this way," she apologized to the man with the bristling black mustache and metal-rimmed spectacles peering down at her, "but I was just about to stop at my friend Anne Deane's for tea when I noticed your carriage. Naturally, I hesitated to disturb her if Michael was sick again, so I—"

"Michael?" he blustered with a bewildered look. "Why, that little fellow's never known a sick day in his life, my dear. No, no, I'm afraid it's poor Anne again. It's the bloody weather here on the island, you know, just as

beastly as our own back home. I've told Lewis any number
of times her lungs simply cannot withstand it."

Sarina thanked him and hurried back to her own carriage.
Michael Steven was fine! He had never known a sick day
in his life. She sank back into her seat with a grateful sigh.
Her son was healthy. Knowing that he was safe and well
made her feel she had been granted the license to live
through another day. That Anne Deane was ill again sobered her for a moment, but the moment quickly passed.
All that really mattered was that her beloved son was all
right. Patience, she counseled herself. She must try to
learn patience. With a last backward glance at the distant
house, she told the driver to take her back to Dragon
Flower Street.

She had become so accustomed to Janson's appearing
promptly at ten that when ten-thirty was struck off in a
single bong by the tall ebony clock in the front hall, Sarina
assumed that someone had overwound it and that it was
running fast. Although she pretended that his tardiness
did not concern her, she nevertheless found she was becoming increasingly short in her greeting to each succes-
sive man who came in the door. As her agitation mounted,
so did the ominous flutterings in her stomach. She pic-
tured the crystal decanter of brandy sitting so temptingly
on the table beside her bed, and hastily tried to divert her
thoughts. She dared not prove Janson correct by trading
one form of addiction for another.

To ease her restlessness, she drifted toward the second
receiving room, where Mei was singing in the exquisitely
sweet voice Sarina remembered so well. She smiled to
herself at the small victory she and Janson had shared
together in convincing the unhappy girl to take that first
tentative step back toward living again. Reassured by Madam
Blue that she was not expected to do more than sing
unless she so chose, she had been singing for three nights
now. Not only was she drawing more men into the music
parlor than ever before, but she was also luring them away
from the gaming tables in the first receiving room as well.
Now, as Sarina walked through the half-empty gambling
parlor, she noticed Tung-tsu standing silently in a corner,
and she greeted him with a warm smile, which he acknowledged with a deep, respectful bow. Although his bruised

face had begun to heal, his nose remained heavily swathed
in gauze and white tape. No one had even mentioned the
unpleasant incident which had occurred in her room the
week before, and she was grateful that Wesley Galvan had
not set foot in the place since that night. Sarina stood in
the doorway of the music parlor for only one of Mei's
songs, and then she returned to the foyer again, even
more restless than before.

By midnight she was so distraught that she asked one of
the parlor maids for a cup of *samshu*. She sipped it slowly,
savoring the warmth that spread quickly through her body
and bound up some of the fraying ends of her taut nerves.
Although it dulled the biting edge of her distress, Sarina
was especially grateful for the brief diversion provided
her by Mei's stopping by to say good night before she
returned to her room again.

"He has not yet arrived?" the girl whispered in Sarina's
ear so that neither of the two men passing them on their
way out could overhear them.

As Sarina smiled and bowed to the two men, she gave
her head a slight shake. When the door closed behind
them, she turned to Mei and said anxiously, "He's been so
punctual, this isn't like him at all. What if something has
happened to him?"

Mei rested a placating hand on Sarina's shoulder.
"Nothing has happened to him, my sister," she assured
her in her gentle voice. "He has sailed an ocean to stand at
your side. Two hours are but a moment in the face of that
other journey. He will come, Sarina. Have patience."

Sarina sighed. "Patience." Again, patience.

"If he is not yet here, it is because he is elsewhere by
necessity and not of his own choosing."

Sarina gave the girl a grateful hug. "I hope you're right,
my sister," she said. She kissed Mei on the cheek and then
watched as she made her way slowly up the stairs to her
lonely room—and the company of her little pipe.

She heard the front door opening and turned toward it
expectantly, just as she had all evening, praying that at last
it would be him. She saw the shadow of a long robe in the
doorway and she hurriedly masked her disappointment
with a polite but artificial smile as she bowed low in her
traditional gesture of greeting. But just as she began to
straighten again, her flesh turned into stone.

Standing there in the foyer, in a black quilted silk robe embroidered with red poppies, silver tree peonies, and green lotus leaves, a black melon-skin cap on his head, was Wo Shue Kwen.

Her mind reeled at the sight of him. Had she been found out and betrayed after all? Nausea forged its way up the back of her throat and flashes of glaring white light began exploding in front of her eyes. Why was he here? Why was he bowing to her as if he were simply bowing respectfully to any stranger he had happened to encounter? Stunned, she blinked her eyes. Was he even aware of who she was? His gaze raked her from head to toe with obvious and lustful approval. She suddenly felt she was observing him from someplace outside her own body when she slowly straightened up from her bow and came face to face with him at last.

"Welcome," she murmured in her breathy whisper. "I am Dragon Flower, your hostess."

"A most lovely name indeed for a woman of such fiery perfection," came the smooth reply in the voice she had never thought to hear again. "But, tell me, Dragon Flower, where is the Madam Blue whose name I have heard spoken these many years and whom I have never had the pleasure of meeting?"

"Madam Blue is already occupied." She gave him her usual reply. "Perhaps some other evening . . ." She allowed her voice to trail off.

"I fear there will be no other evening, my beautiful Dragon Flower," he sighed. "I return tomorrow to my home. Perhaps an exception this one time?" From deep inside his robes he drew out a black silk pouch, which he proceeded to bounce up and down in the palm of his hand.

Disgusted, she nonetheless managed to honor him with her sweetest smile. "I am forbidden by Madam Blue to accept such generous gifts."

She watched his expression subtly changing as he tucked the pouch back inside his robe again.

"If you would be so kind as to follow me, I will acquaint you with the many delights available to you here," she told him.

"And are you not one of those delights yourself, my

exquisite flower?" he asked as he followed her into the gambling parlor.

She half-turned, and with her eyes carefully narrowed, replied, "Although your words are most flattering, Dragon Flower is only your hostess."

He paused for a moment before one of the gaming tables and reached inside his robes again. Sarina took advantage of his obvious interest in the game and decided against showing him the rest of the house as she was expected to do with each new caller. Giddy with the knowledge that her disguise was shielding her from the man she feared and loathed most in the world, she did not want to endanger herself by remaining with him any longer than necessary. Favoring him with another smile, she bowed to him and began backing toward the door.

"While I amuse myself with these games of chance, my lovely Dragon Flower," he called out to her, "would you not see if perhaps good fortune will be mine with Madam Blue as well?"

"As you wish," she deferred to him, her frozen smile barely concealing her contempt for his supreme arrogance.

Her strength gave out just as she reached the staircase. She used the banister to help her up the steps, but she stumbled and nearly fell just as she reached the landing. Regaining her balance, she tottered down the hallway, half-falling against the door of Madam Blue's bedchamber as she knocked and pushed the door open at the same time. The frail figure sitting in her chair by the window, sipping a cup of tea, glanced up in alarm as Sarina staggered into the room.

"I can't go back downstairs tonight," she gasped, sinking to her knees at Madam Blue's feet.

"My dear child, what has happened to trouble you this way?" she demanded.

"The first day I came here," Sarina blurted out, "when Mei told you I was in fear for my life . . . The man I was running from is downstairs right now."

Madam Blue set down her cup. "Did he recognize you?" she asked.

"No." Sarina shook her head.

"That, at least, is a blessing."

"He was asking for you," she said grimly.

"Then let us not disappoint him," the woman declared as she pushed herself up from her chair.

"You're going down there?"

"Someone must remain at the door, my dear, and it was my duty long before it was yours." She patted Sarina on the shoulder as she hobbled toward her closet. "Now, help me to dress, and then you must describe for me what this villainous creature looks like."

When Madam Blue was dressed, Sarina handed her her silver-topped ivory stick and walked with her to the door.

"Now, you return to your own room," the older woman instructed her, "and bolt your door. I will send Mr. Carlyle up to you as soon as he arrives."

"But how did you know he wasn't here?" asked a shaken Sarina.

Madam Blue patted her cheek affectionately and smiled. "If he were here, my dear child, you would not have had to come to me. Now, do as I say."

Sarina waited until Madam Blue had begun to descend the staircase before she left the room and hurried back down the hallway again. She looked in on Mei, and when she found that the girl was already asleep, she heaved a sigh of relief and softly closed the door. Locking her own bedroom door, she rushed over to her bedside table and picked up the crystal decanter. It banged noisily against the side of her glass as she poured some brandy into it.

While she toyed with the snifter, she nervously stalked the room, cursing Janson for encouraging her to depend on him and then letting her down. What a fool she was to have trusted him! She ground her teeth together and continued her restless pacing. But what if he had not intentionally disappointed her? she argued with herself. What if something had happened to him? What if Wesley Galvan had found out Janson's name and had decided to settle accounts with him? No. She shook her head. Wesley Galvan was high-spirited, but certainly not vindictive. Or was he? She gulped down half of her brandy.

There was nothing detaining Janson but his own headstrong and independent nature. Perhaps she had frightened him off by hinting that she preferred him in her bed to sleeping alone now. She damned herself for her own stupidity, for admitting to him what she had only just come to realize herself. She drained her glass. Business.

That was it. He had had a number of business appointments that afternoon. Any one of them could have detained him.

When she heard the knock on her door, she was so unprepared for it that she let out a little scream. She was just about to rush over to the door on winged heels, but something small and contrary inside her held her back. He had kept her waiting all evening. Now it was his turn to wait. The knock came again, rapid and insistent. She smiled wickedly and walked in measured steps toward the door. My, he is impatient, she thought, placing her hand on the brass door handle. He was hammering angrily now. She decided she had teased him long enough. With a cool smile on her face, she threw back the bolt and opened the door.

Madam Blue took a tiny step forward and collapsed in Sarina's arms.

Sarina wrung out a fresh cloth and draped it across Madam Blue's forehead. Her eyelids fluttered open and then closed again, as if the effort of keeping them open was simply too great. Sarina had half-dragged, half-carried the slumping woman to her bed before Madam Blue had fainted, and now, while she waited for her to come round completely, all she could do was watch over her with loving concern.

Finally the remarkable blue eyes opened again and remained open this time. Sarina removed the damp cloth, and as she smoothed back several fine strands of white hair from Madam Blue's high forehead, she gave her a warm, reassuring smile.

"The gods manifested a peculiar generosity when they sent you to me in search of sanctuary, my dear Sarina," the woman said in a voice still weak with shock. "For it would seem that you and I share something of a common past."

"I don't think I understand," replied Sarina.

The sky-blue eyes focused sharply on her face. "Wo Shue Kwen" was all she said.

Sarina gasped.

There was a strange distance in those blue eyes now, as if the woman were already sinking back into some long-forgotten yesterday as she murmured, "Like you, he did not recognize me."

"You knew him?" Sarina whispered incredulously. "You once knew Wo?"

The woman nodded, her eyes still focused on that distant memory, and the voice drifting up to Sarina could have been the voice of someone else. "I was a girl then, and my name was Ch'in Ling. My father was Chinese, my mother British, and we lived, along with my two brothers, on a large silk farm outside of Shanghai. My marriage had been arranged—to the son of a lifetime friend of my father's who owned a silk farm far larger than ours. But unlike most young people whose marriages have been arranged, we met and fell deeply in love, and because of my love, I gladly surrendered my virtue to him." She paused for a moment to moisten her lips before she continued.

"Shortly before our marriage was to have taken place, his father, a greedy and ambitious man, broke his trust with my father and betrothed his son to the daughter of a man who owned a vast tea and poppy plantation and whose own betrothed had recently died of the pox. The word of a Chinese father is law, and like any obedient son, my lover obeyed his father. And so, while I lay alone with my grief and my shame and the blossoming seed he had planted within me, he and a stranger exchanged their vows before the ancestral tablets in his father's house. Then, on that most consecrated of all nights, when a husband takes his new wife to his bed for the first time, he came to me and asked me to become his favored one."

Sarina buried her face in her hands and moaned. She saw not only a young Ch'in Ling and a young Wo Shue Kwen being brutally torn apart by the cruelty of tradition, but Mei and Chen and another stranger named Lao Kuer T'ai, and her heart grew heavy and cold.

"I refused him," said Madam Blue. "Although he pleaded with me, weeping as I had seen no man weep before, I sent him away. He had taken our love and tainted it by offering me the lowly position of his whore. In my anger, I would punish him by denying him our love and the child he did not even know I was carrying. I was proud, Sarina, and because my heritage was a blending of two cultures, I

refused to bow to the duplicitous laws of Chinese tradition.
And so I left Shanghai and never returned."

"And the baby?"

"Kwen's first son?" Madam Blue smiled, her lips curling
in contempt. "I rid myself of the seed his love had left
inside me, and I was cursed by the gods for my action by
never again being able to bear a child."

Tears were sliding in twin paths down Sarina's face.
"I'm so sorry," she sobbed, "I'm so terribly sorry." She
bent and kissed the woman on the forehead and then
gently stroked one of her silken cheeks.

"For some time after, I allowed my anger and my grief
to guide my steps," Madam Blue continued. "I became the
whore Kwen would have had me be. I sold strangers the
use of my body so that I could eat, but I gave no one
access to my heart. Soon, no feeling remained in me at all,
neither love nor hate, merely an exalted emptiness. I even
forgot the girl I had once been, and so Ch'in Ling ceased
to exist and Madam Blue was given life instead."

"And that was thirty years ago?" questioned Sarina.

"Yes"—she nodded—"thirty years. And tonight I have
been forced to remember what I had trained myself once
to forget."

"And now that you've seen him again," asked Sarina in
a hoarse whisper, "do you still love him?"

Madam Blue laughed. "One cannot undo in a single
moment, my dear Sarina, a pattern which thirty years has
woven. No"—she shook her head—"I do not love Wo
Shue Kwen, nor do I hate him. Perhaps, one day when
you trust me enough, you will tell me of your own dealings with the man I knew only as a boy. And please, my
dear, erase that fear from your eyes, for he will never
learn from these lips that you are here. You are as precious to me as any child I might have borne, had the gods
directed my steps along a path far different from the one
they themselves chose for me. Now, let me lie here awhile
longer, and then I will return downstairs."

"You can't mean that!" Sarina was aghast. "I won't allow
you to do it. There's no reason for you to submit yourself
to something which can only cause you more pain."

"It is only my body which pains me, Sarina," Madam
Blue insisted, "and it was my body which betrayed me

tonight, sending me into your arms like a weak and foolish child."

"Please, don't be so stubborn. You can't go back!"

"There is something I must do before the night slips
past us and the gods snatch back this moment which they
have bestowed on me. As there is a purpose in all things, my
dearest Sarina, so there is a purpose to this fated encounter."

Sarina studied the woman's closed eyes and tried to
grapple with the feelings raging inside her. How could she
ever tell this woman, who looked upon her as her own
daughter, that Wo Shue Kwen had wanted her for his
concubine too? And Mei. Should she tell Madam Blue
about Mei, the girl Wo's son had loved but could not
marry? The girl Wo had banished to live in the brothel of
the woman he himself had been forbidden to marry all
those many years ago? It was mad, she decided, mad and
absurd.

There was a soft rapping at her door. Madam Blue's
eyes flew open, and the two women stared at each other.
The knock came again, and Sarina got up from the bed
and tiptoed over to the door.

"Yes?" she called out in her whispery Dragon Flower
voice.

"It's Janson," came the equally low reply.

Sarina stiffened. "I'm already in bed."

Madam Blue began gesturing to her, but Sarina stood
her ground.

"I don't believe you," Janson said softly. "Now, open the
door."

"Good night, Janson."

"I think you'd better let me in, Dragon Flower." He
fairly spit out her invented name.

Madam Blue was struggling to her feet.

"I'm tired, Janson, and I'm following your advice and
having some brandy before—"

"Do you know who's downstairs in the gambling parlor?"
he demanded, his voice still lowered, but harsh with
exasperation.

"Yes, I do."

"He came by my office this evening and caught me right
in the middle of a meeting with some other silk growers. I
had to interrupt the meeting to speak with him, because—"

"You knew he was here in Hong Kong?"

"He was furious with me for not having discussed my decision with him, and he thought that by coming here himself, he could convince me to change my mind. I practically threw him out—"

"You knew he was in Hong Kong and you didn't warn me!"

"He hasn't been in Hong Kong for thirty years. How the hell was I supposed to know he'd sail into port, show up at my office, and then head straight over here!"

Madam Blue seized Sarina by the arm and shook her. "Do not be as stubborn as you have accused me of being."

"Who's in there with you?" hissed Janson.

"That is none of your business," Sarina retorted.

"Do not play this game with the heart of a proud man," warned Madam Blue, but Sarina refused to heed her advice.

He had kept her waiting, he had caused her to worry about him, but worse than that, he had known Wo was in Hong Kong and had done nothing to warn her.

"Sarina," he whispered urgently, "if you're doing this to punish me for being late, I apologize for that, but it couldn't be helped. I was still in that meeting when Kwen showed up after ten, and I had to finish it after I finally managed to get rid of him. As soon as the other men left, I came directly here. When I noticed him downstairs, all I could think of was finding you and making sure that you were all right. You *are* all right, aren't you?"

When she said nothing, he rapped lightly on the door again. "He didn't recognize you, did he?" He waited a moment and then said, "Sarina, are you listening to me? You're safe. He has no idea where you are—he even tried to wheedle it out of me, thinking I might know. Sarina? Dammit, say something!"

She heard him give the door a savage pound with his fist, followed by what she was certain was a kick. Then, before she could stop her, Madam Blue was unlocking the door.

"Please, don't," Sarina cried, reaching for the handle, but it was too late.

The door swung open. The corridor was empty. Janson was gone.

"Sarina!" The woman turned on her, fire in her blue eyes. "You are a fool!"

24

Wo Shue Kwen raised his head from the blue silk cushion and accepted the second pipe she had warmed for him. She had drawn the curtains to enclose them in a tent of clearest blue, separating them by a silken barricade from the jarring clamor of the world outside, and he felt the peace of their private world gradually entering his body and saturating his senses. He inhaled deeply, drawing the acrid smoke into his lungs, and then he exhaled it through his nose. Above the twin funnels of the mist he had released, he could see her watching him, refusing the pipe herself, preferring to serve him instead. It was impossible to determine her age, for beauty such as hers knew no age, although signs of its encroachment were there in the gentle gnarling of her elegant white hands and in the tremor she made no attempt to disguise.

She had not spoken to him since she had returned to the gaming parlor and beckoned for him to follow her. He had suspected who she was because of the reverence being shown her by the others as they passed, and when she clapped her hands twice and the blue silk tent was immediately emptied of its five occupants, there could be no mistaking her identity.

He yawned and stretched out languorously on the cushions to revel in his victory. He had secured for himself the services of a woman whose prowess had been legend for thirty years, and although this was the first time he had paid for a woman to pleasure him, he knew this was no ordinary woman. He was well pleased. A man of his stature deserved no less than Madam Blue herself.

When she moved closer to him, her face was no more than a wavering ivory image sheathed in the blue of the sky. He closed his eyes and allowed the power of the opium to lift him up and far beyond himself. Her warm breath was like a spring breeze against his face, and he sighed and raised his face to the breeze. He shivered as the pointed tips of her long scarlet nails began slowly to trace the outline of each of his features, leaving him to feel as if she were searing the imprint of his entire face upon the very surface of his brain. His eyebrows burned, as did the skin of his eyelids. His nose twitched. He opened his mouth, and following the bidding of that fiery nail, he left it open, open and burning.

He turned his face to the side as her breath warmed his cheek, sweeping out toward one delicate and sensitive ear. He shuddered over and over while her tongue teased circles around the rim of his ear before snaking its way inside the narrow channel of the ear itself, to flick and probe, withdraw and probe again. And all the while, her breath grew warmer as it fanned him. He groaned, and she withdrew, using her tongue to lap its way gently around his face, grazing each of the burning features her nails had traced. When she lazily circled his mouth, his tongue darted out and tried to capture hers, but she laughed, a throaty rustle of laughter, and then she drew away from him.

He trembled when she kissed the corners of his mouth, then dotted tiny kisses across his upper lip and nipping bites along his fuller bottom lip. As she lapped hungrily at the tender inner flesh of his mouth, he groaned again, thrusting his body into the air once, then twice, and then falling back down again. She sought out his tongue, and he offered it to her thankfully, holding it still, a rigid staff, while she spun tantalizing circles all around it. She had yet to touch his body, and he was already stiff and heavy.

When she removed his robes, he was adrift on a wave of desire so intense that his body was undulating, rising and falling, as the wave itself crested and ebbed. He was lost among blue gossamer clouds, where puckish sprites nipped and lapped and tugged at his flesh, each sprite enticing a separate part of him with subtle artistry. One pulled the fine hairs on his chest, another drew prickling circles around each hardened nipple, still another stroked his stomach with a touch as delicate as a feathered wing.

Two worked to pry his legs apart, spreading them wider

and wider with gentle insistence, and then spreading them wider still. Then they all gathered in the throbbing center of his parted legs, all of them dancing there on sharp little feet. Some stooped to tug at his curling brush, to lap at his dewy skin and nip at the two great orbs which cushioned his mighty scepter, rising above them, a proud banner, heralding his manliness.

He caught his breath. His body arched expectantly. A moistened sheath was fitting itself over the head of him. Slowly, slowly, the silken wetness descended, molding itself to his shape, pulling him higher and drawing all the remaining breath out of him. He whimpered as the jaws of that velvet vise clamped tightly around him. A moment passed, its grip relaxed, freeing him, and then it rose upward again. It spiraled down, capping him, cupping him, enclosing him, and then just as swiftly spun away once more. He followed its beckoning path, straining to plunder its taunting sweetness on his own.

He was panting as he sought to match each glorious celestial thrust with a parry of his mortal soul. He bucked and raged, his head thrashing from side to side, slick with his own wetness and her heavenly nectar, straining, seething, gnashing his teeth, clawing at the blueness that was oblivion awaiting him. With one final heaving thrust, he hurled himself up, up, up to meet her at last, screaming as the explosion tore ecstasy's honeyed juices from his wretched body, spilling himself into the boundless vessel of the sky. And when he had spent his seed and his fury, she released him to tumble on his earthward journey all alone.

He woke slowly several hours later and reached out for her. His hands closed around nothingness. His eyes flew open. All around him was the translucent blue of the silken tent, lighted by the single oil lamp hanging from the ceiling above his head. He was strangely light-headed, yet fatigued at the same time, as though he had recently waged a fearsome struggle he could not quite recall. And to his surprise, he was fully dressed.

He pushed himself into a sitting position and rubbed the final vestiges of sleep from his eyes. It was only then that he noticed her there, sitting, not on a silken cushion now, but on a low cushioned stool, her arms at her sides, her hands like trembling birds fluttering just above the floor. His eyes were drawn down to the magnificent ring she was wearing on the index finger of her left hand, and something deep within him began to stir.

The ring was a broad band of rare pink jade carved into small plum blossoms. At the center of each blossom was a tiny diamond, and twisting through the field of flowers was a smiling dragon, its regal head and elongated body sheathed in tiny glittering emeralds, its eyes two blazing rubies. He had seen a ring like it just once before. Even then he had thought it to be the only one of its kind. And he wondered how she had come to own one so very similar.

From the ring, his eyes traveled slowly up to her face, to her narrowed eyes, which were regarding him so solemnly. Veiled before by the smoky shades of night, obscured by the vaporous haze of the pipe, her eyes had remained no more than darkened slashes in her whitened face. Now, as she met his gaze directly, her eyes began to widen, widening enough for the lamplight to glimmer across the surface of each brightening orb and to reflect their startling blueness back to him. It was at that moment that the light which kindled the very life force within him sputtered and went out.

"Oh, no." It was a long, drawn sigh spun from his lips, urged upward from his soul, echoing in his ears, turning back upon itself over and over and over again. "Oh, no, it cannot be." What foul deceit had seen him pay to lie with the woman he had once loved with all the innocence of his youth, and to whom he had given that very ring she was wearing as a pledge of that love? How could the gods, whom he had served so faithfully, have chosen to play him so falsely?

"No, Ch'in Ling, no," he moaned, covering his face with his hands, blocking out the sight of the woman he had lost more than thirty years before, the woman whose image time had dimmed, but had never erased completely. He had searched for her through the years, never once thinking to look for her in the gutters of Hong Kong, never once suspecting that the woman known as Madam Blue had been the Ch'in Ling he had vowed would be the mother of his sons.

Madam Blue clapped her hands twice and the curtains of the blue tent parted. Wo fought them with what remained of his strength, but they lifted him to his feet as if

he were a paper dragon. Still she said nothing. She simply
sat there, her face expressionless, watching as they dragged
him from the tent.

"Ch'in Ling!" he cried out to her, his legs trailing like
useless stumps of wood behind him. "You have used me as
faithlessly as the gods themselves have used me. We are
not finished with each other, Ch'in Ling," he shrilled. "It
is not finished between us yet."

His voice faded. She heard the front door close and she
allowed her shoulders to sag. She had made love to him
and she had remained untouched and unmoved through
it all, her body performing, a thing apart from her mind,
as if he were simply another of the many faceless men
with whom she had shared but brief moments of her long
life. To think that the past they had lived without each
other would have been their future together had the gods
dealt more fairly with them. *It is not finished between us yet*,
he had said. Should she take him at his word? Would he
dare return again? She sighed. It had been over between
them for thirty years, and the wound, once so raw, had
healed without even a threadlike trace of a scar.

Rising slowly from the stool, she swayed for a moment
on uncertain legs, while her eyes remained fixed on the
tiny jeweled flowers which encircled her finger like the
innocent pink blush of a spring morning. It seemed to her
that she had lived two lifetimes since a young man had
pledged his love to her with that ring on a spring morning
thirty-three years ago, when the plum trees were in bloom
and the future lay ahead of them. As she made her way
through the sleeping house, she reminded herself that the
plum trees would soon be in bloom again. But never again
would there be such a love as theirs.

By the time she had reached her bedchamber, her bittersweet recollections had all been returned to her memory
for safekeeping. Kwen had indeed been wrong. It *was*
over between them.

Sarina had managed to sleep fitfully through the early
hours of the morning, torn between wanting to use Mei's
pipe and wanting to prove to herself that she could manage without Janson there beside her. Her moments of
sleep were jumbled whirls of black dragon robes and pointing fingers and fists pounding on her door and a pair of

scarlet lips calling out fool, fool, fool to her while she covered her ears and shook her head and shouted for them to leave her alone. Now, as she lay huddled in her bed, her knees drawn up to her chest, staring through the partially drawn curtains at the bleak gray smudge of morning, she absently stroked the empty place next to her. It was cool where it should have been warmed by the heat of his body, just as she was cold without the warmth of his arms around her, the strength of his chest cushioning her head, and the comforting balm of his voice to soothe her.

"Oh, Janson, Janson." She whispered his name as she continued to smooth the already smooth, cool sheet, the anger of the night before dissipating, burning itself out, leaving only a sad, wistful loneliness in its wake.

When the agonized howl of a man shattered the silence of the house, she threw back the bedcovers and ran to the door. Her hand on the door handle, she hesitated. It could only be one man's voice she was hearing. She backed slowly away from the door and put her hands over her ears.

"It is not finished between us yet!"

The words screamed in shrill force near the bottom of the staircase penetrated the protective shield of her fingers and echoed through her brain. What had she done to him, Sarina wondered, to have provoked such a bellow of pain from a man who prided himself on his self-containment? She took her hands from her ears as the front door slammed, and her first impulse was to rush to Madam Blue and hold her in her arms and be her comfort should she need it. But something held her back, something which warned her that she should not intrude upon the privacy the woman would be needing now far more than companionship. For thirty years of waiting had finally been repaid in the dusky hours of a single night, and it was perhaps a triumph too painful to be shared with another.

Would Wo make good his threat, she wondered, and return to Hong Kong again to finish whatever lay between Madam Blue and himself? Janson had assured her that she herself was safe. But for how much longer? She had managed to fool Wo and successfully elude him this time, but what if he *did* return and caught her unawares and unprepared? She stared dismally at her tumbled bed. Even if Janson were there with her, would that be enough to keep her out of the vindictive grasp of Wo Shue Kwen? She smiled wanly. She had managed without Janson for one night; that in itself was a victory of sorts, and yet she realized with a bit of a shock that what she had unthinkingly blurted out to him the day before had finally been confirmed for her. She did not want Janson Carlyle to leave her bed at all.

She took great pains with her toilette later that morning, lining her eyes subtly with blue and using a touch of rouge on her cheeks and mouth. Then she arranged her hair in a cluster of loosely twining curls on top of her head and freed several tendrils to softly frame her face. She slipped into her most elegant day gown, a high-collared, long-sleeved *cheongsam* of blue brocade with a modest slit cut up one leg halfway to the knee, and patiently fastened each of its tiny side buttons. Drawing on her long blue cloak, she carefully draped the hood over her hair and picked up her small blue silk reticule from her dresser. As she left the house, she stopped a passing carriage and told the driver to take her to the offices of the Carlyle Trading Company.

It was a wide single-story gray stone building fronting the harbor on Market Street. The portly gentleman who was leaving the building just as she was walking up the steps politely doffed his hat to her and held the door open for her. She dimpled prettily for him and glided into the front office, which was ringed by wooden benches and filled with men talking together in small groups, who obviously preferred standing about to sitting down. She swept up to the crowded counter, smiling to herself as a number of men drew back and allowed her to pass.

"Mr. Janson Carlyle, please," she announced to one of the harried Oriental clerks in a loud, clear voice, which brought the conversations around her to an abrupt halt.

"You have appointment see master Carlyle?" chirped the young man without looking up from the ledger he was studying.

"I most certainly do," she replied haughtily, warming at the continued silence in the place.

"Come this way, please." He was vaguely gesturing to her with one hand while turning the page of the ledger book with the other. "Third door left."

"Thank you." She nodded imperiously as she followed his pointing finger around the counter and down a narrow corridor to the appropriate door. She took a deep breath and rapped smartly on the door and then waited until he finally called out for her to enter.

"Have a seat," he said without glancing up from the papers he was working on. "I'll be with you in a moment."

Her eyes swept the large, well-appointed room with approval. The walls were hung in an ivory paper lightly patterned with sprigs of crimson berries and bright green bamboo shoots. The dark wood floor was partly covered by a crimson-and-green woven silk rug, and the low sofa set against one wall, as well as the two armchairs facing the vast mahogany desk, was covered in crimson silk. It was a surprisingly elegant office for the casually attired man who was working in it, the sleeves of his white shirt rolled back to the elbow, his cravat hanging open around his neck, and the first three buttons of his shirt undone.

As she settled herself in one of the crimson chairs, she licked the lips she had rouged such a short time ago and nervously folded her hands in her lap. Her eyes were riveted to the curling black hair exposed by his open shirt, and she recalled the springy softness of that hair as it had flattened against her cheek and curled around her fingers and . . .

"Now, how can we help you?" he asked, setting down his pen.

"I think you already know the answer to that, Mr. Carlyle," she purred.

His head shot up. "What the . . . ?"

"Good morning, Mr. Carlyle," she said sweetly.

The scowl slowly retreated from his face. " 'Morning," he mumbled. He picked up his pen again and leaned back in his chair. "You here because you have something to ship?"

She dimpled for him and cocked her head to one side. "As a matter of fact, I'm here to deliver something."

"Oh?" He began to nibble on the end of the pen. "And what might that be?"

She hesitated for a moment and then said, "An apology. I wanted to apologize for my behavior last night." Looking into his green eyes was like staring straight into the glare of the sun. She blinked and lowered her gaze, focusing instead on the pen he was now tapping against his bottom lip. "When you didn't come by at ten, I became worried, and then I became angry with you for keeping me waiting and for making me worry. And so"—she looked down at her hands—"by the time you knocked on my door, I was furious with you and decided not to answer it."

"But you managed to find someone else to keep you company in the meantime."

She shook her head. "No, that isn't true."

"You sure it wasn't our friend Mr. Galvan in there helping you to keep your mind off your worrying?"

She should have known better than to come here and apologize. The mocking tone in his voice was far worse than his anger. "Why are you always so infuriating?" she demanded. "Can't you simply accept my apology like a gentleman, or is being a gentleman just too difficult for you?"

Janson raised a skeptical eyebrow. "Judging from some of the company you've been keeping lately, Sarina, I'd say you're hardly qualified to be a judge of who's a gentleman and who's not."

She was on her feet, her eyes blazing. "I resent that remark, Janson. You've not only insulted me, but you've insulted everyone I know. And since I obviously offend your sensibilities, I suggest you look elsewhere for your own companionship from now on."

"Thank you, Sarina," he said, tossing the pen down onto his desk, "I'll do that."

A wave of panic engulfed her. She had come hoping to bring him back, and she had succeeded only in driving him further away. The spasm of fear clutching at her was as vicious as the cramps those first nights without the pipe. But she refused to be defeated by him again. She squared her shoulders and threw him a cold, withering look. Something flickered across his face. He looked away. And then, as if he had hastily considered the alternatives, he pushed back his chair and came around the desk to stand in front of her. They stood there facing each other like two adversaries, their eyes locked in defiance, their stances firm as they both waited, each determined to let the other be the first to weaken.

It was she who broke the stalemate between them. She turned and started for the door. And so it was he who accepted the defeat she had dealt him by going after her. He caught her by the wrist and spun her into his arms. His hands plunged inside her cloak and closed around the silken smallness of her waist. Her hood slid from her head as she arched her back, twisting her upper body as far away from him as she could. He slid his arms up along her back, drawing her closer and closer to him, until her breasts grazed his chest and only inches separated their parting mouths. Their lips touched briefly once, and then again, until they each chose to deepen their kiss, where-upon they melted into each other's mouths, the two of them breathing as one.

He pressed her head to his shoulder and buried his face in the sweet gilt of her hair. "Sarina," he whispered as he raised her face again and kissed her on the forehead. Each time he kissed her, he murmured her name. He left no part of her face untouched, and then, just before their lips met again, she cried out his name, joining his name to hers. When they kissed, they clung and swayed together as the moments passed and time fell away.

"Sarina," he said urgently, cupping her face in his hands, "I want you to leave Madam Blue. Tell me where you want to live and I'll arrange it. A small house, a large house, in the city, up on the hill, anywhere, but let me take you out of that place."

It seemed an eternity had passed before what he was saying finally reached her. She had come here hoping to share a few more nights with him, and he was offering her much more than that. He was offering her what he had sworn he would offer no one.

"A house?" Her voice was quaking with excitement, but she cautioned herself to tread warily.

"Anything—everything—you want."

"Here in Hong Kong?"

"Or in San Francisco, wherever you want it to be," he said. "How much longer do you intend to hide out in a brothel?"

"Until I know that I'm safe."

"Kwen sailed for Shanghai this morning, Sarina, but he could return at any time. You can't remain where you are and expect to escape him forever."

"What other choice do I have?" she baited him carefully.

"I've just offered you one."

She clenched her fists to steady herself as she said quietly, "You're willing to marry me so that I won't have to stay with Madam Blue?"

Janson's brows shot upward. "Marry you? No, I didn't say anything about marriage, Sarina. I simply said I'd buy you a house."

She wheeled about and headed for the door again.

"Sarina, come back here!" He bolted after her. "Does it have to be marriage or nothing at all?"

"I told you once before I had no intention of becoming your whore!"

"Don't make it vulgar, Sarina."

"Why not?" she challenged him. "You yourself suggested I was nothing but a whore when you accused me of being with Wesley Galvan last night."

"I was just as upset as you were about last night," he admitted reluctantly. "We both said things we didn't mean."

Her eyes were narrowed spitefully. "So now that I'm respectable again, I'm good enough to keep house and to play the whore for you—but *only* you."

"Stop it, Sarina!"

"Tell me, Janson," she continued bitterly, "do you plan to live in the house you want to buy for me, or should I simply expect you to call whenever you happen to be in port?"

"Sarina!"

"How many other cities have women living in houses you've bought for them, Janson, waiting for your ship to dock so that they can spend a few blissful days or weeks with you before you leave again?"

"There *are* no other houses and there *are* no other women," he hissed.

"And you expect me to believe that!"

"Yes, I do."

"Why?"

His teeth were clenched, his eyes stormy, as he snarled, "Because I want you, you silly little fool. I want to be with you, make love to you, wake up with you in my arms and know I won't ever have to share you with anyone else."

"Then what you want is a whore."

"I don't want a whore!" he shouted. "I simply don't know if what I want is a wife."

Sarina cringed, imagining all those men outside roaring

with laughter as Janson's words reverberated through the building. When was she going to realize that what he felt for her was nothing but lust? It was no more than what Wesley Galvan felt and no more than what Wo Shue Kwen had felt. In spite of her protestations to the contrary, she knew that she wanted Janson as much as he wanted her. But standing so close to him, their wits and their pride equally matched, and their separate secrets still secret from each other, she finally admitted to herself that what she felt for him was far more than simple lust.

She had fallen in love with Janson Carlyle, desperately and irrevocably in love with him. And she was in agony. She was in agony because she could admit her love to no one but herself, and because Janson Carlyle simply did not love her in return.

Would it change things between them if he knew they had a son? she wondered as she watched him angrily pacing the floor. What difference could it possibly make? Michael Steven was not theirs to have. He was the child of Anne and Lewis Deane. There was no proof of her having given birth to him, no witness to Kwen's treachery. What use could there be in telling a man who wanted no children that the one he had was alive and walking the earth as the child of someone else?

"I can't accept your offer, Janson," she finally told him, her voice flat and dull, "and I won't even consider leaving Madam Blue. She and Mei are the only loyal and loving people in my life, and they both need me."

He stopped his pacing and trained his troubled gaze on her. "I need you too," he said.

But not enough, she wanted to tell him. *Not enough.* She turned the handle of the door.

"Don't give me your final answer now, Sarina. I'll still be in Hong Kong for a while, so you can think about it before you have to make up your mind."

But as she closed the door of his office, all she could think about was where he would be when he left Hong Kong and where he would be going after that.

25

As the weeks passed, neither Sarina nor Madam Blue mentioned the visit of Wo Shue Kwen again, nor did Sarina ever tell Mei about it. Each evening she stood by the front door, prepared to see that dreaded face again and hear that silken voice she had once found so comforting; but each morning, she slipped into her lonely bed, thankful that her fears had gone unrealized for another night. She was sleeping fitfully again, but she was sleeping nonetheless, without the pipe, without any brandy, and without Janson Carlyle beside her. In spite of his persistence, she steadfastly refused to change her mind and accept his offer, and after a while he stopped asking.

It had taken all of her fortitude, but she had stayed away from the hill and number eighteen Casuarina Road ever since the fateful night of Wo's visit. It was no longer because she believed the Deanes had been warned about her, but because seeing her son was more painful to her than not seeing him at all. She had been foolish to think that it could have been otherwise. She was no more content with bits and pieces of her child than she was with the bits and pieces of his own father. The separations were too wrenching, the times apart fraught with too much uncertainty, the times together too brief and unsatisfying.

But one day shortly before Christmas, she weakened. Michael Steven was nearly a year old. It had been more than two months since she had last seen him. The day was mild and a feeble sun licked the ground; surely, she thought, Anne Deane would be out and about today. But later that afternoon, when the carriage slowly circled the block several times and there was still no sign of either

Anne Deane or the pram, Sarina made up her mind to return every afternoon until she saw the woman again.

Three days later, her persistence was finally rewarded. As they approached the small park on Banyan, she caught sight of the back of Lucy Greer's cheerful red cape and excitedly climbed down from the carriage. Coming up behind the girl, Sarina was disappointed to discover that she was not wheeling the pram at all. She was alone. When she called softly to her, the girl turned around very slowly. At first she appeared not to recognize Sarina, but when she did, only her eyes brightened; the rest of her face remained pinched and drawn. Sarina's chest began to constrict in fear.

" 'Ullo, mum." Lucy Greer acknowledged her with a slight nod of her head. "This is the first bit o' time I've 'ad to meself in days. My mistress Deane's passed on, you know, goin' on two weeks now."

"Oh, no!" Sarina's eyes widened in shock. "I'm so sorry to hear that.".

" 'Er lungs never were no good," the girl said. "The doc, 'e says it was a miracle she even lived as long as she did. The mister's takin' it real bad, 'e is, and little Michael, now, 'e's too young to understand about these things, but 'e knows there's somethin' diff'rent. I think 'e knows 'is ma's dead."

No, she's not, Sarina wanted to shout, *she's alive! Anne Deane may be dead, but she wasn't Michael Steven's mother. I am and I'm alive.* Suddenly her thoughts began to tumble about, tripping over themselves as they skittered like a child's wooden blocks, helter-skelter, inside her head.

"And much as I 'ate doin' it, mum," Lucy went on, "I've given poor Mr. Deane my notice. It ain't seemly a young girl like meself livin' alone with a man, now, is it? So I've found meself a position four streets up a ways as nanny to two girls in a big 'ouse with both a ma and pa to keep things respectable. You wouldn't be knowin' of someone, maybe a widow woman or the like, needin' a position, now, would you?"

"No." Sarina shook her head. "No, I'm afraid I . . ."

She clamped her mouth shut in time to give her addled brain a moment to think more clearly. A widow. She nearly laughed out loud. Her seafaring husband could conveniently have died—as he had lived—at sea. She was aware of Lucy studying her with a puzzled expression on her face.

"I was wrong," she blurted out, "I was wrong, Lucy. I *do* know of someone."

"Why, that's bloody marv'lous," the girl beamed. "Could you send 'er 'round right away, then? My other family's waitin' for me kinda impatient like, you know."

Right away. Again Sarina tried to think. She had told Janson she would never leave Madam Blue. How could she do it now, while he was still in Hong Kong? Once again she was conscious of Lucy's bewildered stare. She thought of Michael Steven. By some fateful sleight of hand, she was being given the chance to share in her son's life, a chance she had never expected to have. She could feed and bathe him, dress him and brush his hair and take him for walks. She would be with him when he took his first steps and spoke his first words. She could tend him and teach him and watch him as he grew up. But most of all, she could give him all of the love she had been storing away for him.

Through a blaze of tears she said in a tremulous voice, "When I said I knew of someone, Lucy, I was speaking about myself."

"You, mum?" The girl gaped at her, and Sarina nodded her head. "You a widow, then?" Again Sarina nodded, and the tears brimming in her eyes made the lie all the more convincing. "Well, now, you and the mister's got need o' each other's comp'ny, just as much as little Michael needs lookin' after." Lucy Greer seemed quite pleased with herself. "You come 'round this evenin' then, mum, and speak to the mister, and I'll make certain 'e don't go givin' the position to no one else."

Sarina dabbed at her eyes with the corner of her white lawn handkerchief and gave the girl a grateful smile. "What would be the best time for me to call?" she asked.

" 'Round seven would be best, I'm thinkin', mum."

"I'll be there at seven, then," agreed Sarina. She would ask Mei to tend the door for her until she returned, and no one need ever know where she had been.

Just as she was preparing to return to the carriage, Lucy called after her, " 'Scuse me, mum, but I don't even 'ave yer name."

Without hesitating this time, she called back, "Thomas. Mrs. John Thomas."

The sitting room, with its gay rose and pale green chintz furnishings and its papered walls hung with framed prints of hunting scenes, seemed to Sarina to be a bit of England transported to one of her most distant colonies. A fire snapped noisily in the grate, warming her far more effectively than the weak tea Lucy had served them, and added a cheery amber glow to the already pleasant surroundings. She burrowed deeper inside her cloak, unable to shake off the uncomfortable feeling that, somehow, she was a trespasser here, in spite of its being her own son sleeping in the nursery on the second floor. Would she have taken tea with Anne Deane in this very room, she wondered, or would they have sat in the formal parlor she had glimpsed briefly when she had first entered the house? Perhaps she would have even sat in the same chair she was sitting in now. She shuddered and hastily set her cup and saucer down on the small oak table standing next to her chair.

As she settled back in her seat again, she studied the wan face of the young widower who was slumped in the sofa opposite her with his chin in his hand. His hair was a thick and wavy deep blond, as was the trim mustache he sported under a narrow, aristocratic nose. His eyes were light brown and dulled with pain, and his pale mouth was set in a tense, unhappy line below his mustache. She doubted, as she watched him, that he even remembered she was still in the room with him.

He had appeared vague and apologetic when they had been first introduced by Lucy Greer, and not in the least bit suspicious. If he had ever been warned about a woman of her description, he had seemed oblivious of it. His questions concerning her qualifications had been as vague as his manner; her contrived answers had been accepted with mildly interested nods and halfhearted mumbles of assent, and he had hardly looked at her directly in the entire hour she had already spent with him. He seemed far more content to stare into the flames and absently stroke his mustache. He was as pale and tentative a presence in his own house as Sua had been in hers, and Sarina wondered if Lewis Deane had always been this way or if the death of his wife had loosened his hold on the world around him.

"And you say you're a widow, Mrs. Thompson?" He was speaking into his hand, and the words were muffled.

"Thomas," she corrected him for the fourth time, and again answered yes to his question.

"Tell me . . ." He scowled as he peered deeper into the flames. "Do you ever get used to it—the loneliness, I mean?"

She was taken aback by his question and so she said, "Two weeks is a very short time, Mr. Deane. Your grief is still fresh. I believe you first have to accustom yourself to your loss before you can even begin to consider the loneliness of it."

He began stroking his mustache again. "You're right, I suppose, Mrs. Thompson. Yes, foolish of me now, isn't it . . . ?" His voice trailed off.

As Sarina clasped and unclasped her hands in her lap, wondering how she was going to manage to live in the same house as this sad and withdrawn stranger, she was suddenly overwhelmed by a flurry of panicky doubts and questions. Would she be placing herself in danger by moving into the house of a man who worked for Wo Shue Kwen? Wo could appear at the door of number eighteen Casuarina Road just as easily as he could appear at the house on Dragon Flower Street. What was she going to tell Janson? Were there any other servants in the house besides the Chinese houseboy? Was she to cook and clean as well as tend her son? How would Madam Blue react to her decision to leave?

Suddenly all she wanted to do was take up her purse and flee. She wanted to tell Lewis Deane that she had made a mistake and that she was sorry, but she had changed her mind about the position.

"Very well, Mrs. Thompson—"

"Thomas," she automatically responded as she was starting to get up.

"Yes, well . . ." He waved her name away with a vague flick of his wrist. "Can you begin immediately, then?"

"I'm afraid I—"

"Is Monday too soon?"

"No, but—"

"Good. Then I'll expect you in three days. Lucy will

show you out." He fumbled for the small porcelain bell on the table in front of the sofa and gave it a ring.

Sarina was wavering on her feet. "Yes, yes, of course," she murmured. "Thank you."

She stumbled out of the room, wondering what she had just done. It was still not too late; she would simply have Lucy tell him that she had changed her mind. In all probability, the poor man had already forgotten that he had even offered her the position.

"Well, mum, did you get it?" bubbled Lucy, wiping her hands on her apron as she hurried into the front hall from the kitchen.

"Yes." Sarina nodded, still dazed and uncertain. "But I—"

"Oh, mum, I'm ever so pleased," Lucy squealed. "You'll be 'appy 'ere, mum, and you'll 'ave the little one all to yerself, you will, just like 'e was yer very own."

Lucy Greer's innocent words banished the last doubts from Sarina's mind.

Sarina studied the faces of the two women seated across from her and waited for their response to her announcement. Her hands were hidden behind her back on the bed to conceal their trembling, but her nervousness was evident in her eyes as she looked first at Mei and then at Madam Blue, both of them sitting in stunned silence by the window in Sarina's room. Finally it was Mei who was first to react. She gazed at Sarina with a warm smile on her face, but it was a smile which failed to reach her dark, shadowed eyes.

"I am pleased for you, my sister," she said in a solemn voice. "You have chosen a path which will bring you much contentment."

"But you don't really approve, do you?" questioned Sarina.

Mei glanced down at her hands. "It is not for me to approve a decision you have made," she replied carefully, "but I had believed you to be already sharing the path of your life with another."

Sarina stared up at the ceiling and tried to keep her voice calm as she said, "The path Janson Carlyle would like to set for us is not the path I want to follow."

"So be it, then," intoned Mei. "In my head I am pleased for you, Sarina, while in my heart I weep."

Janson was not Chen, Sarina thought bitterly; he would never risk his life out of love for her, as Chen had risked and possibly forfeited his for Mei. Love! This made her laugh out loud. Janson Carlyle knew nothing about love.

"My dear Sarina . . ." Now Madam Blue was breaking her silence. "Like Mei, it is not for me to approve or disapprove, but I do believe that you are running away from your own fears, preferring the blandness of comfort and contentment to the uncertainties of a fierce and passionate love."

Sarina would have cut her short had Madam Blue not held up her hand and glowered at her to keep still.

"There is nothing more tedious than the slow withering of a comfortable state of being, Sarina, and nothing more glorious than passion, even as it begins to fade, as fade it must. By choosing to deny yourself desire's flame, preferring instead the spent ashes of another's flame, you will have denied yourself one of life's most precious experiences. For myself"—she sighed—"I will miss you as a mother misses her own daughter whose path has taken her far from the gates of her home, but I will also grieve for you, my dear, for accepting another woman's man and child rather than accepting the challenge of securing for yourself a man and a child of your own."

Their words cut deep and Sarina wished she could have told them the truth, to prove to them how wrong they were. But she would never tell either of them the truth, just as she would never reveal it to Janson. Let them think whatever they wished, she decided grimly, at least she knew, and for now it would have to suffice.

"Am I to be returned to my duties, then, as keeper of the door in three days' time?" asked Madam Blue, breaking the rising tension with a laugh in her voice and a mischievous spark in her eyes.

Sarina looked hard at Mei. The girl refused to meet her gaze.

"It is but several short steps from the music parlor to the front door," suggested Madam Blue, following Sarina's lead.

"And you already know all of the appropriate Chinese

phrases," teased Sarina gently, to be rewarded by a flicker of a smile on Mei's serious face.

"But the pipe," Mei protested, looking from Sarina to Madam Blue and then back at Sarina again. "My need is too great. The pipe will never permit me to do it."

"Perhaps you will come to believe that you may one day live without the pipe," Madam Blue said.

"Perhaps"—she shrugged—"but I am still uncertain as to whether I care to live without the peace it brings me."

It was then that Sarina decided to take Mei's life into her own hands. If Madam Blue knew the truth about Mei, it could provide them with a bond to ease the pain and fill the void of her leaving, and it might give Mei the loving support she so urgently needed. Her eyes were bright, her tone determined, as she turned to Madam Blue and said, "Did you know that Mei was sent to you by Wo Shue Kwen?"

"Sarina!" Mei's eyes cried betrayal, but Sarina shook her head and held up a finger to her lips.

She was watching Madam Blue as she registered first shock and then wonder.

"You were sent by Kwen?" she whispered.

Mei, still glaring fiercely at Sarina, reluctantly nodded her head.

"You fell into disfavor with him?"

At Sarina's nod of encouragement, Mei finally turned to face the older woman, and in her gentle voice said, "I was the forbidden love of his son, Chen."

For a moment it appeared that Madam Blue might not be able to sustain the blow Mei had delivered her, but as she slowly recovered her composure, Sarina knew that by unleashing the truth about Mei she had given them both something far more precious than her own truths. When Madam Blue gazed up at Sarina a moment later, her eyes were brilliant with tears, and in her eyes was her message of thanks. Mei looked from one to the other again in complete bewilderment.

"He was to marry another?" asked Madam Blue.

"Yes," whispered Mei.

"And you refused to become his favored one?"

Mei swallowed hard and shook her head. "He refused out of pride to ask me to accept what he considered to be the lowliest of stations."

"You would have accepted, then?"

Sarina was hardly aware of holding in her breath.

"He was my master as well as my love," said Mei. "I did his bidding and I followed where he would have had me follow. But, yes"—she sought Sarina out with her eyes, and Sarina felt the breath rush out of her—"I would have suffered whatever the gods would have meted out to me to remain at his side always."

Sarina choked back a sob. "Damn him," she moaned, "damn him and his stubborn pride." Chen's words came back to her then, those words whispered with such urgency and such assurance in her room that night. *I know what she would say, for her pride is as great as mine.* To think that he had lost everything because of his own pride, when he could have had it all. She winced as she saw the pointing finger of Madam Blue, heard her accusing her of the very same thing. Fool, fool, fool. The word repeated itself over and over inside her head. Like Chen, she was a prideful fool, and like Chen, she was going to lose everything.

"Sarina, are you all right?"

She heard Madam Blue's voice cutting through the thickening wall of her own stubborn pride and she shook off the woman's concern as she would a bothersome fly. Her head came up, her back stiffened. She was not losing anything but what she could never have. And what she was gaining by her decision was something she wanted more than life itself, more than Janson Carlyle himself. Her son!

"Did you know, Mei," she said, wiping her burning eyes and staring intently at the shaken girl, "that before I left the estate, I pleaded with Chen to live? I begged him to stay alive so that one day, if the gods were kinder, the two of you would be reunited again."

"As long as Wo lives, we will never be together," returned the girl with an unhappy sigh.

"Would you return to him, then," continued Sarina, "if he asked you to become his concubine?"

"Oh, yes." Mei's eyes were shining, her face transformed by the radiance of her love for Chen, as it had always been transformed in the past.

"Then I'm asking you to live, Mei," Sarina said, her

voice gentle, but at the same time edged with steel, "live for that day I promised Chen he would have."

While Mei was considering what she had said to her, the look Sarina gave Madam Blue promised her her own truths one day, and the woman nodded her head in silent understanding. With a weary sigh Sarina got up from her bed and started slowly across the room.

"I'd better go back downstairs now," she said. "Janella will never forgive me if Felicity lures her naval officer away from her while she's tending the door."

"Wait, Sarina," Mei called out to her. "I will come with you," she said, hastily getting out of her chair, "and you must teach me all that I will have to know."

Sarina put out her hand to her and Mei took hold of it and gave it a hard, grateful squeeze.

"You must wake me, Mei, when Sarina has finished with you for the night," said Madam Blue, leaning on her walking stick as she pushed herself to her feet. "We have much to talk about, you and I."

The evening before Sarina was scheduled to leave Madam Blue, Janson responded to the message Tung-tsu had delivered for her to his offices by appearing at the door of her room promptly at seven. She was dressed for her final evening as Dragon Flower, and the small traveling bag Madam Blue had given her was sitting open on the floor at the foot of her bed. Janson strode into the room in his brisk, matter-of-fact way, hands thrust into the pockets of his dark trousers, and came to an abrupt halt when he noticed the half-packed bag.

"Going someplace?" he asked her.

"Obviously," she snapped in exasperation. She immediately cautioned herself to remain calm, for this was the confrontation she had dreaded the most.

"Do you plan on telling me where you're going, or is that a secret?"

"I'm doing exactly what you've been advising me to do for some time now," she explained. "I'm leaving Madam Blue."

He folded his arms across his chest. "And where exactly are you leaving for?"

"Not too far from here." She smiled wickedly, enjoying

his growing impatience. "And you won't be able to fault me for my choice of companions from now on."

One black boot was beginning to tap out a staccato rhythm on the bare floor.

Sarina picked up an embroidered silk shawl and began to fold it as she announced calmly, "I'm going to work as a nanny for a little boy whose mother has just passed away."

The tapping slowed. "One of your bereaved clients, no doubt?"

She stifled a giggle. "Hardly."

"How did you happen to find out that this fellow, whoever he is, needed a nanny?"

"From the nanny who's leaving," she replied airily, dropping the shawl into the traveling bag. Deciding she had better put an end to his questions, she changed her tone. "I thought you would be pleased, Janson. I even thought you would approve of my decision. After all," she goaded him, "isn't respectability something you've always wanted for me?"

He sank onto her bed and raked his fingers through his hair. "I don't understand you, Sarina," he said, staring down at the tips of his boots. "I've asked you to leave here and move into a house of your own, and you've refused me. A stranger, some man with a child, has asked you to work as his nanny, to share *his* house with him, and you've accepted. Is this how you intend to spend the rest of your life, living in different strangers' houses as a servant and taking care of their children? Is this man going to be any different from Kwen?" he demanded, his temper rising. "You said yourself he's a widower. How long do you think your precious virtue will remain intact with him?"

"If you had ever seen him, you wouldn't even be asking me that," she fired back at him.

"I don't care what he looks like, dammit, he's still a man and you're still going to be living under his roof."

"And you'd prefer me to be living under yours instead!"

"I've given up on that notion, Sarina," he told her wearily. "A man will subject himself to only so many rejections before he begins to feel like a goddamned fool." He got to his feet and touched her lightly on the cheek. "Good luck, Sarina," he said; then he turned and strode out of the room.

"Janson!" Dropping the dressing gown she was folding,

she ran after him. She got as far as the doorway and then she stopped. It was better this way; she could hardly have expected it to have been otherwise. She bent down and picked up her dressing gown and continued with her packing, while she gritted her teeth and told herself that it no longer mattered what Janson Carlyle thought of her or where he went after he left Hong Kong.

Nothing mattered to her now, except her beloved child.

26

Spring was Hong Kong's shortest but loveliest season, so when Sarina woke late one March morning to the sweet perfume of the camellia bush below her window, she hugged her pillow to her chest and smiled. It was Sunday. Even Michael Steven now sensed that Sundays were special days, for he would sleep later, and when he woke up, it would be to Lewis Deane's beckoning arms instead of hers. It was an arrangement she and Deane had worked out between them, which allowed her some time to herself while permitting him that private time alone with his son.

Madam Blue had been wrong. Never before had Sarina known such peace and contentment. Each day melted predictably and uneventfully into the next. The boundaries of her world were defined by the expanding perimeters of Michael Steven's world, and she wanted little else. She took all of her meals with him, played with him, and walked him in his pram when the weather allowed it, acting the doting nanny and trading stories and bits of advice with the other nannies wheeling their own charges. Then, in the evenings, she would bathe him and put him to bed, often remaining in his room for several hours, sitting silently in the large cane rocker in the corner and watching him as he slept. Soon it seemed that the pattern of her life had always included Michael Steven in it.

Every one of her days was filled with the glory of a thousand shared experiences with her son, while every night was reserved for reliving each precious moment in her head. Each new tooth, every word he added to his vocabulary, each new bit of food he tried was a triumph they would first share together and which she would then cherish later privately. He was a beautiful boy, a perfect

replica of his father, whose sweet disposition seemed somehow to have come from Anne Deane; and Sarina often
wondered which parts of him, besides his golden hair, had
actually come from her.

Sarina turned over onto her back and gazed up at the
canopy above her head. In one of his few expansive
moments, Lewis Deane had told her that the furnishings
in her room had been in Anne's room when she was a girl
and living in Sussex. The furniture was delicately carved
and gracefully curving Hepplewhite, and although they
had subsequently changed the coverlet and the draperies
on the bed, the pattern of small nosegays of purple violets
festooned with long, trailing pink ribbons was almost identical to the original. The same fabric had been used for
the two slipper chairs standing on either side of the tall
chiffonière and for the valance and richly swagged curtains covering the window. It was far different from the
austere starkness of the room she had known as a girl
growing up in Oregon, thought Sarina with a wistful sigh;
it was the kind of room every young girl dreamed of
having.

She drew the covers up over her head, raised her knees,
and burrowed inside the tent she had fashioned for herself.
It was warm and protected in there, much like the protective mantle Lewis Deane still wore draped around him to
keep him safe from all intrusion. As she had expected, he
remained no more than a gentle and unobtrusive shadow,
both in his home and in her life. He worked six days a
week in his office near the harbor and spent his evenings
with Michael Steven until it was time for him to be put to
bed. He was an attentive and adoring father, never raising
his voice in reproach or his hand in discipline. Lucy Greer
had once said that Anne Deane had lived only for her son,
and it seemed the same was true of Lewis Deane; to him
Sarina, whom he still occasionally referred to as Mrs.
Thompson, existed only as a vague appendage of his son's
life.

She and Deane were still virtual strangers to each other,
content to continue living as strangers, sharing nothing
but their concern for Michael Steven and the most basic of
pleasantries during those infrequent moments spent in
each other's company. He took his early breakfasts and
late dinners alone in the dining room, eating the meals

prepared for him by Bridget Bromley, the fifty-seven-year-old widow he had hired to cook and clean when Anne had taken to her bed for the last time. The sprightly Englishwoman left each evening at eight and returned the following morning at seven, and Sarina found her irrepressible good nature a welcome antidote to the dour houseboy, Zhen, who slept in a small room off the kitchen and looked after the marketing and the heavier household chores as well as tending the gardens. There seemed to be little other use for a formal houseboy; no one ever came to call, and Lewis Deane had no friends on whom he ever called. From the gossip of the other nannies, Sarina discovered that their employers led a far different life from the reclusive Deane, attending lavish parties and dividing the rest of their leisure time among the racecourse, the polo field, and the cricket grounds.

Giving one final languorous stretch, she threw back the covers and finally got out of bed. Sifting through her scanty wardrobe, she impetuously settled on the newest and most elegant of the day gowns she had recently purchased with some of the generous wages Lewis Deane was paying her. As she began to dress, she hummed softly to herself, thinking of the afternoon she would be spending with Madam Blue and Mei, just as she spent every Sunday afternoon with them. But when she encountered some difficulty with one of the buttons on her new gown, she began to frown and the humming stopped. Suddenly all she could think about was Madam Blue and how badly she had deteriorated over the last two months.

She could no longer fasten any of the buttons on her own gowns by herself. Bending down was now impossible for her, and the stoop to her back, whenever she walked or sat, seemed to grow more and more pronounced each time Sarina saw her. It pained her to see the skin on that exquisite face becoming creased and waxen, while the sparkling brilliance of her remarkable blue eyes refused to dim and her indomitable spirit refused to be vanquished.

Sarina pushed the button through the stubborn buttonhole at last and turned to consider her hair. At least Madam Blue had Mei with her, she thought, reaching for her brush. The girl was like a blossom reborn. If she was not the radiant Mei of the summerhouse, she was once again the enchanting Mei of the music room, and the tie Sarina had known would bind the two women together had grown stronger and tighter with time.

As she worked patiently at her hair, she invariably found herself wishing what she wished every Sunday—that she could bring Michael Steven down to Dragon Flower Street with her. But it was a wish she knew would continue to go unfulfilled. One glimpse of the boy and they would know. She was grateful that neither of them ever mentioned Janson Carlyle to her anymore, and she refused to ask if either of them knew of his whereabouts. She had not seen him since that last evening at Madam Blue's more than two months before.

At first her days and nights had been filled with thoughts of him and a terrible longing to be with him, while all the time she knew how impossible such wishes were. But as the weeks passed and her new life began to consume her days, Janson's hold on her weakened. Soon all that remained of him was the fearsome image which stalked her nightly dreams. He was Hades, rising from a bank of sulfurous smoke to carry her, a resisting Persephone, down to his dusky kingdom to share eternity with him among the flames. And she would wake, her body still smoldering with the heat of her nightmare and that old, familiar ache deep in her heart.

She turned slowly in front of the pier glass and studied herself in her new gown. As much as it smelled like spring outside her window and looked like spring inside her room, she decided with a satisfied smile that she was the very blush of spring itself. The high-necked gown of pink-and-white-striped taffeta had a small bustled train and a short draped front overskirt above a series of pleated flounces edged in stiff white lace. The bodice was a lush cascade of lace, as were the cuffs of the full long sleeves, and as she pinned several large white and deep pink silk peonies among the curls set high above her forehead, she realized that she would require no rouge at all on her cheeks, for the pink of the gown had already suffused her skin with a luminous and natural rosy glow.

She ate a light breakfast alone in the kitchen, and just as she was getting up from the table, Lewis Deane poked his head around the corner. "You're looking rather like spring this morning, Mrs. Thomas," he said brightly, startling her by his unusually animated tone of voice. "I thought we might take Michael Steven out for a bit before you set off for the afternoon." She was even more taken aback when he gallantly offered her his arm.

They could very easily have been the loving parents of Michael Steven from the way they were being greeted on the street by the people they passed. With Deane proudly wheeling the pram and acknowledging with increasing joviality the extravagant compliments being paid his son, Sarina tried to look properly respectful of the man who was her employer by hanging back a bit as they continued their walk. All three of them were so fair, she suddenly thought, it was not difficult to mistake them for a contented, little family. A tremulous beating of dark, feathery wings inside her caused her to turn away from Deane's profile and concentrate instead on the back of her son's head as he sat up in his carriage, his arms around his favorite toy, a flop-eared dog made of dark brown cotton and filled with down, and gazed curiously around him.

They were approaching the park on Banyan, where the orchid trees and palms were greening and bits of pink and white were starting to show again on the azalea bushes and flowering almond trees.

"Would you care to sit awhile, Mrs. Thomas?" asked Deane, pushing the pram over toward the bench she had once shared with Lucy Greer. "That way Michael Steven can muck about as he wishes. I think he's finding his pram rather tiresome these days. Perhaps he's outgrown the thing."

But Sarina had stopped listening to him. Something was wrong. Even while they were walking, she had felt it. She glanced about them, hastily scanning the orchid trees and the palms and the clutch of silk-cotton trees off to the right of them. It was the same foreboding she had felt that afternoon in the gardens of Wo's estate and then later again that night in her room. It was the feeling that she was being watched.

Fear slithered like a twisting serpent down the length of her back. Was it Wo? Was it one of his men? Had they found her out after all? She swayed dizzily for a moment, reaching out for the arm of the bench and catching hold of the arm of Lewis Deane instead.

"Is there something wrong, Mrs. Thomas?" he inquired. "You look rather distressed."

His brown eyes were troubled, his face concerned, and as he continued to scrutinize her, it was as if he were finally seeing her for the first time.

Sarina offered him an apologetic smile and quickly took her hand from his sleeve. "I'm sorry," she said. "It's nothing, really." Bending over the pram, she put on her gaiest voice. "Now, then," she exclaimed, "shall we release our young man from his prison?"

"Yes, let's," agreed Deane, reaching into the carriage for the dog Michael Steven had dropped.

Their hands touched. He glanced up at her and their eyes met. His mustache twitched imperceptibly and his face began to color. Flustered, Sarina drew her hands away. It was he who finally picked up Michael Steven, she who retrieved the dog. She shivered in the wake of what had just passed between them. His look of open admiration had unsettled her far more than the look she was certain was being trained on her by a pair of eyes she could not see.

Janson cursed again at the sight of Sarina with Lewis Deane. Not until he had seen them coming down the flagstone path together had he known that Lewis Deane was the occupant of number eighteen Casuarina Road and the man whose son Sarina had left Madam Blue to care for. A telltale ache was beginning deep inside him, and he absently rubbed his chest with the heel of his hand. He waited another moment and then peered cautiously around the trunk of the silk-cotton tree and stole another hasty look at them. He recoiled when he saw them bending over the pram, freezing momentarily while they gazed into each other's eyes. Then he watched Sarina turning away, while Deane lifted the boy into his arms. Janson flattened himself against the tree and pressed his thumb and fingers hard into the lids of his eyes, as if that could erase what he had just seen.

"My God, Sarina," he groaned, "what the hell have you done? What kind of a goddamned game are you playing?"

Why Deane? He obviously had no inkling as to who Sarina was, and from the way he had been looking at her just then, he was not likely to go packing her off to Wo

Shue Kwen even if he did know. Either Sarina had lied or she had managed to convince herself that Lewis Deane had been interested in her only as a nursemaid for his child. The man was obviously infatuated with her. Janson had even noticed the gown she was wearing, and it was certainly not the kind of uniform worn by any of the nannies he had ever seen before. Nanny! He snorted. Nanny and mistress combined was more likely.

He never should have come back. He should have sailed directly to Canton after leaving Shanghai, as he had originally planned. He had hated himself for following Sarina's hired carriage to discover just where she was going that Monday morning when she had left Madam Blue, and now he hated himself even more for returning to Hong Kong and passing by the house on Casuarina Road for three straight days in the hopes of seeing her again. He glanced out at her one more time and then just as quickly ducked back behind the tree again. Dammit! Those golden eyes of hers missed nothing. He could have sworn she had been staring directly at him.

The ache was now in his groin. It was an ache which nothing could dispel, neither his work, nor his plans, nor his nightly dreams. Nothing was able to quench his thirst or slake his appetite for this bewitching golden-haired angel he had been yearning for and running from for nearly two years. No woman he had held since first holding her had had the power to arouse and tease and torment him as she had. And yet, there she was, with still another man. He grimaced. She was now touching the side of Deane's face with the boy's hand, using it as if it were a glove between her own hand and Deane's cheek. Now they were both laughing. Janson strained to catch a glimpse of the boy's face, but all he could see was the back of his golden head. All three of them were so fair, so golden, he thought bitterly; what a beautiful golden family they made.

He turned away, pressing his cheek against the rough bark of the tree and welcoming its savage thrust on his skin. Any pain was better than the pain he felt at being played for a fool again. Sarina had her clerk and her child now and she had her house; she had finally gotten exactly what she had always wanted. It was time he learned to leave her alone, time he realized that he had had no right to ask a woman like her to be content with what he himself had offered her.

Pushing himself away from the tree, he started back toward his carriage. He took his handkerchief from the breast pocket of his coat and held it up to his bleeding cheek, but as he tucked it into his pocket again, he was stunned to find no trace of blood whatsoever on the square of white linen. It was soiled instead by the tears he never even knew he had shed.

Sarina sat back on her heels and watched Michael Steven crawl to the edge of the blanket and then rise on shaky legs to stand by himself.

"Good boy," she applauded him, "good Michael Steven."

With a toothy grin he turned to her and clapped his own hands together. "Good," he mimicked her, "good Seeven." Then he toddled off to examine a white azalea bush.

They were sitting on the warm grass in the garden behind the house, where the flowering almond trees were now in full bloom, their tops fanning out like small pink clouds against the blue of the sky. The rockery, so carefully tended by Zhen, was now an artful patchwork of pink and fuchsia, yellow and white and green, and the scents of all the different flowers were blended into one glorious perfume. A pair of tiny white butterflies fluttered soundlessly by. A plump yellow-and-black-striped bee hovered just near Sarina's head before flying off and disappearing above the box hedges, and Sarina gave a low, contented sigh and stretched out on the blanket with her chin in her hands.

Suddenly she stiffened. Around one side of the house, a shadow had just appeared, lengthening ever so slowly as it crept stealthily forward. Cold fear stabbed at her insides. It was far too soon for Zhen to be returning from the market. She scrambled to her feet. Bridget was at home with a cough, and Deane was at his office. Dashing after her son, she pulled him, shrieking in protest, from the azalea bush he had been examining so curiously.

The rays of the sun slanted the growing shadow across the grass ahead of the approaching intruder. It stretched and grew, a fearsome living thing, dark and ominous, an alien presence among the harmless shadows cast by the flowering trees. She was halfway to the stone steps leading up to the kitchen door when the figure emerged from the shadows into the full glare of the sun.

"Janson!" His name burst from her lips in horror.

Pressing her son's face to her chest, she inched closer and closer to the steps. With his face pressed against her so tightly, Michael Steven became frightened and began to cry. Terrified of smothering him, Sarina took her hand away from his head, but his howls grew louder. Desperate to shield his face, she raised him higher, cushioning him there against her shoulder, as she kept backing toward the stairs and away from the man who was advancing on her.

"Sarina . . ." His eyes were pleading with her to stop and to hold still. "I didn't mean to startle you, I just had to see you."

His face was paler than she remembered, or was it simply the way the sun was filtering through the branches of the trees? His stride, usually so bold and purposeful, now seemed slower, almost hesitant. Alarm spread through her at the sight of him so uncertain. Had he been ill?

Michael Steven refused to be comforted. As soon as he began to squirm and kick, Sarina stopped and, without thinking, set him down again. All she could see was the misery on Janson's face. For a moment their eyes held, while she searched his strongly chiseled features for some sign of what was wrong.

"Janson?"

She moved closer to him, close enough so that if she wanted to touch him she could do so by simply putting out her hand. He turned from the sudden concern on her face to take his first look at the boy, who was no longer crying, but was standing next to Sarina, snuffling softly, while holding on to the folds of her skirt with one small hand. His hair was the same sun-silvered gold as Sarina's, and his eyes . . .

Janson gasped. A searing pain shot through him, consuming his chest and engulfing his entire body in a flash of scorching heat. "My God!"

He stared at the clear green eyes and saw his own eyes gazing back at him. If he were still a child himself, the face of the boy standing in front of him would have been his mirror image.

"Janson?"

He felt himself slipping away from her. He was stagger-
ing backward as if he had been shot by some internal gun
whose bullet had pierced his heart. His hand went up to
cover the hole in his chest where the bullet had lodged,
and he let himself slump slowly to the ground.

"*Janson!*"

She fell to her knees beside him and saw the terrible
grayness in his face. Cradling his head in her arms, she
called out to him, crooning his name over and over
again, while her tears fell softly down upon his upturned
face.

He could hear her calling his name, but for the moment
he lacked the strength to answer her. The pain had passed.
It had flared through him briefly and was gone, a grim
reminder of his own mortality and nothing more. It had
been the shock, exploding in the wake of that fleeting
pain, which had shaken him from his feet. Dear God in
heaven, he wanted to cry out, he had a son! A son! That
precious extension of himself which he had never thought
to have, that part of him he had never dared to create.
Sarina had given him a son!

"Janson, please. Oh, Janson, answer me."

Answers. He needed so many answers. He had to find
the strength again to ask her all the questions for which he
had no answers. As he slowly opened his eyes to look up at
her, his hands reached up to clasp her face.

"Oh, Janson," she breathed, "Janson."

She covered his face with grateful kisses.

"I'm all right, Sarina," he assured her.

"But—"

"Ssh, I'm fine."

He kissed her warmly and gently, and when she tightened her grip on him, he tightened his hold on her and
they deepened their kiss, while she sank beside him on the
grass and lost herself in his embrace. It was several minutes before they separated again and Sarina was able to
finally stretch out her arms to their son. With a gurgling
cry he skittered into her open arms and collapsed in a
quivering bundle on her lap.

"What's his name, Sarina?" asked Janson, his eyes never
leaving his son's face.

"Michael Steven," she told him.

"Michael Steven." He repeated the name as though he

were repeating the words of a prayer. "And he's ours, Sarina, yours and mine?"

"Yes." She nodded. "He's ours."

Janson put out his hand and touched the top of his son's head. Then he ran the tips of his fingers tenderly over his face, tracing each of the boy's perfect features in breathless wonder, while Sarina held him still. After a while she sat Michael Steven on Janson's lap and watched Janson wrap his arms around his son for the first time. They sat that way for some time, Janson holding on to Michael Steven and Sarina just watching them in their gentle beauty.

"Why didn't you ever tell me?" Janson finally asked her over the top of his son's head.

"You said you never wanted to get married, much less have children," she replied curtly, but she lowered her voice as she hastily added, "and it wasn't until a few months ago that I knew for certain Michael Steven was my son."

"I don't understand."

She hesitated, still needing some time to recover from the shock of their confrontation and its frightening aftermath.

"Sarina, you've got to tell me," he pleaded. "I have a right to know."

She nodded her head. "Yes," she whispered, "yes, I know you do."

The time she had doubted would ever come had, in fact, come at last, and after carrying her secret alone for so long, she was suddenly relieved to be able to share it with someone, especially him. She struggled for a moment to find the right words, and when she did, the truth poured out of her in a purging rush, as she told him of Wo's treachery and Li's truth and how she had come to be with Lewis Deane. By the time she had finished, she felt as though she had just run a race which had been interminably long and lonely, emerging both exhausted and exhilarated, and knowing that at long, long last the race was finally over.

Janson put his son back on his feet and watched him scamper off to examine the white azalea bush again. Then he reached for Sarina. "My angel," he murmured. "My poor sweet angel." He began to stroke her hair while he rocked her in his arms to comfort her and ease some of the pain she had endured alone in stubborn silence for so long. He felt helpless in the face of her agony, helpless and chastened, wanting only to right the wrongs perpetrated against her and to make up for so much wasted time.

"I want to talk to Lewis Deane, Sarina," he told her. "I want to tell him the truth and claim my right to my son."

"No." She shook her head. "You can't, Janson, not just yet, not when he's still struggling with his grief over his wife's death. He has nothing in his life now but his work and Michael Steven. You'll destroy him if you take that boy away from him now."

"But what about me?" he argued. "That man has had my son for as long as he's been alive, which is a hell of a lot longer than I have."

"Take Michael Steven now," she said quietly, "and Wo will find a way to destroy you. Then he'll take me back with him, Janson, and return Michael Steven to Deane."

"Why are you so damned protective of Lewis Deane, Sarina?" he asked, his voice hardening as he studied her face. "You haven't fallen for him, have you?"

She bridled at his insinuation and pulled away from him. "I seem to remember your accusing me of being in love with Wo as well, and you were wrong then, just as you're wrong now."

"Am I so wrong?" he persisted. "Look around you, Sarina. You've gotten what you want. With very little effort, I'm sure you could even get Deane to marry you, and then you'll have everything."

She pushed herself to her feet and faced him defiantly. "How could you even begin to know what I want?" she spit. Then she turned her back on him and picked up her son and headed for the house again.

"I want my son, Sarina!" Janson called after her.

She paused at the top of the steps. "You can't have him," she returned coldly. "He's my son, too."

He was on his feet and starting after her when he suddenly stopped. Everything had changed. Without his knowing it, a force far greater than his own determined will had wrenched the control of his life from his grasp and set him on a far different course than the one he had charted for himself so long ago. He glanced up at the empty doorway and saw them there in his mind, both of them so beautiful, both so golden, impossible to separate one from the other. It was time for a new course. One day, he would find the courage to explain it all to her, and he could only hope that she would understand and forgive him. But that was one day. He still had today to salvage.

He took the stairs two at a time. The door was unlocked. Had she known, he wondered, had she known he would come after her? *How could you even begin to know what I want?* She had hurled that at him, an accusation and a challenge, and it was a challenge he had finally decided to accept.

"Sarina!" He stumbled blindly through the strange house, peering into every empty room while he called out her name. "Sarina!" His heart thumping, he took the second flight of stairs just as quickly as he had taken the first. "Sarina!" He flung open the door to the white-and-yellow nursery and found it empty.

She was wrong. He knew exactly what she wanted. He had always known, and it had been his reason for running. He was panting now, and he was tired, tired of running. He wanted to stop.

He threw open the door and stepped into light. "Sarina!"

She turned from the window, the sun a halo encircling both her and the boy. She stood there without saying a word, a golden blaze of celestial perfection, and the sight of her there took his breath away and broke down that final barrier of resistance inside him.

"I'll wait, Sarina," he said quietly as he walked slowly toward her, "but I'll wait for only a little while, and then, no matter what the consequences, I intend to go to Lewis Deane and get our son back for us." He reached out to caress her face. "And then, my Sarina, my beautiful Sarina, we'll be together, the three of us. Always."

She raised her head and looked into the wondrous green of his eyes, and she found at last what she had waited so long to find. Michael Steven twisted around in her arms and put out one small hand to touch Janson's cheek, and the three of them continued to stand there in the streaming sunshine, heartbeat-close.

"I love you, Sarina," murmured Janson, his voice a

husky whisper. "Forgive me for ever having hurt you, my angel, because I think I've always loved you."

She closed her eyes as his mouth claimed hers, and the demons from her nightmares vanished forever.

27

The sun flicked a lazy tail of fire across her face. Turning onto her side, Sarina tried to close the draperies on the bed without having to sit up, but it was impossible. With a hasty peek at Janson, she slipped carefully from underneath the covers and crouched on her hands and knees while she drew the curtains together, enclosing the bed in a cooler world of purple violets and trailing pink ribbons, where only the two of them existed. Janson stirred, slid his hand across the sheet, and found that the space next to him was empty. His eyes flew open and he sat up with a start. Seeing her sitting there watching him with a mischievous smile deepening the dimples in her cheeks, he let out a low growl, grabbed a handful of her hair, and pulled her down beside him again.

"Did you think I'd run off?" she giggled, snuggling up against him.

He nuzzled her throat with his mouth. "I thought I'd lost you to my competitor across the hall again," he said.

"Shame on you, Janson Carlyle," she reproached him, "for calling your own son a competitor."

"He is, you know," he insisted. "He seems to want you just as much as I do."

"Well, he's happily asleep, sir, and I'm all yours."

"Are you, Sarina?" he murmured, kissing her hungrily on the lips.

In answer to that she wrapped her arms around him and pressed her body tightly against his. In the middle of their kiss he moaned and responded to her tender urging with a hungry thrust at her. She ran her hands up and down the length of his back, kneading his taut muscles and stroking the satin smoothness of his skin. Then she began to undulate rhythmically against him, while her pouting softness which was crushed against his hardening strength grew warm and moist.

"What a magnificent temptress you are, my angel," breathed Janson, raising his head to look into her eyes, which were glazed with the intensity of her desire.

She opened her mouth for another kiss and he hastened to oblige her. Some moments later it was she who broke their embrace to whisper, "Make love to me, Janson, make love to me. Please."

He circled her mouth with the tip of his tongue and she shuddered. "Is that what my angel wants?" he asked her. "Hmm? Is that what she wants?"

"Oh, yes," she sighed, "yes."

As his mouth closed over hers again, his hands began their exquisite journey across the gentle contours of her body, and where his fingers led, her body followed. On her own, she traced the hard edge of his spine with both thumbs locked together; then she spread her fingers and fanned them over his narrow hips to clasp the firm roundness of his buttocks.

"Sarina," he groaned as one hand found him and closed tenderly around him.

She molded him in her hands, stroking and fondling that precious part of him which she ached to plunge inside of her at that very moment. She wanted him to pierce her, pin her to him and hold her there. She wanted to feel him tunneling deeper and deeper inside her, until neither of them knew where one of their bodies ended and the other's began. Releasing her hold on him, she seized him by the buttocks again and arched her back, telling him of her burning need.

"Oh, Janson, love me," she cried up to him, "love me now."

The sweet moisture coating his fingers told him that she was ready, and he raised himself above her on his knees. As always, the beauty of her face at that moment just before he took her made him stop while he savored one final look at her. When her fingers closed around him once more, he shut his eyes and allowed her to guide him into her welcoming warmness. Gliding slowly through the silken wetness of that channel, and feeling it spreading open before him, he suddenly shivered. Never had he loved this way before. Never had his hunger been so tempered by the need to cherish and protect and share. Gathering her into his arms, he surrendered all of himself to her.

Lashed together by their common yearning, they advanced and retreated, plunged together and then pulled apart with increasing urgency. He rolled onto his back and took her with him, thrusting harder and deeper to keep himself inside her. On her knees above him, she drove him even farther into her. Clutching his shoulders, she braced herself for each new battering thrust which coaxed another new burst of fiery feeling from her.

From where his finger was now so insistently stroking rose that familiar curl of delicious agony. Her legs began to weaken, her arms grew heavy, and she began to moan as the heat mounted in a tightening, tingling spiral. The feeling spread through her in ever-widening circles and her low moan rose with it, billowing upward, lifting her, as the feeling itself was lifting her, up and beyond herself.

As soon as he felt the surging rush of her release, he used the waves of her completion to carry him up to his own release.

She was the first to stir. Raising herself on one elbow, she gazed down at his face, at the black lashes lying in fringed crescents against his cheeks, at the straight slash of his nose, at the mouth so generously hewn from the sculptured strength of his face, so relaxed now in sleep. As she looked at him, she realized with a sudden catch in her throat that this man, as much the needy child as he was the father, was hers.

"I love you, Janson Carlyle," she told him softly. "I love you more than one person should ever love another, and sometimes that frightens me. But I just can't help myself, I don't know of any other way to love you."

To the contentment of her life with Michael Steven, Sarina had finally added passion and a love which grew stronger and more complete with each moment she and Janson spent together. They had been sharing two stolen hours of loving almost every afternoon for three weeks now, taking advantage of Michael Steven's naps, Zhen's daily marketing, and poor Bridget Bromley's cough, which had turned into pneumonia. As much as Sarina cherished their times together, each parting was a wrenching tear in the gathering fabric of her life, and today's would be the most difficult of all.

After postponing his departure for Canton over and over again, Janson had finally set the following day as his sailing date, and this time he had sworn to honor it. He would be gone for at least two months, he had warned her as gently and as patiently as he could, because securing another major Chinese port had been a part of his expansion plans long before she had come into his life, and those plans were already months behind.

With one last, lingering look at him, Sarina slipped out of bed and began to dress. Zhen would be returning shortly from the market, and it was nearly time for her to wake Michael Steven from his nap.

"Sarina!"

She fastened the final button on her gown and drew back the draperies on the bed to find Janson scowling up at her.

"I hate it when I wake up and you're not here."

"But I'm never that far away," she chided him, sitting down on the edge of the bed and taking his hand.

"I know this is going to sound foolish, Sarina, but sometimes my love for you scares the hell out of me."

She could scarcely believe that he was putting her own thoughts into words. Moving closer to him, she asked him why.

"Because, dammit, I'm afraid of losing you!" He drew her head down to his chest, and his voice in her ears was low and fierce. "I've lost almost everyone I've ever loved, Sarina. I was five years old when my father died of a heart attack at the age of twenty-nine. When I was eighteen, my mother died in a boating accident in San Francisco Bay. My older brother, Markham, died when I was twenty-four. He died of a heart attack, Sarina, at twenty-nine, just as my father had."

She caught her breath. The pieces of the puzzle that was Janson Carlyle were beginning to slip slowly into place at last.

"Don't you see"—his tone was anguished—"I've lived with the deaths of the people I've loved most in the world for a very long time, and all my brother Garrett and I have done is wonder if Markham's death was just coincidence or if there was something in our blood which would kill us at twenty-nine too."

Sarina thought of Michael Steven, the son he had sworn he would never have, and her sudden stab of fear drained all the strength from her body.

"Well, I've made it past that goddamned number." Janson sighed. "And now Garrett has too. Somehow I thought that once I'd made it, I'd feel safe, as if it would magically guarantee me immortality, but I still don't feel safe. My way of fighting back was always to live as quickly as I could with as little feeling as possible, but you've changed that for me, Sarina, you and Michael Steven." He kissed the top of her head and then dug his fingers into the luxuriant tumble of her hair. "What we have now, my beautiful angel, is what I purposely left out of my life before, and that's why I'm afraid—I'm s℩ l afraid of losing you one way or the other."

She recalled Chen's parting words to her while he lay on his bed with his own agony and grief, and as she slid her arms around Janson, hoping her nearness might ease some of his pain, she repeated those words to him.

To her surprise, he began to chuckle, and as the tension slowly left his body, he said, "I think I owe Chen my apology, Sarina. He wasn't as big a fool as I thought he was." He gave her a light peck on the mouth and then started to sit up. "I guess I'd better leave," he announced, his voice slightly gruff now, as though he had allowed her to catch too close a glimpse of him and he needed to establish some distance between them again.

When he was dressed, he held her in his arms and squeezed her tightly. "Don't look at me that way, you witch," he teased, "or I'll never leave. Stop pouting, Sarina, you wouldn't want my shipping business to collapse because I was negligent and spent all of my time just making love to you, now, would you?"

"I don't think I would mind that at all," she replied, boldly running her hand along his thigh.

He grabbed hold of her hand and twisted it gently behind her back. "I love you, Sarina," he declared. "Remember that and never doubt it once while I'm away."

"And do you still intend to speak to Deane when you come back?"

"Damned right I do," he answered. "We've waited long enough, Sarina, and although I feel sorry for the man, I want my boy back. I want both of you back."

She clung to him for another moment and then walked with him to the kitchen and unlocked the back door. This was the way he always came and went, while his carriage waited for him two blocks from the house. When he kissed her good-bye one last time, it was with a fierce longing, and when he dashed down the steps, she was thankful that he continued straight through the garden without looking back once.

"I love you, Janson," she whispered to the empty air as a lonely ache settled deep inside her.

After another few moments she turned the key in the lock with a resolute click and went back upstairs to wake up their son.

The clinging mist of early June took the island by surprise and laid siege to the city. It clamped vaporous tentacles around the floating villages of junks and sampans in the harbor, looped itself around the wooden stalls and shanties and godowns cramped together in jumbled confusion along the waterfront, and slowly snaked its way up the hill toward the Peak.

From the docks, the fetid stench of unwashed bodies and refuse left exposed too long to the sun rose in a noxious cloud that not even the occasional cool breeze could dissolve. Fungus and mildew, unheard of on the hill and at the Peak, sprang up for the first time, as if from nowhere, on silken walls and priceless antiques. It oozed between the cracks of every window and door. It crusted mirrors and oil paintings and crystal chandeliers, and it turned even the finest sheets damp and musty.

It began in the rat-infested alleys behind the cluttered stalls and crowded shops. It extended one bony finger and then another as it poked its way into the sleeping houses and the bobbing boats. One hand reached out to touch the youngest and to claw at the oldest and the weakest. It prodded screams of pain from the children, squeezed cries of horror from the parents, and forced rattles of death from the old ones.

It hovered impatiently near the docks at midnight, when

the first contaminated bodies were dropped into the murky
water of the harbor, with only a hasty prayer chanted over
the makeshift graveyard. And when the night grew too
short for the living to bury their dead in secret, they
buried them during the day, while it reached out to them
now with both hands.

Plague.

It plunged a stake of fear into the heart of every inhabi-
tant on the island. Some immediately fled, others moved
higher up the Peak, while most people simply remained
where they were and waited. In Chinatown, the death toll
rose daily. Soon the dead could no longer be carried by
the sick and the dying to either the harbor or the burial
grounds, and so they were simply left to decay in the
streets. They were eventually collected, like rotting debris,
and thrown into large shallow graves, and sent to their
rest with a muttered prayer for their souls and a thick
coating of lime.

High on the hill, the wealthy closed their shutters and
barricaded themselves inside their slowly decaying homes.
Soon Lewis Deane no longer made the trip to his office on
the waterfront. Three of the men who worked for him
had fallen ill and one had already died. He remained
inside the house with Sarina and Michael Steven, and like
his neighbors, he waited. One afternoon Zhen took his
wicker basket and in spite of Sarina's protests set out for
the market. He died some days later. Now there was no
one to fetch their food.

The house grew damper and hotter and Sarina finally
gave up trying to wipe away all of the fungus she found.
No sooner had she cleaned one contaminated surface with
a rag soaked in carbolic acid than the festering slime
appeared on yet another surface. But the one room she
still attempted to keep scrupulously clean was the nursery.

Late one night there was a shift in the wind, which had
been sweeping up the hill from the harbor for so many
days, and Sarina and Deane walked through the house,
throwing open all of the windows and doors to air out
their stifling tomb. Their reprieve was short-lived. It was
not long before the wind shifted back again, and the foul
odor of rotting garbage and decomposing flesh forced
them to close the windows and bolt the shutters and retreat inside their miserable prison once more.

The following morning, Sarina awoke to the sound of someone's wretched moans. Terror gripped her as she swung her feet to the floor and slipped into her dressing gown. Michael Steven! He was sick. They should never have opened the windows. Panic propelled her across the hall to his room, but the nursery was dark and still. The moans were louder now. With an icy feeling of dread, Sarina knew that it was Lewis Deane who had been stricken.

"Don't come in, I beg you, Mrs. Thomas," rasped the weak voice from the bed when she opened the door to his room. "I am far from a pretty sight, and I daren't risk infecting either you or the boy."

The stench of his vomit nearly sent her reeling backward. But she pressed her hand over her nose and mouth and inched cautiously across the floor.

"Please, Mrs. Thomas, you must leave," he whispered hoarsely as he began to cough. "You should not be in this room."

In the semidarkness she watched the spasms of his coughing throttle him until he was panting and gasping for breath. She put her hand to his forehead, felt the clammy heat consuming him, and immediately ran downstairs to the kitchen and filled a porcelain basin with cold water. Grabbing up a towel, she returned to his room and began to sponge off his face. In spite of his continued protests, she stripped away the soiled bedcovers and put fresh linens on the bed. Then she undressed him, and while he lay there, weak and silent, his skin streaked with sweat and his body shaking, she sponged him off and helped him into a long clean dressing gown.

"I'm so very thirsty," he moaned. She touched his lips. They were cracked and dry.

She filled a glass with some water from the pitcher on his nightstand and held it up to his lips. "Drink it slowly," she cautioned him, "and take very small sips. Otherwise you won't hold it down."

He did as she told him, and when the glass was empty, she laid his head back on the pillow and continued to sponge him down in an effort to lower his fever. Soon he was vomiting again. She held his head over the porcelain basin as he brought up a bit of water and then green globules of bile. Closing her eyes, she tried to pray to occupy her mind and keep her from retching herself.

When he finally collapsed into an exhausted sleep, she closed the door to his room and carried his soiled sheets and clothing outside to the metal bin they used for trash. Then she boiled several kettles of water and filled the tub behind the screen in her bedroom and stepped into it. With a bar of strong lye soap which Bridget used for the laundry, she scrubbed her skin until she was red and sore. Then she added her own dressing gown to the clothes already in the bin and set a match to it.

On the second day of Lewis Deane's illness, he complained of a continuing pain in his head. Sarina found some laudanum among his late wife's various medicines and gave him a teaspoonful every three hours to dull the pain and enable him to sleep for a while. When the laudanum ran out, he was in agony again, and she sought to distract him by reading to him from the Bible.

"Anne!" he cried out in his delirium each time Sarina bent to sponge him now or raised his head for some water. "Anne, my Anne, bless you for helping me. Bless you." Then he would fall asleep, only to wake after a few minutes, calling out for his beloved Anne again.

Large swellings had formed on either side of his neck and deep in the pits of his arms, making his breathing difficult and causing him to lie on his back with his arms outstretched. When Sarina came to sponge him down just before midnight, she noticed the carbuncle in his groin for the first time, and she knew that unless the deadly boil broke, Lewis Deane could not possibly live much longer.

She collapsed into bed after tending to the sick man, her body strained with fatigue, her hands red and raw from the lye, and her stomach growling from hunger. She and Michael Steven were eating only *congee* and dried biscuits now because the rest of the food in the house was finally gone, and she dared not risk going down to the market herself. As she tossed and turned in the suffocating clamminess of her room, she could hear her son whimpering unhappily in his sleep in his own room across the hall. She longed to go to him and comfort him, but she had been trying to keep away from him as much as possible, so afraid was she of infecting him, should she herself already be infected.

In the morning, she pushed herself out of bed and peered cautiously into Lewis Deane's sickroom. Faintly, very faintly from the darkened room came the sounds of his labored breathing. His lungs were clogged with mucus now, and when he breathed in, it was no more than a hoarse tug of air, followed by a brief whistling gasp as he breathed out again. The room was so hot and foul-smelling that Sarina threw open the window and flung back the shutters to allow some air to circulate through it. Deane was trapped within a dome created by his own illness and she hoped that the change of air might provide him with a cooling respite for a while. But as she turned from the window, a scream rose and caught in her throat.

Lewis Deane's skin was now tinged a dusky blue. He was dying. Sarina stumbled toward the bed, her eyes wide, her heart pumping in an awkward rhythm inside her chest. She heard him suck in some air, hold it for an instant, and then finally release it in a long, shuddering sigh. She waited. The air was suddenly still. She waited and listened, but there was no further sound from the man on the bed. His terrible battle was over at last. With shaking fingers she closed the staring eyes and the gaping mouth and drew the coverlet over his face. Then she walked slowly out of the room.

She opened the front door, and clad only in her nightgown, stepped out onto the front porch. She was numb inside, numb and weak with fatigue and fear, without the strength to even weep for the gentle man who lay dead inside the house. There would be no need for Janson to speak to Lewis Deane now, for by his death he had unwittingly relinquished their son to them. Sarina put her head in her hands and whimpered softly to herself. The sounds were neither joyful nor despairing, but rather a series of small, fretful puffs born of sheer exhaustion.

In the eerie silence of the deserted street, the clip-clopping of a horse's hooves brought Sarina's head up sharply. Raising her arm, she signaled to the two men in the wagon passing by. One of them tugged hard on the reins, pulling the dappled gray nag to a halt just in front of the house. Both men, dressed in rumpled blue uniforms, their faces covered with white bandannas, jumped down from the wagon and started up the walk.

They were British soldiers, members of the Whitewash Brigade, pressed into service by the government on the island to remove the dead from their homes and bury them in vast common graves beneath a covering of lime and earth. Without a word, Sarina led them to the room where Lewis Deane was lying and watched as they lifted him from the bed and carried him out of the house.

"This the only one, mum?" asked one of the soldiers from behind the cloth protecting his face.

"Yes."

"God spare you, mum," said the second man as they started back down the walk.

She stared after them, dry-eyed and still numb. But when she saw them toss Lewis Deane's body into the back of the wagon as though he were a sack of potatoes, a howl of angry protest burst out of her, and the tears began at last.

Later that morning, Sarina put Michael Steven into his pram and locked the front door of the house. To remain there would be to slowly starve, and she was terrified of staying in a house which had now seen two deaths from the dread contagion. She wheeled the carriage down Casuarina Road, past the silent, shuttered houses and the green lawns and the trim box hedges, past the little park on Banyan abloom with azaleas and roses and pinks, and started down the hill.

When she reached Queen's Road, the streets began to narrow and the blue of the sky faded to a drab and dirty gray. Washing fluttered in the tepid breeze above her head. She was assailed by the cries of fruit vendors and vegetable hawkers, by the stench of fresh fish and steaming pork stew, by the sight of ragged children playing among the sprawled bodies of the dead, and by the sick, lying stretched out in the alleys on bamboo frames so that their departing souls would haunt the streets and not their homes when they finally died.

Lifting Michael Steven out of the pram and into her arms, Sarina walked up the steps and knocked on the door of the shuttered house on Dragon Flower Street.

When the tiny, gnarled woman opened the door, the blue eyes in the creased and waxen face began to glow with the brilliance of the sky on a cloudless day. Her ivory walking stick clattered to the floor. "So you have come home, my daughter," was all she said as she held out her arms for Sarina's child.

28

Madam Blue moaned and Sarina wrung out a fresh cloth and draped it across the woman's burning forehead. Her eyelids fluttered weakly, opening for a moment, and then closed again.

"Would you like me to comb your hair for you?" asked Sarina, knowing how much that seemed to please and comfort her.

Madam Blue managed a weak nod and Sarina reached for the wide ivory comb on the bedside table. The woman's hair lay unbound around her shoulders, a fine ebony stream divided by a broad band of silver, far wider now than it had been when they had first met a year ago. While she gently combed the silken black hair, Sarina kept up a steady patter of conversation to keep Madam Blue's mind distracted from her terrible pain and the spasms racking her emaciated body. She told her about her father and her girlhood in Oregon, about Janson and Michael Steven, and about her life on the estate of Wo Shue Kwen. There were no longer any secrets left between them. The day Sarina had come home to Dragon Flower Street was the day she had finally told Madam Blue the truth about herself.

"You have such gentle hands," whispered Madam Blue through dry and cracking lips. "You were blessed with hands destined to hold the fragile sweetness of love in them and to be held by love in return." She looked up at Sarina with those startling blue eyes which even her illness could not dim. "I am pleased there are no secrets between us now," she said. "Knowing that my chosen daughter has found the love I myself had wished for her, I can go to my ancestors with a glad heart."

The effort of speaking exhausted her. Her eyes fell shut again and her head nodded slightly to one side. Sarina blinked back a fresh rush of tears as she laid the comb down on the table and walked over to the shuttered window. Nowadays it seemed she was viewing everything around her through a thickening veil of tears. Day and night had long blended into one continual haze of lamplit blue, death was as familiar to her as the reddened tips of her fingers, and terror had found a permanent home within her heart. Five of the girls in the house had died before her arrival, two had died in the four days since then, seven had subsequently fled the contaminated house, while Mei and the last two girls were preparing to leave for the small cottage Madam Blue owned just outside the city. For Madam Blue herself, such a journey was now too late.

"Sarina . . ."

At the rasping call from the bed, Sarina turned from the window and hurried to the woman's side.

One twisting finger was pointing at the mahogany dresser on the opposite wall.

"In the top drawer you will find a small sandalwood box," she said. "Bring it to me, please."

Sarina located the little box, painted in an intricate design of leaves and flowers, still smelling faintly of sandalwood, and brought it over to the bed.

"Open it," commanded the failing voice, "and put the ring on my finger."

It was the most unusual ring Sarina had ever seen, a magnificently carved band of pink jade with a smiling emerald encrusted dragon winding its way through a field of diamond-dotted flowers. Without having to ask, Sarina knew, and her own hands were trembling as violently as Madam Blue's as she tried to find a finger large enough to hold the heavy ring.

Her voice was thick with regret as she said, "I'm afraid it will only fit on your thumb now."

The woman gave her a wan smile. "Then my thumb it shall be," she declared. With the ring safely on the thumb of her left hand, she folded both hands across her chest and sighed. "You will bury me with this ring, my dear Sarina," she told her as, once again, she closed her eyes.

Her grief clogging her throat, Sarina paused only long enough to change the cloth on Madam Blue's forehead before she fled the room. Closing the door, she leaned up against it, wiping at her tears with the back of her hand and fighting down her need to scream and scream until she finally lost her voice. Just as all the muscles in her aching body were screaming for a release from their ordeal, so she was longing for some surcease too.

"Sarina?"

Startled, she glanced up. Mei was signaling to her from the top of the stairs. She was waiting to say good-bye. Sarina stumbled down the hallway, the fingers of her right hand lightly trailing along the wall, and sagged weakly into Mei's arms. Over the girl's shoulder she could see Janella and Ariadne, the hoods of their blue cloaks drawn up over their heads, standing silently in the front hallway below.

"You still refuse to come with us?" asked Mei one final time.

"You know that I can't leave her," Sarina replied wearily. "She needs me, Mei, and as long as she's alive, I'll stay and nurse her."

"But you risk falling ill yourself each moment that you remain here," the girl protested. "She will die in the arms of her ancestors, Sarina, whether you are here to hold her head or not."

"She gave me a home, Mei," Sarina said in her tired voice, "and she gave me love and loyalty. Would you want me to turn my back on her now when she needs me? I've loved her as though she were my own mother, and if she's going to die, let it be in the arms of someone who loves her."

Mei's dark eyes filled with tears. "I have loved her as well, my sister, and yet, as you once urged me to live, now I am urging that of you. Even she has pleaded with you to save yourself, for your life still lies ahead of you, while hers, my dearest friend, is nearly over. Come with us, Sarina, where, away from the certainty of death, we may breathe in the hope of life, and perhaps the gods will spare us."

Sarina thought of the little house Madam Blue had described to her in the countryside just outside Victoria. A wood-and-bamboo cottage, it was set among orchid and camellia trees, with a large, flowering plum tree standing on either side of its front door. There was even a small brook behind the cottage, alive with tiny gold and silver fish, where she and Michael Steven could go wading. She could smell the camellias now, feel the coolness of the water on her bare feet, and taste the honeyed sweetness of the sun on her tongue.

"Sarina!" Mei had started to cry.

Sarina clasped both of Mei's shoulders and gave her a little shake. "Please don't cry, my darling Mei, this isn't good-bye. We said good-bye once before, and yet we found each other again." She hugged the girl and felt the convulsive shaking of her slender body. "We'll both pray," she said, "and then, once this is over, we'll be together again, I swear we will."

Mei pressed a kiss onto each of Sarina's cheeks. "May the gods protect and spare you, my sister," she sobbed as she turned and hurried down the stairs without looking back again.

May the gods spare you. It was the same prayer the British soldier had said for her after Lewis Deane had died. Was she to watch everyone close to her die, then, before she herself was struck down? The front door slammed shut. Sarina jumped. Suddenly the house seemed too large, too silent, the barrier between herself and death too fine. With one hand pressed to her throbbing head, she started up the stairs to the last room on the third floor, where Michael Steven ate and slept in isolation, with only his flop-eared brown dog and a handful of wooden blocks for company.

Just outside his door, she paused. The hand which had been massaging the pain in her head had worked its way down to her throat. She swallowed hard and again felt the dry soreness she had spent most of the morning trying to ignore. She winced as her fingertips grazed the slight swelling in her neck behind one ear, while her thumb touched the telltale lump on the other side. Her legs began to shake. She reached out for the wall to support her slumping weight. She was sick!

"Oh, God," she whimpered, doubling over, her head in her hands. "Oh, please, God, not now. Not now."

Michael Steven! She dared not go in to him. But there was no one left to tend him now; all the others were gone. Terror straightened her up again and sent her charging across the hall to one of the bedrooms overlooking the street. She raised the window and threw open the shutters, praying to God that she was not too late. Leaning out of the window, she screamed out Mei's name.

But all she could see was the back of the hired carriage as it disappeared down the street.

"Come back!" she shouted in futile desperation. "Mei, please come back. Mei!"

She fell to her knees sobbing, her forehead pressed against the windowsill. What a fool she had been not to have sent Michael Steven away with Mei and the others. What a selfish fool she had been to risk his life by keeping him with her rather than having to endure another separation from him. In her anguish she pounded the wooden sill over and over again with her fist, while all of the pent-up fear and grief and rage surged out of her in one cleansing torrent. She cried until she could barely breathe. When her nose was clogged and her throat was raw and her eyes were swollen into two narrow reddened slits, she finally stopped her crying and pushed herself to her feet.

She made her way downstairs to her own room again, where she scrubbed her hands and face with lye soap and water and then patted her stinging skin dry. Recalling the bandannas worn by the British soldiers to protect them from the stench of the dead, she tore a wide strip from one of her petticoats and tied it over her nose and mouth. Then she climbed back up the stairs to the third floor and went into her son's room, quietly closing the door behind her.

Wo Shue Kwen stood on the deck of the ship, his arms folded across his chest, his brow furrowed in impatience. The harbor was coming into view at last. To ease his mounting agitation, he began to stalk the deck, his long robes sweeping the wooden planks behind him as he paced back and forth, taking long, angry strides. Would he be in time? he wondered, damning himself for the pride which had held him prisoner and kept him away from her all these months.

Although she had bested him and made a mockery of the love they had once shared, there was a continuing ache in his loins which not even his cherished Li's ministrations could soothe, a yearning which none of her skills could satisfy. Lust was an appetite easily gratified, while love, on

the other hand, was that purest of experiences only the
very blessed were permitted to share. He and Ch'in Ling
had been so blessed.

Fear plucked at his heart and danced in maddened
circles around his head. What his pride had begun, the
pestilence might have already completed. He slammed his
fist down hard on the wooden railing.

"Let me be in time," he called above the howl of the
wind in his face. "Please let me arrive in time."

As the ship cut through the waves, continuing to close
the distance between its proud, thrusting bow and Hong
Kong harbor, Wo fell to his knees and began to pray.

Janson could hardly blame the captain for having insisted
on dropping anchor in mid-harbor, some distance from
the docks. Nor could he fault the sailors for having agreed
only to lower a small rowboat over the side of the ship for
him, while refusing to accompany him ashore. Why should
they risk their lives? he reasoned to himself as the carriage
finally turned off Banyan and onto Casuarina. It was his
woman and child he was going after, not theirs. He ham-
mered the carriage door with his fist, impatiently keeping
time with the horse's clopping hooves as they drove down
the deserted street and stopped in front of the white
stucco house with the closed gray shutters.

He bolted from the carriage, hurrying up the flagstone
path and up the steps to the somber gray front door. It
was locked. He used the door knocker first and then he
used his fists. Cursing under his breath, he went around
to the back, broke the window in the kitchen door, and let
himself into the darkened house. Moving swiftly from
room to room, he found nothing but silence and the
stench of sickness and carbolic acid and neglect. By the
time he stumbled back to the carriage again, his chest was
heaving, his insides were churning, and he was shaking
like a man with the ague.

Were they dead? Had he arrived too late? He leaned up
against the side of the coach and began nervously drumming his fingers on the window. He had cut short his trip
as soon as the news of the outbreak had reached Canton,
but too many vital days had been wasted in trying to
round up a crew, in spite of his having offered enormous
cash sums to anyone willing to sail with him to the plague-

ridden British colony. And now that he was finally here,
where was she?

"Madam Blue on Dragon Flower Street," he barked to
the driver as he opened the door of the carriage and
jumped back inside.

It was the only other place she could be.

The rapping came again.

Sarina focused dimly on the woman gasping for breath
in front of her and wondered if it was Michael Steven
banging on the wall of his room for attention, or simply
her own breath rattling noisily in her chest. She coughed,
turning her head quickly to one side, and coughed again.
Touching her forehead, she found it warm and filmed
with perspiration. Her cheeks were hot and there was a
dull, insistent ache behind her eyes. The fever had already
begun.

Once again the house reverberated with the sound of
knocking. Each thud echoed painfully inside her head as
she finally forced herself to acknowledge that there was
someone at the front door. With an anxious glance at
Madam Blue, Sarina struggled to her feet and worked her
way slowly across the floor, every step she took sending a
charge of agony exploding from the ball of her foot to the
roof of her head. Gripping the banister, she started down
the stairs, her palms so slick with perspiration that she
could barely maintain a weak grasp on the wooden rail.

She shuffled through the front hall to the foyer and
then paused for a moment to listen. The angry hammering began again. It required all of her diminished strength
just to draw back the bolt and open the door ever so
slightly.

"Sarina!"

She staggered backward and tried to close the door
again.

He wedged his foot in the door and forced it open.
"Sarina, thank God you're all right." But a closer look at
her flushed and sweat-streaked face and he felt his joy
shrivel and die inside him.

Her heart stumbled and then soared, and then just as
quickly faltered again. He had come for her! But it was
already too late.

"Please, Janson," she whispered hoarsely, waving him

away as he advanced on her, "please go away. It's not safe for you here."

He reached for her, but she slid away from him. "Sarina," he cried, anguish tearing at his heart. He was too late. Too late.

"Oh, Janson." She could barely make out his beloved face. "Lewis Deane is dead. All the girls are gone, and Madam Blue is dying."

"And Michael Steven?"

"By some miracle, God has spared him. Take him with you, Janson," she said, backing toward the staircase. "The room at the end of the hall. Third floor." She gestured weakly with one hand. "Take him with you and let him live."

"I'm taking both of you with me, Sarina." He closed the gap between them and pulled her into his arms. Weakly she tried to fend him off. His lips found the hollow of her throat. He felt the swellings there, tasted the salt on her skin and the heat of her fever. "My darling, my precious darling," he crooned to her, "I've come for both of you. Both of you, do you hear me?"

"No." She shook her head.

"Yes!"

"I won't leave her," she insisted. "I won't leave Madam Blue. I won't leave her to be thrown into a common grave with strangers and covered with lime. I've promised her, Janson, I've promised her dignity."

"Sarina, for your own sake," he pleaded, "and for Michael Steven's sake, break your promise to her. She'll understand, she'll forgive you."

"But I won't forgive myself! I left my father on a hillside among strangers. I won't leave her to the same fate."

He pressed her head to his chest and stroked her damp hair in mounting desperation. "I love you, Sarina, and I don't want you to die. Please come with me . . . come with me now."

She leaned against him, trembling with an urgency far greater than the effects of her climbing fever. With all her heart, she wanted to live. She wanted to live for this man and for the son she had borne him. But she was already too ill, and she knew that only God's chosen few ever recovered. To go with him now would mean infecting them both—Janson, with his own heart as his enemy, and

Michael Steven, for whom she had fought so long and so hard. No, she shook her head, she could not do it for the sake of the few days left to her.

"Take Michael Steven to your ship, Janson," she told him as she began to cough again. "Take him and leave Hong Kong while you're both still healthy."

"And you're prepared to sacrifice yourself for the sake of an old woman?" he demanded, his voice harsh and bitter in spite of himself.

"When Ch'in Ling dies, I'll have lost my only mother," she said softly.

"Ch'in Ling?" Janson was frowning. "Who's Ch'in Ling?"

Her smile was vague, a strange, sad smile lit by some inner vision only she could see.

"Sarina!" He seized her by the shoulders and shook her. Was she delirious? "Sarina!"

"One day I'll tell you about Ch'in Ling," she murmured, turning away from him and starting up the stairs.

He put his arm around her waist, helping her to take one painful step after the other, until they reached the second-story landing. There she stopped and refused to go any farther.

"Take Michael Steven now, my darling," she whispered, steadying herself against the banister. "Hurry, please." The strength was draining from her legs. The pain, unbearable now, swelled in front of her eyes and blocked her view of the man she loved and whom she knew she would never see again.

He came back down the stairs with their son in his arms, squirming and fighting inside the blanket covering him from head to toe. In one small hand was clutched his flop-eared brown cotton dog.

"I'll be back for you, Sarina," Janson told her. "As soon as Michael Steven's on board the ship, I'm coming back for you. And God forgive me for saying this, but I hope that for all our sakes, she's dead by then, because even if she isn't, I'm still taking you with me."

He was halfway down the stairs when she called out to him, "Janson! Please, Janson, hold me for just another moment."

He set his son down on the floor in the hall and bounded back up the stairs to her. Seizing her trembling body, he crushed her to him. Deep in his soul seethed an ache so great that he wished he could die right then with her in his arms.

"Oh, God, Sarina, my beloved, how can I leave you?" he moaned. He held her away from him and looked down into her anguished face. "We'll take her with us," he decided, suddenly hopeful again. "That way we can all leave now."

"And contaminate your ship?" She should never have weakened. She should never have called him back. "You're a fool, Janson," she hissed, using the last of her strength to push him away from her. "Can't you see for yourself that I'm dying?"

His face went white.

"Save my son," she told him hoarsely. "It's his life you've got to think of now."

Without another word, Janson clattered down the steps and lifted Michael Steven into his arms. "I'm coming back for you, you stubborn fool, no matter what you say!"

His shout echoed through the empty house, and she cracked a feeble smile, a smile which vanished the moment she heard the front door close.

She collapsed in the chair beside Madam Blue's bed and reached out for the tiny gnarled hand lying so limply on top of the coverlet.

"Sarina?" came the fading whisper.

"I'm here, Ch'in Ling."

"You did not go with the others?"

"No."

"You're still the fool you always were, you know." Madam Blue began to cough, bringing up specks of blood which Sarina was now too weak to wipe away.

"Yes," Sarina sighed, "I know." She tightened her grip on the warm, dry hand as she leaned back in her chair and closed her eyes.

She opened her eyes and tried to sit up, but the pain in her head forced her back again. A spear of amber light knifed its way into the room, and she winced as the light struck her full in the face. Who had opened the shutters? Who had drawn the curtains? She moaned, trying once more to rise, only to slump weakly in her chair again. She rubbed her eyes with her hands, wishing she could wipe

away the stubborn white strands which were threaded
across them and making it impossible for her to see clearly.

It seemed that two turquoise-and-purple pheasants were
strutting through a forest of shimmering green leaves not
far from her. Now they were bending over Madam Blue.
Sarina called out to them. She had to brush them away.
She had promised Madam Blue that she would look after
her.

"Ch'in Ling," she cried, stretching out her hand to brush
the pheasants away. Where was Ch'in Ling?

The pheasants moved again, and Sarina could see that
they were climbing up the back of a robe and that above
the robe wavered the ashen face of a man. When the man
in the pheasant robe stepped back from the bed, she was
finally able to see Ch'in Ling.

"No!" The hoarse scream ruptured the air and brought
her barking cough to the surface again. The figure on the
bed was stained a dusky blue.

Sarina's eyes rolled upward. She smelled the jasmine
wafting toward her on wings of cool night air, felt the
rustle of silk against her skin, and heard the laughter of
the children as they followed her up the stairs of the small
white house. And at the top of the stairs, his hands lost
within the folds of his sleeves, stood a smiling dragon.

Wo Shue Kwen closed the staring blue eyes, and their
glimmering brilliance was lost to him forever. He had
been too late, arriving only in time to hold her within his
embrace before the final weak beat of life had fluttered
from her withered body. In her death, she had cried out
to him, never knowing that he had been there with her, he
who had loved her all those years ago, and had been
prepared to love her still. With a broken sigh he kissed the
pale, cold mouth and prayed that her departing spirit
would fly swiftly to the hallowed home of her ancestors.

He slid to his knees beside the bed and clasped his
hands to his chest. Deep inside him, grief and joy were
now equally matched and battling one another for mas-
tery of his soul. He closed his eyes and offered up his
thanks to the gods for restoring Sarina to him, even while
they had been robbing him of Ch'in Ling. To think that in
their strange and beneficent wisdom the gods had set

Sarina there where he could find her, in the one place he had never thought to look for either of them.

As he rose to his feet again, his eyes fell on the pink jade band on the thumb of Ch'in Ling's left hand. He hesitated for only a moment before sliding the ring from around her stiffening finger. She had no further need of it. He had given her that ring as a pledge of life as well as of love, and both were over for her now. He tucked the ring into the pocket of his robe, and when he bent to lift Sarina into his arms, his heart swelled with joy.

"One day I will learn the truth of how you came to be here, my golden lotus," he said. "But now, with the help of the generous gods, I will make you well again. And then, my precious blossom," he pledged, "you will live to bear me many sons."

29

The sky was blue. A billowing white cloud floated past them, and Sarina held Michael Steven's hand up to show him that the cloud was nothing but a large fluffy white pillow. He shrieked with delight and gathered up some of its gossamer lightness, forming it into a ball which he tossed high into the air. Gilded by the sun, the ball slowly descended, falling with a gentle plop into Janson's lap. He picked up the golden orb and spun it around and around in the palm of his hand. It shone like a mirror, and Sarina saw all three of them reflected over and over again in its brightness. When Janson threw her the ball, she caught it easily. The arc it made as it traveled through the air was golden, like the ball itself, and Janson took one end of the arc and used it as he would a rope, wrapping it around the three of them until they were bound tightly together. When the rope ran out, he fashioned a lock from the ball in Sarina's hands and snapped it over the end of the rope, telling her that they would remain bound that way together always.

"Janson . . ." She sighed, feeling safe now with the warm golden band wrapped around her.

Wo Shue Kwen ground his teeth together in frustration when he heard her call out Janson's name. But she was quieter now, enabling him finally to take his arms from around her waist and continue bathing her face with the cloth soaked in jasmine water. He knew that the jasmine water would help draw out some of the fever raging through her body. It was a remedy he had learned long ago from Qi Ting-fang, and Qi was one of the few men whom Wo held in deep esteem.

Rinsing a second cloth, he drew back the covers and

began to bathe her body. As he stroked each golden part of her flesh, he felt none of the lust which the sight of her nakedness might have otherwise inspired in him. He had sworn to keep his thoughts pure, his mind cleansed of all indecent desires, if the prayers he had offered up to the gods were to be answered. He needed for her to be well again, and anything the gods demanded in exchange for her life, he would gladly bestow on them: thank offerings of jade and pearls, spices and tea, silk and the blessed poppy.

He had to have his golden lotus restored to him. She had a glorious destiny yet to fulfill.

Janson stood in the tiny garden behind the house on Dragon Flower Street, his head bowed respectfully, while the two young Chinese sailors patted the final bit of earth over the grave of Madam Blue. It was what Sarina had wanted, he knew, forcing himself to hold still in spite of his impatience to be off, as the men continued with their prayers. He studied the faces of the two men praying over the grave he had found them digging when he had returned for Sarina as he had sworn he would. In their dark eyes burned a hate to equal his own.

They had apparently accompanied Wo Shue Kwen to the house from the harbor and had been ordered to dig the grave for Madam Blue while Kwen waited for them in his carriage out front. It had been left to Janson himself to inform the two men that Kwen had abandoned them, for there had been no other carriage nearby when he arrived. Now, by their solemn nods in his direction, he knew that they were finished at last. Reaching up to one of the branches of the flowering plum tree spreading above the grave, he tore off several sprigs of the pink blossoms, and dropping to one knee, pressed them into the mound of freshly turned earth.

"Go with the smile of the gods to join the spirits of your ancestors," he said, "and may they grant you the peace of eternity."

It was a prayer he had heard many times before during his years in the Orient, and yet he had never thought to deliver it himself one day. He rose with a sigh and turned from the grave to the matter at hand. Sarina.

"Come with me," he ordered the two silent men, and they obediently followed him to his waiting carriage.

In exchange for their passage off the plague-ridden island, they had promised to point out to him the Jardine and Matheson ship on which Wo had sailed from Shanghai to Hong Kong. As Janson settled back in the hard leather seat, his hand closed over the handle of his pistol. Kwen's blood was like a sour metallic taste already alive in his mouth.

Wo held the pipe to her lips and watched as she breathed in the acrid smoke, only to cough it out again almost immediately. He tried to convince himself that some of the soothing smoke was better than none at all. Each time the pipe cooled, he warmed it again and held it up to her mouth, willing her to draw on it more deeply, so that it might ease her pain and reduce her fever, while she slept and allowed her tortured body to heal itself.

The hours passed. He left the stuffy little cabin to stand up on deck, where he could breathe in the freshness of the sea air. At one with the stars lighting the black face of night, he tugged deep, gratifying gulps of the clean air into his lungs and felt it purify him. If only he could carry her up on deck, he thought, perhaps the brisk chill of the air would cleanse her as well. But the frowning curve of the silver crescent moon warned him that his were merely the foolish hopes of a desperate man.

In the bruise of early morning, a faint stain of apricot and turquoise fanning upward from the sea, he walked on deck again and used his glass to scan the lightening waters around them. It was then that he saw the ship. It was flying the red-white-and-blue flag of the United States of America, while below it fluttered a triangular pennant, its large gold C emblazoned on a half-green, half-white field— the flag of the Carlyle Trading Company.

Hatred and fear coagulated his blood and congealed into an angry fist which began hammering against the walls of his chest. How had Janson known? He ransacked his mind for the answer. Those two sailors. The treacherous dogs! He would see them flogged for this. After he had dispensed with Janson Carlyle once and for all.

"Jettison all of your cargo!" he ordered the captain.

"And if that does not add sufficiently to our speed, then throw overboard all that is not secured."

He would gladly throw the entire crew over the side if that would provide the ship with the wings it needed to outdistance the pursuing Carlyle. Slapping the spyglass anxiously against his thigh, he strode across the open deck and then picked his way carefully down the flight of steep, narrow steps to her cabin, praying with each step that the boil in her groin had already lanced by itself and that her recovery had begun.

Sarina floated contentedly down the winding stream on the back of a large white swan. The sun was a warm caress on her back, the down of the swan's belly soft beneath her fingers, the long, graceful neck a cushion for her head. But soon a dark gray cloud passed by overhead, nudging its way across the blueness of the sky, and gathered its fellow clouds about it. They spread like a sooty blanket across the smiling face of the sun, and in the sudden chill she began to shiver.

She was shivering so violently that her teeth had cut her tongue. He dabbed at the cut as best he could with the tip of the jasmine-soaked cloth, then flung the cloth aside and leaned over her, gathering her into his arms, so that the heat of his own body might enter hers. She was whimpering, emitting tiny pathetic squeals like a young animal crying out for its mother. He hugged her even tighter, urging his strong soul to join with her weakening spirit and make her whole again.

Just then the captain called down to tell him that they were approaching the harbor of Shanghai. At last! Wo pulled himself reluctantly from Sarina's trembling body and pressed a tender kiss onto her eyelids. Soon they would be home and Qi would tend her as he had tended her before.

With the crushing weight finally removed from her chest, Sarina was able to breathe more freely. When his lips brushed across her eyelids and his soft breath fanned her cheeks, she felt her body growing warm again beneath his tender gaze. She longed to look into his face and see his love for her shimmering in the depths of his remarkable green eyes. Eyes the color of emeralds, the color of

the forest on a sun-spattered morning. There was a trace
of a smile on her mouth as her eyelids fluttered open.

Her smile faded and his name died on her lips. The
eyes studying her so solemnly were not green at all, but
black. They were the color of a starless night, the color of
a tomb. Janson was gone. He had heeded her pleas and
fled with their son to life, abandoning her forever to Wo
Shue Kwen. With a shuddering sigh she closed her eyes
again and took her first willing step toward the outstretched
arms of death, which had been waiting so patiently for her
for so long.

Wo climbed back on deck and made for the stern of the
ship and the captain, who was battling with the wheel.

"Why have you ordered the sails trimmed?" he demanded above the howling wind.

"We must reduce our speed," came the shouted reply.

Wo seized the younger man by the shoulder. "I told you
to gain speed, not reduce it. How dare you disobey my
command!"

"We are too near the shoals now," barked the captain,
shaking off Wo's hand. "We must reduce our speed or
risk being flung upon the rocks and dashed to pieces."

"Do not trim those sails!" Wo bellowed. "I am ordering
you to do as I say, or I will have you locked below."

"I am the captain of this ship," the man retorted sharply.
"My orders are obeyed here, not yours."

With a snarl of rage, Wo shoved the younger man out
of the way and sent him sprawling facedown on the deck.
Grabbing hold of the wheel himself, he seized control of
the ship. He had sailed many times in his youth, and now,
with the great spoked wheel clenched in his grip, he felt a
surge of exhilaration and power.

When the captain lunged at Wo and tried to tear him
from the wheel, Wo's shout brought two of the men from
the estate scrambling to his aid.

"Take him below and lock him in his cabin!" ordered
Wo, watching with smug satisfaction as they dragged the
young captain away from him.

In sole possession of the wheel and of the ship, he threw
back his head to the wind, felt its frenzied lash upon his
face, and tasted the salt spray of the sea on his tongue.
This was a freedom unknown to him on land, where even

the swiftest horse was no match for the sleek steed now at
his command.

Suddenly the ship tipped sharply to one side. Wo lost
his footing and the wheel spun out of his hands. Around
and around it whirled, while he grabbed desperately for
it, feeling his arms being wrenched from their sockets
when he finally managed to catch hold of it again. Straining and heaving, he fought to right the teetering ship. It
lumbered back, stabilized briefly, and then lurched out of
control again, bucking and tossing like the most ornery of
animals, refusing to obey its master's call.

Men were now spilling onto the deck, all of them
shouting, some of them pointing frantically. He turned his
head and saw the rocks. They were portside one moment
and starboard the next. Panic closed his throat. How was
he to see them? How was he to know where to steer?
Several of the men began running from one side of the
deck to the other, picking out the most prominent rocks,
gauging the distance for him with their hands and chart-
ing a path for him as best they could. Following their
signals, Wo wrestled with the heavy wheel, sending the
ship on a shimmying, zigzagging course through the treacherous shoals.

When a piercing scream rippled through the ship, it
took Wo a moment to realize that it was not a scream at
all, but the screeching, rending sound of the hull splitting
open. In spite of his efforts to hold it steady, the ship
seemed to possess a will of its own now. Its bow lifted into
the air for one terrifying moment, like a horse rearing on
its hind legs, and then came crashing down again. Men
were scattered everywhere. Many of them were thrown to
the deck, some were flung over the side, and others were
hurled through the air like arrows shot from a bow.

Wo picked himself up from the deck. He staggered to
his feet, watching helplessly as the wheel spun away from
him again. The ship was now plunging wildly through the
waves on its own. Jagged pieces of wood hurtled through
the air, water gushed like small geysers from the many
leaks springing open in the battered deck, while all around
him, men were falling to their knees and praying. Their
foreheads touching the wooden planks, some clutching
little red pouches in their hands, they began to wail, "Ma

Chu! Grandmother Ma Chu, spare us, we beseech you. Spare our lives, Ma Chu. Ma Chu!"

There was a second ear-splitting crash as the ship flung itself against another series of rocks. With a whistling roar, one of the three mainmasts began to fall. It struck the deck like a mighty tree falling to the forest floor, and where it lay, wood splintering, white masts ripped and fluttering, rose howls of agony and shrieks of death so fearsome that Wo clapped his hands over his ears and began to run. He skidded through a pool of bloodied sea water and nearly tripped over the blood-soaked leg of a dying sailor in his rush for the stairs. Bile rose in his throat at the sight of so many maimed and screaming men strewn about the deck like broken, bloodstained dolls, but all he could think of now was Sarina. He had to reach Sarina.

He was thrown into the cabin on his hands and knees by another pitch of the anguished ship. Rising to his feet in the cold salt water, he fought his way toward the unconscious figure rolling perilously close to the edge of the bunk. His long robe weighed him down, slowing his steps so that he felt he was walking against the wind, waist-deep in mud. When he reached the side of the bunk, with a heaving grunt he lifted Sarina into his arms and began to thrash his way to the door again.

The water had saturated his robe and was now eddying around his knees as he neared the steps leading up to the deck. Hoisting Sarina across one shoulder, he placed his foot on the bottom stair. It crumbled and gave way beneath him. Struggling to maintain his balance, he reached, with every straining muscle in his body, for the second step, and found, to his relief, that it would bear his weight.

The ship was listing to one side when they reached the deck. Wo slipped and slid across the briny wood planks, slick with sea water and stained red with blood. Above the howl of the wind and the splintering of the ship's hull he could still hear the screams of the injured and the last rattles of the dead. A bloodied hand, three of its fingers ripped away, reached up to him from beneath a fallen spar. Whether it was the hand of a dead man or one still clinging to life, Wo did not know. Nor did he care.

He stumbled over to the rail, where two young sailors were lowering a small rowboat over the side. He laid

Sarina gently on the deck and bent to help the men. The
ship lurched and all three of them lost their balance,
falling heavily to their knees. Wo was the first to recover
his footing. He played out the last bit of rope and watched
as the little craft splashed down into the waves. As he
stooped to pick up Sarina, one of the sailors pushed past
him and scrambled over the side. A moment later, the
second one started after him.

With a savage cry Wo hauled him back onto the deck by
his neck. Taking a small jeweled sword from his belt, he
shouted, "Carry her down first or you are a dead man."

The man grunted in compliance and bent to pick up
Sarina. While Wo watched, his eyes devouring her pale
face with its glorious spill of golden hair, the man shouldered her effortlessly and clambered over the side with
her.

Once she was safely settled in the bobbing craft, her
unconscious form slumped against one of the sullen sailors,
Wo sheathed his knife. Just as he was hoisting up his
drenched long robe, he felt the hands of another sailor
digging into his shoulders and shoving him out of the
way. Slipping back, steadying himself against the rail, Wo
reached once more for his dagger. When the sailor had
lifted one leg over the side, Wo raised his arm and plunged
his knife deep into the man's back. With a gurgling cry the
man reeled backward. He thudded to the deck, arms and
legs splayed, eyes staring, mouth gaping, dead.

The ship shuddered and slammed its battered body into
another rock, tearing loose the last of its three masts. It
began to fall with an eerie, high-pitched wail, sweeping
through the air, with its white sails thumping noisily in the
wind. Like a bird swooping down from the sky, it dived
toward the deck and toward the man whose both hands
were gripping the rail, while one foot was poised to carry
him safely over the side. Wo Shue Kwen glanced up and
his eyes widened in terror.

"*No!*" His scream was the scream of a man who knows
that the gods have turned their backs on him forever.

The mast struck him on the head and his fingers released their hold on the rail. He fell onto the deck, his
final glimpse of her no more than a golden blur being
cradled by another. He was not aware of any pain. His lids
fluttered and closed over the fading blackness of his eyes.

His fingers relaxed, his hands opened, palms upward as if in humble supplication. With his last breath he breathed her name.

And then Wo Shue Kwen released his spirit to join the hallowed spirits of his ancestors.

Janson ordered the anchor dropped and a boat lowered over the side. He had witnessed the entire debacle in mounting horror, and now all he could see was the fleet of small rowboats bobbing and weaving about on the waves as they left the foundering mother ship to die on the rocks. All four men rowed swiftly, backs bent, muscled arms tugging at the oars, and yet in the high waves of the choppy sea they seemed to be making no progress at all. Janson leaned forward in his seat, the spyglass raised to one eye, scanning the boats for some sign of her, some hint of gold, a wind-tossed curl raised as a banner to lead him to her.

The boat plunged into a trough and rose again, bucking the foam-capped turquoise waves to ride the crest of a surging swell and then plummet down into yet another darkened trough. The men were panting, their shirts and trousers laced with sea spray and sweat. The heat of the sun steamed and dried the salt on their faces, caking their eyelids and crusting the corners of their mouths. Janson peeled off his shirt and used it to wipe his streaming face and chest. Then he tugged off his boots and rolled his trousers up to just below the knees. He checked his pistol, making certain that it was dry and serviceable, and then tucked it back into the waistband of his trousers.

They were overtaking two of the boats now. Janson tensed and held his breath. It seemed an eternity before he released his breath in a dispirited sigh. There was no sign of her on board either of the boats. They passed a third and then a fourth, and still there was no sign of Sarina. His heart plunged deeper than any of the ocean troughs. Was she already dead? Were both she and Kwen dead? Only two boats remained now. As they neared the first of them, Janson braced himself, scarcely daring to look and risk being disappointed again.

"Sarina!" Her name spun in a spiral of joy from his dry and stinging lips.

She was there, a sinuous golden wisp curled at the

bottom of the boat, while the two sailors with her rowed desperately for shore. He signaled to his men. The boats rubbed together, brushing sides, bouncing off one another, and then slammed together once more. The two sailors stared wide-eyed at the pistol Janson was pointing at them. Dropping the oars, they raised their hands above their heads.

"Grab hold of our boat!" Janson barked at them in Chinese, and in their haste to obey him, they nearly capsized.

With two of his own men helping to keep both craft lashed together, Janson dropped to his knees and began leaning over the side, reaching slowly for Sarina. His boat tipped precariously for a moment, but it quickly righted itself again. His arms closed around her at last. He drew a deep, steadying breath and then lifted her into the air. Panting from the exertion, he sank back onto the floor of the boat with Sarina cradled in his arms and her head resting against his shoulder.

"Take us back to the ship," he shouted to his men, "and for God's sake, hurry."

The time for vengeance was past. It was obvious that Wo Shue Kwen was dead, for only death could have forced him to relinquish his hold on Sarina. Janson pressed his lips to her forehead and brushed back the hair from her eyes.

"You're safe now, my darling," he murmured. "You're safe at last. Now you've got to fight, Sarina, fight for my sake and the sake of your son. Please, my angel, I beg of you. Live."

30

"Blessed be the Lord, because he hath heard the voice of my supplications. . . ."

The voice penetrated the mist enfolding her. It was the voice of her father reading one of his favorite Psalms from the pulpit of St. Clement's, renewing the faith of those whose faith had faltered.

"The Lord is my strength and my shield. In him hath my heart trusted, and I am helped. . . ."

It was the prayer he had urged her to repeat again and again when she had lain ill with the fever the doctor had said would kill her, just as it had killed her mother.

". . . therefore my heart greatly rejoiceth, and with my song will I praise him. . . ."

It was her father's Psalm, but it was not her father's voice at all. She began thrashing about on the bed, lashing her head from side to side as she tried to put a face to the voice that was again pleading with her to live.

It was hopeless. Janson closed the Bible, her father's own Bible, with the man's favorite passages still clearly marked, and rested the heavy book on his knees. He wearily rubbed his tired eyes with both hands, then stretched his arms above his head to ease his cramping back. What else could he do? he fretted, idly tracing one finger over the gold lettering embossed on the Bible's worn black leather cover. What could he do to instill the will to live in her? He hugged the book to his chest, the precious book he had retrieved from Sarina's room at Madam Blue's, and stared despairingly at her while she continued to toss deliriously on the narrow bunk.

An entire day had passed since he had brought her aboard the *Briny Breeze*, a day during which he had not

once left her side, not even to visit with their son. He had
sponged and fanned her, forced small amounts of water
into her, and read to her from her father's Bible until his
throat was dry and sore. And yet nothing had seemed to
reach beyond the protective mantle she had wrapped
around herself.

He must have fallen asleep sitting upright in his chair,
because it was dark when he was jarred into awareness by
a shrill scream of pain from the bed. The Bible thudded
to the floor as he sprang to his feet. Scrambling to light
the oil lamp on the nightstand, Janson saw Sarina tearing
at the covers and clawing at herself as though the bed-
clothes were aflame. Throwing the covers back, he immediately saw the reason for her acute distress.

The carbuncle deep in her groin had burst, sending a
stream of clear liquid spilling down her legs. His heart
lifted. In spite of her pain, the bursting of the deadly boil
meant that she now had a chance to live. It took all of his
strength to force her down onto the bed and hold her
there until she ceased her struggling and grew quiet again.
Relaxing his grip on her for a moment, he reached for the
cloth soaking in the basin of water on the nightstand. Just
as he was about to wash out the oozing sore, he thought
better of it and dropped the cloth back into the basin
again.

The draining wound required cleansing with something
far stronger than water. He recalled the hunting accident
which had seen him take a bullet in his thigh. One of the
men had removed the bullet and poured half a bottle of
rum into the bleeding wound. The memory of it still had
the power to make him wince. It had been the stinging
shock of the rum, more than the removal of the bullet
itself, which had finally caused him to pass out.

His mind made up, he crossed the cabin to his bureau
and picked up the full bottle of gin sitting on it, yanking
out the cork with his teeth. To his dismay, Sarina was
beginning to flail about again, her fingers straining to
scratch at the gushing sore. Racing back to her bedside, he
clamped one large hand around both of her wrists and
pinned her arms above her head. Then he slanted his
body across hers and raised the bottle.

"Forgive me, my darling," he whispered in her ear.

"Forgive me for hurting you. But this way you have a chance to live now, Sarina. Fight, my angel, fight."

As he poured the gin over her leg, her shriek of agony forced a rage of tears to his eyes. She went limp beneath him. He emptied half the bottle into the site of the lanced boil before he released her arms and pushed himself into a sitting position again. Taking several deep, bracing swallows of the gin himself, he set the bottle down on the floor and went to fetch several fresh towels. He patted her dry and then tore one of his clean shirts into strips. After carefully binding her open wound, he drew the covers over her again and sat back in his chair to wait.

It was dark. She was lost in the blackness of his eyes. From far away, someone was calling her name. Shielding her eyes with her hand, she peered into the distance and heard him call to her again. His voice seemed to be coming from the edge of the forest bordering the ebony pool which held her prisoner. As she watched, a shy sliver of opal moonlight ignited the top of one of the trees. When he called her name again, she began wading toward the tree, toward the sound of his voice, but the cold black water reached out with inky fingers and tried to hold her back.

The moonlight flared through the branches of the tree so that its greenness shone like a beacon in the blackness. She stretched out her arms and forced one foot in front of the other, leaning forward from the waist as she strained to break free of the grasping, plucking fingers all around her. She was panting now. Heat droplets formed on her skin and trickled into the cold water, warming the icy pool and weakening the strength in the hands which sought to keep her bound to them.

As she neared the shoreline, the light from the benevolent moon transformed the glimmering tree with its spreading branches into the image of a man whose arms were stretched out to her in silent supplication. Gasping, she set one foot on the shore and reached for the hand he was extending to her. There now remained but a single ebony finger tangled in the golden tendrils of her hair. As she fell to her knees on the ground, her hand touched his at last, and the inky finger slid away from her, disappearing beneath the surface of the pool, releasing her forever.

She raised her head slowly and lost herself again in the greenness of his eyes.

"*Janson!*"

He was instantly on his feet. Sarina was sitting bolt upright in bed, her eyes wide, her head thrown back as she continued to scream his name. He pulled her into the circle of his arms, kissing her forehead, rocking her against him while he talked soothingly to her in an effort to calm her.

"I'm here, Sarina," he hushed her, "I'm here, my angel. You're going to be all right now. You're going to be just fine."

She stirred in his arms and raised her head to examine his face. What she saw made her gasp. His eyes were green, not black. Doubting what she had seen, she squeezed her eyes shut and then quickly opened them again. But his eyes remained green. She touched his cheek and felt the roughness of the stubble on his chin. Janson! It was Janson who was there with her, not Wo. She was suddenly aware of the gentle rocking of the ship, and for the first time she began to wonder where she was and how she had come to be there.

"Janson?" She was still uncertain as she whispered his name, afraid that saying it out loud would make him vanish and put the other one, the dark one, there in his place. "Janson . . ." She repeated his name once more, and when his eyes remained green and his arms tightened around her, she wrapped her own arms around his neck and began to cry.

"You're safe now, Sarina," he assured her. "You're on board the *Briny Breeze* and we're docked in Shanghai harbor. Michael Steven's on board and he's healthy and strong, my angel, and missing you as much as I've missed you."

After a little while he unwrapped her arms from around his neck and laid her gently back on the bed again.

Her head was throbbing, there was a dull, drawing ache in her leg, and her body felt bruised and raw. But she was no longer afraid. Their beloved boy was close by. Janson was with her, and together they would fight to make her well again. She drank some of the water Janson offered her, and when the dryness in her throat had eased, she asked him the first of the two questions she dreaded having to ask.

"Where is Wo?" His name, as she said it, was like bile on her tongue.

"He's dead, Sarina," came the muted reply.

She closed her eyes. A spasm of relief and remorse shuddered through her as Janson recounted for her the story of the shipwreck and her narrow escape.

"I sent some of the men from the *Briny Breeze* back to save whomever they could and to recover as many bodies as possible," Janson continued, "but they're still searching for Kwen."

Sarina braced herself. "And Madam Blue?"

Janson shook his head. "I'm sorry, Sarina."

She choked back a sob.

"We buried her in the garden behind the house," he told her.

"Did you bury her with her ring?" she asked as the ache deepened inside her.

Janson frowned and shook his head again. "She wasn't wearing a ring."

"Oh, no," she groaned. "I'd promised her. She begged me, and I'd promised her, just as I'd promised to hold her, so that she could die in the arms of someone who loved her."

Janson looked down at her and smiled. "I believe she did, Sarina."

What he was saying made her catch her breath. Of course. The figure in the pheasant-patterned robes. It had been Wo. He had kept his promise to Ch'in Ling, but it had been too late. He had arrived just in time to hold her before she died. Sarina turned her face to the wall. Suddenly she was very, very tried. And as much as she loved the man bending over her so caringly, she needed to be alone.

Sensing her withdrawal into her own private pain, Janson got up from the bed and walked quietly from the room.

"I refuse even to consider eating another mouthful," protested Sarina, pushing the tray away from her.

"But you need your food," Janson insisted, sliding the tray onto her lap again. "Just a bit more of the pudding. Come on, Sarina, it's Michael's favorite, isn't it, Michael?"

He glanced over at the small boy sitting cross-legged on the bed, intent on pulling out one of the eyes on his

brown cloth dog. At the sound of his name, he looked up
and grinned.

"See?" Janson boasted, ruffling the boy's hair with his
fingers. "He's waiting to finish it if you don't, and judging
by the little belly he's developing, he doesn't need it half as
much as you do."

Sarina grimaced at his tactics and spooned another bit
of the rich, creamy pudding into her mouth. In spite of
her protests, she enjoyed being pampered by Janson. His
coddling and attention were helping to put a safe distance
between her and the pain of losing Ch'in Ling and the
terror of her own harrowing brush with death. Never had
she felt more loved or cherished than in the days since her
recovery had begun, with Janson hovering over her and
their son playing beside her on her bed. Only occasionally
did she wonder if Michael Steven sensed that the first parents
he had known were gone and that others had taken their
place.

"All right, stop looking like a martyr," Janson griped
good-naturedly, finally removing her tray. Then with a
dramatic flourish he swept back the bedcovers and held
out his arms to her. "How about a walk up on deck?"

With one arm wrapped about her waist and Michael
Steven holding tightly to his other hand, Janson led them
on a slow turn around the gently bobbing deck. Sarina
shook out her hair, feeling each strand being teased and
tickled by the breeze as she drew in breath after breath of
the tangy sea air.

She scanned the harbor with the eyes of the innocent
she had been two years before. She saw again the crowded
sprawl of junks and sampans, smelled the cooking fires,
and smiled at the brown-skinned ragtag children laughing
and playing aboard their floating homes. The docks were
bristling with a hundred ships' masts, the wharves were
lined with towers of cargo, some of it being loaded, much
of it waiting to be stored inside the vast godowns fronting
the harbor. Beyond the piers were the dilapidated wood
shops and shanties and the narrow winding streets alive
with vendors and hawkers, rickshas and sedan chairs, itiner-
ant peddlers and chains of stumbling blind beggars.

Lifting her eyes, she gazed off into the distance in the
direction of Wo's estate, and an old familiar longing rose
up inside her. Her eyes misted, and when she leaned her

head against Janson's shoulder, she was glad for the tightening assurance of his arm around her waist.

"Sarina . . ." His voice was soft in her ear. "I have something to tell you, something I just found out myself this morning."

She tensed, her mind alert, her body prepared.

"Chen's alive, Sarina."

Both hands flew to her mouth, muffling the cry of joy springing from her lips and catching the splash of her happy tears.

"When my men recovered Kwen's body from the wreckage of the ship and brought it back to the estate for burial, it was Chen who greeted them. When he learned whose men they were, he sent a letter back with them. Chen's the landlord now, Sarina, and he's asked me to meet with him as soon as possible to discuss resuming our business dealings."

She could scarcely contain her excitement. Chen was alive! He had heeded her words as she had heeded his. He had fought as she had fought, and they had both lived.

As if divining her next thought, Janson said, "In his letter, Chen asked if I knew of the whereabouts of Mei."

Sarina gulped.

"Do you know where she is?" he asked. "Do you know if she might still be alive?"

"All I know is where she might be," Sarina answered tonelessly. *Oh, God*, she prayed, *please let her still be alive. Let me keep my promise to them as I kept part of mine to Madam Blue.*

"Where is she, Sarina?"

She caught the urgency in his tone and quickly told him.

"Now that Kwen's dead, Chen can bring Mei home again," said Janson, "but do you think she'll accept it, Sarina, do you think she'll agree to being his concubine?"

Her heart sank. "So he's married."

"Yes."

She released a low, dispirited sigh. "Yes, Janson," she said, a touch of sadness in her voice, "she'll agree to it. Chen once told me that Mei wasn't like Li, but what he never knew was that she wasn't like Ch'in Ling, either."

Janson frowned. Again that name Ch'in Ling.

With his arms around her and her eyes fixed on that distant place she could still see so clearly in her mind, Sarina finally told him about Ch'in Ling.

Michael Steven was napping and Sarina was strolling the deck with Janson when Chen's letter was delivered to the ship one week later. Scarcely daring to breathe, she watched as Janson broke the seal and hastily scanned the contents of the letter before shoving it into her shaking hands. She knew by the grin on his face even before she too read Chen's bold, scrawled message. Mei was alive. She had been found alive and well with Janella and Ariadne and had returned with Chen's men to the estate the day before. Sarina's face was glowing as she turned to Janson.

"They're together again," she sang, her heart bubbling with gladness. "Oh, Janson, I kept my promise to them, I kept my promise." She fell into his arms, laughing and weeping, and the two of them clung to each other and swayed together on the deck.

After a few minutes Janson held her away from him and said, "They want us to visit them, Sarina, before we leave."

"Just when are we leaving?" She hesitated to ask.

"The day after tomorrow."

Sarina winced.

"I promised my brother that I'd be home in time for his thirtieth birthday, my angel." Janson tipped her face up to look at her. "Now, you wouldn't want me to start breaking *my* promises, would you?"

"No," she sniffed bravely. Then, pulling a face, she pouted. "But I have nothing to wear."

"I was prepared for that," he declared with more than a tinge of pride. "A woman by the name of Chiang Tan was only too pleased to make up several gowns for a beautiful golden-haired missy whom she remembers most distinctly." One dark eyebrow arched playfully at her gasp of astonishment. "Just over a year ago, I believe you left her with a number of unclaimed gowns, not to mention one very drugged servant."

"And my new gowns—they're here?"

"They are indeed."

Sarina laughed and linked her arm through his. "Then

come along, Mr. Carlyle," she purred. "I'll be very interested in seeing if your taste is as good as Wo's was."

Janson took the mirror down from the wall of the cabin and held it at various heights and angles so that she could see herself in the shimmering silk robes she had selected for their visit to the estate. She was like the radiant blush of a spring sunrise, aglow with luminous pinks and fresh dew-dappled green. Against a background of palest pink silk, sinuous branches bursting with small pink almond blossoms and tiny green leaves were entwined about large, full tree peonies in a deeper shade of pink. Clusters of pink silk almond blossoms adorned the golden spill of curls crowning her head, and a pair of pink silk slippers peeked out from beneath the hem of the gown. Emeralds blazed at her ears and throat and on one slender wrist— belated gifts, Janson had hastened to explain, for the birthdays he had missed these past two years.

"Pleased?" he asked, and Sarina answered him with a happy little nod. This was how Chen and Mei had grown to know her; this was the way she and Janson wanted them to remember her.

Leaning the mirror up against the wall, he came up and wrapped his arms around her. They met in a clash of hungry, yearning mouths, the fires of their mutual desire consuming them and promising to see them bound that way together always.

"We'd better leave right away," Janson's voice, husky with his need, whispered, "or we'll never get to say goodbye to them."

During the carriage ride out to the estate, they sat with their son between them, his golden hair a tousled nest of curls in spite of Sarina's efforts to tame them, one hand in hers, the other clutching his poor one-eyed brown dog while he gazed about him at the passing countryside. Her heart was pounding, brimming over with joy and anticipation as they drew up before the familiar black iron gates. She caught Janson's reassuring nod, felt his gentle squeeze on her arm, and then, through a gathering veil of tears, she saw them.

Chen was opening the carriage door himself. She was barely aware of being lifted into his arms and set down on the ground in front of him. She was not touching the earth at all, she was suspended inches above it on a cloud the texture of a dream. His lips grazed her cheeks and his hands tenderly cupped her face, while he smiled at her and showed her that he was the Chen she had known long ago and not the one she had left behind. He was dressed in the traditional white robes of mourning. There were faint lines around his gentle black eyes where no lines had been before, but his youthful handsomeness had matured into the proud majesty of a man. Wo Chen had become at last the son his father had wanted him to be.

"The gods have looked with favor on all of us, my friend," he told her. "You have found what my cherished Mei and I had wished for you so long ago. And now that you have returned to us, we welcome you to the house Mei spoke of on that distant night in the summerhouse. It is far grander than our farm in Canton was to have been," he admitted, his smile wistful, his eyes a mixture of acceptance and regret, "but it is, as that humble house would have been, a house filled with love."

She stepped forward then, as if on the mist of a memory, the Mei of the music room, once more the radiant Mei of the summerhouse. Her hair was simply bound again in two braided coils looped about her delicate ears, her face luminous without a trace of rice powder or rouge. Her gown was white, embroidered with mauve magnolia blossoms and turquoise butterflies, and on the index finger of her right hand was a ring set with a turquoise the size of a quail's egg.

"Li is gone, my sister," said Mei, following Sarina's startled gaze.

"I have banished her, Sarina." Now it was Chen speaking. "She and her three daughters will now live in a house my father counted among his many possessions in Shanghai, and my honorable mother will no longer be forced to dwell in the shadow of her treacherous presence."

"Do not grieve for her, my sister," soothed Mei, hugging Sarina close, "for she wronged each of us."

"I know," Sarina admitted, thinking more of the girls than of Li at that moment, "but without Li, I might never have found my son again."

"Perhaps the gods would have found some other way to lead you to him," provided Chen.

"Perhaps," Sarina conceded in spite of her lingering

doubt. She moved closer to Mei and lowered her voice as she asked, "Did you tell Chen about Ch'in Ling?"

The girl nodded. "There are no secrets between us and no place for bitterness within us now. Although the differences between Chen and his father were many, Chen mourns him as every obedient son mourns one who has gone to join the ancestors of his family."

"And Janella and Ariadne?"

Mei smiled. "Once the pestilence has safely passed, they will attempt to locate those from the house who may still be alive and urge them to return. It is Janella who is prepared to assume the position of Madam Blue, and it is her hope that one day the house will be again as it once was."

A sudden whimper from Michael Steven brought Sarina back with a start.

"I believe our little man grows hungry." Chen laughed, hoisting the boy into his arms. "Come, my friends, it is a timely reminder to all of us."

With Janson striding along beside him, Chen carried Michael Steven into the house, while Sarina and Mei followed some steps behind them. In the dining room, an older and slightly wizened Sua greeted them with no more than a shy inclination of her head, and Sarina wondered if the woman had ever forgiven her for speaking so boldly to her before the ancestral tablets in the shrine on that long-forgotten morning. It hardly mattered now. Chen was alive, standing in his father's place, with the woman he loved standing proudly at his side.

As they seated themselves at the table for the elaborate luncheon Chen had arranged in their honor, Sarina felt she was taking a step backward in time. She found herself looking into a distorted mirror image of that first day two years before, when she had sat at this same table, a stranger then as she was still very much a stranger now. Where Wo had sat, Chen was sitting, and in the beautiful Li's place, there was Mei. Sua was bowed before the place once set for Chen, while in her own chair sat Chen's new wife, Lao Kuer T'ai.

In spite of her lovely face, her ornate robes of yellow and orange and deep blue, and her skin atwinkle with topazes and sapphires, she was simply a gaudy shadow beside Mei; and Sarina could not help but pity the girl and

the bleak, loveless future which lay ahead of her. She stole
a hasty glance at Janson then, who was deep in conversation with Chen. Sensing her eyes on him, he looked over
at her and smiled. Her heart skipped a beat, tripping
giddily inside her as their eyes met and held. Feeling the
color flame in her cheeks, she reached for her ivory
chopsticks, while she wondered at the mysterious power
he still held over her.

The meal was over all too soon. Janson carried their
sleeping son out to the carriage and laid him down across
the seat. Then he turned to Chen and clasped his hand,
sealing both their friendship and their agreement to resume their business dealings.

"It may please you to know," said Chen, one arm draped
lovingly around Mei as he spoke, "that I have ordered the
entire poppy crop destroyed. We will soon be planting tea
instead. Since Lao Hong Han stubbornly refuses to divulge the secret of the blending for his jasmine tea even to
his own son-in-law, I thought it only fitting that I devise a
blend of my own."

"Well, you certainly have my approval," applauded
Janson, "and the Carlyle line will be more than pleased to
handle your shipping and distribution for you when the
time comes."

"So be it." Chen beamed, taking his arm from Mei's
shoulder to clamp both hands firmly around Janson's.

Mei caught Sarina's eye and they reached out to each
other at the same time.

"You will be greatly missed, my sister," murmured Mei
as she clung to Sarina. "Promise me that you will return
before too many tides have flowed and too many seasons
have passed."

"I promise," whispered Sarina, her voice breaking.

"Go with the smile of the gods to warm your path, my
beloved sister," Mei prayed, "and may they bless you and
those you love with a long life and much happiness."

"And I wish the same for you, sweet Mei. Love and
cherish Chen as you would your own husband, and give
him sons, my sister," she said fiercely, "give him sons."

Mei kissed Sarina one last time. Then, with her dark
eyes brimming, she stumbled away from her, to be immediately replaced by a tearful Chen. Wrapping Sarina in his
arms, he said, "Hold us in your hearts as we shall surely

hold you in ours, my dearest friend, and we will never be separated."

"Oh, Chen, I'm going to miss you terribly, both of you," sobbed Sarina, burying her face against his shoulder, "but I shall keep you close to me in my heart and in my prayers, always."

He pressed a kiss onto the backs of both of her hands and then he was tucking something hard and cool into the palm of one hand and closing the fingers around it.

"This was hanging from a cord around my father's neck when they found him," he told her. "I believe he had meant to offer it as a pledge to a love which the gods had decreed was never to be. It is yours now, Sarina, as perhaps it was destined to be."

He handed her into the carriage and then closed the door. As the carriage started down the drive, Sarina turned around in her seat and waved to them. She continued to wave until the black iron gates grew too small and the figures standing in front of them faded into darkened blurs and slipped into the places lovingly reserved for them within her memory. Then she opened her hand.

In her palm lay the pink jade ring.

Janson slipped the pink jade ring onto the third finger of Sarina's left hand. They had exchanged vows on the deck of the *Briny Breeze*, beneath a benevolent moon, just as the ship was sailing out of Shanghai harbor. As it had once bound the hearts of two young lovers in another time, forever joined in eternity in the presence of their ancestors, so the ring would unite the two of them and their younger love, for now and ever more.

Great Reading from SIGNET